REBEL SWORD

DEREK BIRKS

DEREK BIRKS

This is a work of fiction.
Names, characters, places and incidents
are either the product of the author's imagination
or are used fictitiously, and any resemblance to any
persons living or dead is entirely coincidental.

Derek Birks asserts the moral right to be
identified as the author of this book.

REBEL SWORD
Copyright © 2024 Derek Birks
All rights reserved.

Acknowledgements

I must thank those family and friends who have helped to make this book possible. Katie Birks has designed and created the brilliant cover and produced the map. Good friend and colleague, historian Sharon Bennett Connolly, has offered helpful advice - especially about aspects of the lives of medieval women.

As ever, I also need to thank, my wife Janet, who joined me on my research trips, traipsing around what remains of Duncliffe Forest, as well as exploring Shaftesbury itself. The remains of Shaftesbury Abbey were examined and many miles were walked. We investigated the much-overgrown site of the adulterine castle in the north-west of the town which dates from the anarchy period and provides the most important location in this story.

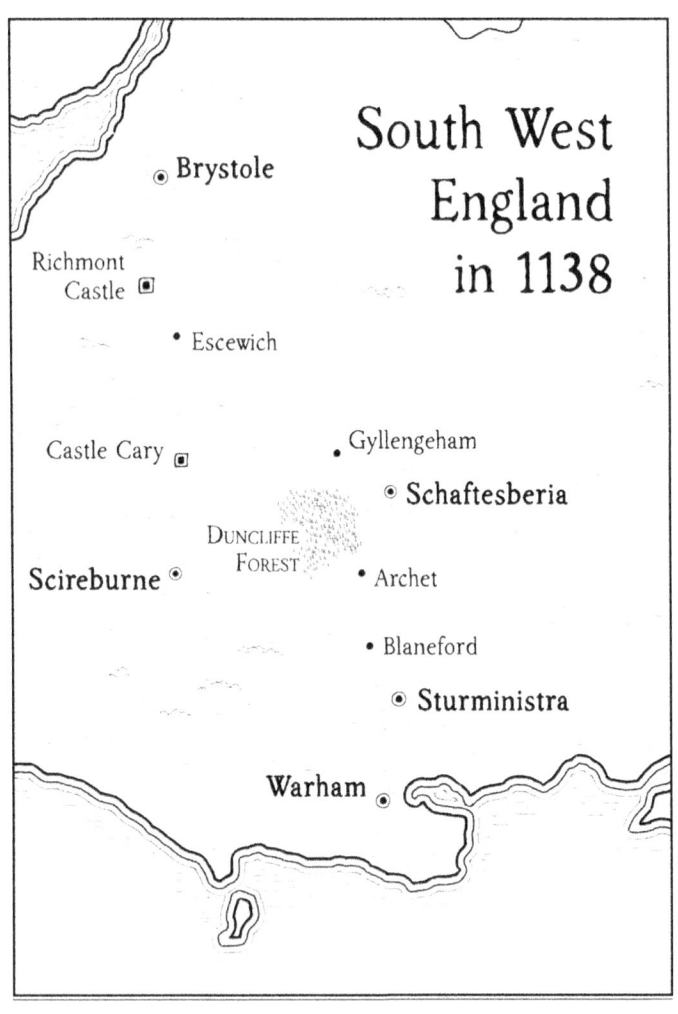

REBEL SWORD

Contents

The Players in Rebel Sword	6
Placenames in Twelfth Century England	7
Part One: Bastard Sword	9
Part Two: Renegade	80
Part Three: Traitor	129
Part Four: Under Siege	288
Part Five: Castellan	334
Part Six: Lord of Schaftesberia	408
Epilogue	445
Historical Notes	448

The Players in Rebel Sword

* indicates an actual historical figure.
*Thomas FitzRobert, bastard son of Robert, Earl of Gloucester
*Robert FitzRoy, Earl of Gloucester
*William FitzRobert, Robert's eldest son
William de Burgh, man at arms to the Earl of Gloucester
Sir Roland de Burgh, knight and brother of William
Thorold le Breton, a comrade of Roland.
Enric, Saxon uncle of Thomas
Adeline de Sarne, young co-heiress
Isabel de Sarne, Adeline's sister
Ralph de Sarne, bastard half-brother to Adeline and Isabel
Aelflaed, an alewife at Escewich
Edwin, Aelflaed's son
Enwyn, Aelflaed's daughter
Eadwulf, Enwyn's son
Wilflaed, a Saxon healer
Sir Roger of Schaftesberia, knight sworn to Robert Beaumont, Earl of Leicester
Folcard, Sir Roger's second in command
Bella, the Abbess of Schaftesberia
Avice, a lay healer at the abbey
Edith, a novice nun at Schaftesberia abbey
Tancred, a young man at arms at Schaftesberia abbey
Berner, a man at arms at Schaftesberia abbey
Selima, the cook at Thorold's manor house
Father Edric, a lapsed priest
Prisoners at Schaftesberia: Edgar, 'Long' Tom, Ranulf, Peter 'the thief', Garth & Jonas
Outlaws sworn to Thomas: Will, 'the liar', Galt, Turstin, Geoffrey & Pain
Men at arms from Brystole: Bernard, Hawk and Renold
Alina, alewife at Osbert's tavern

Placenames in Twelfth Century England

During the early middle ages, English placenames were very varied in their spelling. What records we have are often from charters and, needless to say, each cleric drafting a charter had his own ideas about spelling. So those interpretations are what we are left with today.

I decided to go with a version of each placename documented as close to the time in which the action is set.

Twelfth Century	**Modern name**
Archet	West Orchard
Blaneford	Blandford Forum
Brystole	Bristol
Escewich	Ashwick
Gyllengeham	Gillingham
Hastynges	Hastings
Schrosberie	Shrewsbury
Scireburne	Sherborne
Schaftesberia	Shaftesbury
Sturministra	Sturminster Marshall
Warham	Wareham

DEREK BIRKS

Part One: Bastard Son

1

9th May 1138 at Brystole

From the threshold of Osbert's tavern, Thomas FitzRobert gazed out upon the unrelenting misery brought on by the excessive spring rains. Long-faced traders, their sodden cowls dribbling onto ruined goods, packed up their stalls and lamented their plummeting income. A cart floundered along the lane towards the castle gate with ferocious rivulets of water surging past its wheels. In the fields across the swollen river, groaning cattle tramped wearily over the same mired grass, turning their pastures into quagmires. Aye, the view from the tavern was depressing; but it suited his mood perfectly.

Hardly surprising, Thomas thought, that folk sought consolation in a place like Osbert's. According to the widowed alewife, Alina, the tavern began life as a seld; and, though Osbert himself was long dead, there was still plenty for sale there. For those who could still afford to pay, ale - and whores - were always on offer.

As a regular patron, Thomas was appalled at the influx of damp and jostling newcomers cramming into his favourite refuge. Most of all, he resented the men at arms who barrelled in and took over the place. When they required more room to accommodate their great muscled arses, they simply cracked a few heads to ease the press. Dripping with Norman pride, they were mostly brutal men, many of whom Thomas observed when he and the other youths trained in the castle yard.

Often the more experienced men liked to watch, ever-willing to poke fun at the younger lads. Some took particular delight in ridiculing Thomas, probably because he was their earl's bastard son; though Thomas suspected that his manifest prowess with any bladed weapon, at such a young age, only deepened their resentment.

For a time, they struggled to discover a weakness in the bastard youth, until one chanced to remark that he fought well, for a Saxon. Thomas, though born to a Saxon mother, had never really considered himself any different from his half-brothers; but the men at arms latched onto the taunt like leeches. Since Thomas was quick to anger, the nagging insult of 'Saxon' was more than enough to lose him several practice bouts in the yard.

This morning he was attempting to salve his habitual melancholy with the aid of copious quantities of ale. After a gentle warning from Alina, he had slunk to the door; but now, eyeing the persistent downpour, he took an unsteady step back inside.

With steam rising from every rain-soaked body, it was close and humid in the tavern. His own lank, rust-coloured hair clung slick to his scalp and sweat dribbled from his chin as he called for more ale.

"You need to stop drinking, Fitz," Alina told him, with a tired frown.

Though she was old enough to be his mother, when she leaned over him, his eyes were drawn inevitably to her damp, near-transparent and amply-filled, linen tunic.

"You're a fine-looking woman," he slurred amiably. "But you should really cover your…"

He should have known better, but the slap on his cheek was hard enough to remind him that Alina was not a woman who suffered fools. It was also loud enough for others to notice and chuckle about. After she left him, Thomas let his heavy head sink down onto the rough wooden board that served as a table. She meant only to help him, as ever; and, of course, she was right. He resolved to stop drinking and prayed that sleep might ease his gloom for a few hours – though, thus far, it never had.

Before he could doze into oblivion, there was a loud crash and a scream from across the room. A brief moment of silence followed, broken, moments later, by an outburst of savage laughter. Levering one eye open, Thomas noted a couple of overturned stools and a blurred circle of men jostling Alina from one man to another. Thomas groaned at what was becoming a popular pastime for the two de Burgh brothers and their comrades.

It rarely got out of hand and soon, no doubt, they would tire of their tame sport. Though all were well-schooled in ways to kill and maim, no-one generally died in the course of their leisure pursuits - chiefly because no sane man would dare to interfere against the two brothers. An ale-sodden youth, however, wild of temper and weary of life, might just be tempted.

Getting unsteadily to his feet, Thomas barked across the room: "Enough! You've had your fun. Now leave her alone."

Every head in the chamber swivelled to look at him and most, no doubt, wondered at this youth who clearly had a death wish. The younger de Burgh brother, William, removed his hand from inside Alina's torn tunic and released his hold upon her waist. For a moment, Thomas thought they were actually going to comply with his order. Perhaps, after all, being the bastard son of their sworn lord commanded at least a small degree of respect.

Alina shrugged off William's arm and walked away. "No 'arm done, Fitz," she said. "Best you go now. We don't want no… upsets in 'ere, do we?"

Thomas grinned back at her and nodded agreement for even he understood that, if he stayed much longer, he would very likely provoke a fight. His intervention had worked, injury had been avoided and thus, it was time to leave. Other patrons relaxed and struck up their conversations once more, relieved no doubt that no blood had been spilled. So, with only a final stare at William de Burgh, Thomas turned to leave.

"Do you turn your back on me, Saxon?" growled William.

Once more a nervous hush descended upon the tavern as all waited to see how Thomas would respond. Had he been sober, Thomas might have noted William's baiting tone; but he was far from sober.

With cheeks flushed and teeth clenched, Thomas replied: "Yes, I do, William; I do turn my back on you – what of it?"

When he took another step towards the door, Thorold le Breton, a close comrade of the de Burghs, stepped out to block his path.

"Come here, Saxon boy," ordered William quietly.

While Thomas was deciding whether or not to comply, he glanced down at the seax tucked in his belt. Most men at arms had a blade upon them but none longer than the seax since the earl had forbidden the wearing of swords in the town. Only those actually on guard duty were permitted to wear mail and carry weapons. The aim was to stop brawls turning into skirmishes where lives might be lost in anger.

Spinning around, Thomas almost lost his balance but, aware of Thorold lurking close behind him, he took a step back towards William. The younger of the two de Burgh brothers had a fearsome reputation but Thomas reckoned that his adversary was at least as drunk as he was. For a few seconds the pair stood, scowling at each other, six feet apart, until Alina thrust herself between them.

"We'll 'ave no fightin' in here," she pleaded. "Your lord forbids it – as you both well know."

Whether William resented her interference, or was simply bent on mischief, he drew out his knife and rasped a challenge at Thomas. "Shall I cut this whore, Saxon?"

There was a gasp from all and even Roland laid a warning hand on his brother's arm and murmured: "Best leave the alewife to serve her ale, eh, brother?"

"Keep out of this," snapped William. "It's time we clipped this Saxon's wings – long past time."

With one arm still clamped around the trembling Alina, William placed his knife point against her throat. Again, Roland urged his brother to release her and even the brutal Thorold made a half-hearted protest. All others, fearful of William's notoriety, shrank into the furthest corners of the room.

"Let her go, William," warned Thomas. "She's done nothing but serve you ale these past months."

"Aye, Saxon, but she's too fond of you for my liking," complained William.

De Burgh's habitual jibe about his Saxon mother was hardly new but, just then, another stab at his pride was more than enough to spark his anger. Very slowly William moved the point of his blade down the alewife's neck towards her breast leaving a thin, bloodied line. Squirming in his grasp, she cried out in fear and Thomas took a step closer, righteous fury welling up in his heart.

No-one else dared move.

"It's me you really want to cut, isn't it?" growled Thomas, slowly easing out his seax. "Every tiny little part of you is just aching to slice a piece off the Saxon's hide, eh? So, stop fondling Alina and play with someone who has a blade."

William gave a grim nod of satisfaction. "Think you can face me knife in hand, boy, and live?" he scoffed.

In one swift movement, he flung Alina aside and thrust his blade at Thomas's chest. Lurching sideways to avoid the flashing steel, Thomas winced when it grazed his shoulder.

"Hold, both of you!" ordered Roland de Burgh; but his plea fell upon deaf ears.

When a fuming William lunged at Thomas a second time, the youth brought up his seax and parried the blow. Both men, swaying on their feet, lurched forward again and this time the seax failed to parry William's sharp blade. Thomas' shirt was sliced open, but little blood was drawn. His seax, however, continued on its upward arc and plunged up to its hilt into William's throat.

Instantly, blood spurted from the wound, splashing Thomas's face, before flowing over his fingers like spilt wine. The other men at arms moved lightning fast to hurl Thomas aside as they fought to save their comrade. But, of course, it was hopeless and, after a few moments of shocked silence, every eye turned to the youth whose hand was steeped in the dead man's blood.

Standing over his brother's corpse, Roland glowered at Thomas and then, drawing out his own knife, stepped forward so that Thomas was obliged to raise his seax. Undoubtedly Roland would have killed him had the door not crashed open to reveal half a dozen guards who rushed in to restore order. Both Roland and Thomas were disarmed while the serjeants attempted to unravel what had happened.

As Thomas was led away, Roland snarled after him: "You're a dead man, Saxon. Even the earl can't save you from this!"

And Thomas knew that the grieving brother was right: he would be marked forever – not as a great earl's son, nor even as a loyal bastard – but as the feral youth who ripped out the throat of William de Burgh.

2

9th May in the Privy Chamber at Brystole Castle

Pinned by the arms, Thomas was hauled roughly along the stone-walled passage, shoulders snagging at the bright red banners draped there. Those propelling him towards judgement were the serjeants who arrested him in the tavern and how they delighted in forcing him down onto his knees in the earl's chamber. With the dried blood of William de Burgh staining his tunic and hands, Thomas knelt before his lord and father, Robert FitzRoy, Earl of Gloucester.

"Leave us," Earl Robert instructed the guards.

With a brief show of reluctance, the men at arms went out without a word leaving Thomas relieved that at least they wouldn't witness his humiliation. To his surprise, there was no immediate tirade of censure from the earl to puncture his bastard son's youthful pride. Indeed, for several moments, the earl said nothing at all. In the solemn silence, Thomas might have pleaded his cause but he had none; a man was dead at his hands and there was no escaping his guilt.

"The man you killed, William de Burgh," said Robert finally. "He was one of my best household men at arms."

"Aye, but he was also a cruel butcher."

"So, you just decided to take his life… for fondling some whore."

"She's not a whore."

"What is she to you then that you troubled to take her part?" enquired Robert.

"She's just the alewife at Osbert's," muttered Thomas.

"Hah, Osbert's – where else?" scoffed the earl. "So, you slew a man for a girl you don't even care for."

"She's not a girl; she's a woman twice my age," said Thomas. "But I'd have done it for anyone so ill-treated."

"Then you'd die a fool's death and I'd have no men at arms left at all," grumbled Robert. "Yes, William de Burgh was a brutal man – but so are most of them; if they weren't, they'd be little use to me, would they? And, if they were not, boy, I'd be lying gutted in some Welsh stream by now."

"But…"

"Who are you to judge the faults of others when you have so many of your own?" demanded Robert. "Hard-edged men are a necessary tool, Thomas; William was useful to me while you are… God help me, Thomas, I can't decide whether you're any use to me at all."

Since Thomas didn't know either, he made no comment.

"Now William's comrades are baying for your blood," continued his father. "And, whatever I decide, I doubt his brother, Sir Roland will let this lie."

"Throw me to your dogs then, if I'm worth nothing to you," cried Thomas. "But at least grant me trial by combat with Roland."

"Hah! Roland would hack you apart in a moment," retorted Robert.

"I can fight," protested Thomas.

"Aye, you can, lad - but only until your wild spirit gets you killed."

There was a rebellious glint in Thomas's eye when he replied: "Perhaps I get that from my proud Saxon mother."

"Aye, she was proud," agreed Robert, "but she was also the gentlest woman I've ever known. So, don't blame her for your temper. Oh, I've heard the taunts of 'Saxon' - but is that truly all that drives you, lad?"

"I'm not ashamed of my Saxon blood," Thomas blurted out. "My great grandfather fought your grandfather at Hastynges!"

"Aye, and died there," growled the earl. "A Saxon thegn who died helping to lose a kingdom. Saxon blood counts for little now, Thomas."

"So be it," groaned Thomas, fists clenched. "Pass sentence and give me the right to defend myself."

"You've shed more than enough blood already," replied Robert.

"But-"

"Be calm, Thomas. Even William's comrades tell me he struck the first blow; but he should not have died for it and, had you shown any sense at all, he wouldn't have."

"I just lost…"

"But it's hardly the first time, is it?" his father pointed out testily. "When I look at you, Thomas, I struggle to see a son of mine."

"I never meant to kill him…"

"Still dead though, isn't he?"

"So, what now then?" said Thomas. Still upon his knees, he felt the full weight of his father's troubled frown.

"This couldn't have come at a worse time," said the earl. "Just now, I need every man I've got – especially brutes like William de Burgh."

"Why now more than any other time?" enquired Thomas.

Robert stared at his errant son for so long that Thomas realised his father must be weighing up whether to confide in him or not.

"Tell me, father," he pleaded.

With a shrug, Earl Robert complied. "Tomorrow, I leave for Normandy to meet my sister, the Empress Matilda. There I shall renew my oath to her as the rightful ruler of England."

Thomas, who rarely paid attention to the petty bickering among those he regarded with indifference, was nonetheless shocked.

"You intend to rebel against King Stephen?" he murmured.

"I do – but you will tell no-one of my intention – not a soul, you understand."

"I swear I will not, father," agreed Thomas. "But what will happen now?"

"My treason will affect all the family – including you. Once I declare for the Empress, the king will seek to destroy me and seize my lands. It'll be a time of treachery, Thomas and even some of my own sworn knights may decide that oaths to a traitor count for nought. The king's favoured lords, like the wretched Beaumont twins, will be only too pleased to prise men and lands away from me. Your reckless killing of de Burgh may well give some encouragement to anyone thinking of deserting me."

"So, let me fight Roland now and settle it before you leave," said Thomas.

"I'll have few enough allies, so I'd rather not lose one of my own sons before the carnage even begins."

"Then take me with you to Normandy then," suggested Thomas.

"I can't take you without making a judgement on what you've done; my knights would not accept it."

"So, what becomes of me?" asked Thomas.

"I'll delay passing sentence until my return and you'll stay here in a cell."

"I won't last a week here once you've gone," protested Thomas.

"Until I return, your brother William will hold Brystole. I'd intended to leave you here with him but, as you say, there are those who will want to take their revenge."

"Then I'll fight them all," declared Thomas. "For I can't see my brother Will protecting me."

"Don't underestimate him," said Robert. "But, in any case, I've arranged a way out for you."

"A 'way out'?"

"I can only pray, Thomas," said Robert, "that, before you throw your life away, you learn that you can't fight everyone on your own. I've just sent word to your uncle, Enric who will help you escape to Normandy. It'll mean you'll be outlawed, but when you join me, you'll be a traitor anyway – unless, of course you plan to join King Stephen instead."

"You'll always have my support, father," said Thomas. "I swear it."

Robert nodded. "Very well. But you'll have to be patient – a lesson for you - and be careful for, even locked in a cell, you'll still be at risk. Roland will be an unforgiving enemy and he has many friends here."

"Very well," agreed Thomas. "But why Enric? He may be my uncle but I was still a boy when I last saw him; and what I remember of him isn't good."

"God's breath, you're so hasty to judge men, Thomas. Like you, he was a young and angry warrior once but when he sought salvation in the crusade, the Holy Land ripped out his heart and all but devoured his faith. Many have told me he fought like a lion, but returned a mere husk of a man. Yet, I believe he's a good man, Thomas."

"So, I'm to stay with him till Normandy?"

"Aye, at least until you join me. But much can happen on such a journey; so, you must learn to make your own choices – better ones than you've made thus far. God knows, we all live or die by our decisions. In life, Thomas, you must choose your path with care; but, once you've done so, pursue it with all your strength, else you and all those you love, will suffer. Now get up off your knees for, when I summon the guards, I'd like my son to walk out of here with at least a trace of dignity."

"Aye, before they throw me into a hole in the ground." muttered Thomas.

Easing himself upright was no mean achievement for, though he might have won the fight with William de Burgh, the serjeants who arrested him had been far from gentle.

Once he was on his feet, his father handed him a small purse of coin.

"You'll need this," said Robert. "And be careful, Thomas. You're a marked man so, never lower your guard – and try to keep out of trouble..."

When he was taken from the earl's chamber into the bailey courtyard, William de Burgh's comrades were waiting for him. Sullen-faced, they knew they dare not touch him within the castle walls but Roland's murderous look spoke plainly enough. Thomas would be vulnerable until Enric arrived to get him out of Brystole. Though he was not enamoured with the idea of spending any time with his taciturn uncle, he could only pray the old soldier would arrive before Roland de Burgh managed to cut his throat.

3

5th June in a small chamber at Brystole Castle

With every passing day, the chamber felt smaller and, being at the level of the cellars and close to the river, the floor and walls remained damp. After so many days locked up - Thomas had lost count of exactly how many - the dripping walls seemed to be closing in upon him. Nevertheless, because of its location, he had to admit that the foul chamber was perfect for keeping a prisoner well-hidden.

Brisk footsteps on the stone flags outside told him he had a visitor, which was an event in itself. He recognised the familiar footfalls of his half-brother, William, the eldest of his numerous half-siblings. Aside from the Castle Constable, the Earl of Hereford, only William knew where Thomas was being held. Secrecy was vital because it appeared that Roland had not travelled to Normandy with the earl; if the knight discovered where Thomas was being held, the youth's life would be measured in hours.

William, four years older than Thomas, was his only – if infrequent - visitor. The half-brothers, with little in common save their father's blood, had never been close. Thomas knew that William only came out of duty, but today, his half-brother had a gleam of purpose in his eyes. Thomas, habitually miserable, did not greet him with any warmth for incarceration had done little to improve his mood.

"Your uncle, Enric is here, Fitz," confided William.

"At last," muttered Thomas. "Where in God's name has he come from, the Holy Land? I've been stewing here for weeks."

"Well, he's here now," said William. "And don't forget you're only here at all because you're a reckless fool."

"Where is he then?" demanded Thomas, peering at the closed door.

"The constable thought it best he should remain outside the castle walls lest Sir Roland should hear of his arrival."

"I suppose," agreed Thomas, wondering whether Roland and Thorold le Breton would have fought alongside Enric in Wales with his father.

"It's all arranged for tonight," William explained. "I'll take you from here along to the river gate. From there, a boat will take you upriver to Enric who'll have your horse and… well, all you own."

"That shouldn't burden him too much," muttered Thomas.

"So, I'll come for you in the night," said William curtly, slipping out as swiftly as he had entered.

∞ ∞ ∞

It was close to dawn Thomas decided, when William eventually returned to his chamber.

"Is something wrong?" enquired Thomas.

"No," muttered William, "but your uncle was tardy – God damn him. It'll soon be light."

Thomas seemed to recall that his uncle had always been unreliable where time was concerned, but he still felt aggrieved; for it was hardly a promising start. Climbing the steps from the cellars, the two brothers made their way out of the main keep and crossed the inner ward. As they passed through the gateway into the outer ward, a faint glimmer of light began to creep into the clouded eastern sky and William mumbled a terse oath. But it was only another twenty yards to the river gate.

"No guard," observed Thomas.

"No, he'll return only when the constable tells him to," replied William.

REBEL SWORD

When they opened the narrow gate, Thomas was relieved to find a boatman waiting.

Turning to offer his hand to his brother, Thomas said: "You've done well by me, Will; and I shan't forget it."

At first, William appeared reluctant to clasp his hand, but finally did so and replied: "I fear more difficult times lie ahead for both of us, Fitz."

"Aye, father told me before he left for Normandy," Thomas murmured.

In the dim glow of dawn, William's eyes revealed his surprise and he whispered: "He confided in you?"

"Aye."

"And… will you support him?"

"Of course," replied Thomas.

"Up to now, you've hardly seemed to care much about the rest of us," complained William.

"I'm as much his son as you are," declared Thomas. "When he needs my help, I'll be ready."

"I pray you truly will," said his brother, "because once father's new allegiance becomes known, the king will rain down his anger upon us all."

"But he won't be able to take Brystole," said Thomas.

"No, just everywhere else. God give you a safe journey, brother."

It was probably the longest conversation the two half-brothers had ever had, but Thomas was glad of it. If his family were going to be under grave threat, then he owed a debt to the father who had willingly acknowledged him after his mother's death and taken full responsibility for his upbringing and training.

When Thomas stepped into the boat, it moved off at once and his fate lay now in the hands of the boatman who, William assured him, was very capable of keeping a secret. Thomas, however, reckoned that being able to keep matters privy did not necessarily mean that a fellow would. Their waterborne journey was short though for, only a mile or two along the Avon, with dawn fast approaching, Thomas spotted a rider and several horses where the engorged river was encroaching on the north bank. The instant he disembarked, the boat sped away back downstream towards the castle and Thomas trudged through the mud towards the tall, thin figure waiting by the horses.

It was more than ten years since he had last seen Enric and his uncle looked even more gaunt than Thomas remembered him. As a boy, he had idolised his uncle as a formidable warrior until Enric had made it abundantly clear that he had no interest at all in Robert FitzRoy's bastard. Thus, after his sister's death, Enric had simply taken the eight-year-old Thomas to Brystole Castle and abandoned him there. Surely his father could have found a better man than the curmudgeonly old Saxon to escort him to Normandy.

"Uncle," he murmured in greeting.

The grey-haired soldier gave a curt nod. "Your father's told me to look after you," he growled and, by his tone, Thomas understood at once that his uncle was no more enamoured with the arrangement than he was. It was, he decided, going to be a long and unhappy journey for both of them.

"Got yourself in the shit again then," said Enric.

"You know nothing about me," replied Thomas.

"Aye," said Enric. "Nor do I want to but I've heard you're a hot-headed fartwit."

"Then why agree to this?" grumbled Thomas.

"Coin changed hands," said the older man simply.

"He paid you? My father paid you, my own kinsman…"

"Aye, half now and the rest when you get to Normandy in one piece."

"Better keep me alive then, hadn't you?" said Thomas.

"Just make sure you don't get into any more bother because, from what every pissmaggot tells me, it's the only thing you're any good at."

"Just do what you've been paid to do, mercenary," retorted Thomas. "I'll ride with you; but mark this: I don't answer to you."

Enric gave a shrug, held out the reins of one of the horses and then mounted another.

Despite his misgivings, Thomas mounted and then contemplated the goods being carried on the third horse.

"That, according to your half-brother, is all you own," said Enric.

It more than likely was, thought Thomas: sword, helm, mail and nothing much else…

"Come on," urged Enric. "It's light now, so we'd best move fast – or at least as fast as we can in this shitmire. I'm told a certain Roland de Burgh wants your head and, if anyone saw you leave, some of those Norman sowsarders will likely follow us."

Though Thomas knew the threat of revenge was real, he wondered whether fighting Roland de Burgh might not be preferable to being harangued by his uncle for a week or two; for it would probably take that long to reach his father in Normandy.

"Do we make for Warham?" enquired Thomas, as his uncle led them off southwards.

"What's it matter to you?"

"It matters because I'm not following you about like a lost dog for weeks."

"Weeks? You'll be lucky to stay alive for days, let alone weeks," scoffed Enric.

"I dare say only a few hours in your company will be too long," said Thomas. "So, just tell me where we're going."

"We'll ride hard to Warham then take a ship to Normandy. So, stop whining and make haste."

Since Thomas was only too happy to avoid further conversation, they rode on in silence for several miles, picking their way along the waterlogged tracks. The flooding slowed their progress so much that Thomas began to wonder whether it would take weeks just to reach the south coast. But, when they were only about ten miles out of Brystole, Enric gave him something else to worry about.

"Shit of a priest, we're being followed," he muttered.

"I feared as much," groaned Thomas. "I reckon that boatman went straight to Roland."

"Aye, I'm sure he paid the boatman well," agreed Enric. "But you should maybe take more care who you piss off."

"You'd know all about that," sniped Thomas. "So, how many are following, do you think?"

"More than one; less than a dozen," replied Enric.

Briefly, his uncle nudged his horse forward into a canter, but the slippery ground soon obliged him to slow down again.

"These horses weren't bred for speed," he moaned. "And, if one goes down in this bog of a track, it'll likely break a shitting leg."

"They can't ride any faster than we can," said Thomas.

"Maybe not, but they're catching us; and, if we stay on this road, they'll have us before nightfall."

"Then we'll just have to stand and fight," declared Thomas.

"Aye, I'm told that's your idea of a plan."

"You've been told too much," complained Thomas.

"We need a place to lie low," said Enric. "I used to know an alewife in these parts – Escewich it was; and we're not far from there."

"How well did you… know this alewife?" muttered Thomas, with a smirk.

"Well. Aelflaed was a lass of good Saxon stock," Enric told him. "Aye, she might give us a floor for the night."

"When did you last see her?"

"Oh, a while back…"

"Will she remember you?"

Enric looked uncomfortable. "Our last days were… well, I've always remembered them."

Enric's revelation suggested to Thomas that he might have to adjust his opinion of his uncle; perhaps the old goat had charms of which he was unaware.

"How far is Escewich?" he asked.

"About twenty miles south – but first we need to lose our sheepswiving friends."

When the road passed close to a swathe of woodland, Enric darted off into the forest of ash and oak, crying: "This way!"

"But they'll see our tracks easily," said Thomas.

Undeterred, Enric rode on until they reached a stream, fast flowing but not too deep. From the moment they splashed across it, the rest of the day was spent laying false trails for their pursuers though it proved more difficult than Enric hoped. Time and again they disguised their direction by using a brook or a stretch of stony ground only to discover that their efforts had failed.

After an hour or so of riding, Enric pulled up.

"Their tracker's no arsewit," he groaned. "I can't shake the beggar."

"So, what now then?"

"We stay ahead till sunset," replied Enric, "and lose 'em in the dark."

"Let's pray we don't lose ourselves," said Thomas.

At dusk, Enric called a halt and, for a time, they sat motionless in their saddles, listening for any sound of pursuit. With the light failing fast, Thomas glanced around him. "I don't hear anyone," he breathed.

After a few more moments, Enric gave a nod. "Aye, on then," he said, setting off once more to walk his mount into yet another stream. Thomas wondered idly whether Enric had been leading him back and forth all afternoon across different stretches of the same stream. Either way, he was utterly lost and could only pray that his uncle was not. Till nightfall, they followed the gently meandering watercourse along a wooded valley until, finally, they left it where they found a gravel bank.

It was not long before Thomas detected woodsmoke in the air.

"Are we close to Escewich," he enquired.

"Aye."

"Are you sure we can trust this alewife?"

"Aye."

"How long since you were last here?"

"Don't know… thirty years, maybe more …"

"Thirty years?" gasped Thomas.

"Keep your voice down, arsewit," chided Enric, "unless you want the whole village out to welcome us."

"But… thirty years," hissed Thomas. "By God, after so long, I doubt she'll even know you, never mind let us stay. I don't know why I'm even following you."

Ignoring his nephew's protests, Enric joined a muddy track which led into a cluster of cottages.

"It's not a big place," he muttered, "but in the night men's fears wax all the greater; so, stay close – and try not to kill anyone…"

Thomas suspected that the sudden arrival at night of two heavily-armed strangers would be enough to cause alarm amongst the villagers and so it proved. Mothers scooped small children into their cottages and more than one man stood in his doorway gripping a staff.

Nonetheless, the circumspect inhabitants of Escewich allowed the two riders to continue through the village unchallenged – no doubt in the hope that they would pass on through. Several, however, looked more apprehensive when Enric pulled up outside one of the dwellings.

"I think this is it," he said, peering at the building in obvious confusion. "But it looks different…"

"Aye and, after so long, so do you, I should think," remarked Thomas. "Well, are we going in, or not?"

Several of the local men were now watching their every move and, Thomas noted, one or two of them carried spears.

"Enric," he whispered. "Make up your mind."

However, the decision was taken out of Enric's hands when a woman's voice sounded from the cottage doorway: "What do you two want outside my door?"

Moments later, the owner of the voice, a stocky woman, emerged to glare, hands on hips, at the two horsemen.

"Aelflaed?" murmured Enric.

The woman peered up at Enric in the gloom. "God take me, it can't be – I thought you must be long-dead."

"You remember me then?"

"I'm surprised you can even remember my name," she grumbled, "when you've not seen me for near forty years."

"You said it was thirty," whispered Thomas.

"I said I wasn't sure," retorted Enric. "It could be forty…"

Aware of a growing crowd gathering around them, Thomas warned: "We can't stay out here."

"Aye," groaned Enric and promptly dismounted to go to Aelflaed.

"I was hoping we might stay the night here," he told her. "You know, talk over old times and… fond memories…"

Standing before her, his words dried up as the warrior appeared to lose his nerve.

"After so long, Enric, I doubt what brought you here was fondness," replied Aelflaed.

"Aye, not exactly," said Enric, lowering his voice to a whisper. "We're sort of … on the run."

Aelflaed gave a dismissive sigh and shook her head. "I'm not surprised to hear that from you, but who's the youth?"

"My nephew, Thomas." Enric hesitated for a moment before adding: "who also happens to be the bastard son of Earl Robert of Gloucester."

Aelflaed gasped. "And why would anyone pursue the earl's son?"

"Long tale, Aelflaed…"

"If you want my help, tell me what he did."

"Thomas killed one of his father's men at arms," explained Enric.

"One of his own?"

"It was an accident," Thomas blurted out.

"The earl's charged me with getting him safe to Normandy," said Enric.

"Not got far, have you?" observed Aelflaed.

While Aelflaed and Enric were talking, the villagers, reassured that the newcomers were not quite strangers, lingered in the hope of discovering some new gossip about their alewife.

"You can stay the night," agreed Aelflaed, "but only to stop all these folk gawpin' at me. And you're to be gone at dawn."

"We're in your debt, Aelflaed," replied Enric, "for you've no reason to help us."

"Reasons?" scoffed Aelflaed. "Oh, I've got reasons, alright."

Turning to the house, she called out: "Eadwulf! Come out and take your grandfather's 'orse."

The villagers, gifted at the last moment a surprising titbit of scandal, stood in stunned silence and then everyone started chattering at once. The spectacle of his uncle utterly dumbfounded gave Thomas a warm glow as he dismounted to lead their horses towards the house.

"Eadwulf!" Aelflaed cried again and then smiled as a slim, fresh-faced youth appeared from the rear of the cottage.

Thomas found himself staring at a tall, wiry lad of about his own age and could not help thinking that it was exactly how Enric must have looked in his younger days.

"It seems we're kin," said Thomas, reaching out a hand to Eadwulf.

At first, the youth regarded Thomas doubtfully before eventually clasping the outstretched hand. With a wry grin, he said: "Ma always said our kinsman would come back one day, but I don't think we ever believed it."

"Nor did I," confessed Aelflaed, "but you'd all best get in before the whole village knows any more of our business."

Once inside, they were introduced to another member of Aelflaed's family.

"This is Enwyn," Aelflaed told them, "My daughter – and yours, Enric."

"A daughter and a grandson," murmured the ashen-faced Enric, as he embraced Enwyn awkwardly.

"So young Eadwulf here is your son, Enwyn," said Thomas.

"No, Enwyn's his aunt," explained Aelflaed, "Because, Thomas, your uncle left me with twins, didn't he?"

"Twins?" choked Enric, in disbelief. "God's nails."

"Eadwulf, best go and fetch your father," ordered Aelflaed.

For the first time, Thomas viewed Enric with something other than disdain, astonished that the grumpy old Saxon had actually fathered children. Although, of course, the fact that he had also abandoned them seemed to fit more closely with what little he knew of his uncle.

"Why did you not send me word?" breathed Enric. "I would have come back if I'd known."

"Hah. Come back to do what? Drink the rest of my ale?" scorned Aelflaed. "And whither would I have 'sent word'? I'd no idea where you were. And well, you were just a boy back then – a youth who came back from the Holy Land with a bloody sword and a head full of demons. What could you offer me, Enric?"

"But I shouldn't have left you so," he said. "I'm sorry, Aelflaed."

"Don't be," the alewife reassured him. "For a long time, the twins had a father – a village man - who did well by us… till the careless bastard caught a fever and died."

"Had I known about the children I'd not have come at all," lamented Enric, "lest I put you all at risk."

"You haven't changed much in forty years, Enric," said Aelflaed bitterly. "The reason you're here now is the same as back then: you're on your way somewhere else…"

"But I stayed with you," remonstrated Enric. "I did care for you."

"Aye, cared enough to leave me for two score years," muttered the alewife.

The awkward silence which followed was only broken by the return of Eadwulf with his father.

"So, this is Edwin," said Aelflaed. "This is your father, Edwin…"

Though Edwin was tall like Enric, Thomas reckoned that he had inherited his features from his mother – which, he reflected, was no bad thing.

"Ah, the absent father," said Edwin. His voice, naturally gruff, seemed to emphasise a dormant resentment awakened by Enric's arrival. The two men did not embrace but studied each other with obvious reserve.

Thomas, sensing the change in mood, suggested: "Perhaps we should leave, after all."

"Thomas is right," agreed Enric at once. "We can't stay here. There's a man pursuing us who'll not give up easily. If he knows you've helped us, he'll show no mercy."

"And why would he? I suppose he's a Norman, isn't he?" replied Aelflaed simply. "But you're not going anywhere – even if some shit-stirrers are after you. My children's only sight of their father won't be him fleeing like a craven dog."

"Would you rather they saw me hacked down?" retorted Enric savagely.

The fierce glint in Aelflaed's eyes told Thomas that her mind was made up but he prayed she would not come to regret her decision. Roland de Burgh might not be as cruel as his younger brother, William, but he was a man of ruthless determination. It would take little provocation for Roland to burn the entire village to the ground.

It was Edwin's intervention that settled the matter. "I've not known you as a father but I'd never turn a kinsman away. A night's rest here for you and your horses will make your journey easier on the morrow. If trouble follows you here, then we'll face it together."

4

6th June in the late evening at the village of Escewich

Edwin insisted that the son of an earl - even a bastard one – should have the straw bed and proceeded to lie down on the floor beside Eadwulf. The gesture of respect was wasted upon Thomas, who was a restless sleeper at the best of times and, just now, with the threat of Roland's revenge hanging over him, he lay wide awake for several hours. Yet, the nocturnal peace of the village, pierced only by the occasional cries of owl or fox, gradually enveloped him. It was the first night he had spent anywhere other than at Brystole Castle since his arrival there so many years before. How strangely different it was, he thought, from a great town in the dead of night.

After dozing for a while, he was disturbed by a tiny, but persistent, sound which seemed at odds with the tranquillity of Escewich. One of Edwin's brace of dogs, lying half on top of Eadwulf, opened an eye, lifted its head and glanced across at Thomas. It was an enquiring look which said: I thought I heard something; did you?

In response, Thomas sat up and, easing his legs off the bed, quietly pulled on his boots. When he stood up and walked towards the door, the dog did not follow - perhaps reluctant to trust someone whose scent was only recently acquired. Before Thomas had taken more than a few paces, silence returned and he stopped; the dog lowered its head once more onto the slumbering Eadwulf's shoulder.

Thomas was returning to his straw bed when he heard a new, but more familiar sound and one that could not be ignored. With a sigh, he retrieved his sword belt and crept towards the door. The dog, he noted with approval, had decided this time to follow him out. It might be nothing of

REBEL SWORD

course but, where Roland was concerned, Thomas thought it was better to be certain. After all, his pursuer would only need a moment with one of the villagers to discover exactly where the fugitives were.

Creeping to the cottage door, he collided with Enric leaving the curtained alcove where Aelflaed slept. Unable to read his uncle's expression in the darkness, Thomas simply gave a shake of the head and murmured: "You old goat…"

Enric responded with an indeterminate grunt and whispered: "You heard something too?"

"Aye."

His uncle proceeded to remove the bar from the cottage door and told him: "I'll go left, you look right – but softly, mind…"

Once outside, they went their separate ways to explore the nearby houses beside the muddy track which split the village into two halves. Keeping by the cottage wall for as long as he could, Thomas stared along the track. With only a sliver of moon hidden beneath heavy cloud, it was too dark to be certain of anything. Yet, the sound - which had now stopped - had seemed so close and unmistakable… the ring of steel striking stone.

The dog, sniffing the air, stayed with Thomas, front paws planted, ears pricked and eyes focussed straight ahead. When Thomas stepped out to peer around the corner of the wall, a crossbow bolt sped past his ear and buried itself in the thatch of the low roof. Though he leapt back, the dog bounded away in the direction of his assailant and Thomas knew well enough when the animal located its prey. Indeed, the savage snarling and ensuing shrieks of pain shattered the peace of the village.

With the alarm now well and truly raised, Enric was soon beside him.

"What happened?" he gasped.

"Crossbow."

"It's that sheepsarder Roland then," grumbled Enric. "And he's got help. God damn the man. I thought, even if he found our trail, he'd wait till morning."

"Roland's not one for waiting, uncle – and he's waited three weeks already to get his hands on me."

"Shit of a priest," muttered Enric, pointing up the track to the west end of the village. "See, those torches."

The crossbow quarrel had shocked Thomas and reminded him that he wasn't in the training yard now. Any mistake tonight and the outcome would not be merely a scratch and a rueful grimace of failure.

"We have to go," hissed Enric. "Else we'll get our kinfolk killed – and their cottage burned."

"I'll get my horse and draw them away to the north-east," offered Thomas. "We can lose them again in the woods there."

"We'll both go," insisted Enric. "I'm supposed to be keeping you alive, remember."

"I'll fetch the horses," said Thomas, "and you make sure Edwin keeps the others inside the house."

Hurrying to the rear of the cottage, Thomas found their mounts tethered under a lean-to roof but, by the time Enric joined him, several torches were advancing along the track towards Aelflaed's cottage.

"There's at least half a dozen of the pissmaggots," growled Enric.

"I'll lead them away," said Thomas. "You bring the pack horse and find me later."

"All I'll find is your damned corpse," complained Enric, but for all his reluctance, he must have known that Thomas was right: the pack horse would slow them down too much.

"Alright," he agreed, "but at least take this."

Retrieving a shield from the pack horse, he held it out to Thomas.

"And don't go taking any foolish risks – you hear me? Just ride away – 'cos I'm still owed half your father's fee."

Thomas gave a solemn nod, but it was surely a little late for caution now; and a reckoning with de Burgh had been inevitable ever since the tavern brawl. Though he had agreed to draw Roland away, he had no intention of fleeing. He would settle the matter now one way or another. It was the only way to protect Aelflaed and her family. If he defeated Roland, they would be safe; if not, then his opponent's thirst for revenge would be satisfied and, with luck, the villagers would be of no further interest to him.

Once Enric was riding slowly away towards the northern treeline, hauling the pack horse with him, Thomas encouraged his reluctant mount in the direction of the flickering torches. Drawing closer, he saw that only Roland was mounted; so, if he could separate the rider from the rest, he might just have a much better chance – albeit still a slim one. As he passed by the houses, doors creaked open only to be slammed shut almost at once.

Desperate to draw Roland away from the village, Thomas hurled abuse at him, calling him a coward and oath-breaker. Only when he was certain he had captured the knight's full attention, did he turn away towards the adjacent east field. With any luck, Enric would soon be nearing the trees on the north side of the field, far enough away to avoid becoming embroiled in what would follow.

The moment Thomas guided his mount into the field, he realised he had made a grave error for, after the rains, the ground was so waterlogged that the cloying earth sucked at his horse's hooves. As his pace slowed almost to a walk, he could hear Roland's shouts drawing ever closer. Even the damned mire, it seemed, could not blunt his adversary's resolve.

One darted look back, however, gave him a whisper of encouragement because it was clear that Roland's torch-bearing foot soldiers, their boots no doubt weighing heavier with every step, were falling well behind. In the darkness, it was impossible to tell how far across the field he was but he thought perhaps halfway. He must turn and fight now before Roland's comrades could catch up.

Sadly, the mail shirt which might save his life was still on the pack horse and it was only thanks to his uncle that he had even a shield. Forget all that, he told himself; think what you're about to do. Christ's blood! What was he about to do?

When Roland's mount closed upon him, Thomas swung his horse around in a tight half circle to face the knight. If he ever had the slightest doubt about Roland's desire for vengeance, it vanished when the knight ripped his sword from its scabbard. His opponent would have observed Thomas at Brystole and would know that, what the youth lacked in experience, he might make up for in speed and power. But Thomas had only ever fought in the castle yard and here, on a lake of mud, every manoeuvre seemed likely to bring disaster.

Keen to strike the first blow, Roland came straight at him, but Thomas parried the slash of his sword easily and let the Norman pass by. Roland attempted to turn sharply and, though his mount skidded, he urged it on, undaunted, to unleash a fury of blows which Thomas met with shield and blade. Roland might, of course, simply have waited for his men to draw closer; but Thomas reckoned that his opponent's impatient desire for retribution demanded that he bathe his sword in the culprit's blood.

Again the knight came on, delivering a shuddering blow that almost unhorsed Thomas. Reeling back in the saddle, he barely raised his shield before Roland's sword crashed into it again. This time, knocked sideways, Thomas did lose his balance and, with a groan, slid from his horse to thud down onto the wet earth. With a roar of triumph, Roland turned back, eager to deliver a killing stroke.

As he staggered back to his feet, Thomas muttered to himself: "Don't panic. Remember your training; you know how to face a mounted man."

But he soon discovered that knowing what to do wasn't always enough. At the moment of impact, all the training drills were tossed aside and pure instinct took over. With Roland's blade hacking down at him, Thomas bore the full impact upon his shield and, ducking in close to horse and rider, raked his sword across the back of Roland's upper leg. At best, it was a shallow wound, but it gave Thomas a tiny spark of hope.

Though he survived another two assaults from the relentless knight with no more than a few cuts and bruises, he failed to inflict any more damage upon his clever opponent. But the longer the struggle lasted, the more frustrated Roland became and his next snarling attack was unleashed with such rage that he splintered Thomas's shield. On the next pass, with only half a shield dangling from his left arm, Thomas saw his adversary's whirling blade pulverise the last remnant.

Seizing his chance, Roland hacked down again and, as Thomas attempted to step aside, his feet slid from under him. With the ground horribly churned up by the trampling hooves, Thomas slithered about as he tried to get up. Moments later, Roland's henchmen arrived, mud-spattered and gasping for breath, to surround the fighting pair.

"Throw down your weapon, boy," ordered Roland.

"Why, to get a quarrel through my back from one of your men?" cried Thomas.

Roland pulled up beside Thomas, looming over him wearing a grimace of satisfaction.

"Believe me, Saxon, when you see death, it'll come from my hand, no other's."

"Very well then," replied Thomas, "but I grow weary of your dithering."

In response, Roland raised his sword, but the blow never came. Instead, the rider gave a yelp when an arrow flew so close that it grazed his chin. The presence of an archer changed everything and both men knew it. Even in the darkness, the horseman offered an easy target so he turned away at once, hoping to evade the next shaft.

Thomas, almost as shocked as his adversary, assumed that his uncle must be the archer; but beyond the glare of the nearby torches, he struggled to work out where Enric might be.

Roland, meanwhile, snarled at his men: "In God's name, put down those damned torches - unless you want to die even quicker!"

His warning came too late for, next moment, two of Roland's men at arms were struck down. If Thomas was confused by the intervention of two archers, the same thought no doubt crossed the mind of every other man in the field. All peered nervously into the shadows that surrounded them and Roland, no doubt deciding he would be safer on foot, leapt from his mount. He would have known that the safest place on the field was right next to Thomas and trudged towards him at once.

Without a shield, Thomas retreated, until he fell backwards over the corpse of one of the fallen men.

His carelessness elicited a savage laugh from his opponent.

"A Saxon so slow that even a dead man can trip him," scoffed Roland.

The barb struck home and, as Thomas lay there, he was seething with anger. Close by the corpse was a discarded weapon and, at the sight of it, Thomas bared his teeth like a hungry wolf. Sheathing his sword, he snatched up the fallen spear. In response, Roland slowed, knowing that now Thomas held the advantage of greater reach.

"Kill him. Kill the Saxon bastard now," roared Roland, instantly sacrificing any desire for personal retribution, in favour of survival.

Let them all come, thought Thomas, and he would kill them all. His new opponents, wove a ragged path towards him in the hope of frustrating the archers. A few, he noted, were wielding clubs but most had spears. However, one man was aiming a crossbow with a quarrel already set upon it and Thomas stalked towards him. But no quarrel was despatched, because an arrow thudded into the crossbowman's side, hurling him down into the mire. His deadly fate only persuaded his fellows to close upon their quarry even faster.

"This way, Thomas!" a familiar voice shouted out of the darkness behind him.

Ignoring his uncle, Thomas headed for his opponents, thrusting his furious spear at the midriff of the first man he encountered. Without a second thought, he twisted the weapon and hauled it out. Though another man faced him, the fellow's boots must have stuck fast in the quagmire, for Thomas was able to sweep his spear aside and cracked his own shaft against his temple. Thrusting the dazed man aside, he strove to reach the others but his own boots were now so caked in mud, that every step required a colossal effort.

No more arrows flew but, out of the night, Enric emerged with axe in hand to stand beside Thomas. "What are you doing?" he railed at his nephew.

"It's called fighting," snarled Thomas.

"We're supposed to be avoiding a fight," shouted Enric.

"Not me!" said Thomas, feeling his rage firing every sinew of his being.

"Fool!" replied Enric, grim-faced. "Don't you ever think about anyone but yourself? Now we'll have to kill every last one of these arsewipes because, if any live, Aelflaed and her kin will suffer for it."

Ignoring Enric's protest, Thomas eviscerated another man at arms and walked on. Roland came at him out of the night and he swivelled, off balance, to bring his spear point to bear. He was too slow and only a fearsome blow from Enric's axe stopped Roland from bringing his great sword down upon Thomas's head. The knight's shield was split in two, but Roland was an experienced fighter and, when the axe blade snagged for an instant in the damaged shield, he carved his sword at Enric. Though he cut him only slightly, the cursing Saxon was forced to give ground. Darting forward, Thomas managed to keep Roland at bay with his spear.

"Enric! Thomas!" cried other voices.

It could only be Edwin and Eadwulf, Thomas reckoned. But, by the time the two Saxons joined them, all the torches lay spitting and guttering on the sodden ground. Hence, with the night sky shrouded by thick cloud, darkness imprisoned all the combatants. Men on both sides peered warily into the black night, fearing death might lunge out at them at any moment.

Enric's grandson moved with astonishing speed over the heavy soil and, in a matter of moments, buried his spear in an opponent's breast. It was hard though, to tell how many of Roland's men remained. Having relinquished his useless shield, Roland had only his sword to swat aside Thomas's belligerent spear. The occasional wild swing of the staggering Enric's axe provided a constant distraction and perhaps that was why Thomas eventually managed to wound Roland with the spear, striking him on the thigh just below his mail shirt.

At once Roland made for his mount which was still only a few yards away.

"Finish the others," Thomas railed at Enric, as he tried to hurry after Roland.

But, in the clinging mud he could move no faster than the wounded knight who was just far enough ahead to reach his horse and remount. Evading a desperate lunge by Thomas, Roland slashed down in one final attempt at revenge. Thomas, swaying to one side, slid down once more into the mud and could only watch, cursing, as Roland's horse carried him away into the night.

"Christ's bones," cursed Thomas, slamming down his spear in frustration.

After a few more moments his reckless spirit evaporated and he slithered back to his comrades, who stood wiping the blood from their blades. But Roland had escaped and, of course, he was the only one with the power to exact revenge upon Escewich. For a time, Thomas and his weary kinfolk scoured the woods for Roland, but it was soon abundantly clear that no amount of stumbling around in the dark would enable them to find him.

When Thomas joined Enric, his uncle punched him hard on the chin, knocking him to the ground.

On his knees, Thomas growled: "What was that for?"

"For being a selfish shitmonger who cares nothing for his kin," railed Enric.

He might have struck Thomas again had Edwin and Eadwulf not dragged him away. Thomas, rubbing his jaw, was obliged to reflect upon what he had done. His enemy might be carrying a serious wound, but Thomas doubted it was a mortal one. Roland was a survivor who would neither forget – nor forgive - his humiliation at Escewich. As soon as the knight's wound was bound up, Thomas feared he would resume the pursuit and Enric was right: the first place he would start was Escewich.

5

7th June, at Escewich

A drear dawn brought dull, sombre clouds to stifle any hint of sunlight and steep the land in drizzle. Thomas, unable to sleep, was still regretting how he had put Aelflaed's family at risk and now he faced the prospect of riding all day with his unforgiving uncle. Peering outside at the murky rain, he decided that, if they left at once, they might yet keep well ahead of Roland. The latter's wound would hold him up for a day at most and, if he was desperate to make up for lost time, he would follow swiftly and leave the villagers of Escewich unharmed.

Roland was, of course, not the only one to receive a wound in the nocturnal skirmish but Enric made light of his torn leg - perhaps because he too recognised the need for haste. While the sleep-deprived Thomas accompanied Eadwulf to prepare the horses, Aelflaed bound up Enric's leg and exacted a promise from him that, as soon as they arrived at Scireburne Abbey, he would ask one of the monks to dress the wound again.

Thus, in a very short time, the two men who had brought such carnage to the village, were ready to leave. In both Enric and Aelflaed, Thomas detected a certain regret at their parting. As they left, he offered a silent prayer for God to watch over his newly-discovered kinfolk; it was the very least he could do.

The ride south to Scireburne took them most of the day for, whilst they would have preferred to travel faster, they were mostly forced to walk their horses. The ground was so waterlogged in places that the road was barely discernible at all, which caused Enric to lose his way several times.

"Last time I rode along here," he explained, "I wasn't much older than you; and that, lad, was a very long time ago."

"We're still going to Warham?" said Thomas.

"Aye, and in case Roland follows sooner than we hope, we need to get there as fast as we can. It may take a few days to get a ship to Normandy and I don't much like the idea of lingering in the port for too long."

"Have you ever been to Normandy?" enquired Thomas.

"I suppose I must have ridden through part of it on my way to the Holy Land," replied Enric. "Didn't care much for it… You should see Naples - now that's a great city – and warmer too."

"Where's Naples?"

"Er, well… somewhere between here and the Holy Land," said Enric vaguely.

"Helpful," sighed Thomas, "very helpful; but I think I'll try Normandy first."

Talk of cities far across the sea caused Thomas to lament how little he had seen – even of England, let alone what lay beyond. But now they had truly left Brystole behind them so, he resolved to bury his past and look only to the future. The events of the previous night had reminded him that at least he could fight well; so, perhaps there was truly hope of a fresh start with his father and he might even become one of his knights. As his thoughts dwelt upon fighting, he noticed, slung across Enric's back, the bow which had certainly saved his life at least once the previous night.

"That bow," he mused. "I meant to ask you where you got it. It seems longer than the one Edwin carried – longer than most others I've seen."

"Found it," replied Enric.

"Where?"

"Welsh borderlands..."

"Care to tell me a little more?" asked Thomas.

"Not much to tell…."

"There never is with you," grumbled Thomas.

"It was when I went with your father a year or so ago to put down that revolt."

"I didn't know you served my father."

"I don't – unless I'm paid for my service."

"Just a mercenary then," murmured Thomas.

"God's nails, it's a lot better than swearing oaths."

Thomas, still curious about the bow, set aside his disapproval of his uncle's faithless lifestyle and asked: "So, you just found that bow lying about in Wales…"

"The sowsarding Welsh used a lot of them - and took a heavy toll with them too. So, I borrowed one to… try it out."

"After last night, I reckon you must've mastered it."

"Aye, I used it last winter for hunting. It'll go further than English bows and…"

Enric stopped talking.

"What?" gasped Thomas, but his uncle motioned him to be silent.

After a few moments, he whispered: "We're being followed again."

"How many?"

"Just one, I think."

"Surely, Roland wouldn't follow us on his own," remarked Thomas. "Or would he? Should we stop and face him?"

Enric gave a shrug. "Could be just another traveller on the road 'cos I doubt we're the only folk fool enough to ride through this rain. Let's wait here in the open and see who it is."

The horseman was coming on at a much faster pace than Thomas expected – or indeed was safe. Thus, the lone rider swiftly caught up with them but they scarcely had time to bid him good day, before he swept past them with only a disdainful wave of the hand. Watching him disappear into the distance, Thomas just grinned and shook his head.

"Now there's a fellow in great haste."

"Aye, far too great haste for his own good," observed Enric. "A youth not much older than you, I'd say – and just as reckless."

"I wonder if he's running away from trouble, or towards it," said Thomas.

"If he carries on at that speed his mount will likely lose its footing and kill them both," said Enric. "And, if trouble's following him, let's pray we're not caught up in it for, God knows, we've enough problems of our own."

No more travellers passed them along the way and it came as a relief when, in the late afternoon they reached their destination at Scireburne. Once they were admitted to the abbey, Thomas prayed that the cares of the past few days could be left outside its gates. The Benedictine monks were most hospitable though the abbot apologised that, because the abbey was in the midst of having its church rebuilt, accommodation for guests was more limited than usual. Since another group of travellers already occupied the whole of the guest quarters, Enric and Thomas would have to sleep in an outhouse near the stables. Scireburne, explained the abbot, was not used to having quite so many visitors at the same time.

Enric, however, agreed with alacrity. "That'll do us very well, father."

"Pity though," Thomas lamented later. "Some cheerful company might have been welcome."

"No; it's better we're on our own," argued Enric. "If strangers on the road find out who you are, they might betray us for a few coins. And… try not to lose that temper of yours."

With a shrug, Thomas acquiesced, though the outhouse proved to be every bit as rudimentary as he feared. Nonetheless, from the thin straw mattresses on the floor, it was clear that it had been used many times before. He imagined that rebuilding a church must take even skilled craftsmen a very long time, especially if the building work was hampered by the inclement weather.

After the monks provided them with a simple meal of pottage and bread, Enric suggested they retire early after the exertions of the previous two days. In the absence of anything else to do, Thomas agreed but, as ever, he found sleep hard to come by. Eventually, he left his uncle snoring noisily and wandered outside to explore the abbey precinct whose buildings were silhouetted against the clear night sky. The rain had petered out during the late afternoon and it felt good to smell the damp evening air as he sauntered around the darkened abbey.

The main abbey guest house lay close by and it crossed Thomas's mind that the youth who had sped past them on the road earlier, could be lodged there. If so, he might have an interesting story to tell and anything was better than solitude. As he approached the guest quarters, however, two armed men, eyeing him with suspicion, stepped out to block his path.

"Who are you?" demanded one, gruffly.

"Just a… fellow traveller," replied Thomas, irritated by their brusque tone.

"Well, these chambers are taken, so clear off," replied the man at arms.

While his initial instinct was to ram a sharp object down the rude fellow's throat, even Thomas knew that a religious house was hardly the place to start a brawl. So, biting back a barbed response, he gave a curt nod and withdrew. His uncle would, no doubt, have approved of his restraint, but the hostile rebuff still rankled with him as he trudged towards the abbey gate.

Out of the darkness, a slurred challenge came: "Who's… there?"

Into the torchlit gateway a portly figure swayed with a pitcher clutched to his breast. Thomas could not suppress a grin since it appeared that the means of alleviating his melancholy might be closer at hand than he thought.

"Holy vessel?" he enquired.

The gatekeeper, staggering awkwardly, released a clearly satisfying belch before whispering: "It's holy water."

"I could lighten your burden," suggested Thomas. "What sort of holy… water is it that you keep so close – the ale sort, or the wine sort?"

"Wine…" confided the keeper. "Holy wine, blessed by the abbot himself."

"And does the abbot know you're drinking his wine?" asked Thomas.

"'Twas the abbot gave it me," chortled the keeper, "'cos of all the extra work I've had… what with the builders and now all you travellers wanderin' in with your mud-caked 'orses. Only the best, for his trusted gatekeeper."

With a sigh, Thomas extracted a small coin from the pouch his father had given him and held it out. "Would this ease your grief at parting with the abbot's wine?"

"Fair enough," the porter agreed at once, snatching the coin with surprising dexterity before handing over the jug of wine and lurching away into the night.

Frowning at the light weight of the jug, Thomas realised that perhaps the keeper was rather more sober than he seemed. Yet, even if he had paid far too much for it, a little wine was surely better than no wine at all. However, after his first swig of the sour liquid, he was not quite so sure. Seeking a quiet place to drink undisturbed, he made for the abbey church which was still under construction and indeed, looked far from finished. Only one or two of the new walls stood above head height and those were still flanked by wooden scaffolding. The masons must have been at work there for many months, but judging by the piles of cut stones amid the debris, they might be employed for many more months, perhaps years.

By day, the stone skeleton of the church scarred the skyline but, torchlit in the evening, Thomas found a certain stark beauty in it. Half a church, he decided, would be an excellent place to reflect and perhaps seek God's blessing for the journey to come – fortified by some of the abbot's doubtful wine. The site, not yet in use by the monks, was suitably deserted; though he hesitated for a moment when it occurred to him that, even though unfinished, it might still be deemed a sacred place. Nonetheless, since he could think of nowhere else, he stepped cautiously into the nave and was relieved that no indignant bolt of lightning struck him down.

The only illumination emanated from a handful of torches whose wavering light gleamed upon the wet stone and shimmered in every puddle. It was so damp that some of the mortar was still soft; but it did not take him long to locate a dark corner, sufficiently dry and out of sight, where he could settle himself down. It was far from clean, but he reckoned that, since his clothing was already stained by blood and mud, a bit of mortar would make no difference.

Leaning his back wearily against the transept wall, he lifted the pitcher to his lips and drank a deep draught. Perhaps he was getting used to the wine for it seemed to taste sweeter than before; all too soon, though, the pitcher was dry. Still, he reckoned he had probably consumed enough to encourage a wine-induced sleep and decided to leave so that he could stretch out upon thin straw rather than hard stone.

Just as he was about to rise, however, he heard raised voices just outside the shell of the church. A young woman was arguing with an older man – a husband and wife, perhaps; or even a father and daughter. In either case, they must be among the well-guarded visitors occupying the guest quarters. The heated conversation moved closer until he heard the girl declare: "I pray you, Sir Roger: just leave me to my prayers! We're in an abbey; so, I'm quite safe here and the guest house is only a few yards away."

"Very well," grumbled the one she referred to as Sir Roger.

Something in the young girl's tone intrigued Thomas for, whoever she was, she was not only irked by the man's presence, but more than capable of arguing her cause. Soon he heard boots tapping away from the church – presumably Sir Roger's. He did not hear the girl's footsteps but, when he turned his head, she was scarcely a dozen yards away, walking down the nave.

She was tall and slight but, since the cowl of her outer garment covered her head, he could see nothing of her face until she stopped in the torchlight and eased the hood back a little. One glimpse was enough for Thomas to hold his breath; and, thereafter, his eyes followed her as she walked further down the nave, weaving a careful path to avoid the rubble under her feet.

Perhaps it was the wine, but Thomas just sat and watched, utterly entranced by the stark beauty of her face. But it was more than that, for he detected a sadness in the girl's countenance that drew him to her. After several great sighs, she knelt down in the centre of the nave, heedless of the stone shards that must surely have dug into her knees. Abruptly, sweeping back the hood of her cloak, she unleashed a tangle of black hair, streaked amber by the torchlight. Green ribbons, which might once have bound her plaited hair, hung untidily now beside cheeks glistening with tears.

Only when she began to speak, did Thomas realise the enormity of his blunder; for the girl was praying and nothing was more private than prayer. Yet, if he moved now, he would certainly disturb her and she would think he was eavesdropping. Better to allow her to finish and wait until she left - except… that meant hearing her prayers. Remaining in the shadows behind one of the unfinished stone pillars, he convinced himself that, if he covered his ears, all would be well. Yet, he did not cover his ears, because of course, his curiosity soon outweighed any feelings of guilt.

"Lord," she began, "I know I've not sought your guidance as often as I should… and perhaps, if I had, my fate would not be what it is now…"

The voice faltered and fell silent for a moment. Thomas was about to peer out to see if the girl was alright when she spoke again.

'Tis no matter now, Lord; but I implore you to watch over my sister, Isabel, for soon we shall be parted. And, though she cares little for me now, I still love her… and so, I pray You, give her the strength to endure the trials she will face and also the wisdom to be a good wife."

Hoping the girl had finished, Thomas stretched out a cramped leg but winced as his boot struck the wine jug he had so carefully placed on the flagstone before him. Tipping over, the jug rolled a few inches before he could snatch it up and hold it still. The girl swivelled around to stare straight at him, distressed eyes attempting to pierce the gloom but, apparently, unable to pick him out in the shadows.

"Who's there?" she hissed, in a voice sharpened by anger rather than fear. "Is there someone there?"

Thomas held his breath and, after a long pause, she looked away and resumed her prayer.

His overwhelming relief was matched only by the depth of his shame. God help him if the young lady ever learned what he had done.

"I also entreat You, Lord," she continued, "to comfort my poor brother, Ralph for the absence of both his sisters will surely trouble him greatly. And… finally, Lord I ask that You forgive my father for what he has willed upon us all; even if I can't yet find it in my own heart to do so… Oh, and please send a plague upon my captors – no, forgive me, I shouldn't have said that…"

Though he could not possibly comprehend the girl's situation, the bitterness of her words moved Thomas. He understood well enough what the word 'captors' meant; so, it seemed that she and her sister were being held against their will. Surely the knight, Sir Roger, must be the perpetrator of the crime and it certainly helped to explain why there were guards posted outside the abbey guest chamber.

Once she had finished, the girl rose stiffly, brushed the debris from her knees and turned to walk slowly back along the nave. Thomas breathed out and stretched his aching limbs. As he made his way back across the nave towards the incomplete entrance archway, he was still struggling to make sense of what he had heard. But there, to his horror, he came face to face with the young girl. Worse still, she did not seem at all surprised to see him.

6

Scireburne Abbey

"I knew it," the young girl growled. "I knew there was someone there. Who are you?"

"I'm, er, Thomas," he blurted out, hoping he didn't sound quite as inebriated as he felt.

"Why are you spying on me, Thomas?" she demanded. "Are you Sir Roger's man?"

"Er, no, no - I'm just a guest here, like you," he explained. "And I wasn't spying."

"You were listening," she snapped.

"I know it looks bad," he said, "but, let me explain, please…"

When footsteps sounded on the cobbled yard outside the church, Thomas guessed that it must be Sir Roger returning and stepped away towards a side arch. All Thomas had to do was remain where he was, and let the girl leave with her escort. But he couldn't; for there was so much more he wanted, needed, to know about her.

From the archway, he implored her: "Follow me, lady, if you will."

But when Sir Roger appeared, he grumbled: "Come, Lady Adeline. It grows late."

The lady, however, did not comply at once and instead, directed a bleak stare at the shadows where Thomas was hiding. Perhaps once, there would have been a locked door in the opening, but during the building there was no door at all, only a couple of wooden scaffold poles wedged across to deter entry. Carefully ducking under them, he passed into the passage beyond and stepped to the right to conceal himself in a dark alcove. From there, however, he could only make out some of what was being said.

"Lady Adeline," Sir Roger was urging, "we have an early start on the morrow."

"A while longer, if you please, Sir Roger," begged Lady Adeline. "You know how much I have to reflect upon."

Thomas could not make out the next exchange of words but he thought the lady sounded compliant and his shoulders sagged in disappointment. What a fool he was to think that any self-respecting young lady would contemplate trusting someone who, at best, she thought a drunkard, and at worst, a black-hearted deceiver. And, God's blood, though he didn't deserve her trust, it saddened him that he would never know her story.

Taking in his surroundings for the first time, he realised with a jolt that he was in the cloister – an area reserved solely for the monks. At any moment, he expected to be hauled out of his hiding place, scolded by an angry cleric and despatched in disgrace to his uncle. Yet, when he was at the abbey gate, he vaguely remembered hearing a bell and decided that it must have been sounding for Compline. How he wished he had paid more attention when he had been taught the monastic hours… but, he reckoned that, if Compline had been and gone, then the monks might already be abed – at least for as long as monks ever seemed to be abed.

A deserted cloister, though he had no right to be there, was exactly the sort of place he craved: secluded and peaceful enough for a guilty youth to reflect and repent. For a time, he waited in his hiding place, to make certain this time that he was alone. When finally, he judged it to be safe, he stepped out of the alcove and there she was, looking almost as surprised as he. For several moments, neither moving nor speaking, they just stared at each other.

"I didn't think you'd come," he murmured finally.

"Nor did I," she replied, her dark, wide-open eyes offering no hint of forgiveness.

"A cloister is… no place-"

"-for a lady?" She nodded. "I'll go then, shall I?"

Reaching out to take her hand, he pleaded: "No, my lady, please stay."

With an icy stare, she pulled away her hand. "I have a knife," she said.

"Where is it then?" he asked.

"I don't need to tell you that…"

"I thought you'd left with… Sir Roger," he mumbled.

"I almost did."

"So, why come back?" he breathed.

"Perhaps to berate you further for being a false coward."

"Well, while you're… berating me – which I deserve – perhaps we could walk."

The fleeting trace of a smile vanished almost at once. "How dare you ask that of me, after what you've done?"

To know you better, he wanted to say, but didn't dare.

"What are you, Thomas?" she asked and, when he did not reply, she added: "I was a fool to come."

Only when she turned to leave, did he blurt out: "I'm Thomas FitzRobert, son of Earl Robert of Gloucester."

Lady Adeline paused and, when she turned back to face him again, he thought her eyes betrayed a trace of doubt.

"If we stay here by the doorway, my lady, we may be seen or heard," he warned and took a step away from her along the cloister. It was just a small step, but it felt like a giant leap. Holding his breath, he offered a silent prayer of thanks when she appeared alongside him.

"I've heard of your father," she said. "Indeed, I think I met his son once when I was much younger, but he was called William. I've never heard of a Thomas."

"I'm one of his bastards," confessed Thomas. "Born of a Saxon mother."

"A half-Saxon bastard," scoffed Adeline, "who skulks in dark corners…"

"I wasn't exactly skulking," he protested.

They walked several more yards in silence until Lady Adeline came to an abrupt halt under one of the torches. "Only the lowest of worms would watch and listen while a lady bares her soul to God."

"Or," he argued, "a foolish youth who sought a quiet place to drink some wine; and thus, was already sitting there when you came in."

In the shimmering torchlight, he could not take his eyes off her face despite the cold contempt he found there.

"Then you should have shown yourself at once," she told him. "I opened my heart… and revealed my deepest fears - and you just drank them in with your wine."

"I only had a little wine…"

"What does that matter?" she retorted.

"It doesn't," he agreed hastily. "I am guilty, my lady, but I'm also most penitent."

"Why didn't you just stay cowering in the dark when Sir Roger came?" she asked. "Why bid me go with you?"

"Because he's your captor," explained Thomas.

"Aye, as you learned from my prayers," she grumbled.

"I was touched by your plight," he said, already far more intoxicated by the girl than the wine.

"My… plight has nothing to do with you," she cried.

"Did you know," he whispered, "that when you're angry, your green eyes sparkle with flecks of gold."

"No, because I don't look at myself when I'm angry."

"Or perhaps it's just the torch light," he suggested.

If he hoped to make her smile, he was disappointed and another uncomfortable silence ensued as the pair faced each other, bathed in the pale glow of the torches.

"I'm sorry if I've angered you," he said gently.

"If?" she groaned. "My plight, my life and my anger - none of these are the concern of a drunken Saxon bastard."

"Perhaps we should argue more quietly," he suggested, "lest we disturb sleeping monks."

"Or perhaps I should just take my leave."

"I could escort you back to Sir Roger…" offered Thomas.

Adeline's response was to set off again along the cloister and Thomas fell in gratefully beside her.

"I'm only half-Saxon," he said.

"I don't care what you are - or anything else about you," she announced. Then, perhaps remembering where she was, she lowered her voice. "Saxon, Norman or damned Infidel… Whatever you may be, you're nothing to me."

"Explain then, lady, if you will," he asked, "why you're still walking beside this drunken, bastard, half-Saxon, who means so little to you."

Lady Adeline stopped again, shoulders quivering. "Because, Saxon, however little I care for you, I care even less for the company of Sir Roger of Schaftesberia."

After that they walked on in silence again until Thomas said: "It's true you've no reason to trust me, but I swear that I want only to help you."

"Help me, how? My father's will condemns me to a nunnery - can you change that? Because, if you can't, there's nothing in all Christendom you can do to help me. Nothing at all."

When she walked faster, Thomas matched her pace.

"That was a sign for you to leave me alone," she told him.

Reason suggested that he should comply, but then he had abandoned reason long before.

"I won't leave you alone," he said. "I should at least take you back to the guest chambers."

Taking her hand once more, he told her: "You have cold hands, my lady. Let me at least warm one of them."

With a weary sigh, she allowed him to clasp her hand in his as they walked in silence onto the next stretch of cloister.

After several minutes, she said: "You've stopped talking, Saxon."

"I thought I was annoying you."

"You were, but I confess that you offer some distraction at least; so, tell me how you come to be here – but just promise me that you'll be truthful."

"I killed a man."

"Do you always start with that?" she enquired.

"You wanted me to be truthful," he said simply. "And, it is, after all, why I'm here."

"Why did you kill him?"

"It was an accident; but sometimes, I struggle to control my… my wild spirit – at least that's what my father calls it."

"Wild spirit?" she said. "Well, if only for the sake of distracting me, tell me more about your troubles..."

So, he told her about the tavern brawl and the death of William de Burgh. After that, he could not stop talking and related the entire story of his journey with Enric and the brutal events at Escewich when he faced Roland. All he omitted was his father's intended treason.

When he had finished, Lady Adeline stopped walking and turned to him. "So, if I understand you correctly: having killed a man, you were sent away by your own father and now you're hunted by a vengeful knight; yet you offer to help me and, in doing so make an enemy, not only of Sir Roger, but his powerful lord, Robert, Earl of Leicester? Is that what you're telling me?"

"Robert of Leicester is no more powerful than my own father," countered Thomas.

"Who, you tell me, is no longer in England. By God, Saxon, your troubles weigh a deal heavier than mine."

"I still want to help you," he insisted.

"I've told you that you can't. My fate - and that of my younger sister - is decided. With our father dead we're at the mercy of his will: my sister must be married and Robert of Leicester, as our feudal lord, is well within his rights to choose her husband."

"But, if you're the elder, why are you not to be married?" asked Thomas.

"I am to become a novice at the abbey in Schaftesberia. So, that's how it must be."

"But why?"

"Have you not heard enough?" she complained. "Must I bare the rest of my soul to you as well?"

"I told you how I came to be here," he said.

"And I regret telling you anything at all," she lamented.

Somewhere close by, a door opened and closed. They both heard it and the approaching footsteps. For an instant, they exchanged a glance of panic until Thomas hauled her a few yards along the cloister to a darkened alcove midway between two pools of torchlight.

Darting in, he breathed: "Come, make haste!"

"There isn't space for us both," she grumbled.

But Thomas pulled her in beside him and they stood there wedged together in the cramped alcove. Holding her close in the darkness, he felt the warmth of her and the thud of her heart beating fast against his chest.

"Be still," he said softly, as the footsteps came closer.

Though she made no reply, he felt her trembling in his arms. "You're safe with me," he assured her. The monk was close now, almost upon them, but all Thomas could think about was the rise and fall of Adeline's breast against him. His face was no more than an inch or two from hers – close enough to press his lips upon hers, if only he dared.

Adeline, her eyes fixed upon him, gave a slight shake of the head and he felt a tiny stab at his belly. The monk passed by without noticing them and both let out a sigh of relief.

"By God, you really did have a knife," he murmured.

"A lady doesn't give up all she has at first meeting, Thomas," replied Adeline, with a dark grin. "But I think the danger has passed."

"Passed?" he muttered.

"You can release me now," she told him. "But thank you for saving me from yet more shame. Being found in a cloister with a young man would have tarnished my poor reputation even further."

"I'm happy to be of service, lady – always."

"There isn't going to be an 'always', Saxon."

Though she drew apart from him, she did so slowly and retained her hold upon his hand as they resumed their walk. Soon they would reach the place where they had started near the obstructed church door into the cloister.

"So, you are content with your lot," he said.

"Content?" the green eyes glimmered with gold. "I'm far from content, Saxon; but I am reconciled to it."

"I still don't understand why your father would do that to you."

Her hand gripped his more tightly as she came to an abrupt halt and glowered at him. "You want the sordid heart of my tale? Then, have it: my father found me with a youth – you understand? So, in his eyes, I was soiled forever - a girl not worthy of any respectable suitor. Now, if you've humiliated me enough, perhaps you'd take me back to the guest hall before Sir Roger comes looking for me."

Dropping his hand, she continued walking on, with Thomas struggling to keep in step.

"I never sought to humiliate you," he declared. "Only to be of service."

Shaking her head, she murmured: "Then listen, Saxon, when I tell you that there's no service you can do for me."

"There is one small service," he replied.

With a weary shake of the head, she groaned: "And what might that be?"

"I could warm your other hand," he suggested and his heart leapt when the lady gave a sigh and allowed his fingers to wrap around hers. Helping her to clamber between the scaffold poles to return to the nave, he led her on towards the guest chamber. Before they reached it, however, they were intercepted by a furious Sir Roger.

Glancing at their clasped hands, he demanded crossly of Thomas: "Who in God's name are you?"

"Just a fellow guest," replied Thomas, forcing a smile. "I came across the lady and insisted upon seeing her safely back to the guest chamber."

Thomas expected Adeline to drop his hand like a hot stone, but instead she squeezed it and kept on walking beside him. Though Sir Roger was clearly tempted to tear the girl from his grasp, he very likely wanted to avoid a disturbance at the dead of night and was therefore obliged to hover around the pair as they sauntered to the door of the guest house. Upon reaching it, Thomas reluctantly released Adeline's hand and, despite – or perhaps because of - Sir Roger's damning eyes upon her, she leant in to Thomas and kissed his cheek.

"Good even, Saxon," she murmured. "And do try to control that wild spirit, won't you?"

When Sir Roger bundled her inside the chamber, Lady Adeline made no further protest. She did not look back, as Thomas hoped she might, before the heavy door slammed in his face and left him alone on the threshold. Bewildered, he returned to the nave of the church where he had first seen her and sat down to recall every detail: the accusing tone in her voice, her gentle face and the gleam in those determined, emerald eyes.

7

8th June 1138 at Scireburne Abbey.

It was deep into the night when Thomas eventually returned to the outhouse, where Enric was still snoring noisily. He was dog-tired when he lay down on the straw bed and, at some point, he must have fallen asleep because, long after dawn, Enric kicked him awake.

"I let you sleep," explained his uncle, "'cos you looked like you needed to. But we can delay no more."

Levering himself up onto his aching limbs, Thomas gave a groan and sat back down onto the low bed.

"It's the damp," remarked Enric. "In that soft life at the castle, you're not used to being out in the rain so much. But where did you get to last night? It's not as if there's anywhere to go."

Having vowed not to tell Enric what happened the previous night, Thomas soon disclosed the entire story. Enric, as he feared, was far from content.

"Not another girl," he moaned, with evident exasperation. "Have you forgotten what happened last time you decided to 'help' a lass?"

"That was an alewife - and I wasn't in love with her," declared Thomas.

"So, last night, you fell in love," chuckled Enric. "God's nails! It doesn't take you long, does it?"

"This is different," protested Thomas.

"Aye, lad, they're all different and yet they're all the same."

"But she's in deep trouble," said Thomas.

"We're in deep trouble too, you witless pissmaggot."

"But this girl is a lady..."

"Oh, excellent, as if that makes any damned difference. Are you listening to me, boy?"

"I have to help her," argued Thomas.

"Pah, your father warned me of this; you do it all the time. It's in your blood – your mother was ever trying to help folk. Not that it ever did her much good."

"I want to-"

"I think I can guess what you want to do with her, Thomas," replied Enric flatly. "And you're not going to. We've got a load on our backs already, and if, as you've told me, this Sir Roger of Schaftesberia is the Earl of Leicester's man, he'll bring us a deal more grief than Roland will. Only a fartwit would risk that for a swift sard-"

"It's not about that, I tell you," insisted Thomas, grim-faced.

"And didn't you just tell me she doesn't want your help anyway?"

"Aye, but she needs it," muttered Thomas.

They did not leave Scireburne until late in the morning for Enric found every possible reason to delay their departure in the hope that Thomas would abandon what he saw as a foolish distraction. But, when they finally rode out of the abbey gateway, Thomas turned east at once onto the Schaftesberia road.

"Hold!" barked Enric. "Our road lies south to Warham."

"You take it then," said Thomas, "but I'm not abandoning Lady Adeline."

"It's not our business, Thomas," said Enric. "She's no kin of yours; so, just leave it be."

Ignoring his uncle's protests, Thomas set off at a dangerously fast pace along the sodden road to Schaftesberia.

"What will it take to make you turn back?" his uncle bellowed after him.

"An arrow in my back!" snarled Thomas, which, of course, left Enric no choice but to follow him.

When his uncle caught up, he urged him to slow down, adding: "Lest you want to break your neck before you even get to the girl."

Thomas, relieved that his uncle had relented, willingly complied. Though he might not want to admit it, he needed a man of Enric's experience at his side. After the brutal events at Escewich, perhaps his uncle was right to be cautious. In truth, his initial confidence was already beginning to waver a little - until he remembered that kiss pressed against his cheek.

Enric advised him that the distance to Schaftesberia was short and, after a while, Thomas began to wonder whether they would catch up with the ladies before they reached their destination. Ahead lay a great swathe of ancient woodland where they were forced to slow further as the muddy road skirted the forest before descending into a gentle dale.

Somewhere ahead of them, they heard shouting, but when they pulled up to listen, the voices were too far off to make out what was being said.

"She could be in trouble," cried Thomas, conjuring up an image of the dark-haired girl who had so beguiled him.

"Before you get any foolish ideas," said Enric, "it's very likely nothing to do with her; and she's got an armed escort, remember, to keep her safe."

"Well, someone's in trouble," Thomas pointed out. "Could it be outlaws?"

"That's more likely, so close to the forest," agreed Enric.

"So, what do we do?" asked Thomas.

His uncle swore under his breath before sliding down from his mount. "Best be prepared, lad - just in case. Come on, I'll give you a hand."

Enric pulled and prodded at the load carried by their pack horse, until, wincing with the effort, he hauled out a heavy, mail shirt, covered in rust.

"Do you really think I'll need that on," grumbled Thomas, "against a few thieves?"

"Against a stray arrow," muttered Enric.

"But you're not wearing any mail," protested Thomas.

"Aye, but only because I haven't got any mail," snapped Enric. "And I'm not you; your father was very clear that he wanted you kept alive."

With a sigh, Thomas bent down to allow his uncle to ease the mail over his shoulders until it hung down below his waist. He had forgotten the weight of it for he could hardly remember the last time he had worn it. Pity there hadn't been time to don it against Roland.

Once remounted, the pair walked their horses on along the road which deteriorated even further at times as it meandered through the fringes of the woodland. Since it was another gloomy day, their watchful eyes scanned the trees for any hint of an ambush. Even after a short time, Thomas felt the strain of constantly staying alert. It was almost midday, he reckoned, and so warm that sweat was dribbling down his cheeks, yet his mouth had never felt so dry.

There were no more shouts; though, of course, that might just mean that the outlaws – if there were any - had now despatched some other unfortunate travellers. On their right hand, the woodland grew ever thicker and encroached upon the disintegrating road. So intent were the pair upon peering into the trees, that they almost missed the wounded man completely. Though he lay slumped at the foot of a birch tree not far from the track, they would very likely have passed him by, had he not cried out.

While Enric kept a wary eye on the forest, Thomas dismounted to examine the fellow's injuries.

"It's the youth who passed us yesterday," he told Enric.

A careful examination under the youth's ragged mail shirt, revealed a stab wound on the thigh.

"I'll need some cloth to bind his leg," he said, but though Enric nodded, he remained mounted and vigilant.

Thomas tossed aside half the load carried on their spare horse before he found a linen undertunic and tore off a length of the cloth. All the while, the stranger said nothing so, as Thomas bound up the wound, he asked: "How do you come to be here alone in the forest, a prey for outlaws?"

Grimacing as Thomas tightened the linen band around his leg, the youth made no reply at first but then, perhaps feeling he owed some explanation to his rescuer, said: "This was not the work of outlaws; and I fear I brought it upon myself..."

"How so?" asked Thomas, as he finished dressing the wound.

"It's no matter to us," interrupted Enric, frowning at Thomas. "But we're bound for Schaftesberia and we'll gladly help you to get there. I'm certain the nuns at the abbey will be able to apply healing salves to your wound."

In reply, the injured man gave a shake of the head and a grim smile.

"I don't think I'll be welcome there," he said, "for those who wounded me will no doubt be going there too."

"What's your quarrel with them?" asked Thomas.

"As I said, your affairs are your own," said Enric briskly, glaring at his nephew. "And we don't seek to pry, do we, Thomas?"

Thomas reached out a hand to help the youth up. "Thomas FitzRobert," he said, by way of introduction. "Son of Robert, Earl of Gloucester."

"Bastard son," added Enric, clearly irked at his nephew.

"Aye, bastard son," said Thomas, "as my uncle is pleased to remind me."

"Ralph de Sarne – and I'm also a bastard son," confessed the youth, "for if I wasn't then none of this would have happened."

Thomas exchanged a brief glance with Enric and gripped the youth's hand all the tighter.

"You were trying to free your sisters," murmured Thomas.

Ralph dropped his hand to the dagger at his belt and, looking Thomas in the eye, he snarled: "How could you know that? Are you in league with their captors? Because, if you serve my enemies, then I'll take no more help from you."

Thomas smiled. "We're not your enemies," he assured Ralph. "I met your sister, Lady Adeline, at Scireburne Abbey and learned of her… plight. I wanted to help her but she rejected my offer."

"Have your sisters been mistreated?" asked Enric.

"I don't believe so, but they were taken by force."

"Were you there?" Enric pressed him.

"No, I wasn't," snapped Ralph. "But our servant told me the girls had been taken and the poor fellow received a cracked skull when he tried to prevent the crime."

"It wasn't a crime," scoffed Enric. "The lord had a duty to take the girls under his protection and carry out your father's wishes."

"I was already protecting them," declared Ralph.

"Not very well though, it seems," observed Enric.

"They've been abducted by a powerful lord who…"

"-has, I'm sure, arranged their futures," said Enric.

"How do you know?" said Ralph.

"Because I know that night follows day, lad," replied Enric, softening his voice a little. "It's simple: your father's dead; so, all must change…"

"They may not have a father, but they do have a brother," argued Ralph.

"Aye, a bastard brother," said Enric, "who can certainly help protect them; but who can't decide their fate."

"The Earl of Leicester had no right to take them by force," railed Ralph.

"The armed escort is surely for their own safety," Enric pointed out.

"Robert de Beaumont, Earl of Leicester," murmured Thomas, as his uncle gave a firm shake of the head.

"Yes, it's he that has lordship over my father's lands," replied Ralph. "Do you know him?"

"No," said Thomas. "I don't know him at all –at least, not yet …"

"Robert de Beaumont is not a man to be crossed," advised a stern-faced Enric.

If he attempted to release Lady Adeline, Thomas knew he would be making an enemy of one of the most powerful men in England. But a wry smile played upon his lips as he realised that, with his father poised to support Empress Matilda as ruler, Robert de Beaumont, one of King Stephen's most loyal barons, would soon become his enemy in any case. Poking his finger in de Beaumont's eye now was, at worst, merely commencing the hostilities a little early.

Before Thomas could embroil himself any deeper in the fortunes of the de Sarnes, Enric intervened. "Either we take you to Schaftesberia Abbey," he told Ralph, "Or we take you to the nearest village. You choose."

"Very well," agreed Ralph, "You can leave me near the abbey. At least I'll be closer to my sisters so, on the morrow, I can try to free them again."

"That's a fool's errand, boy," declared Enric. "You've damn near got yourself killed the first time."

"We'll help you," offered Thomas.

"No, we won't," growled Enric, laying his hand upon Thomas's shoulder. "We can't do that! We've still got Roland after us."

"That's true enough, uncle," replied Thomas, fixing Enric with a determined stare. "But I have to do this…"

Indeed, the moment he first heard Ralph's name; Thomas had made up his mind. God must have heard Lady Adeline's prayers, he told himself, and guided him to her wounded brother. And now… he would risk all for the sake of a brief kiss upon her cheek.

Before Enric could stop him, Thomas pulled himself up onto his horse, feeling again the weight of the chain mail, but this time a little comforted by it.

"Wait here with Ralph," he instructed his uncle, snatching a spear from the pack horse.

"No!" yelled Enric, but it was too late for Thomas was already urging his mount on along the track.

As he cantered away, he adjusted his belt and, for peace of mind, eased his sword in and out of its scabbard several times. The armed escort had to be travelling slowly for the ladies wouldn't be riding astride their mounts and in places the rain-worn road was barely passable. Indeed, the parlous condition of the road was amply demonstrated when his own horse skidded so much that he was obliged to rein it in a little. Desperate though he was to overtake them, he would do Adeline precious little service if he never reached her.

Only as he hurried along the track did he even begin to consider how he intended to persuade Sir Roger and several men at arms to surrender the ladies to him. He had scarcely travelled fifty yards, when he heard another horse splashing along behind him and, a moment later, Enric was shouting at him to pull up. Though Thomas slowed to a walk, he was in no mood to change his mind.

"I'm not giving this up," he cried.

"Then you're a cock-driven fartwit," Enric berated him.

Enric was probably right for, the moment Thomas glimpsed Adeline in that shell of a church at Scireburne Abbey, he had fallen for her. Thus, where she was concerned, there could be no compromise – and no going back, whatever the cost.

"Do you have the slightest idea what you're doing?" demanded Enric.

"I'll overtake them before they're clear of the forest."

"And then what?" pressed Enric.

"I'll tell Sir Roger to release the ladies."

"From what you've said about him, I don't reckon he's going to do that."

"Most likely not," agreed Thomas. "So, I'll just have to persuade him."

With a shake of his head, Enric said: "You're good in a fight, Thomas – no doubt about that; but if you don't show a bit more wit, you're going to die very young – most likely today."

"So, stay out of it then," said Thomas. "It's not your fight."

"Hah!" said Enric. "I can hardly take your body back to your father with that pitiful excuse, can I? However foolish you are, lad, your fight's always going to be my fight."

"Very well then," acknowledged Thomas. "Let's go to it."

Enric gave a sigh of resignation. "I think there's a bit of a ravine up ahead where the road starts to rise before the town," he said. "Best take them on there while they're slowing down. But listen, Thomas: I'm not keen on butchering men just 'cos you want to swive some girl."

"I want to free her, uncle, that's all."

"Aye, so you say," grumbled Enric. "Go on then, ride on."

"And where will you be?"

"I'll cut through the forest edge. Don't worry, I'll be close if you have any trouble…"

"If?" grinned Thomas.

"Aye, and just remember: this was your choice," warned Enric, as he left the track and slowed to veer off into the woods.

Though a little chastened by Enric's dire warnings, Thomas remained committed to his task. If he intervened by force of arms, events would swiftly run out of his control – as they had when he attempted to defend Alina. Perhaps he had been right to do so then; but was he right now?

"God will be my judge," he murmured, as he urged his mount forward to follow the track east.

Soon, as Enric predicted, it began to slope upwards, so Thomas rode on faster and caught up to the two rear-most riders when the column was still deep in the ravine. There was scarcely room for him to pass by them, but he forced his way through and glimpsed the two young ladies a little further ahead. Adeline, sitting straight-backed upon her mount, was speaking to her sister who was slumped more awkwardly in her saddle. Their spirits would be low, he reckoned, if they had just seen their half-brother struck down.

"Good morrow, ladies," he called brightly, as he rode up behind them.

Lady Isabel squeaked in surprise, fear written across her pale, round face and both girls pulled up at once. Sir Roger, a score of yards further on at the head of the column, darted a worried glance behind and, seeing Thomas, also came to a halt.

As he greeted them, Thomas forced a grin. "And how are you two ladies this morning?"

Swiftly recovering her composure, Adeline met his good cheer with a scowl, while Isabel merely blinked at him in confusion.

"You must be Lady Isabel," said Thomas, but, while the lady offered a hesitant smile, she still regarded him warily.

"What are you doing here, Thomas?" demanded Adeline.

"You know him, sister - is he a friend then?" enquired Isabel.

"No… he's not," declared Adeline. "He is Thomas FitzRobert, son of Earl Robert of Gloucester."

"Son of an earl?" gasped Isabel, immediately much more interested.

"It's an honour to meet you, Lady Isabel," said Thomas.

"Bastard son," spat Adeline, causing Thomas to wince.

"What in God's name are you doing here?" roared Sir Roger, riding back to face Thomas. "We've had enough trouble already."

"I'm just a fellow traveller on the road to Schaftesberia, Sir Roger. Perhaps I could accompany you."

Since the whole escort had now come to a halt, Thomas weighed up where he should strike first to make good their escape.

"I bid you leave these ladies in peace," ordered Sir Roger. "I fear they are far too tired for idle chatter."

For a moment Thomas simply stared at the girl whose prayers he hoped to answer, willing her to give him even the smallest sign of encouragement, but instead Lady Adeline said: "Sir Roger is right. We're not good company – and neither are you. So, please ride on."

"Surely I might bring you some welcome… distraction, my lady," he suggested.

At once those eyes flashed back at him; but she looked exhausted and her voice was steeped in sadness when she replied: "I fear, it's too late for any more distractions, Thomas."

"Be on your way, boy," grumbled Sir Roger. "You may be Gloucester's son, but it won't stop me having you tossed into the bracken on your bastard arse."

Having faced much worse jibes since he first came to his father's court at Brystole, Thomas ignored the knight's insult and replied: "This is the king's road, and I yield to no man upon it – no man…"

"But I serve Robert, Earl of Leicester," declared Sir Roger, "and there is no greater man in this realm under the king."

"Except perhaps, my father," countered Thomas.

"Your father?" laughed Sir Roger. "Your father's been absent from the king's court so long that many begin to question his loyalty…"

As if to emphasise his authority, Sir Roger laid his hand upon Thomas's arm.

Thomas stared down at the knight's hand, inclined just for a moment to hack it off; but, mindful of Enric's advice, he took a moment to choose his words.

"Whoever you serve, Sir Roger, you do not rule me. So, remove your hand, or I'll be obliged to remove it for you. I've no wish to shed your blood but, if you provoke me, I will."

With evident reluctance, Sir Roger withdrew his hand.

"Thank you," said Thomas, feeling the sweat on his palms. "And I trust that you intended no insult to my father."

Sir Roger had clearly had enough but, through gritted teeth, he growled: "No insult intended. Now, will you ride on?"

In only a few moments, the atmosphere around the wagon had become far more tense. With Sir Roger glaring at him, the other mounted men rested their hands upon their sword hilts or gripped their spears more tightly.

Thomas, his eyes fixed upon the ladies, nudged his mount closer to them. Though Lady Isabel looked ever more bewildered, her sister rested a reassuring hand upon her shoulder. Staring at Thomas with pleading eyes, she murmured: "I am promised to Abbess Bella at Schaftesberia. You can't save me so, just leave us, please…"

Isabel, he noted, was quick to shrug off her sister's hand; so, sisterly love was clearly rather limited. Edging closer to Adeline, he leaned in and looked into those green, gold-flecked eyes.

"Better keep your heads down, ladies," he warned.

Adeline reached out a hand to clutch his arm. "No, Thomas," she gasped. "There are too many…"

Glancing around at the scattered escort, he knew that she was right: there were too many. But still he grinned back at her and replied: "Aye, lady, but it's never stopped me before…"

"See him off, Folcard," Sir Roger told one of his men at arms. "Like that other wretched youth."

"You'll find, Sir Roger, that I'm not like that 'other wretched youth'," Thomas warned.

"See the bastard off!" Sir Roger snarled at the rider nearest Thomas.

Swiftly, Thomas slid his spear out of its restraining leather loops, and drove his horse forward. Though the fellow had drawn his sword, he greatly underestimated the force Thomas would bring to bear. The spearpoint scraped past a half-raised shield, struck the man at arms full in the chest and passed clean through his mail shirt. Abandoning the spear in his victim, Thomas swept past and, drawing out his sword, clubbed down the one called Folcard with its hilt.

When Lady Isabel shrieked in alarm, her horse was hauled aside by her sister. Yet, in the close confines of the narrow, steep-sided valley, there was nowhere to flee. In a blur of movement, a furious Sir Roger ripped out his sword and closed upon Thomas. Though he had reduced the odds a little, Thomas couldn't afford to be hemmed in by Sir Roger and the remaining two horsemen - nor could he fight off all three at once.

He cursed his uncle for suggesting the ravine which limited his freedom to manoeuvre - and where was Enric anyway, he wondered as he parried the first of several angry blows from Sir Roger's sword? The answer came almost at once when one of the soldiers coming at him was hurled from his mount with an arrow embedded in his shoulder.

At once, Sir Roger broke off his assault to peer up at the forested slopes above the road. The remaining guard too, eyed the higher ground with obvious apprehension.

"If you leave now, Sir Roger, you'll be spared," said Thomas.

Sir Roger gave a shake of the head. "If you abduct these ladies, you will make a mortal enemy of Earl Robert of Leicester."

"I say these ladies don't belong to him," replied Thomas. "Indeed, you may tell Robert de Beaumont that Thomas FitzRobert claims lordship over the de Sarne lands; so, the two ladies are now under my protection."

"What?" cried Sir Roger, aghast. "That's nonsense, boy. You've no rights to those lands and you know it. My lord has the law upon his side."

"I dispute the earl's claim," said Thomas.

"Defy the Earl of Leicester and you defy the king himself," declared Sir Roger, "And, believe me, your father will feel the heat of that too."

"Oh, I've no doubt of it," agreed Thomas. "Now, go, while you may, and take your wounded men with you."

But Sir Roger stubbornly refused to move until another arrow thudded into the soft earth beside his mount, causing it to rear up. Only then, seething with rage, and probably feeling no small measure of embarrassment, the knight brought his horse under control and nodded to the remaining men at arms to retreat.

"Let us go, ladies," invited Thomas.

"Go? Go where?" cried Isabel. "Sister, what's happening?"

"This is a grave mistake, Thomas," hissed Adeline.

"We can argue about that later," he replied, "but, just now, you need to ride - as fast as you can."

"To what end, Saxon," protested Adeline, distraught. "The earl will simply take us again; this isn't a rescue, it's just a stay of execution!"

"Ride," pleaded Thomas.

"I don't know you and I'm not going with you," complained a defiant Lady Isabel.

"If you do, I can take you to your wounded brother, Ralph," promised Thomas.

"Ralph is still alive?" cried Isabel.

"We feared they left him for dead," lamented Adeline.

"No, he's just wounded. Come, I'll take you to him."

Despite their reluctance, the opportunity to see their injured brother proved sufficient incentive for the sisters to accompany him and they set off back along the track.

With Isabel ahead, Adeline rode beside him, grumbling: "This is folly; they're certain to come after us."

"But they won't dare follow us… yet," said Thomas, with a grin.

When the blow came, it felt like a hard punch in the back, low down on his left side. With a grunt of pain, he lurched forward in the saddle. Feeling for the wound, he grimaced when his hand struck a quarrel protruding from his lower back. The blood upon his fingers warned him that his time was short.

He glanced across at Adeline who stared back at him, open-mouthed. "Thomas?" she cried.

"Ride on," he urged. But, when he tried to press his own mount forward, a wave of agony bent him low over the horse's neck and Adeline's gasp sent a further shiver through him.

"Keep going!" he yelled, wracked by pain. "Ralph's close by."

At the mention of her brother's name, Isabel continued along the road, but Adeline slowed.

"You're hurt," she said.

Forcing himself upright in the saddle, Thomas replied: "A slight wound only… it was just the shock of it… Go on, I'll be close behind."

To his relief, Adeline rode on and thus did not witness him sinking forward again to cling onto the horse's mane, panting and sweating like a fool. Hanging on grimly to steady himself, he took shallow breaths to help dull the agony; but, as he rode, swaying to and fro, the stabbing bouts of pain threatened to overwhelm him.

Though Isabel was almost out of sight, Adeline remained close, darting her eyes back at him. Twisting his expression into what he hoped was a smile, Thomas drove on, praying that Enric was not far behind. It could only have been a mile or so back to where they had left Ralph, but to Thomas it seemed to take forever. With the crossbow quarrel burrowing back and forth through his flesh every time he moved, he could feel his strength ebbing away, yard by yard. By the time Thomas finally arrived, Ralph was already hugging Isabel but Adeline was still mounted, staring back at him as he slumped forward with the forest spinning around him. When he crashed to the ground, his only consolation was her cry of concern.

Part Two: Renegade

8

8th June in Duncliffe Forest near Schaftesberia

Thomas came to with Enric's wrinkled face peering down at him.

"Where…?" he mumbled.

"We're in Duncliffe Forest with a healer I know," replied Enric. "Don't worry, lad, we're well-hidden and Wilflaed will look after your wound."

When Enric moved away, the two de Sarne sisters leaned over him, frowning.

"You should never have taken us," asserted Isabel crossly.

"Not now, sister," murmured Adeline.

"But he had no right to interfere," declared Isabel, before turning away in disgust.

Thomas was relieved when her peevish face was replaced by that of Adeline; until she told him: "She's right, Thomas; for no good can come of this."

Her censure wounded him almost as much as the quarrel still lodged in his back – almost…

"We demand to be returned to Sir Roger at once," persisted Isabel.

Thomas, despite his agony, couldn't let her demand pass unanswered.

"Not… going… to happen," he croaked, sweat dripping from his nose to trickle into his sparse beard.

But however much he protested, the raw pain told him that, for the time being, events would lie far beyond his control.

"Just stay alive, you young fool," grumbled his uncle, ushering the two ladies away.

It came as a blessed relief when an older woman elbowed Enric aside too and bent over him. His respite though, was short-lived for, without warning, he was unceremoniously bundled over onto his chest which sent another jolt of pain spearing through his back. Perhaps, he thought, it was a lightning bolt from the Lord.

"By Christ," he gasped, "I pray you're not the healer."

"Pray again then, lad," advised Wilflaed, "for I'm the only healer you're going to get."

By the time she and Enric started to peel off his mail shirt and tunic, Thomas was past caring who she was, for the agony sent him swooning in and out of consciousness. But only when Wilflaed began to examine the wound itself did the real torture begin. One moment her savage examination of his lower back sent him into a faint and the next the slightest tug on the quarrel jerked him awake again.

When he tried to crawl from the table to escape her probing, Enric scolded: "Hold still, lad and let Wilflaed work!"

"But she's killing me," groaned Thomas, trying to get up.

Thrusting him back down hard, Enric forced a wedge of rough, sour-tasting leather between his nephew's gritted teeth and growled: "Chew on that then."

When the time came to extract the crossbow bolt, Enric was obliged to restrain him more firmly for, though Thomas could not even see Wilflaed, he could feel her fingers stabbing into his throbbing back like a sheaf of knives.

"I need another hand," he heard the healer gasp. "If I don't get this bolt out fast, he's gonna bleed to death."

Enric, already fully engaged in holding Thomas down, looked to Adeline.

"You, girl," he flung out the words. "God's nails, come and help – unless you actually want him to die…"

Craning his neck, Thomas had a glimpse of a shocked Adeline sitting beside the wounded Ralph.

"Stay with your brother," he murmured, before passing out again.

∞ ∞ ∞

Thomas awoke in a different room that was both smaller and darker; and it was Enric he saw first, leaning against a timber partition.

"Had me worried, lad," said Enric, gently pressing a hand upon his nephew's shoulder. "Thank God Wilflaed knows what she's doing."

"I've never been wounded before," muttered Thomas. "Not even the smallest scratch."

"Well, you have now; and it's left a damned great hole in your mail shirt," complained Enric.

"By Christ, it feels sore..."

"And it'll feel sore for a while longer yet," promised Enric. "Though the way you get into fights, you'd better get used to it. Didn't I warn you not to get involved with those damned girls? Didn't I tell you they'd bring us nothing but trouble? And now look at you. You're a simple fartwit, Thomas."

Too weak to protest, Thomas was relieved when Adeline appeared behind his uncle. Enric, offering only a curt nod to the young lady, stalked out.

"I fear your uncle despises me, Saxon," she said, perching on the end of the narrow straw bed where Thomas lay.

"No, he must truly like you," said Thomas, with a feeble chuckle, "else he would just ignore you."

"Are you feeling… better?" she asked.

"Now that I see you."

"Your uncle's right," she muttered. "You are a… fartwit, was it?"

Perhaps she perceived how her response crushed him for she gently pressed a hand upon his chest. It was a simple show of concern but, when he grinned at her, she snatched the hand away at once and stood up.

"My hands are not very… clean," she stammered. "I tried to wash off the blood, but…"

"Ah, and how is Ralph?" he enquired.

"Recovering well," she replied, turning to go. "But it's not his blood that clings so stubbornly to my fingers…"

"What do you mean?" gasped Thomas. "Are you hurt?"

"No, Saxon," she replied on her way out.

For several hours he was left to rest undisturbed and it was almost nightfall when Enric, wearing his customary long face, returned to sit with him. Though it was thoughtful of his uncle to do so, Thomas would much rather have spent the evening with Adeline.

"How do you know Wilflaed?" he asked Enric.

"Ah, well… when I came back from the Holy Land, I was a forlorn bastard," explained Enric. "I didn't seem to fit in anywhere, so I suppose I sought the company of other Saxons to remind me of the old days… and that's how I found Aelflaed. But I was restless, Thomas – and I couldn't stay anywhere for long. I knew I'd bring Aelflaed nothing but misery, so I left and just wandered… all across the south. Here in Duncliffe, I stumbled across Wilflaed who lived with her old mother then. It was Wilflaed who found a way to truly heal me."

"You were wounded in the wars?"

"Not as you might think," confessed Enric. "Salves and potions couldn't heal me, lad; I needed help of a different kind, for I'd brought the torment of the wars home with me. It was Wilflaed who took that hurt away …"

"Don't tell me she's another lass you seduced."

"Alright," said Enric. "I won't tell you that."

"I was in jest," declared Thomas. "Christ's bones, you did, didn't you? I can see now why it took you so long to return. Did you lie with every lass between Warham and Brystole?"

"No - but that's my business," snapped Enric. "It's long in the past now so just leave it. God knows we've more weighty matters to chew over now."

"Aye, such as what happened on the road," complained Thomas. "I thought you were watching my back."

"I was," snorted Enric, "else you'd be dead by now because you were careless. You should've had your eyes on Sir Roger's men, not that pretty little vixen's arse."

Ignoring the rebuke, Thomas enquired: "Did you get that crossbowman?"

Enric gave a solemn nod. "I did, but you must know that Sir Roger will come for those girls. He's not just going to give up, lad, for he's no choice; he owes Robert of Leicester a young heiress to be married and a novice nun for Schaftesberia Abbey."

"But you said we're well-hidden here in the forest," argued Thomas.

"Aye, for now, but not if he's bent on finding us," replied Enric. "And he will be."

"So, what do we do?" asked Thomas. "Where should we go?"

"Oh, so now you want my advice," grumbled his uncle. "Now that you've all but buried us by making an enemy of a knight sworn to Robert, Earl of Leicester. Neither will take this well, Thomas. They'll not rest till the ladies are recovered and you, Ralph and me will be hanging from the nearest gibbet because that's where your swiving cock has led us."

Contemplating whether he should tell Enric the truth about his father's intentions, Thomas said only: "I dare say that Robert of Leicester would have become my enemy soon enough."

"What in God's name does that mean?" cried Enric.

"You'll know in time," remarked Thomas, with a grim stare that warned his uncle not to delve any further.

"Well, we'll not be safe for long, Thomas," insisted Enric. "And Sir Roger will be watching the roads so you can forget about finding passage to Normandy."

"I forgot about that at Scireburne Abbey," murmured Thomas.

Lowering his voice, Enric said: "She's just another girl, lad; and one that's promised to Schaftesberia Abbey."

"Aye, but she's not there yet, is she," argued Thomas.

"If you force her, you're no better than her captors."

"I've no intention of forcing her," hissed Thomas. "I just want to give her a choice."

"A choice, why? Who has a choice? Not many women and, least of all, heiresses to some scrap of land. She won't be the first, Thomas, or the last, to find her way into God's service – and there are far worse fates."

"If you're so troubled by what I've done then just leave," growled Thomas. "I never sought your company in the first place."

"Without me, you'd already be dead," scoffed Enric.

"Aye, I can't deny that," conceded Thomas, "but I will decide my own path, uncle – even if you don't like it."

"I've already worked that out," observed Enric.

For some time, the pair remained in glum silence while each pondered their predicament. At length, Enric said: "We'll have to stay here until you and Ralph are fit to ride; but any longer than a few days and, even in a forest this thick, we'll be found."

"Very well," agreed Thomas, though his thoughts had long ago strayed elsewhere and his uncle knew it.

"Still fixed upon that girl," he muttered.

"Don't know why," lamented Thomas. "She hasn't come to see me again…"

"Aye, that's women for you," counselled Enric. "One moment they're holding onto your hand and mending your chain mail, the next they don't even give a fart about you."

A day or two earlier, Thomas would have questioned what Enric knew about women but recent revelations suggested that his uncle might know rather more than he did.

"Wait," breathed Thomas. "When was she holding my hand?"

"Oh, I don't recall exactly," said Enric, with a wry grin. "Most likely after she helped Wilflaed dig that damned quarrel out of you. Though, as you say, the lass isn't holding it now, is she?"

Thomas had been sitting up while he talked to Enric but, once his uncle left him, he lay down on his right side to relieve the pain. Conflicting thoughts shuffled through his head until he drifted off into a fitful sleep haunted by Adeline de Sarne.

When he next awoke, it was fully dark save for the dull glow of a dying rush light emanating from somewhere in the main chamber of the cottage. He was not aware of Adeline until she moved and, even then, he wondered if she had just stepped out of his dreams.

"I'm sorry if I woke you, Saxon," she whispered. "I couldn't sleep and I wondered… how you were."

"Better," he said.

Smiling at him, she said: "Your uncle is worried about you; he told me so."

"If you've managed to squeeze a few words out of Enric, you've done very well. But I doubt he asked you to come in here."

She gave a shake of her head, which sent her tangled hair tumbling over her shoulders.

"Sweet Lord, forgive my uncovered hair," she groaned. "I must look like a wanton with it hanging loose."

"You're forgiven," he murmured.

"You were not the Lord I was asking..." she replied.

"Your hair looks… wonderful."

She smiled. "However many fine words you use, I can't stay here with you."

"Yet the first time we met, you kissed me," he murmured.

"It was a kiss of farewell – a touch upon your cheek," she explained briskly. "And I only did it to annoy Sir Roger."

"Yet here you are..."

"Your uncle insisted upon telling me all about you," said Adeline, changing the subject. "He seemed very keen to reveal that you were sent away for killing a man."

"But I've already told you that," groaned Thomas.

"Yes, you have," she agreed. "But it was different hearing it from someone who loves you."

"Pah, I doubt Enric has the slightest love for me," said Thomas. "He's only looking out for me because my father told him to – and paid him."

When she rested her hand upon his chest, he knew it was just another of those instinctive gestures that Adeline would make towards anyone in distress; but he welcomed it all the same.

"He told me you've been repairing my mail shirt," he said.

"It gave me something to do," she replied carelessly. "It will look whole but it won't… I mean, if a blade finds the join, it'll slice right through you."

"You didn't need to do it… you're a lady… and your fingers will be chafed and sore."

"It's not the first chain mail I've sewn together," she replied. "Though I confess it was difficult to mend such a large hole and I fear your mail shirt is not so long now as it was. But I should leave you in peace to rest."

"No," he protested, pressing his hand upon hers. "If you leave me now, you'll most definitely not be leaving me in peace."

She smiled and left her hand beneath his.

"It was my blood on your hands, wasn't it?" he said. "My uncle shouldn't have made you do that."

"Is a girl not allowed to help?" she asked. "You have a strange idea, Saxon, about what ladies may do. And, at the nunnery, I'll not be treated as a lady so I should get used to it. Also, it was better to help than sit, listening to your pain."

"Well, I'm still alive," he breathed, "so thank you."

"I'm relieved," she whispered. "Even if I did warn you not to interfere."

"Forgive me, I just couldn't let you be taken," he said. "But now, hearing your sister's complaints, I understand that she didn't want to be rescued. So, I suppose, I've only made things worse."

"Yes, you have," agreed Adeline. "Isabel has dreamed of little else but marriage these past two years. For her, it's a welcome escape to a better place and she believes that I too will find some peace at Schaftesberia."

"But when I look into your eyes," he murmured, "I know you'll find no peace there."

"Then stop looking into my eyes," she said, though hers were locked upon his. "My fate is what my father decreed in his will and I must accept it. As for Isabel, well, every lady is destined to marry and become one of her husband's chattels. Through her, he will gain the de Sarne lands."

"While you, the elder, are disinherited," groaned Thomas, "unless, of course, you were to marry someone - like me…"

"I have no leave to marry anyone, Saxon," she declared. "And why would I even think of marrying a youth who deceived me from the first?"

With that brutal riposte, she tore her hand from his grasp and slipped away into the gloomy cottage interior leaving a bewildered Thomas to reflect how the world could turn so swiftly sour.

9

9th June at Wilflaed's cottage in Duncliffe Forest

Watching Thomas FitzRobert sleep, thought Adeline, was to witness the fitful, twitching slumber of a tortured soul. Surely, in the end, such a man must be consumed by his demons and ruin anyone foolish enough to put their trust in him. If Wilflaed had not despatched her to wake him, she would have kept away. But, now she was standing over him, she could not deny the warm flush in her cheeks.

When Thomas turned onto his back and gave a low moan, she reached out to touch his brow. It was a natural gesture to calm him but, when those blue-grey eyes flickered open, she dropped her hand to rest it lightly upon his shoulder.

Squinting up at her, he murmured: "My lady?"

For a few long moments they regarded each other in silence until Adeline blurted out: "You should get up, Saxon."

"I would have you wake me every morning," he said.

"Wilflaed sent me," she explained hastily, praying her confusion was less evident than it felt.

"Then I thank God for Wilflaed," he replied, smiling up at her.

Overwhelmed by the feelings he awoke in her, Adeline drew back a pace as she replied: "Indeed, you should thank her for saving your life."

Thomas shifted his weight to sit up and winced. "What does Wilflaed want?" he enquired.

"Wilflaed?" muttered Adeline, distracted by the blanket falling away from Thomas's bare chest.

"You said… she sent you."

Dragging her eyes from his torso, Adeline mumbled: "Aye, she did. She wants you to get up."

"But shouldn't I be resting?"

At that moment Wilflaed thrust her head into the small, curtained-off alcove. "Rest is for the dead, Thomas," she announced. "So, start moving."

"Do you want to look at the wound?" he asked.

"Don't need to look at it," retorted Wilflaed. "I can smell it's fine. Just leave the cloth bound to it till it starts to fray. By then you'll have a nice scar forming to impress your young lady."

Adeline looked away and Thomas replied glumly: "I don't have a young lady."

But Wilflaed simply laughed and said to Adeline: "Help him up, then, lass."

Turning back to face Thomas, Adeline hardly knew where to look but extended a hand to help him to his feet. Once he grasped it, she really didn't want him to let it go, so she walked beside him as he took his first tentative steps through the cottage and outside.

Gripping her hand more tightly, he asked: "Where is everyone?"

"Be calm," she said. "Isabel is doing for Ralph what I am doing for you."

"I truly pray she isn't," muttered Thomas, with a mischievous grin.

"I mean helping him to walk on his injured leg," scolded Adeline. Though, as a reproof, she had to admit that it was a very feeble one. "Wilflaed is out collecting herbs and I think Enric must be with her," she added. "Are those two…?"

"I've no idea," replied Thomas. "Until this past week I thought I knew my uncle but it seems I hardly know him at all."

He came to an abrupt halt, his fingers crushing hers, but she bore it, knowing how much pain he was suffering. The moment he realised her distress, he relaxed his grip and lifted her hand to kiss it.

"Your pardon," he murmured.

"Perhaps we should go back," she said, her voice suddenly very small and hoarse.

"No, please, walk with me just a little longer," he pleaded, never once relinquishing his hold upon her hand.

And so, she let him walk on, though she knew his wound was sore and he should rest. They completed two more slow circuits around the cottage but, towards the end, she was obliged to thread an arm round his waist to bear some of the weight. When they returned, finally, to the cottage, she carefully helped him back to his bed.

"I shouldn't have allowed you to walk so far," she said.

"It was my choice… and having you by my side was…"

"Painful?"

"No, well, yes; but it would have been much more so without you."

"So, you say, Saxon," she murmured.

"Why do you keep taunting me with that jibe?" he said.

Wrongfooted by his complaint, she replied: "I… I don't use it to taunt you; it's just how you first explained to me who you are. I use it with… affection."

"I suppose you'll never forgive me for what I did when we first met, will you?" he lamented.

She made no reply for it would not help either of them to admit she had forgiven him even before that night's end.

"What should I call you then?" she enquired.

"Fitz is what the other lads called me in the training yard," he told her.

When he clasped her hand, she pulled it gently away. "This is not real, Fitz," she said, though the words cut her.

"It feels real to me," he replied softly, searching her eyes until she looked away.

"My sister must go back to Sir Roger," she said. "And I must go with her; she's so young to marry and knows nothing of men."

"While you do," he said, with a smirk.

"Now who's taunting," she replied. "But, promise me, Thomas that you won't force us to remain here."

Wrapping his hand over hers again, he replied: "I'll never force you to do anything. If you truly wish to leave, I'll take you myself. But never ask me to stop caring for you."

With a trembling heart, she felt a powerful desire to just lie down there beside him on the straw. But, of course, that would only make matters worse, so she sat down instead, leaving her hand in his. How, in such a short time, had she become so mindlessly besotted with this blood-haired youth? Weak-spirited and wanton, her father had called her; perhaps he was right. Perhaps, after all, she deserved to be confined to a nunnery.

For the rest of the morning, she remained by Thomas's side, though few words passed between them. In the end she only left him when her sister came to berate her for ignoring Ralph; though Adeline knew that it was not her brother that she had displeased.

10

10th June at Wilflaed's cottage in Duncliffe Forest

The next morning Thomas was not awoken by Adeline and, instead, was condemned to take his exercise in the company of his uncle.

"You're a quick healer by the look of it," remarked Enric, adding with a grim chuckle, "which is just as well, given that trouble finds you quicker than flies find shit."

Thomas, brooding because he was not with Adeline, managed only a grunt in response.

"We'll do a wide sweep around the cottage," Enric explained. "And yes, we'll keep one eye on the de Sarnes as well."

Thomas nodded absently, wondering how he could possibly extricate Adeline from her fate. It brought him no pleasure to observe how much the growing friction between the sisters distressed her. Since Isabel fretted more with every passing hour, her bitterness increased the tension in the cottage and Wilflaed's rudimentary woodland home was far too small to accommodate such uneasy company for long. Sooner or later, Thomas could see that someone's nerve would break.

While Adeline attempted to heal the rift with her sister, her prolonged absence grieved Thomas beyond words. Throughout the day – their third at the cottage – the pattern was repeated and, by evening, though his body already felt much stronger, he struggled to conceal his misery. Having Adeline so close, yet utterly out of his reach, seemed worse than not seeing her at all.

Using his wound as an excuse, he took to his bed early though he felt a pang of guilt as he did so. Everyone else was obliged to sleep on the cottage floor and he supposed that, now his wound was showing signs of improvement, he should surrender the bed of straw to the two sisters.

Irritated though he was by Isabel's obduracy, he resolved that on the morrow, he must allow the ladies to sleep there.

That night, having dozed during the early evening, he lay awake, wrestling with problems that were entirely of his own making. The solution, of course, was self-evident: return Lady Isabel to Sir Roger; and, since Adeline could not abandon her sister, she would have to go too. From the outset, though she had told him he could have no future with her, he had simply refused to listen. How bitterly she must resent his attentions for, all that day, she refused even to look him in the eye. She had tried to make him understand and now, finally, he did; yet, when he fell asleep, he could not help wishing it was otherwise.

In the middle of the night, he was awoken by a cold, but soft, hand easing him to the far side of the bed.

"What is it?" he gasped, but at once chill fingers pressed gently against his lips and then, to his astonishment, Adeline lay down beside him.

"This is but a dream," he murmured, but the light pressure of her body against his suggested otherwise. "Is it truly you?"

"Well, it's not your uncle… and would this hand be so cold in a dream?" she asked, resting her palm upon his shoulder.

"I missed you all day," he breathed.

"Then you must learn not to miss me," she whispered.

"Then why, in God's name did you come?" he groaned.

"Do you want me to go?" she asked.

"No, no…"

"Perhaps I came to warm my hands," she replied softly, entwining her fingers in his.

"Aye, perhaps you did…" he agreed.

"In the chill of the night, I just wanted to be with you," she murmured. "So, it seems I'm just as… wild-spirited as you are – or as foolish."

For a time, neither uttered another word as they lay together and when Thomas, captivated by the steady beat of her heart, put an arm around her, all she said was: "Take care with that wound."

"This isn't going to help, is it?"

"It'll be fine if we just lie still," she replied.

"I didn't mean the wound…"

When Thomas awoke, Adeline was still in his arms, her head upon his chest. But the dawn light was already filtering in and he could hear movement elsewhere in the cottage. It took only a gentle shake to wake her but she gasped in panic.

"Be at ease," he told her. "For we have only lain here…"

"Yes, but we've lain here all night," she hissed, scrambling into a sitting position and swinging her feet to the floor. "My sister will find me gone and-"

Her words dried up when the curtain was swept aside and her sister was standing there, quivering with anger. Before Adeline could remonstrate with her, Isabel stormed out of the cottage.

"Oh no," breathed Adeline. "I'll have to go after her, or God knows what she'll do!"

"I'll come with you," said Thomas. "I can explain."

"Explain, Thomas – how?" wept Adeline. "I can't even explain it myself. She already thinks me a whore; so, believe me, there's nothing you could say to convince her that I've not sinned – again. When we talked that night at Scireburne, I knew I should have walked away at once. And now, all I've done is heap more misery upon us both."

Sobbing, she wrestled to put on her boots, while Thomas, brushing away the tears running down her cheeks, tried to help her.

"It's my fault, not yours," he said. "I should have just let you be."

Adeline stood up, embraced him and pressed her lips to his cheek. "Aye, you should; but, you didn't. And I led you on – persuading myself that it was only to annoy Sir Roger - until I found that it wasn't."

The moment she fled across the threshold, he was already pulling on his boots to follow but Enric came in and said firmly: "Leave the ladies be, lad, 'cos we need to talk."

Several times over the past two days, his uncle had been out watching in the woods; but this morning he reported that Sir Roger's men had been observed in several parts of the great forest.

"We can't stay here much longer, Thomas," he said. "They're getting too close. So, whatever we're going to do, we need to do it tomorrow."

"Very well," agreed Thomas. "I know what has to be done: we'll take the pair of them to Schaftesberia."

"What?" cried Enric. "After all this damned trouble."

Thomas stared nonplussed at his uncle. "But I thought you'd be pleased. You never wanted me to free them in the first place."

"No, I didn't but, now we've abducted them, I don't see how we can just go back… And well, by Christ, Thomas, you've just spent the night with her."

"Don't tell everyone," hissed Thomas.

"Everyone already knows," retorted Enric.

"But we were just lying here…"

"Aye, well that's usually when it happens," remarked Enric.

"But it didn't happen," protested Thomas.

Enric gave a shake of the head. "If you say so – but do you really want to take her to the abbey at Schaftesberia?"

"No, of course I don't; but it's what she wants," cried Thomas. "So, what else can I do?"

"Well, I suppose it makes a change for us to be ruled by her dull wits instead of yours," groaned Enric.

"Just leave it," growled Thomas.

"Aye," groaned Enric, "but if we're taking the ladies to Schaftesberia tomorrow then we'd best leave early. I'll make sure all's ready."

For the rest of the day, Thomas was on his feet testing out how well his wound was healing. Since he was able to wield his sword for a time and could mount and dismount without undue discomfort, he reckoned that, if he was careful, all would be well and he thanked God for Wilflaed's healing skills.

Adeline spent almost every moment trying to bridge the chasm that had now opened up between the two sisters; so, once again, Thomas saw little of her during the day. By the evening it was clear that her sister had not forgiven Adeline, so he knew there would be no more nights spent in her arms. He must cherish every glimpse of her before he gave her up forever. Whenever their paths crossed during the day, Adeline darted him a hesitant smile which only made his heart ache even more.

Ralph, at least, was willing to speak to him and, in the afternoon, the two wounded youths took a walk together for the first time. Though both were already tired, it was preferable to returning to the chill atmosphere in the cottage. For the first time, Thomas noticed how similar Ralph's countenance was to his elder sister and the siblings shared the same black hair, though Ralph's was cut shorter than most men.

"I suppose I should be angry with you," said Ralph, "but Adeline insists that you were not at fault and did not take advantage of her."

Unable to think of a suitable response, Thomas continued walking in silence.

"She has been taken advantage of before," Ralph confided, "which is why my father condemned her to a nunnery."

"She did tell me that your father saw her with another man."

Ralph gave a shake of the head. "It was just a young stable lad who found himself spellbound by my beautiful, passionate sister. I don't think either of them knew what they were doing but father whipped them both and turned the boy off the estate."

"He whipped his own daughter?" cried Thomas, incredulous.

"Aye, she still bears the scars – and not only upon her back. In father's eyes, she shamed his whole family that day - hence the nunnery…"

Beside his companion, Thomas, quietly seething, said only: "Then it's as well your father is already dead…"

"What will you do with my sisters?" asked Ralph.

"In God's name, what am I to do, Ralph?" protested Thomas. "I've no power over their fate, any more than you do. Adeline wants to ensure her sister's happiness in marriage and prevent any dispute with your lord, Robert of Leicester. There's only one way to do both those things and we know what that is."

"But you can't take them back," argued Ralph. "Neither of us wants that."

"Adeline's made up her mind and I will respect that," insisted Thomas. "So must you - or you'll lose both your sisters. Whether you choose to come with us to Schaftesberia is up to you, but don't try to stop us."

"I thought you were my ally in this," complained Ralph.

"I am only ever – and always - Adeline's ally," said Thomas.

"She's but a girl – what does she know about anything?"

"You need to listen to her, Ralph," said Thomas, "because, by the saints, she's probably got more sense than both of us."

Leaving the crestfallen Ralph to stew upon his words, Thomas wandered back to the cottage but did not stay there long. At dusk, he took yet more exercise, this time with Enric who, after they had circled the cottage twice on an extended perimeter, pronounced himself content that Sir Roger's men were not yet getting any closer. Even so, the pair did not hurry back to the cottage and, when they arrived, the rush lights were burning low and only Wilflaed was still awake.

"Even if we leave here before Sir Roger finds us," Enric told her, "He might still come here and threaten you."

"He's only to ask at the abbey and they'll tell him where I live," she said, with a rueful grimace. "But then it wouldn't be you if you didn't bring trouble to my door, would it?"

"I'm sorry," muttered Enric.

"No, you're not," she scorned, flashing a rueful smile.

Glancing around the chamber, Thomas's eyes lingered upon the cloth draped across the other end of the room beyond which lay the two young ladies. He had completely forgotten that he was going to give up his bed so, with a guilty sigh, he turned away and left Enric and Wilflaed to talk, which they often did for an hour or more in the evening. Whether they exchanged any more than words, Thomas had no wish to discover.

Long after the rushes smouldered out and it was quiet enough in the cottage to hear Ralph's snoring, Thomas, as ever, lay wide awake. The morrow would bring him much distress and, if he slept, he feared that his dreams of Adeline would be dark indeed. When, eventually, weariness drew him into slumber, his dreams were every bit as bitter as he feared. In the small hours of the night, he dwelt in a pit of black despair and even the light pressure of a woman's lips upon his could not release him from his torment. How evil was such a dream that teased and tore at his heart?

Only when he felt her slide into the bed beside him, did he realise he was awake and that she had come to him again. Her arms slipped around him and he gasped at her nakedness for her shift was rucked up to her waist and she was icy cold.

"Why are you here?" he breathed.

"If you have to ask that," she whispered, "perhaps I should go."

"But you're shivering."

"I was standing watching you for a long time."

"You're so cold..."

"Aye," she murmured, "and a little terrified."

"Of me?"

"Of what I feel, of what I'm doing here in your bed and of what dread punishment I shall bring down upon us both."

"Let's not speak of that then," he said.

In the narrow bed she was so pressed against him that he could feel every contour of her body. Kissing her full on the lips for the very first time brought all his senses alive. It was a long, sweet kiss during which their legs somehow became entwined and he discovered that not all of her was cold. As his loins responded to her touch, he knew that, in a moment he would not be able to stop.

"Are you certain this is what you want?" he asked.

"Aye, but don't ask me again, lest I say no. I wanted to be with you at least once before I shun men forever."

"So, this is one last night together..."

"Our first true night together - and our last…"

"It should be the first of thousands," he argued. "If we just say the words, we are married."

"Without the permission of my guardian, or your father?" she said. "How futile that would be. No, we'll say no words, swear no oaths and have no regrets."

As they moved against each other, her shift somehow rode up to her neck. His skin tingled as he stroked her trembling body; moving his hands slowly down her back, he paused where the skin was rough.

"The scars of my wicked past," she gasped, pulling away from him. "Of course, I should have told you. You must be shocked…"

"Ralph told me…"

"Damn him - he shouldn't have," she said bitterly. "It's my shame to confess, not his."

"It's your father's shame," he told her. "And, in any case, we all have our scars."

Slowly he slid his hands from her back down onto her buttocks and along her smooth thighs. Gulping in several deep breaths, she lay against him, allowing her fingers to explore him and he winced as she touched the wound.

"I'm sorry," she hissed, "Just trying to find the best place to warm my hands…"

"Allow me," he replied, guiding her icy fingers to a place where they swiftly melted upon hot flesh.

"I'm not sure what I'm doing," she muttered, but since her long legs soon wrapped themselves around him, he decided that Adeline's body was a quick learner. Her raw passion thrilled him though, when the moment came, it passed all too quickly and he was left disappointed. He had wanted their union to be more than just some short-lived coupling in the dark. All the same, they lay together as one, grinning and kissing, kissing and grinning until sleep captured them.

He awoke because she kissed him, but her erect nipples pressing hard against his chest would have been more than enough to arouse him again.

"When you said," he murmured, "that you wanted to lie with me *at least* once…"

But her lips stopped any more words and what her hands were doing elsewhere rendered him beyond speech.

11

12th June at Wilflaed's cottage in Duncliffe Forest

"Wake up, Thomas!" cried Ralph. "Wake up – my sisters have... gone."

His voice faltered at the sight of Adeline's tousled black hair emerging from beneath the woollen blanket beside Thomas. Then, before the two shocked occupants of the bed could disentangle themselves, he muttered: "Isabel's gone; and it's your fault - both of you!"

Moments after Ralph left them, Enric came in to report that Isabel had indeed taken one of the horses. Standing on the threshold, staring at the lovers, he gave a mournful shake of the head.

"I'll be outside, Thomas," he said. "When you're ready to leave."

Trembling in Thomas's arms, Adeline gave him a bitter smile. "Only a few sweet hours together and already the punishment begins."

"Ralph's wrong," argued Thomas. "It's not our fault; we're in love."

"No, we're in a dream," sighed Adeline, easing him aside.

"Do you regret it then?" he murmured.

"Aye," she replied briskly. "I do; and now I have to go after her."

"You stay here," he told her. "I'll go with Enric."

"You can hardly sit on a horse, let alone ride one," she cried.

"I can ride well enough," he lied. "Stay and make your peace with Ralph, for he needs you too."

Not without some difficulty, Thomas persuaded her to remain with Ralph and Wilflaed at the cottage. When he went out to join Enric, Adeline did not even look at him but he shrugged off the disappointment, knowing how guilty she must feel. Then, just as he was about to leave, she ran to his side and clasped his hand in hers.

Kissing his cheek, she breathed: "No, Thomas, I don't regret it. I don't regret it at all."

When he rode away with Enric, his whole body was afire but only partly from the discomfort of riding. Though it was perhaps an hour or so after dawn, the dull grey morning offered poor light beneath the thick canopy of beech and oak in the depths of Duncliffe forest.

Lady Isabel had probably left the cottage moments after dawn, so the wretched girl could be as much as an hour ahead of them. Even if she had ridden with very great caution at first, she must be at least a mile or two ahead which, in the forest, was some distance. Thus, he doubted they would overtake her before she joined the road to Schaftesberia and rode for the abbey as fast as she dared. Their pursuit, though necessary, would very likely be futile.

Only God knew how much the furious Isabel would tell the abbess and Sir Roger, but Thomas reckoned that it would not reflect well upon those who had held her, nor her sister. Though he suspected there was little malice in Isabel, the strict sense of duty which drove her towards her marriage would, he feared, also lead her to condemn her sister's wanton behaviour. He doubted that the abbey would reject Adeline simply because she had lain with Thomas, for no doubt the abbess was to receive a generous endowment for taking the girl in. Yet, he did not want Adeline's reputation sullied by gossip.

He should have foreseen what Isabel would do because she had been complaining since her arrival at the cottage. Her concern for her wounded brother might have blunted her initial outrage, but not for long. Having endured for several days the rough hospitality of Wilflaed's cottage, Isabel must have regarded Adeline's growing intimacy with Thomas as the last straw.

The two men rode in silence, with Enric's sharp eyes picking out the tracks of Isabel's mount while Thomas brooded gloomily. When they emerged abruptly from beneath the tree canopy onto the muddy road, Enric pulled up at once and cast an eye along to east and then west.

"She'll be at Schaftesberia by now," muttered Thomas.

Enric gave a grunt though Thomas couldn't decide whether it signalled doubt or agreement. Neither man was keen to urge his horse forward and take the road east; because, once they did, they risked all.

"She knows where Wilflaed's cottage is," said Enric. "And they can follow her tracks all the way there. We should go back to the cottage, get the others and leave while we still can."

"But Adeline won't leave without Isabel," declared Thomas.

"Aye, and I doubt Wilflaed will leave her home either," added Enric miserably. "What a mess of shit you've dragged us into, nephew."

"I should go to Schaftesberia alone," said Thomas.

"And do what?" cried Enric. "Even if you're not arrested on the spot, you can hardly drag the girl back to the forest; you'd be no better than those you're so keen to condemn."

"Adeline will want to know that her sister's safe," insisted Thomas.

"Tell me honestly: where exactly do things stand between you two?" Enric enquired.

"I'm in love with her – in case you hadn't noticed."

"Love, eh?" scoffed Enric. "Well, Thomas, I'd worked that out; but love is a shit-stirring mistress."

"So, I've learned," said Thomas, "And I don't know what Adeline thinks from one moment to the next."

"Ha!" cried Enric. "Nor will you ever."

"It's all so… raw. Until last night I just assumed she'd leave for Schaftesberia with her sister and forget all about me."

"Aye, and better for her – for all of us - if she had," said Enric. "Now we're deep in the mire, Thomas. We've got a wounded, vengeful Roland de Burgh hunting us; and you have to pick a quarrel with the Earl of Leicester - of all people. Is there anyone else you'd like to cross? King Stephen himself, perhaps?"

"Ah well, that'll come soon enough," muttered Thomas.

Enric darted his nephew a sharp look. "I asked you before what you meant; this time, I want an answer, lad – a straight answer."

Thomas gave a weary sigh. "You might as well know, I suppose. My father's gone to Normandy to declare for the Empress Matilda."

"What?" cried Enric, in disbelief. "God's nails! I see now whence you get your foolishness."

"You must tell no-one." instructed Thomas sternly.

Enric gave a bitter laugh. "Oh, aye, because I'm sure to shout about that to every man I meet. And there was me thinking that, if things got worse, your father might help us. Now I find that you're both up to your balls in treason."

"Enough," declared Thomas. "I'm going to Schaftesberia – are you coming, or not?"

"Wouldn't miss it," grumbled Enric.

"Have you been there before?"

"I was a youth last time I went there – the only time I've been there…"

"Good. So, at least we won't find any women there you might have lain with," said Thomas.

"I told you: there were no others," said Enric. "Just Aelflaed and Wilflaed."

"Aye, so you say…"

Though Thomas knew he could not persuade Isabel to return to the forest, there was still a chance that he might convince her not to reveal where her sister was. And, if he could reassure Adeline that her sister was unharmed, she might forsake a life in the abbey and leave with him.

"Watch out!" cried Enric.

Deep in thought, Thomas was slow to react before his horse slid sideways where the road had been washed completely away by the heavy spring rains. With startling agility, the mare recovered her footing but not before she had hurled Thomas face down into the mud.

Enric pulled up, wearing a broad grin instead of his usual taciturn expression.

"There you are, lad," he remarked, grinning. "No good comes from dwelling on a lass; better to look where you're going. Anyway, we're close to the town now; for the two roads from the west meet here."

"They do?" said Thomas, for whom the junction resembled only a small lake.

"Aye," said Enric. "We'd best head south of the old town."

Thomas, his face and hands caked with mud, just gave a shrug and, relieved that he appeared to have done no damage to his wound, remounted his horse. In future, he resolved, he would pay more attention to the road.

"The old town's up there," said Enric, pointing to a great spur of rock which rose steeply ahead to overshadow all else around.

Having taken what Enric assured him was the right fork in the road, they headed up a gentle rise towards the town.

"The lady will likely make straight for the abbey," said Thomas. "So, where is it?"

"You'll see soon enough," replied Enric. "It's east of the old town."

Moments later, as they approached the high plateau upon which the town stood, Thomas saw the lofty tower of the abbey church. Enric stopped to stare up, not at the abbey tower, but towards the nearer high ground looming above them to their left. A grim frown cast a shadow across his uncle's face.

"What's amiss?" demanded Thomas. "What have you seen?"

Pointing up the slope, his uncle muttered: "That wasn't there last time I was here."

That seemed hardly surprising to Thomas if Enric had last visited as a young lad; but it didn't explain his uncle's worried expression.

Stabbing a finger at the wooden building perched on the promontory, Enric growled: "That castle up there looks very new to me."

When Thomas turned his attention to the fort, he reckoned he could actually hear hammering and, at the top of the steep slope, he could make out the raw scar of a freshly-dug ditch. Beyond that, he glimpsed a wooden palisade that, by the sound of it, was still being completed.

"Aye, a new castle," he remarked, "and not yet finished…"

"This isn't a place to linger," observed Enric, riding on to where the road forked again. One road appeared to wind up towards the town, but Enric followed the other, narrower lane which skirted the steeper ground but continued alongside the mighty hill upon which the town and abbey stood.

Passing a small church, Enric remarked: "Now, I remember this place though. St. James, I think, but it looks in need of some repair."

It was not the only thing in disrepair, thought Thomas, for the town rampart perched high above them appeared to have fallen away in places and there were whole stretches where he could discern no defensive wall at all.

"Many a merchant or pilgrim will go through St James to make their way up to the market or the abbey," Enric told him.

"Is that how we're getting in?" enquired Thomas.

"No, it's a bit too open there for us," explained Enric. "Others will head for the main gate to the abbey, but not us."

After a few more yards, Enric turned off left along a lane which led uphill.

"There's another way into the abbey then."

"Aye, for those who know," confirmed Enric, as if he entered the abbey covertly all the time. "Don't worry, lad; I'll get us in."

But when they reached the top of the slope, they were faced by a stone wall which appeared to enclose the entire abbey precinct. Beyond it lay the great west end of the abbey church with its square towers of bright new stone. It was the largest building Thomas had seen outside Brystole and he could not help but gaze up at it in awe.

Scratching his head, Enric said: "God's nails, the abbey's got bigger. I reckon they were rebuilding the church when I last came and now, they've changed everything else by the looks of it. There used to be a gate along here somewhere…"

"Perhaps they've done away with it in all the rebuilding," suggested Thomas.

"Nuns have washing like everyone else," said Enric, "and the lay laundresses use the lane we've just ridden up to take the laundry down to dry. Come on, let's look a bit closer."

Leading the way along the lane, he was almost at the top when he gave a grunt of satisfaction and indicated a small gate set back in the wall.

"There we are," he said. "I knew there'd still be a way through."

Staring at the gate, Thomas remarked: "But it's shut, uncle."

"Not at this hour of the morning," replied Enric, with a knowing grin.

Dismounting, he approached the gate and gave it a gentle shove. When it swung open, he explained: "Some things don't change. When the girls come back up with the washing, they'll have their hands full. So, though it looks shut, they just leave the gate unbarred."

"Are we going in then?" asked Thomas, irritated by Enric's confidence.

"Best you wait here in the alley with the horses," his uncle advised. "We daren't attract too much attention; I'll slip in quick and find out if Lady Isabel's here."

"How?"

"Simple. If you want to know the comings and goings of an abbey, you ask an usher. Now, you just wait here, 'cos I'll not be long."

Pushing open the door, Enric passed swiftly through leaving Thomas waiting in the alley, feeling very exposed. The longer he stood there, the more his confidence in his uncle diminished and, when a sudden uproar came from within, he knew Enric must be in trouble. So, leaving the horses tethered in the alley, Thomas slipped through the gateway into the abbey.

Once inside, however, he came to an abrupt halt for he had no idea where Enric had gone. Creeping across an open yard, he went to every door and listened for a rumble of voices on the other side. Where were all the lay servants, he wondered? At the third door, he heard voices approaching but, before he could move, the door was flung open and Enric crashed across the threshold into him.

As both men tumbled down onto the cobbles, Enric cried: "What are you doing here, you fartwit? You're supposed to be with the horses."

Hurrying back towards the gate, they found their path cut off by several men emerging from other chambers.

"Shit!" cried Enric. "Now we're truly buggered. Why didn't you just stay outside?"

Enric led a bewildered Thomas back further into the labyrinth of timber buildings so that very soon the youth was utterly lost. Worse still, a growing crowd appeared to be pursuing them which only added to Thomas's confusion. Several women had joined the throng and, by their apparel and baskets of clothing they clutched, they could only be laundresses.

"Do you know where you're going?" demanded Thomas.

"Peace," hissed Enric. "It's all coming back to me…"

"These folk shouldn't be our enemies," declared Thomas, as he followed Enric into yet another small courtyard, seeking somewhere to hide.

"No," replied Enric. "But just now they are…"

"But why are they so angry?" groaned Thomas. "Christ's bones! What did you do, uncle?"

But before Enric could enlighten him, they entered a narrow passage off which an empty chamber beckoned. Enric fled inside at once and Thomas, following close, shut the door behind them. For a while they listened for any sounds of pursuit but, to their relief, the hue and cry appeared to have subsided.

"Well, that was awkward," said Enric, puffing out his cheeks. "Still, with luck, they'll go about their business now."

Just then footsteps thudded on the ground outside and someone slammed into the door, wrenching it open. For an instant the fellow stood framed in the doorway and then, swiftly he was gone; but not before the door slammed shut and the two fugitives heard the unwelcome grate of a heavy bolt being drawn into place. Hurrying to the door, Thomas found it shut fast and turned to face Enric.

"You've condemned us, uncle," railed Thomas. "What in God's name have you done?"

"It was an honest mistake," protested Enric, "but, I might have… offended someone. It's a bit hard to explain."

"Try," snarled Thomas.

"Well, I only asked one of the laundry women to show me the stables and she did – which I took as a kindness. There, sure enough, I found Lady Isabel's horse and I was about to go back to tell you when the woman… well, she… I think she might have misunderstood why I wanted her to take me to the stables…"

"What happened?" enquired Thomas, already fearing the worst.

"Well, she was coming on a bit strong so I thought the best way to discourage her was to give her quick peck on the cheek – by way of thanks for her help."

"But she objected?" said Thomas.

"Oh no, I think she was up for more than that – good-looking woman by the way… for her age – but then one of the ushers came in."

"I thought you were looking for an usher."

"Well, not just then, I wasn't; and it was rather… awkward…"

12

12th June in the afternoon at Wilflaed's cottage in Duncliffe Forest

Adeline lounged upon the straw bed where she had lain with Thomas and shamelessly given herself to him. Would the Lord condemn her for one sinful night on the eve of a whole eternity spent in His service? Certainly Isabel had.

Once, in the time when their father loved them both in equal measure, she had been so close to her sister. But his affection for his elder daughter was swept away on that careless summer afternoon when reckless innocence led her to the stable. He was a boy about her age, not yet sixteen and, looking back now, she saw that he was utterly unremarkable. Yet, at that one moment, he awoke a tide of passion in her that seemed to rise from nowhere.

In the steaming heat of that stable, her carefree childhood was cast aside as the pair fumbled away her maidenhood. But, when a shadow crossed the threshold, that one moment of desire served to define her forever in the eyes of both her father and sister. After that day, and the whipping that followed, neither looked at her as they had before.

After enduring two long years of shame and regret, she accepted her disinheritance as inevitable. But only after her father's death, did she learn that the full severity of his punishment was lifelong penance in a nunnery. The misery of it had weighed her down… until that damp night at Scireburne Abbey when Thomas FitzRobert stirred in her feelings she had never felt in that stable.

"Come, my lady," said Wilflaed, startling her. "You can't lie abed all day."

"Thomas said to stay inside the cottage," murmured Adeline.

"Well, it's not his cottage," Wilflaed pointed out. "I've herbs to collect and I think you should come with me."

As Adeline had observed, Wilflaed foraged in the forest almost every day to gather the many diverse ingredients she needed for her healing salves and lotions. Reckoning she would be safe enough with Wilflaed, Adeline accepted the offer and, abandoning a disgruntled Ralph, accompanied the healer into the forest. If she was honest, it was a welcome distraction.

To Adeline's surprise, Wilflaed avoided using the most well-worn tracks and instead picked her way, without the slightest hesitation, among the most densely-packed trees. Keeping up with the Saxon required all of Adeline's concentration. Occasionally, the older woman stooped to point out some plant or other; but, though Adeline was keen to learn, she absorbed very little knowledge that morning. Wilflaed must have noticed for she suddenly stopped to confront the young lady.

"What? What is it?" asked Adeline, smiling at her. "Do I have leaves in my hair – or a spider, perhaps?"

Wilflaed shook her head. "No, lass, you just have a bit of a glow about you - and it's not hard to see why…"

"Well, I've no idea why," said Adeline, feeling a hot flush spread across her entire face.

With a shake of the head, Wilflaed replied: "You might tell yourself that, my lady, but I knew the first moment I saw you with Thomas that you'd fallen for him."

"I haven't 'fallen' for him," protested Adeline.

Taking her hand, Wilflaed said: "If you say so, my lady; but if I were you, I'd hold onto love while you can. God knows, you may never know it again."

"I'm really not sure how I feel about Thomas," lied Adeline, as she recalled every step of their walk around the forbidden Scireburne cloister and the warmth of his hand folded around hers. It was she who kissed him first – even if it was only a mere brush of her lips against his cheek.

"Perhaps your head hasn't caught up to your heart yet," mused Wilflaed.

"I assure you," she told Wilflaed, "that my head and heart are as one on this. I have a duty to others…"

"Does that include Thomas?" enquired Wilflaed. "For he's clearly smitten with you. Even when Enric carried him in bleeding, that youth's eyes never left you."

"I didn't notice," muttered Adeline but, before she knew it, a fierce longing was scorching through her.

Overwhelmed, she lurched, weeping, against a young oak and Wilflaed wrapped her arms around her.

"We've scarce spent a few hours together," sobbed Adeline. "And now I've sent him after Isabel and he'll likely never return."

Taking her by the shoulders, Wilflaed looked her in the eye. "I never marked you for a weak-spirited lass," she said. "Nor, I think, does Thomas. You've a strong spirit, lady, so you'd best start showing it."

"But even if he does come back, there's no future for us," cried Adeline.

"I know you're bound for the abbey; but it was you decided to lie with him," Wilflaed pointed out. "So, how do you think he feels now?"

When Adeline started to weep again, Wilflaed grumbled: "Cast aside your doubts, lady, because either you love him or you don't. Love never takes the easy path; and, by God, it'll twist and turn before it ends. But you have a strong heart; so, if you love him, you'll walk through fire to be with him. Now take a deep breath and show me no more child's tears."

When Wilflaed released her, Adeline felt stripped bare by the healer's stark appraisal. Gulping down a breath, she struggled to clear her head. What did a simple healer know anyway? It mattered not whether she loved Thomas, for she was destined to spend her life with the nuns at Schaftesberia – unless, of course, that was just one twist in their tale of love…

She had to admit that Wilflaed's directness had helped a little; for, somehow, she felt refreshed and perhaps more ready to face whatever troubles lay ahead. As they returned to the cottage in the afternoon, walking arm in arm, the sound of approaching horses brought them to a nervous halt at the edge of the trees.

"Could it be Thomas and Enric, with news of my sister?" whispered Adeline, gripping Wilflaed's arm tightly.

But, when she took a step forward, Wilflaed held her back. "That's a wagon," warned the healer.

"Why would they bring a wagon?" murmured Adeline, noting Wilflaed's worried countenance.

Lingering on the treeline, Wilflaed peered across the clearing at several figures approaching her cottage until her tense shoulders relaxed and a smile lit up her face.

"Curse my foolishness," she said. "I've lost track of the days but it must be Wednesday. It's not Thomas, or Sir Roger; it's Avice!"

"Avice. Who's Avice?" enquired Adeline, still a little apprehensive.

"Avice helps in the abbey infirmary," explained Wilflaed, "and I've known her half my life."

"She doesn't look like a nun," observed Adeline.

"She's not," replied Wilflaed. "She's a lay worker living at the abbey."

Still eyeing the visitors warily, Adeline breathed: "There are two men at arms with her…"

"Aye, but don't mind them; they're only to keep her safe through the forest. She comes every week to collect herbs and… have a gossip. But, with all else going on, I'd forgotten she'd be coming."

"So, you trust her."

"With my life – and yours," Wilflaed assured her. "It may be that Avice will have news of your sister if she reached the abbey. Shall I ask her, my lady?"

"Yes, yes," gasped Adeline. "Ask her, please."

"Very well, child, but… just to be certain, keep out of sight for now. I've no reason to mistrust her companions, but any man can be bought…"

While Wilflaed went to greet her friend at the cottage, Adeline waited uncertainly among the trees, whose soft green leaves whispered gently in the breeze. How much, she wondered, would Wilflaed reveal to the abbey healer? Since she could see no sign of Ralph, she guessed that he must be keeping his head down. Wilflaed and Avice seemed to talk forever and their easy manner with each other certainly suggested their friendship was a long and comfortable one.

When Wilflaed called out to Adeline, she was still a little reluctant to abandon the safety of the trees for the open clearing. However, the appearance of Ralph at the cottage door gave her the courage to emerge from hiding. Despite her hesitation, the moment she met Avice, Adeline felt utterly reassured by the woman's sunny disposition.

"Avice vouches for her two companions, Tancred and Berner," said Wilflaed. "And I thought it best that she met you in case asking about Lady Isabel arouses suspicion at the abbey. Avice should know for whom she takes such a risk."

Avice studied the young girl, looking steadily into her eyes for a few moments before she spoke.

"Though I've not seen a recently-arrived young lady," said Avice, "I do know that early this morning there were several comings and goings at the abbey – and the abbess sent straight to the castle for Sir Roger."

Adeline gave a sigh. "Then it surely must have been Isabel."

"Perhaps," agreed Avice, "for Sir Roger arrived very soon and, not long after, he rode out again in great haste. When I return, I can enquire what happened."

"Isabel will have told him where we are," groaned Ralph. "She'll have betrayed us, I'm certain."

"She believes she's helping me," murmured Adeline.

"Aye, perhaps," said Wilflaed, "but it won't be safe here any longer for you two. Till Thomas and Enric return, you'd best hide out in a shelter I know in the forest. If no-one comes after a day or two, then we'll know your sister hasn't betrayed you after all. Now fetch your cloaks while I pack you some bread and cheese."

"I'd best return to the abbey," said Avice, "and, if I learn any more, I'll send word with either Tancred or Berner."

Ralph limped back into the cottage at once but, before Adeline could follow, a band of horsemen burst out of the trees. By the time she cried out a warning to her brother, the riders had already surrounded the small building and the all too familiar figure of Sir Roger dismounted, grim-faced. With no time to flee, Adeline awaited the inevitable, praying that her brother would have the wit to lie low inside. But, of course, moments later, Ralph hobbled out of the door with sword in hand.

"No, Ralph!" cried Adeline. And even her brother, when he saw that he was utterly outnumbered, tossed his weapon down onto the grass.

"A wise choice, boy," said Sir Roger, eyeing the youth with distaste. To his men at arms, he said: "If he even twitches, cut him down where he stands."

"There's no-one else here," declared Wilflaed.

"Be silent, you old hag," growled the knight. "I promised the abbess I'd not harm you – unless you give me cause - so, where's Gloucester's Saxon bastard?"

With anger building inside her, Adeline replied: "You won't find him here."

"So, says his whore," scoffed Sir Roger.

Stung by his insult, Adeline retorted: "I told you: he's not here."

"Yet your dear sister swears that he is," retorted Sir Roger. "And let's just say I prefer to take her word on it than yours."

"He was here until he left to find Lady Isabel," explained Wilflaed.

Despite her assurances, Sir Roger appeared unconvinced. "Spread out and search the nearby woods for the renegade," he ordered his men at arms.

"Thomas isn't in the forest," insisted Adeline.

"Thomas, is it now?" mocked Sir Roger, his steely eyes full of contempt.

"I've not seen anyone else here," declared Avice. "And I trust, Sir Roger, that you do not doubt my word." Adeline wondered at the woman's calm authority and even Sir Roger seemed to consider his response with care.

"Of course not," replied the knight. "But I'm sure you are needed at the abbey, so please do not let me detain you."

Avice, not to be dismissed so lightly, replied: "I shall remain a little longer to complete my business here and… to bear witness."

"As you please," agreed Sir Roger, through gritted teeth.

When his searchers returned empty-handed, the knight seized Ralph and forced him down onto his knees.

"Sir Roger!" protested Avice.

"Remain if you must," muttered Sir Roger, "but don't presume to interfere in my business here."

Putting a blade to Ralph's neck, he turned to Adeline.

"On your brother's life, tell me where your lover is – now."

"Leave him!" Adeline implored him. "What I told you is true: Thomas FitzRobert set off at dawn to find my sister."

"Well, *lady*, if that's true, you should know that he failed," replied Sir Roger, "for she now resides in the safety of the abbey."

"She was safe here," argued Adeline.

"Well, from tomorrow, thank God, she'll be another man's burden," said Sir Roger.

"She's to be married on the morrow?" muttered Adeline, shocked. "And now I suppose you will take me to the abbey too."

For the first time Sir Roger smiled before replying: "Fearing that your presence in the nunnery might corrupt others, I advised the abbess to refuse to take you in as a novice."

"What?" cried Adeline. "You've no right to do that."

Ignoring her interruption, Sir Roger continued: "Despite hearing from your own sister how you have whored yourself to Gloucester's bastard son, the abbess took some persuading. Indeed, only when I offered to let her keep the sum your father bequeathed to the abbey, did she warm to my suggestion."

Utterly bewildered, Adeline asked: "So, if I'm not to go to the abbey, what will become of me?"

"I'll be acting as your guardian on behalf of Robert of Leicester," replied Sir Roger and something in his tone sent a chill creeping down Adeline's spine.

"Since you're unworthy of a good marriage," he continued, "I've agreed to take you into my household."

"I don't understand... what would I be in your household?"

"A servant," replied Sir Roger, "since there's but a small difference between a serving girl and a whore."

"No!" gasped Wilflaed. "You can't do that to a lady."

Only when one of the soldiers pinned her arms behind her back, did the healer fall silent.

"I warned you not to give me cause." Sir Roger spat out the words to reveal his utter contempt for the Saxon woman.

"Sir Roger, I cannot believe the abbess would condemn a young lady to live thus," protested Avice.

"This wanton wretch long ago besmirched her father's good name," scoffed Sir Roger. "And now he's in his grave, she's done so again; so, she'll get no charity from me. But, if she accepts her fate, she'll be as well-treated as any other servant."

Adeline did not even bother to argue; for she was surely guilty as charged.

"And my brother?" she murmured, glancing across at a distraught Ralph.

"He did not abduct you so, he's free to go," replied Sir Roger, "as long as you both behave yourselves."

"Very well then," agreed Adeline, affecting, with the utmost difficulty, a contrite, almost submissive manner. "Will you allow me a moment to say farewell?"

Sir Roger gave her a curt nod. "A moment only, while they saddle your horse."

Embracing her brother, she could feel his seething rage.

"Be calm, Ralph," she whispered. "You can't rescue me this time – and Sir Roger's right: this is my own doing. So, just let it lie…"

Avice clasped her hand and whispered: "I shall find out more at the abbey, I promise you."

When Adeline turned to Wilflaed, the healer took both her hands and then wrapped her arms around her.

"Don't give up hope," she murmured. "Because Thomas will come for you - you do know that, don't you?"

"Better he doesn't," said Adeline. "You tell him that from me."

Before the two women drew apart, Wilflaed replied, with a bitter smile: "No matter what you or I say, my lady, Thomas will still come."

"But I'll no longer be the lady he's come to know," lamented Adeline.

"If you think that'll stop him," lamented Wilflaed, "you don't know Thomas very well at all."

"Enough, girl, make haste," ordered Sir Roger.

Sir Roger's captain, Folcard stepped forward at once to help her to mount but as he did so, he pressed his palm against her breast and murmured: "Mmm… Very firm…"

Once, such lewd impudence would have brought the perpetrator a slap across the face, but she suspected that his idle groping was nothing compared to what she would soon face in the depths of Sir Roger's household.

"Gently, Folcard," chided Sir Roger. "Remember that only a moment ago the poor girl was a lady."

Looking into Folcard's eyes in that dark, stubbled face, Adeline knew that it was just the start of his interest in her. Only when Sir Roger chuckled at her embarrassment, did her fragile restraint disintegrate and she snarled: "Thomas FitzRobert will come for me. Aye, and he'll come for you too!"

To her surprise, Sir Roger's smile broadened. "Oh, I'm counting upon that, my dear – and, believe me, I'm not the only one that's keen to meet him again."

13

12th June, in the evening, at Schaftesberia Abbey

"Trapped," grumbled Enric, "like two damned rats in a sack."

"You must have caused very great offence, uncle," complained Thomas. "Though why am I surprised about that?"

"What about you?" retorted Enric. "You're the arsewit that's always getting us into trouble."

"Well, not this time," said Thomas. "But perhaps, if I simply explain to the abbess who I am, she'll accept our apologies."

"Best you don't tell her your name," advised Enric.

"Why not? I'm not ashamed to be the son of Earl Robert of Gloucester-"

"Bastard son," Enric reminded him.

"Even the bastard son of an earl should not be troubled by a mere knight like Sir Roger," insisted Thomas.

A noncommittal grunt from his uncle brought their conversation to an end; but, while Enric remained in stoic silence, Thomas fidgeted before getting up to pace around the room. When, finally, the door opened, he darted to it only to encounter a brace of armed men on the threshold.

"You're to give up your weapons and come before the abbess," announced one of the pair.

Exchanging a glance of resignation with Enric, Thomas relinquished his sword and belt. The soldier accepted their weapons and led them out of the chamber between two rows of buildings with his watchful comrade following close behind.

"I suppose the abbess will be under the Earl of Leicester's thumb too," Thomas murmured to his uncle.

"Perhaps," agreed Enric, "but this isn't just a nunnery, Thomas; it's a shrine that has some power of its own. I doubt the abbess here would allow herself be bullied by any man – except perhaps the king."

"So, you think she may not take Sir Roger's part," said Thomas.

"I didn't say that," muttered Enric.

"Once I tell her who I am, all will be well."

"Don't," warned Enric. "And don't mention Lady Isabel. Better the abbess thinks we just wandered into trouble here by accident."

"Well, one of us did," said Thomas, aggrieved.

As at Scireburne, the abbey was in the midst of major building work so that the men at arms were obliged to take a circuitous route to lead them across the abbey precinct. Eventually, they were brought before the abbess, unmistakable by her dress and bearing. Without even a glance at Enric, she focussed her entire attention upon Thomas, fixing him with a solemn glare. Though Thomas hoped the abbess would view them charitably, her unforgiving countenance suggested otherwise.

"I am Bella, Abbess of Schaftesberia," she announced. "I'm told that you have trespassed upon the holy precinct of this abbey and shown great contempt for those who live and worship here. What have you to say for yourselves?"

"Reverend Mother," began Thomas, "that was not our intention and we humbly ask your pardon; though I truly don't know how we have caused such offence."

"Offence?" growled the abbess. "The women under my care are not whores for you and your servant to paw at and fondle."

Though Thomas darted a venomous look at Enric, the latter appeared to be studying the floor closely. Eager to placate the abbess, Thomas opted for honesty.

"I am Thomas, son to Robert, Earl of Gloucester; and I take full responsibility for the actions of my… er, servant – who you may be sure will be severely punished."

Thomas was a little surprised when the abbess did not react at all to his identity, but her next words struck him like a hammer.

"And what about your father, Thomas? Do you also take responsibility for his actions - his treason?"

"Treason?" gasped Thomas as, slowly, he understood what was happening.

"Your father has declared for the Empress Matilda in Normandy," announced the abbess. "Sir Roger of Schaftesberia told me so this morning."

"I didn't know that, Reverend Mother," said Thomas, which was at least half true.

"However," the abbess continued, "I would not condemn a man on the actions of another; so, if you give me your oath that you have no intention of joining your father's rebellion against King Stephen, then I shall not call you traitor."

Speechless, Thomas turned to his uncle, who simply mouthed: 'Swear now; repent later.'

"Well?" enquired the abbess.

To swear would be to deny his father, thought Thomas; yet, not to swear would leave him locked up and unable to help Adeline. And, it was inevitable that Sir Roger, with Isabel's help, would soon find Wilflaed's cottage.

"Is it so hard to swear loyalty to your anointed king?" prompted the glowering abbess.

With a sigh, Thomas replied: "I regret, Reverend Mother, that I cannot swear such an oath."

"Pissmaggot," muttered Enric, in disgust.

"I see," said the abbess coldly. "Then let us also consider the other crimes which Sir Roger has brought against you of murder, abduction and rape."

"I've done none of those things," retorted Thomas.

"So, you did not abduct the ladies, Adeline and Isabel de Sarne from Sir Roger's care?"

"I freed them," explained Thomas, aware that Enric was shaking his head in despair.

"Yet both ladies told you not to…"

"Well, aye, but-"

"You then killed one of Sir Roger's men at arms," continued the abbess, who had clearly been well-informed by both Sir Roger and, very likely, Lady Isabel.

"I may have caused his death, but it was not murder – it was mortal combat."

"A combat which you began," said the abbess.

"Aye, because Sir Roger wouldn't release the ladies to me," said Thomas.

"But he was charged with their safety and those same ladies both pleaded with you to leave them alone, did they not"

"Aye, but they were prisoners..."

"And then you forced yourself upon the Lady Adeline," continued the abbess.

"I did not!"

"But you lay with her."

"Well, I… that's true, but she-"

"Then you are condemned by your own words," grumbled the abbess. "You may be an earl's son, Thomas, but it doesn't put you above the law."

"No, but-"

"Lock them in a secure place," the abbess ordered her armed guards. "I'll send for Sir Roger at first light."

"You're mistaken, Reverend Mother," cried Thomas as he was borne away – more roughly than before – and his uncle with him.

This time they were bundled into a different chamber, stone-built and closer to the heart of the abbey. When the door closed firmly upon them, they could hear that at least one man was posted outside. Inside, there was a pisspot and not much else. Enric regarded their unpromising prison for a moment before sinking down onto his haunches.

"So, what now?" asked Thomas.

"Don't ask me," retorted Enric. "You were the one so keen to give your name; now she's got half a dozen reasons to hold us."

"How was I to know that my father had revealed his true loyalties?"

"You knew he would though, sooner or later," said Enric.

"Not that it matters," Thomas muttered. "She would have condemned us on the word of Isabel alone…"

"Aye, true enough," agreed Enric, "though not for treason…"

"As long as we're trapped here, Sir Roger has time to find Adeline," groaned Thomas, "and there's nothing I can do about it."

Part Three: Traitor

14

12th June in the late evening at Schaftesberia Abbey

"Open the damned door!" bellowed Thomas, slamming his fist at the timber – not for the first time that evening.

"I think that's oak," muttered Enric, sitting on the cold, stone-flagged floor with his back against the wall.

"I'm just reminding them we're here," snarled Thomas, crashing a boot at the foot of the door.

"They know."

"But this is a gross offence against my father," cried Thomas, slapping the stone wall with the flat of his hand.

"He's a traitor," Enric pointed out. "Anyway, you've been offending him for years..."

"That's different," snapped Thomas, continuing to prowl around the room like a caged animal.

"I've not seen you like this before," said Enric.

"Why would you?" grumbled Thomas, aiming another kick at the timbers. "You don't know me at all."

"Though your father did say…"

"What? I suppose he told you I can't control my temper," said Thomas, all too aware that his frustration and fury were getting the better of him.

"Only that you sometimes… struggle to do so," replied Enric. "Makes me wonder whether you're worthy of that fine young Lady Adeline."

His uncle's calculated rebuke struck him like a slap in the face and his anger subsided as swiftly as it had arisen. A wild-tempered youth was the very last thing Adeline needed right now; so, Thomas slumped down, sullen-faced, beside his uncle.

It must have been an hour or more later that Thomas was surprised to hear the door being opened to admit a woman carrying a tray of bread and cheese. When she set it down on the floor, she bent close to Thomas and whispered: "I'll return later; be ready."

Before he could reply, she was gone, closing the door firmly behind her.

"Did you hear what she said?" he asked Enric, but his uncle, already busily tucking into a chunk of bread, gave only a brief shake of the head.

"She said she'll be back."

"Aye, to collect the tray," said Enric, "so let's make sure we leave no crumb upon it."

"I don't think she meant that," murmured Thomas, though he did begin to question whether he might have misunderstood the woman's hastily uttered words.

Enric, concentrating on the food, gave a groan of satisfaction. "By God, Thomas," he observed, through a mouthful of food, "even prisoners eat well in this place."

"Sweet Christ," said Thomas. "I'd rather not be here sampling their food at all. We should've been more careful – or rather, you should've been."

"Just swallow your pride, lad and take some food along with it." And with a sly chuckle, Enric wolfed down some more bread and cheese.

Though Thomas decided to eat, the consumption of each morsel was punctuated by a deal of muttering and cursing. When every crust and crumb was gone, Thomas said: "You know it's not for me that I worry."

"Well, it ought to be," declared Enric, "for we, lad, are up to our necks in the shit."

However, despite their perilous situation, Enric seemed to have no difficulty in settling down to snatch a little sleep. While he nodded off at once, Thomas remained wide awake but, with little light in their cell, he struggled to gauge the passage of time. Occasional sounds from beyond the chamber door told him little and the minutes seemed like hours as he waited for the woman to return.

Marking each successive bell as the nuns were summoned to prayer, he thought of Adeline at Compline; for it was after that hour they walked the Scireburne cloister together. Now he had abandoned her and, since Isabel must have revealed where her sister was, Sir Roger might well have brought her to the abbey by now. She could be here, somewhere nearby, and neither would know how close they were to each other.

His dark thoughts were interrupted by a sudden torrent of water and he wrinkled his nose as Enric made a generous donation to the pisspot. Later, men's voices sounded outside the door – very likely just comrades having a few words while the guard was changed. Only when he heard the bar being lifted out of its slot, did he realise that someone actually intended to enter. Leaping up, he aimed a kick at Enric who had fallen asleep again.

"Get up!" he hissed.

Enric was still on his knees when the door opened wide to reveal a figure with a blazing torch in hand. Once his eyes adjusted to the sudden flare of light, Thomas recognised the woman who had earlier brought their food.

"Thomas FitzRobert?" she enquired softly.

"Aye," agreed Thomas. "Do I know you?"

"No," she replied, "but we share a friend – Wilflaed."

"Wilflaed?" cried Thomas.

"Be quiet," ordered the woman, "unless you want to rouse the whole abbey."

"But-"

"Do you want to leave this place, or not?" demanded the woman.

"Aye, lead on," urged Thomas, hauling Enric to his feet.

The woman was already out of the door when Enric hissed: "Wait. Are you sure about this? Some stray woman turns up and you just meekly follow her?"

"I do if she's offering me a way out," said Thomas.

"But it could be a trap," warned Enric.

"We're already in a trap – thanks to you," said Thomas. "Let's just see where she takes us."

Following her out of the cell, Thomas almost collided with a young man at arms and came to an abrupt halt. Without a word, the youth handed Thomas and Enric their weapons which they accepted gratefully.

"That's Tancred," whispered the woman, as she swept past the guard. "But we must hurry. If I'm seen with you, it'll be the end of my days here."

Reaching a door into an adjoining yard, the woman slowed to lead Thomas and Enric through while Tancred pulled it carefully shut after them.

Ahead, another armed guard awaited them but it appeared that he was holding their mounts at the small gate which the pair had used to enter the abbey precinct. Whoever their rescuer was, she must have much influence at the abbey.

"I trust you can find your way from here," she breathed.

"Aye, thank you, mistress," said Thomas, "but why would you risk so much for men who don't even know your name."

"Because a young lady asked me to," replied the woman.

"Adeline!" gasped Thomas, clutching the woman's hand. "Is she here?"

"No, Thomas, and she won't be coming. Your love is now in service to Sir Roger of Schaftesberia… But you must go now. Go to Wilflaed and she'll tell you all. Now, hurry!"

Thomas and Enric led their mounts through the outer gate but before the woman shut it after them, Thomas whispered: "Please, your name, I must know your name."

"Avice," she breathed, before closing the gate gently behind them.

Swiftly Thomas mounted his horse but was surprised to find that Enric was staring back at the gate.

"What did she say her name was?" asked his uncle.

"Avice," said Thomas. "Come on, or we'll be caught here."

"But… she definitely said Avice," persisted Enric.

"Christ's bones, aye, Avice – but I reckon the less you know about her the safer she'll be."

Slowly, Enric mounted his horse and followed Thomas down the slope alongside the old town wall. As they descended towards St James, Enric was unusually quiet and Thomas knew that something was troubling him. Since it could hardly be their escape, it had to be Avice.

"Do you know that woman, Avice?" he asked.

Enric did not reply at once but then muttered: "No, lad. I don't think I do…"

"You don't seem very sure," said Thomas.

"Her voice," said Enric, "reminded me of someone I knew long ago. But, even if she was that woman, she wouldn't want me telling every man who she once was."

And that, it appeared, was all Enric was prepared to say about the mysterious Avice; so Thomas rode on, head down. When they reached the escarpment below the old town, he pulled up to gaze, stern-faced, at Sir Roger's burgeoning fortress on the hill.

"Adeline will be up there now," he murmured, shooting a malevolent glare at its new timber ramparts.

"Don't you even think about going up there," advised his uncle. "You can't just wander in and fetch her - not this time. We'll go to Wilflaed first, as Avice said."

"No, I don't think so, uncle. If she's there, she needs me now."

"No-one needs an arsewit," argued Enric. "Why can't you just accept that you can't free her from her fate? Everyone else has – even the girl herself!"

"Oh, I'll accept it, uncle - when I'm dead," said Thomas.

"Which you very soon will be if you go up to that place."

"One man might get in where an army would fail," said Thomas. "The castle's barely finished. I could slip in and get her out before anyone even noticed."

"No, Thomas," repeated Enric. "That would be madness."

"Perhaps to you, uncle," replied Thomas bitterly. "But for me, madness is living without her. Not that it matters, because it's not up to you."

"They'll be expecting you," warned Enric.

"Aye, but they won't expect me so soon because Sir Roger's been told that we're imprisoned at the abbey. So, there's a better chance now than later."

"I suppose that's true enough," conceded Enric grudgingly.

"Good. It's settled then," said Thomas briskly. "Wait for me on the Scireburne road with our mounts."

"But you've no mail," said Enric. "And you're certainly not fit for a fight."

"Aye, but if it comes to a fight, uncle, I can't win; so, I just need to be swift and quiet."

"If you're taken, Thomas, they'll not treat you well. Don't forget your father's a traitor."

On that point, Thomas thought, his uncle was probably right; because, with his father in Normandy, it was likely that the full wrath of King Stephen would be directed at the rest of Earl Robert's family. His half-brother, William and perhaps others of his family could hold out at Brystole Castle for it was almost impregnable. He, on the other hand, was at large and about to leave himself dangerously exposed.

Yet, he shut out such fears and concentrated only on how he might free Adeline. If he could not reach her then at least he would have seen inside the newly-made fort and identified its weak points. Thus, when he returned later, armed for war, he would have a better chance of taking the castle and freeing her – not that he had any men with which to do so…

"Sooner or later, uncle, my father will come back," declared Thomas. "And, when he does, I plan to greet him with my lady, Adeline at my side."

For a moment he thought Enric had acquiesced, but his uncle tried one more argument to dissuade him.

"Have you thought at all about what sort of life you'll be condemning that girl to?" he asked. "You're an outlaw now and that's surely no life for a lady…"

"She's strong and brave-"

"Aye, but every single day she's with you, her life will be at risk," declared Enric. "Roland, for one, will never stop looking for you."

"Roland has few men left with him," said Thomas, "unless you know different…"

"What I know is that there'll be others – men desperate to please the king – or Robert of Leicester. They'll hunt you down, Thomas, and your lady will never know peace."

"But she'll be loved, uncle."

"She'll be loved whether she's with you or not."

"Then I have to give her the choice at least," insisted Thomas, "to come with me, or not."

"Aye, if you can even get in…"

"You'll wait for me here then?" murmured Thomas.

"What else am I going to do?" grumbled his uncle.

Thomas grinned back at the older man. "If I don't return by dawn, you should go back to Ralph and Wilflaed. If I am taken, I doubt I'll be leaving that fort alive. I'm sure you'll be disappointed not to bury me yourself, uncle, but someone ought to go to Normandy to tell my father how I died and I think that had better be you."

Enric gave a solemn nod as Thomas dismounted and, retaining only his seax, entrusted both horse and sword to his uncle. The two men clasped hands briefly before Thomas walked away up the long slope towards Sir Roger's fort. He did not once look back for all his attention now was focussed upon gaining silent entry to the castle.

"I'm coming, my love," he breathed and, despite what he had told Enric, he had no intention of leaving Sir Roger's fort without her.

15

Afternoon on 12th June at Sir Roger's fort in Schaftesberia

The ride through Duncliffe Forest and along the road to Schaftesberia afforded Adeline far too much time to contemplate how she would spend the rest of her days. If Sir Roger truly intended to condemn her to base servitude, the outlook would be bleak indeed. Labouring in the castle kitchen would seal a film of smoky grease into her skin forever; while, in the laundry, her soft hands would be rubbed red and raw. But though such drudgery might test her stamina, she dreaded more being a servant of the bed chamber. There, to her certain knowledge, serving girls could be pawed over and abused at will; and the crafty gleam in Folcard's eye seemed only to give substance to her fears.

Their arrival at Schaftesberia came as a welcome distraction from her grim conjecture. Sir Roger led the small party up a steep slope to reach what she imagined must be the old town gateway – though much of its weathered frame appeared to have rotted away. Though the town stood on her right hand, Sir Roger had built – or rather was still building - his new fortress upon a small spur of land that speared out towards the north-west. Hence, the riders veered left off the road onto a newly-repaired wooden bridge across a broad ditch which separated the castle from the town. Passing through the timber gateway, Adeline could not help noticing that, though it looked finished, the palisades adjoining it still had several gaps.

In the cramped yard beyond the gate the horsemen dismounted and, before Folcard or anyone else could attempt to manhandle her down, Adeline slid awkwardly to the ground. As Sir Roger barked orders at everyone, she waited full of dread to learn where she would be sent. When he told her to follow him into the tall wooden tower which lay at the heart of the castle, she was trembling all over. But, since dumb insolence would hardly help her cause, she obeyed without argument in the hope that, if she complied, Sir Roger might treat her with a little favour.

The knight led her into what was a large, if inevitably gloomy, chamber raised up a little above ground level. Since it occupied the entire base of the tower, she assumed it was a hall for Sir Roger and his household men. On one side was a small, rough-hewn dais which served to elevate Sir Roger above all others.

"This place will do for it," announced Sir Roger.

Adeline, fearing what 'it' might be, stared at him blankly. Perhaps her mind was addled by the shock of capture, or the tiring ride, or perhaps she was just a simpleton; because, by the time she understood what was happening, the ceremony was about to begin.

"Stop!" she cried in alarm. "You intend to marry me?"

"Did you really believe I was going to put you to work?" laughed Sir Roger. "In case you've forgotten, you're still your father's daughter. And, while he has chosen to bestow his lands upon your sister, nothing is certain, my lady. So, I've no intention of wasting you in my kitchens – at least, not if you behave."

"But, as you say, my sister inherits," muttered Adeline.

"Yes, and tomorrow your sister will marry Thorold Le Breton and, well… how can I put this kindly? She will not be Thorold's first wife nor, I suspect, his last…"

"So, you seek my inheritance?"

"Your father assumed that, as a nun, the question of your marriage would not arise; but, since you're not going to the abbey now, the disposal of your marriage belongs to your lord, Robert of Leicester and he has awarded that right to his most loyal knight - me…"

"And you would take me to wife despite my sullied reputation?"

"You may have whored yourself out to FitzRobert," retorted Sir Roger. "But that doesn't concern me. I've sons enough from my first wife and your only purpose in this marriage is to live long enough to bring me your father's lands – all of them."

"Well, say what you please, I'll not marry you," declared Adeline. "And you know well enough that I'm of an age where the church will not recognise the marriage unless I consent."

Sir Roger gave her a wry smile. "Very well, my lady, I'll not force you," he agreed, surprisingly affable. "I can be a little patient and you will be treated here with respect – though you may not leave the castle. Think on this, lady, if you will: sooner or later, your beloved FitzRobert will come here to free you; and, when he does, I shall take him. Then perhaps you'll think again about the wisdom of rejecting my proposal; for I swear, lady, that the one man you will never marry is Thomas FitzRobert."

After her blunt rejection of his proposal, Sir Roger dismissed her to a small chamber on the uppermost floor of the tower. It was tiny and dark with the west wind blowing through the gaps between the fresh timbers of its walls - a damp and draughty room that would be her home for the foreseeable future unless she relented.

Hours later, she was still in shock for, having steeled herself for a life of hard toil with little respite, the sudden marriage proposal had caught her utterly unawares. In a matter of hours, she had gone from being a novice nun to a servant and then back to an heiress again. In one respect it mattered little because each of those outcomes left her a prisoner. She saw now that Sir Roger had plotted his course cleverly by exploiting her relationship with Thomas. He anticipated, no doubt that, though she might reject his proposal now, she would very likely change her mind if he were to offer her the life of Thomas in return.

Her refusal of Sir Roger's private offer of marriage was not known to everyone else in the castle. She was seen simply as a lady fallen far from grace and thus little better than the lowest whore. Folcard, or perhaps one of his comrades, must have put such a story about for she noticed that the servants did not defer to her at all. Worse still, when men passed her on the stair or in the hall, her disgrace was evident from their lustful glances. When, at dusk, she ventured out onto the highest rampart above her chamber, she was greeted by a burst of raucous jeers from the leering soldiers in the yard below.

Later, as she lay in the darkness on her thin straw bed, her soul burning with shame, she wondered how she had so willingly given herself to Thomas. If she had not done so then she would probably be safely ensconced at Schaftesberia Abbey… for life. But though she had scarcely known the youth more than a few days, she did not regret for an instant the few sweet hours spent with him. For better or worse, what was done could not be undone and she could only pray that he would come for her. Then, an instant later, she was gripped by a dark fear that Thomas would not come. Indeed, what would she do if Thomas never came?

She thought too of Isabel who, close by at the abbey, would soon be embarking upon the very journey that she had just rejected. Adeline prayed that her sister would find some true affection in her marriage; but from Sir Roger's sardonic description of Thorold le Breton, she feared that it was unlikely. To be sure though, if anyone could discover a husband's gentler side, it would surely be sweet Isabel.

Curled up on the straw that smelt of damp oak, she realised that she was still dressed in her torn and mud-stained clothes. It was as if she dared not shed them lest, somehow, she would be letting go of Thomas too. It was foolish, she decided, for he would want her to do whatever was needed to survive. The same was true in her dealings with Sir Roger for, though she had rebuffed him, she must still offer him humility and respect. If she was civil to him – behaved, as he put it – then he would ensure that she was safe, fed and rather better attired.

Feeling a little more secure, she dropped off to sleep but awoke with a gasp from a grim nightmare where Thomas lay dead on a bloody field and she was trapped in a loveless marriage to Sir Roger. A shiver flitted down her spine when, out in the yard, she heard the knight barking abuse at one of his hapless sentries. Not long after, came the scrape of a boot on the stair and so she braced herself for a scolding from Sir Roger.

Another footfall came, this time on the landing outside her door and it occurred to her that there was another man in the castle who might dare to approach her: Folcard. When her door creaked open, she couldn't decide whether to cower on the floor in submission or lunge at her visitor with all the strength she had. The door was half open when she made up her mind to put up a struggle.

Her left fist struck the intruder full on the cheek and brought a satisfying grunt of pain. But next moment both her wrists were seized, bringing her brief resistance to an end.

"I'll scream," she snarled.

"I'd really rather you didn't," whispered Thomas, releasing her.

"Thomas?" gulped Adeline. "How can you be here?"

"I just… walked in."

Wrapping her arms around him, she crushed him to her breast. "I knew you'd come, but just not so soon."

"It was… on my way," he said, with a chuckle.

"But Sir Roger's expecting you," she warned. "You can't be found here."

"Aye, I was hoping not to be found," he said, drawing a little apart from her so that he could kiss her cheek. Before Adeline knew it, his lips moved to hers and the kiss lasted a very long time until they sank down to the bed, folded together. Tasting the sweat upon him, she realised that he must have climbed up to the castle on foot.

Examining his cheek with gentle fingers, she murmured: "I've hurt you; will you forgive me?"

He laughed. "I'll have a bruise, that's all – and you must never beg my forgiveness… for anything."

Still holding her close, Thomas surveyed the dingy chamber. "He keeps you like a dog," he observed.

"He wants me to marry him," she said.

"I don't blame him," said Thomas, with a wicked grin. "So do I."

"This is deadly serious, Thomas."

"Well, did you accept?" he enquired.

"No, I refused him," she retorted, punching him on the arm.

Just for a moment, doubts flooded into her head until Thomas breathed: "I'm very glad of that, my lady."

"Not that it matters," she said, with a sigh, "for everyman already looks at me as if I'm a whore."

His response was to kiss her lips once more and she wished they could just lie there together until they grew old and grey.

"Well, we can't have that, can we?" he said. "We must make an honest woman of you. So, Lady Adeline de Sarne, I would take you to wife. What say you to that?"

"I say you can't, Thomas," she muttered.

"Can't I? I'm the grandson of a king – how can you reject such a suitor? You've only to say the words and we'll be wed."

Just for a moment, she hesitated, holding her breath at the prospect of sharing her life with this wild, half-Saxon youth with a trickle of royal blood running through him. Marrying him would likely unleash a whirlwind of woe for them both; and yet… all love was surely a leap into the unknown. Every kiss they shared reminded her how much she had missed him, how much she wanted to be close to him, to feel his touch, to feel one with him – and, aye, to be at his side no matter what trials faced the two of them.

A heartbeat later, the words gushed out: "Thomas FitzRobert, son of Robert FitzRoy, Earl of Gloucester, I do take you as my husband in the sight of God."

"Then, before God, we are man and wife," he murmured. "But you know it doesn't count if we don't lie together..."

"But we have lain together," she teased.

"Aye, but that was before…"

"Shouldn't we be making our escape?" she whispered.

"We've plenty of time," he assured her, stroking her breasts. "No-one's going to be stirring for hours yet."

"Even so, husband, we'd best not delay… at least not for too long."

"We'll have to be quick then."

"Aye," she agreed, "though… not too quick."

∞ ∞ ∞

Their youthful ardour spent, the pair lay asleep, legs entwined, on the narrow bed – until Adeline started awake in alarm.

"Thomas," she hissed, "we've lain here too long."

"Aye," he acknowledged. "Perhaps it is time we moved."

"Past time," she gasped. "What have we done?"

"Come on, wife," he said, offering his hand to raise her up.

When she slipped off the straw, he embraced her again while she hastily pulled down her shift and skirt, astonished how shameless she had been with him – not for the first time, of course. But at least, she was no longer a whore…

Brushing her fingers over his hand, she felt the scars of fighting there – so many scars for one so young.

"You've a darkness in you, Thomas," she groaned. "And I fear it's kindled something dark in me."

"Have you changed your mind already?"

"No," she said earnestly. "And I never will."

"We have to go," he said, "else it'll be daybreak."

"Are you sure we can do this?" she asked. "There must be two score men at arms here and you're just one man with a knife."

"Aye, but I know the lie of the fort now – so don't worry, I'll get you out."

"And then what shall we do?"

"We'll live as man and wife," he insisted, eyes bright with eagerness.

"Will we, Thomas?" she said. "Robert of Leicester granted my marriage to Sir Roger and neither lord will allow our vows to stand – and the church will surely take their part."

"Then we'll fight them," he said.

"And live outside God's law – in mortal sin."

"I'm already living outside the law of man," declared Thomas. "And, if God's law serves only wretches like Sir Roger, then I'll reject that too."

She fell silent for, though she could not deny the love she bore him, she could not help but fear for their souls.

"Where would we go?" she asked.

"To my father in Normandy and you can be sure that, once the Empress Matilda rules, she will approve our marriage."

"I don't feel sure of anything, Thomas."

He cupped her face in his hands. "Don't worry; all will be well."

She nodded, wanting so much to believe him.

"Now, wait here while I take a look down the stair," he whispered. "Keep the door closed till I return - oh, and you might want to put your boots on."

She had hardly noticed her bare feet rubbing on the rough-hewn planks of the floor but hurried to pull on her boots. Then, as she waited on the threshold, ready to move swiftly, she felt the flush of anticipation in her cheeks. Whatever the risks, she was committed to this man now, body and soul. For several moments she waited, growing ever more tense until, finally, she could contain her anxiety no longer and eased open the door.

Footsteps sounded on the stair below; but was it Thomas, or someone else? Peering out from the threshold, she could see little by the waning glow of a rush light, but dared not go out until Thomas returned. After a few more minutes, her chest began to tighten with worry and, as more time passed, a grim dread grew in the pit of her belly.

16

The early hours of 13th June, at Sir Roger's fort at Schaftesberia

Thomas had lingered too long. Christ's bones, he could have lain with Adeline all night. But now he would have to spirit her out at an hour when some of the servants could already be stirring. Cursing his folly, he was forced to admit that, for once, his uncle might have been right: love was a bitch of a mistress.

Finding his way into the fort had not been difficult; neither the ditch nor the earth rampart was finished and few sentries were posted. However, with dawn now fast approaching, getting back out again was unlikely to be so straightforward. As he crept down the tower's wooden staircase, every timber seemed to creak alarmingly under his weight. After a particularly loud protest from the boards beneath his feet, he paused for a moment, fearing a warning shout or cry of alarm.

When all remained quiet, he continued down to the floor below where two chambers were located. Through the open door of one, he heard formidable snoring and could not resist peering inside. By the glow of a wavering rush light, he had little difficulty in recognising Sir Roger, sprawled upon his back and rumbling like a sleeping hog.

Despite the urgent need to escape, Thomas was drawn further into the chamber, for here lay the perpetrator of Adeline's misery - alone and at his mercy. Involuntarily, his hand strayed to the hilt of his knife. One swift strike was all it would take; but he hesitated and, for what seemed like an age, he tarried there. He had killed other men; this was surely no different. But of course, he knew in his soul that it was. William de Burgh's death was unintended; but to butcher the defenceless Sir Roger in his sleep would mark Thomas forever as a Godless murderer.

As his fingers released their grip upon the knife hilt, somewhere outside the tower a door slammed which set a pack of dogs a-barking. Abruptly Sir Roger's eyes flicked open and, seeing Thomas looming over him, the knight bellowed at once for help. Stepping back in alarm, Thomas had scarcely reached the doorway before two bleary-eyed guards blocked his exit with swords drawn.

"Disarm the coward and bind his hands," ordered Sir Roger, as he clambered out of his bed.

Thomas had little choice but to surrender his blade and submit to being thrust down onto his knees with his hands wrenched taut behind his back. If only he had just walked past that open door…

"You came here for her." Sir Roger spat out the accusation.

"Aye," replied Thomas, forcing a grim smile. "As you knew I would."

His buoyant response brought a hammer blow from Sir Roger's fist. "God's truth, you've been with her, haven't you? I can smell the wretched whore all over you."

Thomas, licking a trace of blood from his lower lip, saw no point in a denial. Instead, he replied: "Each time you call my lady a whore, your death comes a step closer."

"You forced your way into my house-"

"I strolled in," scoffed Thomas. "No-one even noticed."

Another savage blow landed, this time to the side of his head.

"You were standing over me, poised to strike," growled Sir Roger. "Had I not been alert, I'd be a dead man."

"You weren't alert," said Thomas. "I could have cut your throat half a dozen times while you slept."

"Why didn't you then?" said the knight, still seething.

"Because I'm no murderer, Sir Roger."

"I'd say Roland de Burgh would disagree," retorted the knight.

"Aye, I stabbed Roland's brother in a tavern brawl; but that's between him and me."

"Well, Roland's complaint will have to wait now," Sir Roger told him, "Because, since your father's treason, your life rests in the king's hands. He's ordered my liege lord, Robert, Earl of Leicester, to arrest and pass judgement upon you."

"You might as well kill me now then," said Thomas.

"I shall send word to the Earl of Leicester that I have you," said Sir Roger. "And, for now, you can join the miserable band of prisoners labouring to finish this fort."

Thomas was barely listening to his captor for he was contemplating how utterly he had failed his new wife. What would she be thinking now? She must feel so let down that she would surely never trust him again.

The dull dawn brought more rain as Thomas was hauled roughly outside to join the unfortunate handful of prisoners who were about to start working again on the palisade and ditch. Since they, no doubt, had already formed a bond through their shared confinement and work together, he was not too surprised that his new companions ignored him. He was very much the outsider and they had no reason to trust him. It was going to be a long day.

Shower after shower drenched the labourers as they attempted to work while slithering about in the mud. Hands slipped, men fell and hammers slammed into flesh rather than timber. So many times did Thomas narrowly avoid serious injury that he began to wonder whether malice rather than chance was the cause.

Later, his misery deepened when he spied a pair of all too familiar visitors coming to pay their respects to Sir Roger. Thorold Le Breton, presumably on his way to the abbey to marry Lady Isabel – the poor wretch - was accompanied by his close comrade, Sir Roland de Burgh. Both men looked astonished to discover Thomas FitzRobert, stripped to the waist and toiling in the mud under the barrage of rain. Though Thorold seemed amused by Thomas's predicament, Roland glowered at him with undiminished enmity.

"Not so proud now, Saxon," Thorold bellowed across the yard, "now that your faithless father has fled to Normandy."

With runnels of rain washing the soil down his torso, Thomas, smiled up at the two knights and shouted: "You may have risen out of the shit, Thorold; but the stench will always follow you."

Clenching a fist, Thorold drew nearer, no doubt frustrated that he was still too far away to club Thomas down with it.

"Leave the youth to his work, Sir Thorold," Sir Roger shouted down from the tower rampart. "Else my castle will never be finished."

Though both Thorold and Roland turned to glare up at Sir Roger, neither man seemed willing to flout their host's authority. The two Normans were not the only ones Thomas found watching him that morning. Just before midday he glimpsed Adeline, staring out from the highest rampart of the tower, despite the rain lashing down upon her. Though he could not discern her countenance, he knew that despair must be written there. When she drifted back inside, his spirits sank as low as they had ever been.

It was early evening when the weary captives, after a hard day's punishing labour, were herded into the small, roughly-fenced enclosure where they would eat, shit and sleep until the next dawn. Thomas, despite his years of relentless training, was bone-weary – as indeed were his fellow prisoners. They were a collection of men united by only one thing: they had all somehow fallen foul of Sir Roger.

Rough-hewn chunks of bread were tossed into the enclosure but it was hardly enough to feed the exhausted labourers. Since there was still some work needed on the bailey palisade, Thomas anticipated another long day on the morrow. During the night he hoped to recover a little of his strength, but he was to be disappointed. A few hours after darkness fell, two men at arms came to drag him out of the stockade. He expected to be taken before Sir Roger in the hall, but instead he was hauled outside the castle gates to a patch of sodden ground where Thorold and Roland awaited him.

Sir Roger might well have denied Roland the satisfaction of killing Thomas, but there were other ways of punishing him. Though Thomas knew exactly what was coming, all he could do was steel himself to try to survive it. Just stay alive, he told himself, reeling as the first punch landed. After that, blow upon blow followed until Thomas lost count. His cheek was torn open, ribs battered and belly pounded before they moved down his torso to his groin and lower body. By the time he dropped onto his knees, every inch of his flesh burned with pain but the bruising onslaught continued as he lay on the muddy ground.

Though determined not to show even a trace of weakness, one kick at his wounded lower back tested his stoic resistance beyond breaking point. When the boot struck, he let out a roar of agony. Oddly enough, his reaction appeared to satisfy the Norman pair who brought an abrupt end to his punishment. Perhaps they feared they might kill him by mistake and incur the displeasure of Earl Robert of Leicester. But, no matter the reason, Thomas was grateful for the reprieve.

With a hammering headache and both eyes half-shut, he was long past rational thought when they tossed him carelessly back into the prison stockade. None of his fellow workers bothered to investigate whether he still breathed; so he lay curled up exactly where he landed until dawn the next day. Only then did the other inmates, perhaps a little taken aback at the sight of his bruised and bloodied body, take the trouble to inspect his injuries.

"By the saints, lad, how are you still alive?" enquired one of the older men.

Thomas groaned, raising a hand as a sign of life whereupon the fellow took his arm to help him up to a sitting position while the other prisoners gathered around him – curiosity now overcoming their initial indifference.

"Sweet Christ, I reckon that head must hurt," observed his helper, whose sympathetic smile took the iron from his deep, gruff voice.

"Everywhere hurts," mumbled Thomas, wondering if he had lost a tooth.

"No broken bones though, by the look of it," the older man pointed out cheerfully.

"No, because that would keep me from my labour," muttered Thomas sourly.

Along with the rest of his body, his jaw ached - probably, he reflected, something to do with half his face being swollen up.

"By God, you've taken a few punches," chuckled one of the other men. "You must have really pissed those bastards off."

"They'll want us to start soon," advised the older man. "Can you stand?"

Thomas had been wondering that himself and, since all eyes were now upon him, it seemed like a challenge of sorts. With a silent prayer, he wrapped his aching fingers around one of the rough palisade timbers and managed – just – to haul himself to his feet. Though his legs felt as weak as a new-born lamb's, he remained upright despite the fire that raged around the quarrel wound.

"As you see, I can stand," he growled.

But when he was clapped on the back by several of his new companions, he almost collapsed again.

"I'm Edgar," said the older man, offering his hand in a firm grip. Built like a stone bastion, the broad-chested Edgar had a scarred face suggesting considerable familiarity with violence.

"You can call me…" Thomas hesitated.

"We're all outlaws here," laughed Edgar, "so, we don't care what name you go by."

Despite that, Thomas decided he had nothing to lose by being honest with these men.

"Thomas FitzRobert," he said, "bastard son of Robert, Earl of Gloucester."

"Hah!" cried Edgar. "Look alert, lads, we've a lord among us! What shall we call you then?"

Thomas shrugged. "As long as it's not 'Saxon', I don't care."

"You got something against Saxon blood?" asked Edgar, with an edge to his voice.

"Hardly," replied Thomas, "since I'm half-Saxon."

"So, what do your friends call you?" said Edgar.

"Friends?" muttered Thomas, struggling to think of any. "Just call me Fitz."

"Good, 'cos we've already got a Thomas," said Edgar, indicating the man beside him. "This is Long Tom."

One or two of the others grinned at the name for 'Long' Tom was of very diminutive stature – though, thought Thomas, he was hardly the first short fellow to bear the nickname.

"Fitz is fine," said Thomas.

"Fitz it is then," announced Edgar.

The rest, content to follow Edgar's lead, introduced themselves. No-one seemed interested in hiding the reason for their imprisonment – indeed some seemed almost proud of their status. Long Tom confessed to being a fugitive from his manor lord and expected to be returned any day.

A young lad called Peter announced himself by revealing that he was a thief.

"Aye, and a bad thief," added Edgar. "Else he wouldn't be 'ere."

"Couldn't steal the pot he pisses in," laughed Long Tom. "But he's handy with a blade and he reckons he's a bit of a gleeman – though I've heard better voices."

Then there was Ranulf, who looked a little older than Thomas. He, it seemed had offended Sir Roger by frequenting the same barn as one of the knight's daughters.

"When he drew his sword, I just ran," admitted Ranulf, with a nervous, self-deprecating laugh. "Thank God, he didn't catch me till his wrath had cooled a bit…"

The revelation caused some mirth among the men, but Thomas did not laugh for the tale reminded him too much of Adeline.

"Jonas and Garth," said Edgar, indicating two powerfully-built men, one with glistening skin the colour of pitch. Thomas had seen several such men in the port of Brystole but had rarely spoken to any of them.

"Which one is which?" enquired Thomas, deciding he had better avoid a wrestling match with both.

"It's easy to tell them apart," explained Edgar, with a mischievous grin, "'cos Jonas is an inch taller and he plays a shawm – or a pipe, if he's a mind to… and he's a Moor, of course."

Moments later, further introductions were halted when the enclosure gate was dragged open and the prisoners were led out to the last unfinished section of palisade. The morning sky looked as forbidding as the previous day and it was no surprise to any of them when the heavens unleashed yet another deluge upon them. For Thomas, it would be the hardest day of his young life. His bruised hands struggled to grip the sodden timber stakes, it was midday before his eyes managed to open fully and his back ached all day.

Yet, despite all, one bright moment illuminated his day and helped him to endure every last fibre of pain. In the early afternoon, with the rain still falling steadily, Adeline walked down to where the men were working. The guards, taken by surprise, seemed unsure how to react since she was, despite her sullied reputation, still a lady and apparently a guest of their lord.

Seeing her flinch at the sight of his battered face, Thomas forced a smile of encouragement for he knew what she was risking just by being there. If Sir Roger already thought her a whore, how would he regard such a wilful act of defiance?

"Have faith," murmured Thomas, when she reached him.

Staring at him blankly, she gave a sudden shiver, though not, he imagined from cold. She touched her fingers gently against his ripped cheek, then bit into her bottom lip until it bled. Her tears mingled with the raindrops streaming down her face and Thomas wondered how long she might have remained there, had a bristling Sir Roger not arrived to order her back to her chamber at once. Soaked through to the skin, she obeyed without a word of dissent but contrived to flash a brave smile at Thomas, before trudging up to the tower with her head held high.

Sir Roger regarded Thomas with ill-disguised hostility.

"Remember that moment," he snarled, "because it's the last time you'll ever see her."

After the knight swept away, Edgar murmured: "By the saints, Thomas, you're in more trouble than the rest of us. By God though, that's some lady, eh…"

"Aye," agreed Thomas, "that she is."

When their relentless day finally ended, the labourers trudged back once more to the stockade, knowing that their work was now done. The knowledge that the fort's palisade was finished, however, was hardly a cause for celebration because for most, the morrow would very likely bring something even worse than hard labour. Thomas, however, was only worried about Adeline, fearing that she would be chastised by her host. He just prayed that Sir Roger would inflict any punishment upon him rather than her.

That night he was relieved that there was no repeat of his nocturnal abduction; Thorold was, in any case, likely to be busy with his new bride, Isabel. Any anger Thomas might once have harboured against Isabel for betraying her sister had long since dissipated. Indeed, he spared a prayer for her because he knew she would need the Lord's help to survive her new marriage.

As they settled down for the night, Will recited a melancholy poem which suited their despondent mood. After that, the prisoners morbidly, though perhaps inevitably, discussed what fate now lay before each of them. When it was the turn of Thomas, he told them that he would be taken before the Earl of Leicester and tried as a traitor. Silence greeted his announcement which demonstrated that, though the group might have accepted him as one of them, his crime was on a wholly different level from theirs.

"They'll hang you then, Fitz," observed Edgar.

"I'll plead for trial by combat," replied Thomas.

"For treason," said Edgar, "Not likely, is it?"

"Perhaps not," Thomas agreed.

"Can you fight then?" piped up Long Tom, in his annoyingly high-pitched voice.

"Aye, I can fight well enough," said Thomas.

"Better try to get away, Fitz," argued Ranulf. "You'll get no mercy from the earl."

"If I can get out, I'll not be straying far from this place," declared Thomas.

"Come back to free your poor comrades, will you?" squeaked Long Tom.

But Edgar just laughed. "I think Fitz means he won't stray far from his young lady."

"I'll be back, lads," promised Thomas, with a defiant smile. "And, once I've freed Lady Adeline, I'll be sure to pay you a visit – if you're still here."

When he saw their faces grinning back at him in the torchlight, he could imagine Enric berating him for even indulging in such a wild fantasy.

17

13th June, outside Schaftesberia

Dawn brought a sudden torrential downpour and, though Enric took shelter under a stand of green-leaved beeches, he was soaked through in minutes. Raging impotently at the anvil sky, he could discern no sliver of sunlight through the dark clouds. The rain, of course, was not the real cause of his frustration, but rather the prolonged absence of his nephew. After a few more hours of watery daylight, Enric had to accept that Thomas was either taken or dead - and there wasn't a thing he could do about it. So much for his oath to Earl Robert of Gloucester that he would keep his bastard son safe.

Not for the first time, he cursed the youth for his foolish pursuit of Adeline de Sarne. It was plain enough to Enric - a man with plenty of experience with failed romances - that the liaison was doomed. From his own youth, he recalled only too well the dream of love being brutally torn from his grasp. The loss all but destroyed him and, only by steeping his hands in Saracen blood, had he survived. All traces of that forlorn love were flayed away and buried deep in Antioch; and, when Enric left the Holy Land, he did so as a soulless killer. In the gloom of Schaftesberia Abbey, a woman's voice had disturbed that ancient memory, but only for a moment.

Shutting out his meandering thoughts, Enric struggled to decide what to do next. Though Thomas had told him to return to the others in Duncliffe Forest, he decided he must wait a little longer. Thomas was a resourceful lad, so Enric still hoped to see him striding down the slope from the castle, clothes sodden and hair flattened by the rain, but alive.

It was around midday that Enric, concluding that God had performed all his miracles for the day, reluctantly took his leave. Leading Thomas's horse in his wake, he was surprised how much it troubled him to leave his reckless nephew behind.

"I'll be back, Thomas," he muttered to himself. "I will come for you…"

On the Scireburne road he passed other travellers, though none offered any greeting for all were hooded to keep out the driving rain. One small group of riders, however, did send a chill down his spine. At their head rode the tall Roland de Burgh with another powerfully-built warrior by his side. It appeared that Roland had enlisted some support in his pursuit of Thomas, which did not bode well. If Thomas was still alive and a prisoner at the castle, Roland might well discover him there and that was unlikely to improve his nephew's chances of survival.

Keeping his head well down, Enric was relieved when the party passed by him without incident and, as soon as he could, he hastened off the road into Duncliffe Forest. Yet, he soon slowed up on the muddy forest track for, in truth, he was in no hurry to reach Wilflaed's cottage. Already, he was thinking that he must break the news to Ralph that his sister was once again held by Sir Roger. The rash youth would probably want to race out to rescue her – again. But this time, surely, he must accept that she was a member of Sir Roger's household – aye, and was likely to remain so till the day she died.

Hence, though the trees trickled water onto his head and shoulders, he just walked his mount for the last few hundred yards and, even when he dismounted, he made no greater haste. As he expected, the weather had kept both Ralph and Wilflaed inside and there he found them, glum-faced. Only then did he realise that they already knew of Adeline's fate.

"That poor girl," murmured Wilflaed, but, ever practical, she made no further comment and instead helped Enric strip off his soaked outer clothing.

Ralph, by contrast, could barely contain his outrage. "We must get her back," he cried. "We must-"

But Wilflaed cut him off with a bitter response. "Peace, boy… Enric already knows your mind; so, just be still."

Ralph, stunned by the harsh rebuke from the usually mild-mannered healer, gaped at her for a moment but did at least fall silent. Then, sullen-faced, he left the two Saxons and withdrew to the inner chamber once occupied by Thomas.

Once Wilflaed had taken off Enric's wet clothes, he flopped down in his braies, exhausted. "God's nails - I need to think," he told her.

"You need to sleep," she argued. "You can think on nothing with an addled head."

"True enough," he agreed. "But, before I sleep, there's something been nagging at me. At the abbey, there was a woman who helped us escape – Avice - who said she was your friend."

"Aye, Avice," smiled Wilflaed. "She helps in the abbey infirmary and she is a friend - a very close friend."

Enric stared at Wilflaed until she blinked and looked away, eyes glistening with tears.

"No, surely not," he breathed, "it can't be her…"

Wilflaed nodded. "By the time I knew who she was and… what she was to you, I'd no idea where you were."

"But you knew that losing her in the Holy Land near broke me. God's nails, Wilflaed, I told you all about her – everything. I thought her long dead."

"I didn't meet her till a few years after you left me," said Wilflaed, "nor even then did I suspect she was the girl you lost in Antioch. How would I, Enric? But, these past few years, we've become so close that, one day, I suppose she trusted me enough to tell me her story. Only then did I understand who she was; but what could I say about you? I didn't even know if you still lived. And how could I tell her that we… that I… knew you."

"Aye, I can see it would've been awkward to tell her about us," acknowledged Enric.

"Aye, and what happened between us was far in the past by then," said Wilflaed.

"Until a few nights ago," remarked Enric sheepishly.

"That?" scoffed Wilflaed, with a dismissive shake of the head. "That was just two lonely people…"

"Do you think Avice knew me at the abbey?" he asked.

"I doubt your own mother would know you now, Enric; and Avice last saw you, what… over thirty years ago?"

"More than forty, I suppose," groaned Enric. "But then, why did she help Thomas and me to escape?"

"Because she was here when Adeline was taken," Wilflaed explained. "So, she knew all about Thomas and, I suppose, when she saw he was a captive at the abbey, she wanted to help. But, by God, she put herself at great risk."

"True," said Enric. "But, if she's no idea who I am then it's best we leave it that way."

"Aye," agreed Wilflaed. "Now, go and toss Ralph off that straw bed; 'cos you need sleep more than that idle beggar does."

Over the years, Enric had trained himself to fall asleep whenever he needed to – even when his own life was in peril. Indeed, on the eve of a fight, when others spent the night praying or shitting themselves, he usually managed to find some brief repose. But this was different, for it was not fear that kept him awake now but guilt - guilt that he had failed to keep his nephew safe. Nonetheless, he discovered that, when a man was utterly exhausted, even guilt could not ward off sleep.

When he eventually awoke, it was early evening, though not yet dark and he found Wilflaed outside with Ralph, basking in the last golden rays of the setting sun. The moment Enric emerged, Ralph leapt to his feet, but Enric raised a hand to forestall any fresh demands from the youth.

"Sit yourself back down," he ordered.

Though Ralph did so, he demanded: "When are we going to Schaftesberia?"

"Not yet," replied Enric tersely.

"So, you'd abandon your own kin as well as my sisters," grumbled Ralph.

"Just listen, you fartwit," warned Enric.

"I am listening," retorted Ralph, without a trace of contrition.

"We've no reason to think that either of your sisters has been harmed in any way," said Enric. "So, just now, I'm more worried about Thomas."

"Do you think he could have been killed?" enquired Wilflaed softly.

"Not unless he decided to make a fight of it and even Thomas must have known it was hopeless. More likely, he's been taken; but don't forget, he's the son of a traitor now. With Earl Robert of Gloucester in rebellion, Thomas may have some value to the king – at least for the time being. So, with luck, he's still alive; I have to believe that."

"So, we must help him escape then," persisted Ralph, "with Adeline."

"If the pair of us go to Sir Roger's fort on our own, we'll fare no better than Thomas," pointed out Enric.

"What then? Who else is there?" demanded Ralph. "If Thomas is Gloucester's son, then won't his family help?"

"Even if they had a mind to, I doubt the earl's kin could help," said Enric. "The instant the earl declared for the Empress Matilda; the king would have headed to the west country. I'll warrant Brystole Castle's already stopped up tight. No, the only hope – and, God's bones, it's a damned slim one – lies elsewhere."

"Where then?" asked Ralph.

But all Enric said was: "I'm leaving at first light; so, if you're coming, you'd best be mounted and ready to ride."

18

14th June at dawn in Duncliffe Forest

At the first glimmer of dawn, Enric embraced Wilflaed and set off once more through the forest to join the Scireburne road. Ralph, since he had nowhere else to go, rode with him. Enric was far from confident that his journey would bear fruit and, the nearer they drew to their destination, the more he began to question what he was about to do. If Aelflaed harboured any remaining doubts that he was a callous pissmaggot, his return to Escewich would surely dispel them. And, however hard he tried to justify it, he knew that Aelflaed would never forgive him.

Before they even reached the village, Enric caught a whiff of burning in the air and, instinctively laid a hand upon his seax. It might, of course, just be woodsmoke; but, as they rode along the track into the village, it soon became evident that it was not. Pulling up at Aelflaed's house – or at least where the cottage had once stood – Enric was appalled to discover that nothing remained but a heap of charred timbers on a scorched patch of earth.

In his haste to dismount, Enric almost fell off his horse and ended up crouching on the ash-covered earth. Brushing his hands over the ground, strewn with debris, he found it cold to the touch. The smell of the fire lingered though around several of the scorched beams. As he knelt there, his mind playing out a succession of ever more terrible nightmares, he heard several villagers approach and soon there were half a dozen women gathered about him.

"God's heart, I prayed we'd seen the last of you," snarled a fierce voice.

"What happened?" he murmured, moving towards Aelflaed.

"What happened?" she cried. "You happened! Not a sign nor word from you in years and then you come back and bring the devil with you."

Her voice, breaking with anguish, tore at his heart. "I didn't know this would happen," he muttered.

"Liar!" she yelled. "You led a Norman knight here and you knew he was after your blood."

"I didn't know what would-"

But Aelflaed cut his feeble protest short. "You knew very well what *could* happen, you son of a turd!" she hurled the bitter accusation at him. "You knew… but you led those wolves here anyway."

"Roland came back then."

"Aye, Roland wasted no time in punishing those who gave aid to you and your bastard nephew. And, since our faithless lord, Gloucester, has fled to Normandy, his estates are seized and what's left of this peaceful little place is now granted to Sir Roland de Burgh."

Aelflaed's words seared through him. "Good Christ," he muttered. "And what of our children?"

"*My* children still live," was Aelflaed's cutting reply. "But Edwin and Eadwulf are made outlaws."

As if the memory was too raw for her to dwell upon, she stalked away from him, towards the north field.

"What?" gasped Enric, hurrying after her. "But where are they?"

At first Aelflaed showed no sign of having heard him, but finally she slowed her pace a little. When he reached her, she turned and, lowering her voice, told him: "For now, they live close by in the forest; but they can't stay there all their lives. It's as well I'm the alewife, else folk might have turned me and Enwyn out too."

"What can I do?" asked Enric.

Aelflaed regarded him coldly. "Do? You can ride away as you did before – and, this time, don't come back."

"I didn't know…"

"You didn't pissing care," she murmured sadly.

He couldn't meet her reddened eyes, knowing that only a spear of accusation awaited him there.

The ensuing silence was cut short by a sour laugh from Aelflaed.

"And… you're still here," she observed. "So, you didn't come here to learn how we were; because, even now, you want more from us, don't you? I don't know why I'm even surprised. What is it you want now, our last drop of blood? Because that's all we've got left."

"Thomas is in trouble," said Enric.

"Oh, poor Thomas," said Aelflaed. "But, as you see, we're in trouble too – and it's all because of him."

"He may already be dead," said Enric.

"Then he's beyond our help, isn't he?" replied Aelflaed savagely.

But Enric knew he could not leave it there. "If Edwin and his nephew are outlawed, they'll lose nothing by helping Thomas."

"You truly are a shit of a man," declared Aelflaed. "You want my son and grandson… Why not just drive your seax through my heart and have done with it."

"If they're already outlawed, they've a better chance with me," he insisted, though utterly weighed down by his guilt.

"Aye, a better chance of being killed," lamented Aelflaed.

"And how long will they last in that forest among thieves and cutthroats?" demanded Enric.

"Longer than they would with you, you cold-hearted arsewipe."

"War's coming, Aelflaed - and that's not my doing. This war will eat up young men for every lord will be recruiting from his lands. Outlaws will either be recruited or killed out of hand. Isn't it better Edwin and Eadwulf fight for one of their own?"

"It's better they don't fight at all."

"The choice will be theirs," he told her. "But, if they fight for Thomas, and his father triumphs, I swear to you they'll be outlaws no longer."

But Aelflaed's stony expression showed no sign of softening. "A pardon will give them small comfort if they're dead…" she muttered, "nor those who mourn them."

"You know I'll do my best to keep them alive," he argued.

"No, I don't," wept Aelflaed. "They weren't raised to be warriors, Enric…"

"Aye, but nor was I," he told her. "They know well enough how to fight – and I'll be by their side."

She nodded, strangely silent at last.

"Thomas is young, but he's a good youth," said Enric. "He'll do all he can for Edwin and Eadwulf."

"Where will you take them?" she muttered.

"Back to Schaftesberia where I pray that Thomas still breathes…"

Without another word, the sobbing Aelflaed walked away to join Enwyn, who was glaring at her father from among the small gaggle of village women. After a last look into his daughter's solemn eyes, Enric returned to Ralph, who had wisely remained by the burned-out house.

"How much did you hear?" enquired Enric.

"Enough," said Ralph. "How will we find them?"

Though Enric knew the answer to Ralph's question, he thought it wiser not to enlighten the youth just yet; because Aelflaed was right: he was a cold-hearted old arsewipe.

Though the forest provided a home for a few innocents condemned by misfortune, it was also the domain of some of the most dangerous villains imaginable. Thus, as they rode around the north field to reach the forest edge, Enric warned: "Be watchful now, Ralph, for there's worse folk in this forest than my kin."

In response, the youth rested his hand upon his sword hilt though Enric wondered whether that meant he was prepared to use it. They rode through the trees with care, for every track was thick with mud but, by dusk, after several hours of searching, they had seen only green-leaved trees.

Disconsolate, Ralph ventured: "Should we go back to the village?"

"There's no going back to that damned village," growled Enric. "We'll make camp here and get a fire going."

"A fire?" cried Ralph. "But everything's wet through."

Ralph's observation was true enough for, after so much rain, dry kindling was scarce; but they managed to start a smoky fire. Enric reckoned it might last for an hour or so and prayed that would be long enough.

"Perhaps the fire will draw in your kinfolk," remarked Ralph.

"Oh, very likely," replied Enric, knowing that it would attract a great many more than just Edwin and Eadwulf.

Leaving Ralph to dry himself off beside the fire, Enric announced that he was going to collect more wood. "If anyone comes, tell them you serve the Earl of Gloucester," he advised.

"But he's a traitor…"

"Aye, but it might make an outlaw think twice before killing you," replied Enric darkly.

As he had promised, Enric did gather more firewood, but he did not return to the camp with it. Instead, he left it at the base of a nearby oak and climbed up into the tree canopy.

"I'm too damned old for this," he muttered, for it was not the most comfortable place to wait. Not only were the branches coated by a thin, slimy layer of green, but water dripped down incessantly from the upper boughs.

It must have been more than an hour later that he was awoken by raised voices and he peered across to his camp where Ralph was being pinned against a tree. His loud protests were probably what had woken Enric, who had to admit that complaining was one of the lad's great skills. But those surrounding Ralph seemed deaf to his pleas and Enric reflected, that perhaps he ought to have woken up a little sooner.

"I serve the Earl of Gloucester!" Ralph was yelling repeatedly.

But, as Enric knew very well, few of Ralph's assailants would care whom he served. If he did not intervene soon, poor Ralph would have his throat cut and Enric would be one fartweed down before he even started recruiting. So, nocking an arrow to his bow, he took careful aim for he was still something of a novice with the Welsh bow and this was not the time to make a mistake. Though he intended his arrow to strike the earth next to one of the men holding Ralph, it actually had rather more impact than he planned. Thudding into the midst of the smouldering fire, it sent a spectacular plume of spark-laden smoke and ash into the night air.

Even before the men could move, Enric bellowed: "Stand where you are, or you're all dead men."

Under his breath, he muttered a prayer that no man would move because, if anyone did, he would be obliged to release his next arrow, already nocked. After that, the group would scatter and events would spiral swiftly out of his control. Mercifully, the outlaws, though they darted anxious glances all around them, remained still. He struggled to identify Edwin or Eadwulf among the half dozen or so that still ringed Ralph. If his kinfolk were not there then he had risked a great deal – including Ralph's life - for no reward at all.

Whatever he did next would be a gamble; but he knew he couldn't fight them all and survive.

"Ah well," he muttered to himself and dropped down from the tree.

As he approached the small crowd of outlaws, he called out: "God give you good evening, fellows. We mean no harm to any here – in fact we bring you an offer."

When the men turned towards him, one grumbled: "God gives us little in this forest, stranger; so, what's to stop us taking what you two have?"

"My name is Enric and I serve Robert, Earl of Gloucester," he told them.

"We don't care who you serve," declared one.

"Well, fellow, perhaps you should," replied Enric, "because war's coming to this land and - as I said - I've an offer to make you."

"War?" scoffed another of the outlaws. "What war?"

"My lord, Earl Robert seeks to replace King Stephen with the rightful ruler, old King Henry's daughter, the Empress Matilda."

As he expected, his announcement was greeted only by bitter laughter.

"We're outlaws," one cried. "We don't care which sowsarder rules, for the law stays always blind to us."

"Not always," countered Enric, "for any man who agrees to serve Earl Robert will earn a pardon."

"Hah," said the spokesman, "Earl Robert can't pardon us."

Enric noted that no-one else offered any opinion so it appeared that the speaker was the acknowledged leader of the group.

"True enough, friend," agreed Enric, "The earl can't but the Empress Matilda can. Serve her well and you'll earn your pardon."

"So, you say," scoffed the outlaw. "But we know nothing of her – or you."

"I do," said another man, stepping forward into the firelight to clasp his father's arm. "This man is my father, Enric and I know he does indeed serve Earl Robert."

"Even so," argued the spokesman, "If Earl Robert is turned traitor, any man who stands with him will be called traitor too."

"Aye, that's true," agreed Enric. "But, since you already live outside the law, what have you got to lose?"

"Our lives," snarled the spokesman.

"Fair enough then," said Enric. "No man is forced to serve."

"So that's it; that's your great offer: death or pardon?"

"Aye, neatly put: death or pardon," agreed Enric. "But it's your choice."

Several men began to drift away into the trees, casting wary glances into the canopy of branches for any sign of another archer. Watching them go, Enric raised his voice to announce: "If any man chooses to serve, let him be outside the east gate of Schaftesberia at midday in two days' time."

Whether or not any of the outlaws would accept his offer, it must have given them pause for thought because all dispersed without any show of hostility. Only Edwin and Eadwulf remained to join Enric and Ralph around the dying fire; and, if he was honest, Enric was grateful just to find his kinsmen still alive.

"You left me alone at the mercy of all those outlaws," complained Ralph, bristling with indignation. "I could have been butchered where I sat."

"You weren't though, were you?" said Enric, with a sly grin.

"But-"

"You need to have a bit more faith, lad," said Enric.

"What you said to us all," said Edwin. "Is it true?"

"Well, first, I wanted to find you two; Aelflaed told me you were in this forest somewhere."

"But, is it true, father?" persisted Edwin.

"Er, mostly," replied Enric.

Edwin nodded, as if he had suspected as much. "Which part isn't?"

Since Enric had no intention of misleading his own son, he replied: "I can't be certain of the pardons - but I believe it can be done…"

Edwin fixed his father with a steely glare. "But the earl isn't here; so, you're recruiting for Thomas, aren't you?"

Enric nodded. "You'll get no lies from me, son. Thomas is in the shit, right enough – could even be dead already."

"Why is it," bemoaned his son, "that I hardly know the damned youth, but I'm not surprised that he's in trouble?"

"Aye, that's my nephew for you," agreed Enric. "So, what's it to be then? Will you stay here in this fair forest for the rest of your days, preying on hapless travellers, or join me in the service of your cousin, Thomas?"

19

Evening on 15th June at Schaftesberia Castle

Dutifully, Adeline took her place at Sir Roger's side for the evening meal in his oak-timbered hall. She did her best to play the submissive lady, smiling thinly at the ribald humour and replying politely when spoken to. All the same, her new guardian made no attempt to conceal his fury over her visit to Thomas earlier in the day. She wondered whether he suspected that the timing of her visit to him had much to do with his blunt refusal earlier that day to allow her to attend her sister's wedding.

What he would do if he learned of her marriage to Thomas, she could only imagine – and it made her shiver with foreboding. Yet, having pledged her life to Thomas, it would take more than fear of Sir Roger's wrath to thwart her. Going to see Thomas was not the rash act of a foolish girl, but the commitment of a steadfast wife to her new husband. And that evening, for every moment she lingered in the hall, in her heart she carried the stark image of a scarred, bruised and mud-spattered Thomas.

Though Isabel had wrought a deal of trouble for her - and even more for Thomas - Adeline simply could not wish her ill and was still irked at missing the wedding. Isabel was still her little sister and, in time, she hoped to mend the broken ties between them. Witnessing the marriage the girl craved so much seemed an ideal way to begin such a reconciliation – if only Sir Roger had permitted it. Instead he had taken the first opportunity to enforce his authority over his ward.

When the meal was nearing its end, Sir Roger dismissed her with a curt nod but, even as she withdrew, she knew that he would not leave the matter there. So, though she craved sleep, she remained awake in case he decided to visit her later that night. Her instincts were sound for he did arrive but, since it was very late, he came to the point at once.

"Lady, we must settle our differences," he said briskly. "Today, you went out of your way to embarrass me."

"Aye, as you did when you kept me from my sister's wedding," she replied.

"Perhaps I was wrong to do so," he said. "But whether I am right or wrong, is no concern of yours. Flout my authority again and it will bring consequences you will regret very much."

"I have treated you with respect," grumbled Adeline, "but your treatment of my- of Thomas FitzRobert – has been brutal."

"What happened to him was not my doing," said Sir Roger, "but... still, you defend that renegade."

Remembering Thomas's fortitude despite the beating he had endured; Adeline could not prevent a proud smile from creeping across her lips.

Seizing her arm, Sir Roger hauled her to her feet, snarling: "Do I amuse you, lady?"

"No, lord," murmured Adeline, doing her best to feign contrition.

"Whatever befalls that youth, I forbid you to speak to him again. Nor, by God, shall you even dare to look at him; because, if you do, I promise you he'll be beaten a great deal more severely. Thus, his punishment lies in your hands, my lady. Do you understand?"

"So, if I stay here as your willing prisoner," she murmured, "Thomas will be unharmed."

"Unharmed?" cried Sir Roger. "What a hapless fool you are. I may promise you that your treacherous lover won't be beaten at my command; but I can't say what will become of him once the Earl of Leicester has him."

Adeline made no reply, lest she revealed the depth of her despair.

Growing more confident, Sir Roger continued: "As for you being a prisoner; you're my ward, my lady, and don't forget it. I require your obedience in all matters but I too have certain responsibilities toward you – for example, the choice of your husband."

"That again..."

"Aye, that again – and be certain, lady, the matter will not go away. I beg you to reconsider my proposal for our union would serve us both very well. You and your inheritance would be in safe hands – which is more than I can say for your poor sister at the mercy of that brute, Thorold Le Breton."

"Let me be plain, Sir Roger," said Adeline. "I will not marry you. There's only one man I'll consent to marry – and you know well enough who that is."

"You live in a world of dreams, lady," said Sir Roger, shaking his head. "You will never marry Thomas FitzRobert because he'll shortly be tried for treason. Even if he's not executed, you'll certainly never see him again."

And his words drove such a spike of ice through Adeline's heart that it was as well he still held her arm, for her legs suddenly felt too weak to support her.

"Marry me," he implored her again, "and you shall have my protection – I swear it."

But she had stopped listening and whispered only: "I've nothing more to say and I'm very tired so, pray let me rest."

When he released her, she slid down onto her knees on the straw bed. Perhaps he regretted his bluntness and took pity upon her for he softened his tone as he left: "For the present, lady," he told her, "just learn to obey and all will be well."

Only after the door closed, did Adeline let out the first of several great sobs of grief. For how, if Thomas was lost, could all be 'well'? Indeed, how could all ever be well again? How she longed to go to him in his wooden cage and wrap her arms around him; but, for his sake, she dared not even try. And, though she could not see him, every feature of his face was etched upon her memory.

∞ ∞ ∞

Dawn found her lying wide awake, having slept only fitfully, so she rose early, determined, for Thomas's sake, to regain Sir Roger's favour. But, as it turned out, a new distraction arrived in the shape of Sir Thorold Le Breton and his new bride, Isabel. The newly-knighted warrior, bound for his recently-acquired manor at Sturministra, was making a gesture of courtesy by paying his respects to Sir Roger before leaving the town. From what little Adeline knew of Sir Thorold, she suspected that he was only courteous when it served his own interests. Sir Roger's favour with the Earl of Leicester ensured that he was regarded as an ally worth the wooing.

At the sight of Sir Thorold's party entering the castle, with Isabel among them, Adeline's spirits soared; for surely, here was the chance she so desperately needed to regain the trust of her sister. But though Sir Roger seemed pleased when Adeline descended to the hall to join him, there was no opportunity to converse with her sister alone. Indeed, from the outset, Thorold hardly permitted his wife to stray from his side. Throughout the visit, Adeline noted that Isabel remained unusually quiet and only uttered a word when her husband addressed her directly. Adeline was familiar enough with her sister to realise that all was far from well with her. The girl looked deathly pale and Adeline feared that married life had given Isabel a rude awakening.

Observing Thorold le Breton, she recalled what both Thomas and Sir Roger had told her about the man and prayed that God would watch over Isabel since she could not. In a desperate attempt to comfort her, Adeline reached out tentative fingers to touch Isabel's hand. To her surprise, her estranged sister clasped her hand and smiled – a reaction which brought tears to Adeline's eyes.

Before Thorold could intervene to prevent it, Adeline drew her sister away to embrace her. Head buried in Adeline's shoulder, she breathed: "He's a beast…"

A moment later the girl was hauled away by Sir Thorold who grumbled: "That's enough idle chatter from you two."

Shocked at his rude manner, Adeline was not willing to relinquish her sister so easily. Ignoring Sir Thorold, she turned instead to her guardian and asked: "My lord, will you not allow but a few moments' discourse between two sisters who last parted on poor terms?"

"I think that would be wise, Sir Thorold," agreed Sir Roger. "A few moments for the ladies - perhaps while I show you my newly-built fortifications."

As Adeline hoped, Sir Thorold had little choice but to comply and at once Adeline swept Isabel into a tiny chamber off the hall where, keeping her voice low, she hissed: "Has he hurt you?"

"Hurt me, sister?" wept Isabel. "He's near torn me apart…"

"Well, perhaps it's simply because you've not… been with a man before," soothed Adeline. "And it can be painful at first…"

"Was it for you then, with… Thomas?" asked Isabel.

Knowing her answer would offer Isabel no comfort at all, Adeline ignored the question and enquired: "Apart from that, has he hurt you in any other way?"

"I have many bruises, sister, and a few cuts where, as my husband tells it, I stumbled and fell. It seems I do not please him, Ade; though God knows, I am trying to be a good wife. He told me it was like… ploughing a furrow through dry clay…"

When Isabel fell to weeping again, Adeline, finding no words to console her sister, simply held her close. It had not taken long, she reflected, for Isabel to become disillusioned with the married life she had coveted so much. Perhaps it was just as well that the girl did not understand how slender and fragile was the thread that kept the pair of them alive. Now that Isabel's husband held the de Sarne lands, he did not need his wife. Like Adeline, Isabel would need to adapt quickly to her new circumstances, or one of her 'falls' might prove fatal.

"Perhaps if our mother had been alive, she would have prepared us better," murmured Isabel.

Perhaps she would, thought Adeline, for having their mother taken from them so young had been hard. Ralph's mother, their father's housekeeper, had done her best; but what did she know about marriage when she had never been married? She had brought the girls up to be capable women, not ladies. Yet, Adeline doubted any young girl could ever be sufficiently prepared to cope with a husband like Thorold le Breton. In any case, the past was in the wind and dwelling upon it would help neither of them now.

"You were right all along," muttered Isabel. "I should never have been so eager for a marriage. I thought it would give me a new life but I am more fettered now than ever before. Because of my foolishness I betrayed you, Ade – who I love above all others – and I beg you to forgive me for it. I think you would have been happy with Thomas…"

"'Tis all done now," said Adeline, not daring to reveal, even to her sister, her new marital status.

"Will he come; do you think?" asked Isabel. "Will Thomas come for you?"

"You've not seen him?" gasped Adeline.

"Seen him? Why, is he here?"

"Aye, because, of course, the fool did come," said Adeline, blinking away the tears that threatened to fill her eyes. "He was taken and cruelly abused; any day now he will go before Earl Robert of Leicester and I fear, sis, that I may never see him again."

Though Adeline wanted to sob out her broken heart, she steeled herself to stay resolute. However much she wanted to spare her sister pain, the brutal, savage truth was what was needed now.

"We must both obey our masters and pray for God's help," she instructed Isabel. "But, if that's not enough, then our lives rest in God's hands - as they ever have."

"Then pray for me, sister," murmured Isabel.

"Aye, and you for me," replied Adeline. "Come, lest we provoke our lords needlessly."

Soon enough, an impatient Thorold returned to the hall bellowing for his wife and Isabel fled to join him. A few moments later, the small entourage left the castle and Adeline stood bereft once more. Scarcely had Isabel been ripped from her embrace, when another visitor entered the castle gate flanked by two men at arms. Having no stomach for more polite conversation, Adeline was much relieved when Sir Roger asked her to withdraw.

Still heavy with worry over her sister's plight, she trudged up the stair; but, instead of returning to her damp little room, she continued on up to the tower rampart. While Sir Roger greeted his new guest below, Adeline strained to peer over the parapet towards the stockade in the hope of catching a glimpse of her new husband. Though she paid little attention to Sir Roger's conversation, one word, drifting carelessly up from the yard, caused her fingers to tighten their grip upon the wooden rail. It was a single name, but it was enough to drain the blood from her face, suck all the breath from her lungs and turn her limbs to sand. Broken, she slumped down onto the bare timber floor, hugging her knees to her breast and weeping as she had never wept before, because her husband was not coming back.

20

Dawn on 16th June, at Schaftesberia Castle

Soon after first light Thomas watched Thorold drag his new bride from Adeline's embrace and, in a typically cruel gesture, toss her carelessly up onto her horse. Clearly Thorold made no allowance for his bride's obvious inexperience as a rider. But, when the poor girl managed to cling on and twist herself around to sit astride the horse, Thomas felt a touch of admiration.

With sadness, he watched Thorold's small retinue depart. "God speed, my lady," he murmured, "for you're going to need every ounce of courage you possess…"

Before the castle gates could close, another horseman entered and Thomas groaned. The arrival of Roland de Burgh and his escort confirmed his worst fears. It was clearly in both men's interests that Thomas did not survive to appear before the Earl of Leicester. Sir Roger would then be free to marry his new ward and Roland would get the revenge he so desperately craved. But at least now Thomas knew: if he gave Roland the slightest excuse, this journey would be his last.

When the two men at arms came for him, Thomas was surprised at the vociferous abuse hurled at them by the comrades he had scarcely known for a couple of days. Several also cheered Thomas or clapped him on the back when he made a show of wrestling with his captors.

"Fitz! Fitz! Fitz!" they began to chant, which must have confounded others in the yard who had only ever heard him called Thomas or 'Saxon'.

Before he was taken out, Edgar looked him in the eye and embraced him like a brother. "Don't forget about us, Fitz," he murmured, pressing a slim, sharp object into his palm.

A moment later, Thomas was hauled roughly out of the stockade with his hands bound securely behind his back. While a smug-faced Sir Roger looked on, the prisoner was led across the yard towards the gate. In vain, Thomas looked for a glimpse of Adeline before he was dragged out of the castle. Having crept in there to save her, his careless folly had now left her utterly alone. Some husband he'd proven to be…

It was a steep and slippery descent down the north-facing hillside away from the town and, for the first hour or so, the rain-sodden Thomas slid and stumbled along behind Roland's horse, deep in his own dark contemplation. Every so often, Roland turned to favour his prisoner with a grim smile of satisfaction and the Norman's obvious delight only seemed to confirm what Thomas already surmised.

Their road, Thomas noted, would take them north, which surprised him since Sir Roger told him that the Earl of Leicester was in Salesberie. Though Thomas could not claim much knowledge of the area, he suspected that Salesberie must be further east. But, of course, whatever their destination, the fate of Thomas FitzRobert would very likely be sealed long before they reached it. The knight's burning desire for revenge was certain to outweigh any recent commitment he might have made to the Earl of Leicester – and, for Roland, nothing less than Thomas's death would suffice.

If only Thomas could survive long enough to reach Robert de Beaumont, Earl of Leicester, then he had a chance because, though the earl was unlikely to look favourably upon Gloucester's bastard son, he would not execute him at once. Thomas would be the earl's prisoner, held for as long as it pleased the king; because, though he was certain to be condemned for treason, he might still have some worth as a hostage in a war where prominent men on both sides might be captured.

Roland was probably praying for Thomas to attempt an escape because it would make it so much easier to kill him out of hand. Hence, Thomas resolved to be a stoic and uncomplaining prisoner. If it came to it, he had the primitive blade that Edgar handed him but the chances of an unarmed man, with his arms bound behind his back, overpowering a mounted knight and two men at arms were slim to say the least.

As he laboured to keep pace with the mounted knight, he kept a close eye upon the pair flanking him who, on that warm, wet morning appeared far from enthusiastic about the journey they were undertaking. Both were armed well enough – indeed one had somehow managed to acquire Thomas's seax – but neither man seemed especially alert. Did their glum demeanour, he wondered, stem from knowing exactly what Roland planned for the journey?

As they crossed the green, rolling uplands north of Schaftesberia, Thomas peered into the distance, wondering whether Roland had already planned where to carry out his summary justice. It would have to be a secluded place off the road and probably in a stretch of woodland. However, for the present, the road ahead, passing across an expanse of open grassland, offered no such possibilities. A mounted knight butchering his prisoner in plain sight, where he might be observed by others on the road, was a risk Roland would be reluctant to take.

Though he did not intend to provoke Roland, Thomas was certainly not going to leave himself defenceless either; so that, whatever occurred, he would be prepared. First, if he wanted to last more than a few heartbeats, he needed to free his hands. Giving silent thanks to Edgar for the small piece of flint clutched in his right hand, he started to put it to work. If he survived the day, he would have a great debt to repay there.

However, the flint edge was less effective than he hoped against the leather cords which restrained him. With hands bound behind his back, the task was made even more difficult though at least that concealed his efforts from the two guards. Working the thin, sharp flint back and forth was slow, painful work since it seemed to be slicing into his hands more than his bonds. By the time he felt the leather bindings loosen a little, his aching fingers were greasy with his own blood. Nonetheless, when he spied a swathe of woodland in the distance ahead, he continued with greater urgency. Working the flint ever faster, he prayed he could release his hands before they reached the forest. He almost cried out when his bonds came free but managed to restrain his triumph. As they neared the tree line, he tried to clear his head, ready to try to make a fight of it.

The moment they entered the trees, Roland came to a halt and swung his mount around to face Thomas. This was the moment and both men knew it.

"Hold him," Roland ordered the two men at arms.

The Norman knight had his hand upon the hilt of his sword when, from the road behind them, came the sound of horsemen cantering ever closer. Muttering a low curse, Roland prepared to wait for the oncoming riders to pass by. Thomas, already wound as tight as Enric's Welsh bowstring, took a breath and relaxed his shoulders as the riders approached. By the considerable noise they were making, it was a sizable party and a darted glance behind him confirmed that it was a band of a dozen or more soldiers. It was no surprise because fighting men would have been on the move from the moment of his father's declaration for the Empress Matilda. Few though, he reckoned, north of Schaftesberia were likely to be adherents of Robert, Earl of Gloucester.

Since the group was travelling at a fast pace, Thomas expected his reprieve to be short-lived but, perhaps intrigued by the lone captive, they pulled up to converse with Roland about his prisoner. Thus, all through the forested area, while Thomas trudged behind the horsemen, they chatted like old comrades with Roland who, Thomas suspected, was fuming with frustration at being thwarted.

Only when the road passed out of the woodland again, did the riders bid Roland good day and hurry on their way. Nonetheless, they had already presented the Norman knight with a problem for, not only had they forestalled his execution, but they had seen that Thomas was posing no threat to his captors. All the same, Thomas had little doubt that Roland, once the horsemen were far enough away, would still take his chance. When they neared another swathe of forest, Thomas felt almost relieved that the waiting would soon be over.

After the road entered the woodland, it ran alongside a narrow, but fast-flowing, stream. There, Roland pulled up and Thomas steeled himself for the coming struggle, wondering how far he could prolong it. Roland, though he might be a little hampered by the wound he sustained at Escewich, was still a formidable warrior. Eleven times out of a dozen, he would defeat even a well-armed and fully-fit Thomas – and, just now, Thomas was neither.

Though his hands were now free, he dared not reveal that until the last possible instant. After dismounting slowly, perhaps savouring his moment, Roland drew out his great sword – and it was a fearsome blade. As the two men locked eyes, a faint smile curled along Roland's lips, but his face was drawn tight in anticipation and his brow was slick with sweat. Thomas was well-balanced on the balls of his feet when, at a nod from Roland, the two men of the escort seized his arms. Despite that, as he waited for Roland to strike, Thomas continued to breathe slow and deep because, if he timed his move badly, the knight's weapon would cut him in two.

REBEL SWORD

As Roland's sword carved down at him, Thomas lunged to his left, hauling the two guards with him. Even as he felt the impact of the knight's blade upon the wrongfooted soldier on his right, Thomas was driving the narrow spike of flint hard up under the other guard's chin. Before the life faded from his victim's wide eyes, Thomas abandoned the stone shard, painted bright with blood, and instinctively stepped back. It was as well he did, for Roland, ripping his sword from the falling body of his own man at arms, swung wildly at Thomas.

Still unarmed, Thomas spied his confiscated seax at the dead guard's belt and bent down to retrieve it. Dipping his head saved his life for he felt the breath of Roland's sword as it slashed just over his scalp. Though the seax was a brutal blade, it would not suffice against Roland's weighty sword. Barely parrying the next blow, he stuffed the seax into his belt, dropped to his knees and lurched sideways.

Several times Roland stabbed at Thomas as he rolled away to wrench a bloodied spear from the limp fingers of the other fallen man at arms. Staggering to his feet, Thomas prodded his opponent back; but it was a brief respite for soon Roland attacked again, swinging his blade in great ranging arcs, unleashing the rage he had suppressed for so long. Armed with the spear, Thomas at least had a chance of keeping the knight at bay. But though Thomas was able to turn the blade aside with his spear and even force his opponent back, he would never land a killing blow and Roland knew it.

Sure enough, he soon launched himself at Thomas with all the fury he could muster, trying to hack aside the spear with the sheer power of his sword arm. With every exchange of blows, Thomas felt the spear shaft tremble and could only pray that his adversary's leg wound would soon compel him to move more slowly. Thus, despite the brutal power of Roland's assault, Thomas tried to keep calm and wait for his opponent to make a mistake. His calm evaporated, however, when Roland's sword blade hacked off the point of his spear. His groan of despair was smothered by Roland's shout of triumph as the knight charged forward scenting victory.

21

16th June in Schaftesberia

For a very long time Enric stared impassively at Sir Roger's castle on the hilltop. Almost two whole days had passed since he last stood there, but not much appeared to have changed. However, since the sound of hammering and sawing no longer reverberated from the ramparts, Enric assumed that Sir Roger was now satisfied with his defences.

"How much longer are you going to look at it?" asked Ralph sourly. "'Cos looking at it won't help us."

Enric nodded, because, for once, the impatient youth was right. In two days, a great deal might have happened within the fort and, somehow, they must discover if Thomas was still alive and whether he was held in the castle or not. If not, then there was very little point in trying to break into it.

"We have to free her, Master Enric," pleaded Ralph. "We have to…"

"Aye, lad," said Enric, "but not till we know what we're getting into."

"What we should be getting into is that damned place," cried Ralph, stabbing a finger at the castle.

"No, not till we know more," said Enric, shutting down any further discussion. "For now, we'd better see if any of those outlawed arsewipes have decided to join us."

"Very well," agreed Ralph, "but, Christ's blood, let's make haste."

Aye, reflected Enric glumly, haste was the other thing at which Ralph excelled; he wasn't just skilled at endless complaining, he was a master of witless haste.

"It won't be noon for several hours yet," remarked Edwin.

"Aye, but we can use those hours to find out what's happened here since I left," said Enric. "Ralph - you can stay here and watch the castle."

"Pah, I can't see much from here," groaned Ralph.

"Even so, mind you stay here out of sight," ordered Enric.

Leaving the frustrated Ralph to fester in his own miserable company, Enric took his two kinsmen along the narrow back lanes of St James up towards the abbey. If any outlaw recruits did arrive, they should gather outside the old town's east gate which was a mere thirty yards or so from the abbey gateway. Yet, Enric was far from hopeful; for what man of sound mind would willingly embroil himself in civil strife when he didn't have to? Nor did he reckon that his spurious promise of a pardon would gain much credence among the outlaws. Only those who were truly beyond hope might come - and desperate men made unreliable soldiers.

Arriving outside the east rampart of the town, Enric glanced across to the abbey gate. Their best hope of getting information would be Avice, but how could he involve her again when she had already risked her position for them? But, of course, he would do so because he was a 'callous bastard' and, like the coward he was, he did not dare see her again and thus sent Edwin into the abbey instead.

"But this Avice won't know me at all," argued his son. "Are you sure?"

"Just ask at the gate for the healer," he told Edwin. "Then tell her that you come from me."

With a puzzled shake of the head, Edwin sauntered across to the abbey gate, leaving Enric and Eadwulf to wait in a nearby alley. Though Edwin appeared to pass through the gate without any hindrance, as the minutes passed, Enric began to regret his decision. What if Avice refused to confide in his son who, as he pointed out, was a stranger to her? When Avice walked out of the abbey gate alongside his son, Enric's doubts only spiralled.

As she approached, he could feel her studying him closely which caused a knot of concern to tighten in his belly. When he saw the recognition in her eyes, his heart almost stopped but her greeting gave no hint of their former intimacy.

"Am I to be at your beck and call now, Master Enric?" she chided him. "I'm here to serve this abbey, not your private quarrels."

"Leave us," he told the others briskly. "And Edwin, keep a watch for any new friends, eh?"

To his great relief, Avice made no protest when he led her away from the abbey gate into the old town. Then, drawing her quickly into a side lane, he blurted out: "I crave your forgiveness, Avice."

"And… for what is my forgiveness required?" she asked, with a trace of a smile.

"Why, for losing you in Antioch… and for not finding you then – or later…"

Avice took a few moments before she replied: "My memories of Antioch are all fond ones, Enric. You didn't lose me; my father stole me away from you."

"But I tore that city apart looking for you," he lamented. "Even when I learned your father had taken you away, no man seemed to know where. And then war just… plucked me up and seized me by the throat."

"Well, it's all done now," said Avice. "I'm still alive and, by God's grace, so are you. So, let's not dwell on past troubles when you seem to have found so many new ones for us to face."

"Us? This isn't your quarrel, Avice."

"Though, you sent to me…"

"Only to learn if you've any news of the de Sarne ladies or… my nephew."

"Ah, the one his enemies call 'Saxon'," said Avice, with a mischievous smile.

"God knows why," grumbled Enric. "The youth's only half as Saxon as I am; but, have you heard anything?"

"I believe he was taken from the castle this morning," said Avice.

Enric, aghast, clasped her arm. "He's already gone?" he gasped. "Then all I'm doing is for nought."

Seeing her wince, he suddenly realised how tightly he was gripping her forearm and released his hold at once.

"And what exactly are you doing?" enquired Avice, her face a mask of worry.

When, just for an instant, he held back, she noticed his hesitation.

"What? You don't trust me?" she cried. "Me? Who would have died for you a thousand times?"

"No, of course, I trust you," insisted Enric, "but… I daren't draw you any further into what I'm doing. God's nails, Avice, it's treason."

"Do you want to shout that a little louder?" she murmured.

"I'll not pull you down into this mire," he told her, "nor can I have you taking mortal risks for no reward at all."

"Only the reward of helping an old friend," she replied.

"You owe me nothing, Avice; so, while I'm grateful for what you've told me, you should go back to the abbey before you're seen with me."

But Avice, not to be so easily dismissed, remarked: "That fellow, Edwin, you sent to me has a little of your countenance, I'd say."

"Aye, as you've guessed, he's my son."

Avice smiled while her silent question hung in the air between them.

"Aye, and I've a daughter too, Enwyn… and a grandson…"

She took a deep breath, he noticed before replying: "Then I am pleased for you, Enric – and your wife."

"No wife," confessed Enric. "And I'm not much of a father either; so, you're not the only woman I've disappointed."

"You never, ever disappointed me, Enric," she said gently. "What happened to me was none of your doing; when my father learned I was with child, he brought me back to England at once-"

"You were with child?" gasped Enric. "I'm sorry, Avice."

"Aye, the voyage took months and, long before we reached these shores, I lost the babe. My father, not knowing what to do with his unchaste, grieving daughter, left me here and returned to the Holy Land."

Enric frowned. "But did he never come back for you?"

Avice gave him a wintry smile. "He never intended to come back – and certainly not for me… So, here I've been, ever since."

"If only I'd known," he said bitterly. "All the time I was searching for you there, you were already here in Schaftesberia."

"As I said, it's long ago now," she consoled him. "So let's leave it in the past and speak of more recent matters."

"Very well," agreed Enric. "You're certain that Thomas has left the fort."

"I overheard Sir Roger reporting to the abbess that Lady Isabel de Sarne had gone with her husband to Sturministra and that Sir Roland de Burgh was escorting Thomas to the Earl of Leicester."

"God's breath, Roland…" said Enric, distraught. "Could you perhaps have misheard?"

"No, 'tis certain. But who is Roland?"

"He's more of a threat to Thomas than any other man in the kingdom," cursed Enric. "The news couldn't be worse. And Lady Adeline - what has become of her?"

"I believe she is well and is now the ward of Sir Roger."

"His ward and, before winter, I'll wager she'll be his wife," said Enric.

Every morsel of news seemed worse than the last, for it seemed that both Thomas and his lady were lost.

A hand clasped his own. "I'm sorry to be the bearer of such ill tidings."

During the long silence that followed, Enric released her hand. "You should get back," he said, "or someone will wonder where you've been."

"I doubt it," replied Avice. "It's common enough for me to leave the abbey to help folk."

"Even so," he said. "Someone might have seen us talking."

"People see me talking to strangers all the time," she said, "but, if it worries you, I'll go."

"It's better to be careful," he said.

As they passed back through the town gate, she told him: "If any man can help your nephew, I know it's you. But, when you do, try to stay alive at least a little longer, won't you?"

Watching her walk back into the abbey, Enric felt more alone than ever and was glad that he had Edwin and Eadwulf with him. When he found the pair, as he feared, they were not surrounded by a host of eager recruits. So, it appeared that his desperate scheme to raise a band of fighting men from among the outlaws had failed miserably. Perhaps, he reflected, it was just as well since there was every chance that he no longer had a young lord for them to serve.

"No arsewipe outlaws hungry for a pardon then," he said glumly.

"Oh, aye, there are," replied his son, "but we sent them to wait out of sight of the abbey gate, lest their gathering caused concern among the nuns."

"You jest," cried Enric. "How many?"

"Only five."

"Well, we won't have those five for long," muttered Enric.

"How so?"

"Thomas is gone."

"Gone? Gone where?" asked Eadwulf.

"God knows," muttered Enric. "God – and probably Roland de Burgh - since he's the one charged with escorting him."

"Roland," growled Edwin, "surely not."

"So, what do we do?" asked Eadwulf

"Nothing we can do," said Enric. "He'll be hours ahead of us by now."

"Can't we track him," suggested Eadwulf.

"We don't know where he's going, or even how he's getting there," grumbled Enric. "All we know is that Roland's taking him to the Earl of Leicester."

"Pah, I doubt Thomas will get there alive," said Eadwulf.

"Aye," sighed Enric. "I should never have let him go into that damned castle…"

With a rueful shake of the head, Edwin replied: "He would have gone whatever you said."

"Aye, you're probably right; but now it's all up to him. And I can't offer those outlaws any chance of gaining a pardon now."

"Well, you have to," declared Edwin. "You gave your word and, on the strength of that, I gave mine too. So, you'll have to find a way to do it, father."

Enric groaned, partly because Edwin had called him 'father' for the first time, but also because his son's words seemed to echo Avice's sentiments.

"What are they like then, our five volunteers?"

"A mixed lot," replied Edwin. "Not sure you can trust them."

"They're goatswiving outlaws," snarled Enric. "I won't trust them any more than they'll trust me. Still, I suppose at least they came. Come on, I'd best take a look at them."

At Enric's approach, the recruits, lounging against an ancient stretch of crumbling wall about a hundred or so paces down the road from the abbey, looked up but did not move. Their gaunt faces were so downcast that he wondered what possible use they might be to him.

"Welcome, friends," he announced with forced good cheer. "I'm assuming that, if you've troubled to walk all the way here, then you're willing to serve Thomas FitzRobert, son of the mighty Earl of Gloucester."

"Aye, where is he then, this Thomas?" enquired one of the outlaws.

An excellent question, thought Enric, who declared: "Joining him will be your first act of service; but, if any man has doubts about doing so, then he should leave now."

"And you swear he'll deliver us a pardon?" asked another, older man.

"Aye," agreed Enric readily, fearing at any moment to be struck down by a blazing divine thunderbolt.

"But we've only your word on that, not his."

Though it was exactly what he himself might have said, he replied testily: "My damned word should be enough for you - but I swear, before you all, that if I lie then my life is forfeit to you."

"A bold oath," said the older outlaw.

"Aye, and an empty one too," muttered Edwin, under his breath.

But when Enric swore the oath, he meant it because he was very well aware that the most likely outcome of Thomas's treason was that every single man there – including him - would lose their lives. Hence, only in the unlikely event that he survived; would he need to worry at all about his false oath.

"Come on then – get up off your arses," he ordered, leading them down past St James to the edge of the town until they found Ralph.

"You've taken your time," grumbled the youth. "So, what've you found out?"

When he heard the news of Thomas, Ralph chewed his lip so vigorously that Enric feared how the youth would react to Adeline's new status. As it turned out, Ralph took it in grim, apparently resigned, silence; but then, without another word, he suddenly leapt up to mount his horse.

"Ralph?" said Enric.

"I'm going for a ride." said Ralph.

"But where?" cried Enric.

Ralph, however, rode off at once without looking back; and all Enric could do was let the youth go. He was not the fartwit's keeper and perhaps it was better that the lad was alone for a time rather than among a handful of strangers. For now, Enric had enough on his hands without looking after the embittered youth. Though he had encouraged the five new recruits to stay on the strength of an empty promise, Enric still had no means of helping Thomas. Since his nephew would either be killed, or face long years of imprisonment, his new recruits were likely to serve no longer than a couple of days.

His predicament brought home to Enric, perhaps for the first time, how much he was drawn to Thomas. So many times, he had seen young men fall - cut down before their time – but, losing Thomas seemed very different. If he was honest, the raw fire in Thomas had also kindled a new purpose in him. But now, as he contemplated losing his nephew, a familiar weariness was creeping back into his very bones.

22

16th June, on the road north of Schaftesberia

Thomas retreated, wafting the stump of his spear shaft to and fro until Roland's persistence knocked it from his grasp. Though he drew out his seax once more, Roland drove him back along the stream towards the outer edge of the woodland where only young birch and ash grew. For the first time, Roland appeared to recognise the well-honed blade Thomas now brandished at him.

"I'll be gutting you, Saxon, with that blade you used to murder my brother," he cried.

"Aye, if you can take it from me," growled Thomas.

Continuing to retreat, he skidded on the slippery stream bank and, off balance, was obliged to leap across to the other side to avoid falling in. He wondered, fleetingly, if he might be able to keep Roland on the far side of the bubbling waters but even that faint hope died when Roland, leading with his sword point, easily vaulted across to propel Thomas back yet another pace. With the end of his short and worthless life only a single sword thrust away, Thomas was filled with regret that he would never see Adeline again, nor regain his father's trust.

Incensed by the cruel injustice of his fate, he felt a wave of righteous anger surge through him, firing new vigour into every fibre of his body. So be it then: he would make his stand and, as in all things, the Lord would be his judge. The instant Roland came at him once more, Thomas surrendered to the cold fury that now consumed his heart.

With a roar of rage, he charged straight at his opponent, batting aside with his seax Roland's half-raised sword and ramming his shoulder at the startled knight. When Thomas then jumped back across the stream, Roland followed, but his damaged leg slowed him just enough to give Thomas a few yards' advantage. Snatching up a sword from one of the fallen men, Thomas turned to face his adversary with renewed belief.

Roland gave him a grudging nod – perhaps of resignation rather than respect – and then drew out his knife. For the first time, the two men were equally well-armed and Roland adopted a more measured approach. But Thomas's belligerent mood allowed no hesitation and, at once, he hacked at the knight's head with his newly-acquired sword. Parrying the first wild swing, Roland appeared to be assessing his opponent as if for the first time. But his circumspect approach ended with a swift hammer blow that almost knocked Thomas off his feet. Clutching at a spindly birch trunk, Thomas steadied himself; but the relentless onslaught continued.

After several more brutal blows, however, a confounded Roland took a pace backwards for Thomas had contrived to block every thrust and slash he had attempted. Drenched in sweat, the two men eyed each other as they sucked in lungfuls of precious breath. When Roland's mouth twisted into a scowl, Thomas wondered whether, in his opponent's cool blue eyes, he detected a first flicker of concern. But, with both men driven on by motives far more personal and visceral than mere fealty or honour, the stalemate could not endure for long.

Across two-yards of forest floor, the knight thirsting for revenge faced the youth desperate to survive. Glaring at his opponent, perhaps Thomas' senses were sharpened by the proximity of imminent death. The blood in his mouth tasted sweet, every woodland sound rang clear, every leaf came into keen focus and the faint odour of sour piss drifted up from one of the fallen bodies. Neither man dared even blink lest it triggered a killing strike by his rival. Blind aggression might have kept Thomas alive thus far but, to kill Roland, he would need a clear head. So, slowing his breathing, he fought to entomb his raging demons.

As he studied Roland ever more closely, Thomas discovered a weakness he had never noticed before: so powerful was the knight's sword arm, that he tended to carry his knife low as if he never expected to use it. When, finally, his opponent's face gave an involuntary twitch, Thomas anticipated the coming blow and met its full, withering force only with his seax. Though he felt the jarring impact all along his left arm, his sword was already carving down upon the knight's left shoulder. Biting deep through mail and flesh, when the blade cracked into bone it brought forth a mournful cry from Roland.

With blood dribbling from the deep wound and his left arm hanging limp at his side, Roland was desperate. Both men knew that his only hope was an immediate and mortal strike; but his wild lunge was easily knocked aside. The seax arced towards his throat and thus, at the end, Roland's death was as swift as his brother's. Somehow, Thomas took no pleasure in the kill; and, as he knelt beside the knight's still-trembling body, he bowed his head to thank God for his survival.

When Roland's blood no longer flowed, Thomas considered taking his mail shirt, but baulked at stripping the knight who had fought so well. He did, however, pick up the dead man's sword to test the grip and weight of it in his hand. It was a fine weapon, he decided, which would suit him well; and perhaps, would serve as a constant reminder of the turmoil that his wild temper could provoke.

Scarcely a week before, killing Roland would have marked the end of his troubles; now it merely signalled the start of even more. It would not be long before the bodies of Roland and his escort were discovered and word of the knight's death would scorch along the road to north and south. There might be no witnesses to testify to his guilt, but it would be all too obvious to the Earl of Leicester and Sir Roger of Schaftesberia that Roland had died by the hand of Thomas FitzRobert. Already charged as a traitor, they would now add several more murders to his growing list of crimes.

With a weary groan, he sheathed his weapons, then retrieved Roland's horse and rode south. Urging his mount into a canter, he soon covered the ground across which he had stumbled earlier in the day. But when, late in the evening, he approached the lofty spur of rock upon which Sir Roger's castle stood, he had no idea what he should do next. Pulling up in the darkness, he could only stare up at the chinks of light which marked the great castle tower where he knew Adeline would be. For, though he might be free at the moment, he was no closer to releasing his new wife than he had been a few days earlier.

His father had advised him to choose his path with care; but Thomas reckoned that neither father nor son appeared to have chosen very wisely. Somehow love and treason had colluded to cast Thomas into a deadly pit of ruin. Whatever he did next would determine not only his fate but the fortunes of those he loved. Adeline might be his handfasted wife but, to get her back, he would have to prise her from the grasp of her lawful guardian. Even if he did, all Christendom would roundly condemn them both and brand her a whore all over again. Perhaps, in truth, she would be far better off if she never saw him again.

Riding across to the stand of trees just off the Scireburne road, he found, as he expected, that no-one was waiting for him. Two days was far too long for anyone to linger so close to the fort, but if Enric had withdrawn to safety, it could only be to Duncliffe Forest. Before he rode away, Thomas took one last, lingering look at the darkened castle; and then he stared more intently, eyes focussed upon the road that descended by St John's. In the gloom, it was difficult to tell, but he fancied he saw a horseman picking his way down towards the road out of Schaftesberia.

Keeping well-hidden among the trees, Thomas continued to observe closely until, finally, the rider joined the Scireburne road. At first, he intended to lie low, assuming that any man riding out of the castle in the evening was likely to spell trouble for him. It certainly couldn't be Sir Roger for he would not travel without an armed escort. It might be a messenger – though it was late to send any man out unless it was urgent. With a shiver, he realised that news of his escape and Roland's demise might already have reached the castle by now. That alone would surely provoke a flurry of messages; but, only by intercepting the messenger could he be sure how much Sir Roger knew.

23

16th June in the late afternoon at Schaftesberia

For once, the fickle sky had cleared but even the sight of hilltop Schaftesberia bathed in sparkling sunshine did nothing to melt the chill in Ralph's heart. The knowledge that his sister's fate hung by a slender thread in the hands of Sir Roger distressed him beyond words. Of course, Adeline had never wanted to go to a nunnery, but at least that chaste path would have preserved her good name. When he heard Sir Roger call his sister a whore, the scales had fallen from Ralph's eyes and he realised that FitzRobert's intervention had only corrupted the foolish girl.

He recalled bitterly how he had welcomed FitzRobert's assistance against Sir Roger; but how wrong he had been. Now Adeline's shameless infatuation with the Saxon dog had seen her fall ever further from grace. It was hardly surprising the abbess decided not to admit her as a novice when, even now, folk in the town were busily gossiping about her as if she was a common harlot. God's teeth, she was a lady and the whole de Sarne family was being sullied by her wanton folly.

Yet, Ralph's love for his half-sister persuaded him that the fault lay not with the weak-willed Adeline but with the crafty Thomas FitzRobert. From the very outset, Gloucester's bastard had taken cruel advantage of a young girl still in shock at being despatched to a nunnery. Isabel had seen it and tried to warn her sister, but by then, Adeline was utterly beguiled by the knave's false promises. But however much he found fault with Thomas, it did not help him devise a means of freeing Adeline from her current predicament – indeed, he could see no way of doing so.

When his meandering course around Schaftesberia finally led him to ascend the steep hill past St John's church up to the old town gates, Ralph wondered whether it was just simple chance that took him so close to Sir Roger's stronghold. But, in a sudden flash of insight, he chose to believe that it must have been the Lord who guided him to Sir Roger's gates, for a possible solution to the de Sarne troubles had crept into Ralph's head.

Sir Roger was widowed, Ralph believed; so, what if he could persuade the knight to marry Adeline himself? But would the illustrious knight be willing to take a bride whose carnal misdemeanours were so well-known and who had no inheritance to offer? Very likely Sir Roger would reject the notion out of hand and Ralph wasn't even sure he possessed the courage to suggest it. Doing so would mean swallowing his pride, but he could think of no other solution to their family's disgrace.

Picturing his sister as friendless, desperate and very likely much daunted by her ordeal, he was certain she would clutch gratefully at such a straw of hope. Nudging his mount towards the newly-constructed castle gateway, he felt a new strength of purpose coursing through him. Until another thought undermined his newfound confidence: what if the bastard FitzRobert would not give her up?

Knowing what a dangerous opponent FitzRobert would be, his nerve failed him and, at the last moment, he pulled up several yards from the gates. But, since one gate lay ajar, the two burly guards posted beside it had seen him approach and he knew there could be no going back.

"What do you want here, fartwit?" grumbled one of the keepers, as Ralph came to a halt.

Why, Ralph wondered, were keepers always so surly? Nonetheless, he resolved to remain calm for he had not come to start a quarrel with anyone, least of all a gatekeeper.

"I've come to see my sister, Lady Adeline," announced Ralph, his voice wavering under their hostile gaze.

The keeper glanced at his comrade, who tried – but failed – to suppress a sly smirk and muttered: "Aye, my lady - and everyman's lady, so I've heard…"

Lips tightening into a hard thin line, Ralph said nothing.

"I'll see if Sir Roger will allow it," added the other gatekeeper. "But I doubt he will."

While the keeper crossed the yard and disappeared into the castle tower, Ralph directed a particularly malevolent stare at the remaining guard, marking him for the grave insult to Adeline. However, as the moments slowly passed, Ralph was obliged to look away, lest he should provoke the man before even gaining entry to the castle.

When at last the keeper returned, he was not alone and Ralph was surprised, and a little disturbed, that Sir Roger himself had troubled to accompany his man.

"You, dismount," ordered the knight and at once Ralph hastened to do so.

"What do you want, boy?" enquired Sir Roger.

Gulping at the hostility in the knight's unforgiving eyes, Ralph prayed that his bladder would not fail him under Sir Roger's fierce scrutiny.

"Why… to ask your pardon, lord," mumbled Ralph, groping for words. "I regret my actions against you and also… I beg leave to visit my sister."

"Very well," agreed Sir Roger easily.

Staring at his host in disbelief, Ralph murmured: "I expected you to think ill of me."

"Oh, I do," replied Sir Roger. "But, now that Thomas FitzRobert is on his way to judgement, the lady needs someone she trusts to advise her. Leave your horse and arms in the yard and follow me."

The news that FitzRobert had been taken away was far better than Ralph could have hoped and he understood why the Lord had brought him to Schaftesberia Castle. Driven by new hope, he scrambled to keep up with Sir Roger as he swept through the modest hall. After following up several flights of wooden steps Ralph joined the knight outside a small chamber.

Without troubling to knock, Sir Roger opened the door and announced: "Lady, your half-brother comes to visit you."

His sister's astonishment was amply demonstrated when she jumped off her straw bed to fling her arms around him with tears rolling down her pale cheeks.

"A few minutes only," warned Sir Roger. "And make sure, lady, that you remember this concession on my part."

To Ralph's surprise, the knight did not linger and appeared content to allow the two siblings to speak privily.

"It is such a relief to find you unharmed," gasped Adeline. "And to have at least one friend in this dread place."

"I'm told FitzRobert has been taken for execution," said Ralph bluntly.

"Trial, not execution," corrected Adeline. "But Ralph, Thomas has been so wickedly abused."

"Aye, but perhaps he deserved to be," argued Ralph.

Instantly he regretted the careless remark for it sparked a fire of anger in Adeline's countenance.

"Deserved it?" she cried. "How does Thomas deserve to be beaten when all he sought to do was help us?"

"It's true," Ralph agreed hastily, "that FitzRobert did help us; but perhaps, Ade, he did so only because…"

His sister's thunderous look warned him that he had strayed onto dangerous ground but he had gone too far now to retreat.

"Be honest, sister, he took advantage of you…"

"You think he sought only to lie with me from the start?" growled Adeline, eyes blazing back at him.

"Well, you can't deny he persuaded you into his bed," he replied.

"I can – and I do deny that, brother," declared Adeline, her every word chilling his very soul. "Thomas did not persuade me; for it was I who went to him."

"Well, when I say persuaded…" Ralph muttered, sinking ever deeper into a dark abyss of doubt.

Gripping his sweating hand in her ice-cold fingers, Adeline looked him in the eye and, in a voice forged from steel, told him: "In my life there are now two sorts of people: those who honour and respect the man I love and those who don't. So, Ralph, which are you?"

Clinging onto her hand, he pleaded: "I'm just your devoted brother…"

As Adeline let fall his hand, she replied: "That's good to hear, Ralph, but it's not enough. If you are no friend of Thomas, then you are dead to me."

"I swear I'm a friend to you both," he cried. "And I'll do all I can to help you."

What she would have replied he never discovered for their conversation was interrupted by Sir Roger, who had returned to escort the visitor out of Adeline's chamber. Having squandered his brief opportunity, Ralph could only mumble: "I'll come to see you again, sister."

"Get out," ordered Sir Roger. "God knows you've had long enough to weep over each other."

When they descended the stair once more, Ralph expected to be swiftly sent on his way but, in the hall, Sir Roger's affable manner returned.

"Come," he said warmly, "sit here with me a while and take some refreshment."

Though Ralph was more than a little wary of the knight's apparent civility, he sat down on a bench across the table from him.

"I could not help but overhear the harsh words from your sister, lad," confessed Sir Roger.

Ralph, astonished that the knight was professing sympathy for his plight, wondered how much he dared reveal of his true thoughts.

"I intend to marry her," announced Sir Roger abruptly and Ralph could see from his expression that he was deadly serious.

Unable to believe his good fortune, Ralph could not think of a response.

"Well?" prompted his host.

"I'm certain you will be a fine husband, Sir Roger," said Ralph.

"You don't sound that certain," replied Sir Roger. "Please - you can be honest with me, Ralph. What say you?"

Still fearing that he was about to be caught in some hidden trap or other, Ralph replied: "Perhaps at first, Sir Roger, I misunderstood your intentions, but the very reason I came here today was to persuade you to marry her."

Sir Roger's countenance gave nothing away. "You don't favour the bastard Saxon, FitzRobert then," he said.

"No," retorted Ralph. "Certainly not he."

His vehement denial brought a smile from Sir Roger and an approving nod.

"You're right, lad," he agreed. "As you now know to your cost, FitzRobert is a very dangerous youth..."

"Aye, I believe he is."

"Since your sister is now my ward, I'll determine whom she marries," explained Sir Roger. "If I were prepared to marry her – despite all her recent, ill-advised actions, what would you be willing to do to help me?"

"I… I don't know, Sir Roger," stammered Ralph, for the discussion was venturing into an area he had scarcely imagined possible. Yet, he felt a great weight lifted from his shoulders for Sir Roger's willingness to marry was more than he could have hoped for. Marriage to a well-regarded knight would go a long way to restoring the de Sarne reputation – and his sister's, of course.

Thus, without hesitation, he enquired: "What would you have me do?"

"I fear your sister will need to be persuaded about the match," said Sir Roger, "hence, I need you to help her see the advantages which are already so clear to you."

24

Early evening on 16th June at Schaftesberia Abbey

Ordinarily a summons from the abbess would have caused Avice no concern at all but to be asked to see the Reverend Mother in the evening was most unusual. Indeed, Avice could not remember any previous occasion and she could only assume that the abbess had discovered her involvement in the escape of Thomas and Enric.

"Come in, Avice," invited the abbess.

"Are you unwell, Reverend Mother?" enquired Avice, ashamed of the hope that lurked in her breast.

Though the countenance of the abbess was grim, Avice reckoned it was not caused by illness.

"I am not unwell, Avice," Abbess Bella replied, "but I confess that my spirits have rarely been driven so low."

It was true enough that Avice could not recall ever seeing the abbess so ashen-faced and drawn. "But you think I might be able to help you," she ventured.

"I'm not at all certain that I should even ask it of you," murmured the abbess. "But when the devil stirs…"

"How does the devil stir, Holy Mother?" asked Avice.

"I believe you know him…"

"The devil?" gasped Avice.

"No, of course not the devil," snapped the abbess, "the youth, Thomas FitzRobert."

Avice, reeling in confusion and hardly knowing what she should admit, replied: "I wouldn't say I know him."

"Yet you released him from here, didn't you?"

When the abbess confirmed her worst fears, Avice dropped to her knees onto the stone-flagged floor in submission. "Forgive me, Reverend Mother. I beg you… I didn't do it for young FitzRobert…"

"For the other then - his uncle?" remarked the abbess, eyebrows raised in surprise.

"I know I've betrayed your trust; but I beg you: please don't banish me from this place that has been my home for so long."

With a shake of her head, the abbess raised Avice up. "My dear Avice, you misunderstand the reason for this meeting; I do not seek to punish you. Having those two men here was more of a problem than a blessing – and you made it go away. So, if anything, it was a betrayal for which I was grateful."

"Thank you, Reverend Mother," cried Avice, weeping tears of relief.

"But… you have some… connection then with the uncle."

Avice looked away when she replied: "Enric's a man who lies deep in my past – or, at least, so I thought."

"Perhaps I'd rather not know why you acted as you did," the abbess told her. "But I've always thought of you as someone I could confide in about, shall we say, secular matters… and I've learned there are far worse things even than betrayal, Avice."

For a moment, the abbess seemed unsteady on her feet and leant against the wall for support. Avice, fearing she might fall, reached out a hand to take her arm and steady her.

"What ails you?" she whispered, her voice betraying the depth of her concern.

"I can scarce utter the words to explain," breathed the abbess.

"Yet, you asked me here to do so," beseeched Avice.

"Aye," agreed the abbess, releasing her grip upon Avice's hand as she attempted to recover her composure. "Let us sit and confront the devil…."

"Young girls have been… taken against their will," began the abbess. "Two of our nuns, who witnessed the crime, were also abducted, including the young novice, Edith - I'm sure you know her."

Avice remained silent as she struggled to absorb what the abbess was telling her.

"Of course, I am no fool," continued the abbess, "and I know such things happen – but so many wicked abductions by one man cannot be allowed to stand."

"I don't know what to say," said Avice. "But you surely don't believe that Thomas FitzRobert is the culprit?"

"When I held the outlaw prisoner with his uncle, I did wonder if it was his doing – until I spoke to the youth and knew at once that it was not. It has taken me a day or two more to piece it all together. Only when I noticed, the day after her wedding, an abrupt change in the sweet, bright countenance of Lady Isabel, did I begin to suspect. To my shame, I was relieved when her husband took her away; for I didn't want to believe what a terrifying night she must have endured. It only became clear to me a little later that, while Thorold Le Breton was here being married before God, his retainers were visiting the local abbey tenants and…"

"It was Thorold?" cried Avice. "But, have you asked the Bishop of Salesberie for help?"

"Of course, I sent to the bishop first," replied the abbess, but her voice hardened when she added: "His reply was swift and blunt: Sir Thorold, he assured me, was merely taking on more servants for his new manor house at Sturministra."

"So, the bishop refused to help," sighed Avice.

The abbess said bitterly: "It seems that *Sir* Thorold is now the king's man – as is Roger, Bishop of Salesberie."

"Then what can be done to save the girls, Reverend Mother?" asked Avice.

The abbess said nothing for a moment but then, taking a deep breath, seemed to reach a decision.

"I've confided in you because I believe you can help me."

"But what can a poor healer do about any of this?" wept Avice.

25

16th June in the evening on the road to Scireburne

Since Thomas was taking the same road as the messenger, at least as far as Duncliffe forest, he risked nothing by following him. He was surprised though how fast the envoy travelled for, not only was it fully dark but much of the road surface lay under several inches of standing water. Even if the message he carried was most urgent, surely only a fool would take such risks - and then it struck him that such reckless riding was reminiscent of a certain youth he knew. Closing the distance to the rider ahead, he cursed his stupidity that he had not recognised the slight figure of Ralph much sooner. But then, the last person he would expect to be riding out of Sir Roger's castle was Ralph.

"Ralph!" he called out and the rider stopped so quickly that he almost fell from his horse.

"Who's there?" challenged Ralph, drawing his sword.

Lest he alarmed Ralph any further, Thomas slowed his pace to a walk and, only when he was a mere dozen yards away, did he speak again.

"It's me, Ralph … Thomas."

"Thomas?" echoed Ralph, without sheathing his sword.

"Truly, it's me," Thomas assured him as he drew closer.

"But you were sent for… trial," muttered Ralph.

"You won't need that sword," Thomas told him.

"No, no, of course not," said Ralph, hastily burying the blade in its scabbard. "But we heard you were taken away by Sir Roland de Burgh this morning."

"I was," agreed Thomas.

"And now you're here… free."

"I am."

"You escaped… from Roland."

"I did, Ralph; though I'm certain that now I'll be hunted down with a little more vigour than before."

"Well, Roland, for one, will pursue you," declared Ralph, sounding almost enthusiastic about the prospect.

"If Roland is to waylay me," replied Thomas, "I fear it will have to be at the gates of Hell."

"Ah, I see," acknowledged Ralph.

"You were just at the castle?" enquired Thomas.

Ralph gave a start. "Oh, yes," he admitted. "Sir Roger allowed me a few moments with my sister."

"That's good – how is she?"

"Alone, afraid and much-troubled."

Darkness could not disguise Ralph's cool, almost distrustful, demeanour; and, from his terse response about Adeline, Thomas understood at once that Ralph blamed him for his sister's plight. He was probably right to do so, thought Thomas.

"I tried to get her out," murmured Thomas.

"And instead, you got yourself caught," said Ralph, suddenly full of scorn. "Aye, she told me as much…."

Stung by the youth's distain, Thomas insisted: "As God is with me, I will free her, Ralph."

"Perhaps you will," conceded Ralph, "but will she be better for it?"

Considering his own growing doubts on the subject, Thomas was unwilling to discuss it any further and instead asked: "Where are you heading?"

"Back to the cottage, of course, to join your uncle. I've nowhere else to go."

"We'll ride together then."

"But surely that's the first place they'll look for you," said Ralph.

Thomas nodded. "Aye it is, but I won't be stopping there long."

Cursing the lack of decent moonlight, Thomas lost his way several times in the forest for, in places, the army of trees was almost impenetrable. Since his truculent companion appeared equally lost, it was long past midnight when they finally reached the edge of the clearing around Wilflaed's cottage. Expecting all to be quiet there, Thomas was surprised to see several horses tethered outside and a group of shadowy figures squatting around a large fire. With a groan, he realised that word of his escape must have reached Sir Roger more swiftly than he hoped. So, of course, they were already there waiting for him.

When he pulled up, Ralph, apparently untroubled, continued to walk his horse out of the trees. Glancing back to Thomas, he said: "Oh, don't mind them. Your uncle's recruited some help."

"Help – but who?"

"I think I'll let him explain," muttered Ralph, leading his mount on towards the cottage.

A bemused Thomas followed on, wondering who could have been foolish enough to join Enric. When the two horsemen approached, a figure left the warm glow of the fire and cried: "God's nails, Thomas; it's a relief to see you safe."

"And you, uncle," replied Thomas. "But who are all these… fellows?"

Drawing Thomas aside, Enric, with a sheepish grin, confessed: "Well, these goatswiving pissmaggots are actually *your* fellows, lord."

"Mine?" murmured Thomas, as he regarded the half dozen men in the firelight. When two of them leapt up to clasp him by the hand, he recognised Edwin and Eadwulf at once. But the rest, he did not know at all; nor they him.

"Explain to me how these are my men, uncle," demanded Thomas.

"Aye, lad," said Enric. "Come inside and I'll tell you all."

But, even after Enric had explained how he recruited the outlaws, Thomas was shaking his head in disbelief.

"You promised them a pardon?" he hissed. "Christ's bones! How, in God's name, did you think I could give them that?"

"I needed men," protested Enric, "to help you – and that wretched lass."

"Call her that again and you'll regret it," snapped Thomas.

Enric held up his hands in submission. "I'm sorry, Thomas; I like the girl well enough - indeed, she's a good lass. But once I knew you'd been taken at the fort, well, there was no hope of just me and Ralph getting you out. So, I had to look elsewhere for help…"

When Edwin and Eadwulf came into the cottage, Thomas said: "You're both outlawed because of me and I owe you a great debt for that; so, if the Empress Matilda does rule, I'll ensure that you are both pardoned. But as for these other men – by Christ, we don't even know why they were outlawed. For all we know, they could all be killers."

"What, like you?" pointed out Enric. "You can ask them if you like, but it hardly matters. We need men who aren't afraid to shed some blood, Thomas; and, if they serve you loyally, then you'll look after them. Perhaps, when this is done, they may not be pardoned; but, as your men, they'll have a hearth to sit at and take their ease."

"Pah!" scoffed Thomas. "When this is done, they'll all be dead – and us with them."

"They made a choice to serve you rather than live like a pack of God-forsaken arsewipes in the forest," argued Enric.

"Aye – and yet here they are living in a damned forest," argued Thomas. "And how many are there anyway - five?

"I recruited them to help me get you out, but now we don't need to do that. Five men will be more than enough now."

"For what?"

"To get you safely to your father in Normandy."

"Not a chance," snarled Thomas.

"Listen, I've thought about it," said his uncle. "You can't free the lady just now, with so few of us – it just can't be done. But, join your father and then, when we return to England in force, you'll have the power to get her back. She's just one life, Thomas when the whole land will soon be at war."

"No, uncle, she's not just one life anymore; she's my wife."

"Handfasted wife? I doubt that'll stand," asserted Enric.

"We've said our vows, uncle; so, either I free her, or I die trying," declared Thomas.

"And what if she dies while you're trying?" argued Enric. "Have you thought of that? Where she is now, you know that she's safe enough; and, the faster we take the road to Warham and get a ship to Normandy, the sooner we'll be back to free her."

"But to leave without her…"

"She'd want you to be safe," added Enric. "And right now, you're the one in most danger – because I'm guessing all that blood spattered on your clothes has something to do with your escape."

"Oh, aye," agreed Thomas quietly. "Most of it is Roland's. I've also got his sword at my belt and his horse stands outside because he no longer requires either."

"Dead?" gasped Enric.

"Aye, and the two men with him," confirmed Thomas.

"God's breath, they'll be hunting you down then."

"Indeed, they will," agreed Thomas.

"And they'll expect you to run…"

"Aye."

"So, they'll look for you here first-"

"-which is why I came here to get you. But we can't stay here long – and you'd better put a man on the Scireburne road now to give us some warning."

"Aye, true enough," agreed Enric, nodding to Edwin who left to see to it.

"You can't lay siege to a castle with half a dozen men, Thomas," murmured Enric.

"Aye, I know that," said Thomas, "but… I swore to free her."

"And you will, lad; you will. But it's less risk to her, if we go to your father first."

Thomas felt his frustration growing, but the mere thought of putting her at greater risk saw him submit to reason.

"Aye, I suppose you're right, you old bastard," he groaned.

"So, it's decided then," said Enric. "We leave at first light?"

"No, I need to think on it," muttered Thomas.

26

Early morning on 17th June at Wilflaed's cottage.

Thomas was so exhausted that Enric had to wake him at dawn and he was not well-pleased.

"We've a long ride," said Enric, "so, you've no time for idle slumber."

Thomas found it hard to disagree but he was still dressing when Edwin hurried in to report movement in the forest nearby.

"Sweet Christ," grumbled Thomas. "Can we not have a moment's respite?"

"Only one man would have business here at this hour," muttered Enric and, when his nephew gave a tired groan, he added: "Are you fit for this, Thomas?"

"Aye, uncle – indeed, it seems I'm fit for nothing but *this*." Glancing at his cousin Edwin, he saw a countenance taut with worry. "Edwin, Eadwulf, find out how many there are," he ordered.

"Aye, lord," said Edwin, hauling his young nephew away with him.

"Damn Sir Roger," cursed Thomas, as Enric helped him don his mail shirt. "Word must have travelled fast; I hoped I'd have more time..."

"Once we know their strength, we can decide whether to take them on or try to lose them in the forest," advised Enric.

"And so it begins again," lamented Thomas, "running and fighting; fighting and running… How did I ever believe that I could free her?"

Sooner than he expected, a breathless Edwin rushed in.

"What, cousin?" demanded Thomas.

"It's…" Edwin paused to catch his breath.

"It's what?" snapped Thomas.

"I think it's that woman from the abbey… Avice," replied Edwin.

"What?" cried Thomas, "not Sir Roger then?"

"Avice?" murmured Enric, looking confused.

"And she's brought another woman," added Edwin. "And two men at arms were hanging back in the trees."

"Could Avice have betrayed us to Sir Roger?" asked Thomas.

"Never," declared Enric. "She comes every week to collect herbs from Wilflaed – that's all it is."

"This early in the day," observed Thomas.

"Cooler to ride now," suggested Enric.

"But she was here only a few days past," murmured Wilflaed.

"Better bring them in, Edwin," said Thomas.

"Er, they won't come in, Fitz; they want to talk to you outside."

"Me? But how does Avice even know I'm here?" grumbled Thomas. "God's breath, I'm hardly awake. Well, if she wants to talk to me, she can come inside. Go and tell her that, Edwin."

By the time Thomas had his boots on, Avice was at the cottage door. Embracing Wilflaed fondly, she nodded in deference to Thomas but, he noted, studiously avoided any eye contact with Enric.

"God give you good morning," said Thomas warily.

"My companion would speak to you alone," said Avice. "So, everyone else will need to wait outside…"

"I don't think so," said Enric.

But Wilflaed, smiling at her friend, said: "I believe it's still my house so, if Avice says we must go, then go we shall."

"Oh, very well," moaned Enric, "we'll go, else this will take all day – and we need to be on the road."

When the much-aggrieved Enric trailed out behind all the others, Thomas remained alone with Avice's cloaked and hooded companion. For an instant wild hope flared and Thomas wondered if Avice had somehow spirited Adeline out of the castle. But when the visitor raised her hood, he found Abbess Bella of Schaftesberia staring back at him.

For several moments, the pair stood facing each other in a tense and awkward silence until Thomas blurted out: "I trust you've not come here to drag the hunted traitor back in chains."

"No," said the abbess quietly.

"How did you even know I was here?" he asked.

"I did not – at least not for certain. But, late in the night, Sir Roger sent a messenger to warn me of your escape and Avice suggested that you might come here first."

"She had no business doing so," growled Thomas. "And I've nothing to say to the woman who surrendered Lady Adeline to Sir Roger like so much livestock."

"I understand," murmured the abbess, though Thomas detected no regret in her eyes.

"That, I doubt," he snapped. "But, since Sir Roger could arrive at any time, I suggest that, for your own sake, you leave at once."

"He won't come yet," replied the abbess, "for he's sent to the Earl of Leicester for more men. Until they arrive, he dares not pursue you."

"Even so, you risk much in coming here, Reverend Mother," warned Thomas. "Duncliffe Forest is no place to come on a whim. So, what's your purpose here?"

"You are my last hope," she told him.

"If an outlawed killer is your last hope, then you must be a very desperate woman indeed."

"Perhaps, but will you at least hear me?" replied the abbess, her voice beginning to tremble with emotion. If she was dissembling, thought Thomas, she was exceptionally gifted at it.

"Very well," he agreed, "but every moment I stand here talking to you, my chances of escaping dwindle. So, what is it you want?"

"Your help."

"Hah! Truly?" remarked Thomas. "Help from a man who, only days ago, you were ready to condemn for a whole raft of crimes."

When the abbess told him of the abductions, his ire began to rise. "So, you come to accuse me because I took the two de Sarne sisters from Sir Roger?"

"No, no," pleaded the abbess, reaching out to clasp his hand in hers. "You mistake my purpose, Thomas. I don't come to accuse you; for I know full well who the villain is. I seek your help against him…"

"Against whom?"

"Sir Thorold of Sturministra…"

"Ah, Thorold is the culprit; of course he is," said Thomas. "I can't say I'm shocked; but this is not my fight, Reverend Mother. You ask too much of me – and of those pledged to me. And, in any case, it could not be done without spilling a great deal of blood – which I doubt you'll want on your conscience."

The abbess gave a solemn nod. "I understand what I ask and I pray that God will understand too," she said. "But, if He does not, it's my soul that will pay the price… And, I assure you that to leave those poor girls with such a monster would weigh more heavily upon me than any blood you shed in rescuing them."

Thomas was obliged to revise his opinion of the abbess a little for clearly, she was deadly serious about freeing the girls. Yet, as he told her, it was not his fight and, by God, he had more than enough trouble already.

"I can't help you," he said finally. "I am about to leave and my men are ill-equipped to match the strength of Thorold's household warriors."

"I understand your reluctance," said the abbess, "but… I fear for Sir Thorold's young bride."

Slamming his fist against a timber post, Thomas cried: "So, after sealing Lady Isabel's marriage to a savage beast, you would now taunt me with his brutal treatment of her."

Unfazed by his anger, the abbess murmured: "Aye, but if you truly love her sister…"

Only then did Thomas understand that she was prepared to use any argument, however base, to persuade him.

"That's no false claim on my part," he snarled at her, "for we are handfasted in wedlock."

Cursing his folly, he warned: "I beg you to tell no-one of that, Reverend Mother, for it will endanger the lady."

"I will not break your confidence," agreed the abbess, "but will you not help me in return?"

"Even if I wanted to, I don't have enough men, horses or weapons for such a bloody task," maintained Thomas.

"I can provide two men at arms, with some horses and weapons," offered the abbess swiftly, her grey countenance now, he noted, grim with resolve.

Still he shook his head. "It'll take more than that to persuade me to fight Thorold."

"Very well," said the abbess. "Let us to the heart of it then – exactly what will it take?"

For the first time, Thomas gave her question genuine consideration for a wild idea had just crept into his head.

"For me to attempt it, you would need to become my… ally," he told her.

"Ally?"

"That means-"

"I know what an ally is," grumbled the abbess. "But how can I promise to help a man who is an avowed traitor against the king?"

"Ah, I see, you would prefer to support a loyal king's man such as Sir Thorold le Breton, who kills, rapes and steals away young girls…"

"No, but… I can't be seen to aid an enemy of the king."

"Then I cannot help you to free those girls," said Thomas. "But may God protect you on your journey out of the forest."

"Wait," hissed the abbess. "I said that I can't be *seen* to help you – but perhaps there may be other ways. What do you want of me?"

"Well, first," explained Thomas, "I expect my ally to believe me when I swear that, whatever I've done, I acted in good conscience."

"Having spoken to Avice, I do believe that, Thomas."

"And I expect my ally to swear an oath."

"The word of an abbess is sufficient for any man."

"No, it's not," retorted Thomas.

For a while, the abbess fell silent but then, to Thomas's surprise, she smiled. "I see that you fight hard for those you love, Thomas FitzRobert," she said.

"Swear that you'll be steadfast for me and I'll try to free the girls," promised Thomas.

"If you can free them, I swear I shall do all I can to help you," promised the abbess.

"Swear before God," insisted Thomas.

White-faced with indignation, the abbess intoned: "Very well, I swear *before God* that I shall help you - is that good enough for an outlaw?"

"I'll leave at noon today," announced Thomas. "Have your two men at arms bring the horses and weapons and meet us on the road south to Sturministra."

"Very well," confirmed the abbess, "And I'll post a trusted man at the abbey's postern gate every day at Prime and Vespers. When you have the girls, bring them to me there and… I pray, Thomas, that God will watch over you and your comrades."

"I expect God's going to be very busy watching over both of us, Reverend Mother," said Thomas.

With a final, solemn nod, the abbess raised her hood and opened the cottage door to leave. By the time she mounted her mule and set off with Avice, Thomas was already regretting what he had promised.

Enric came in at once. "What the devil did she want?" he growled. "Avice wouldn't tell me anything."

When Thomas explained, Enric retorted: "Well, I trust you sent her away empty-handed."

"Not exactly," sighed Thomas.

"Tell me you didn't agree to…"

"I did."

"Has imprisonment addled your sowsarding wits?" cried Enric. "We can't do it, Thomas – we can't face Thorold and live!"

"Perhaps not, uncle," conceded Thomas, "but we're going to try."

"So, instead of fleeing to the coast as we should be, we're going to get ourselves killed," protested Enric. "This is some vain gesture to help your wife's sister, isn't it?"

Resisting the temptation to crack his uncle's stubborn head against one of the timber beams, Thomas explained: "It's more than that, uncle. With the abbess on our side, our hand is much stronger."

"It doesn't matter whether the abbess helps us or not," declared Enric. "'Cos these men aren't trained soldiers, Thomas. God's nails, they can barely wipe their own arses."

"Whether we flee or try to take Thorold's manor, these men will need to fight. At least this way, they'll have more weapons and horses."

"You can't ride a horse if you're dead…"

"Well, I've given my word, uncle so, stop griping and get the men ready," ordered Thomas. "And, while we're gone, Wilflaed had better go to the abbey, for 'tis certain Sir Roger will come here."

Of course, his uncle saw his decision as rash, but there was at least a little sound reasoning behind it. For one thing, the moment Thorold learned that Thomas had killed his great comrade Roland, he would be coming after him anyway – very likely with a lot more men than he had at the moment. This way, at least Thomas might be able to strike first. Then there was Isabel, whose rough treatment he had witnessed only for a moment; but he knew that, if Adeline was by his side now, she would beg him to help her little sister.

Thorold, however, was a ferocious warrior and Thomas expected his retainers to be forged from the same steel. Though he could justify what he was undertaking, he was not foolish enough to believe it would be easy. Yet, with the advantage of surprise and two additional men at arms, there was at least a chance that he could deliver a swift blow and free the girls at the same time as removing a dangerous adversary. Just as likely, of course, Thorold would bludgeon him to death and his fine vows to Adeline would be scattered to the four winds.

27

17th June at dusk on the road south from Schaftesberia

The evening light was beginning to fade as they forded the river Stur, where their tired horses churned up the river bottom. Skirting the small settlement of Sturministra, Thomas pulled up in a stand of alders close to the riverbank. Scarcely a glimmer of sunset remained when he despatched Edwin and Eadwulf to scout the manor house. The rest of the company, especially those who were poor horsemen, were grateful for a long overdue rest.

Thomas was much relieved to have arrived there at all; for the journey had not started well. Before they even set off, Ralph, no doubt overeager to depart, startled his horse just as he was in the act of mounting. The resulting fall gave the youth a nasty crack on the skull and an injury to the arm with which he attempted to break his fall. All of which meant that Thomas was forced to leave Ralph behind - a great pity because, despite his faults, he was at least a fair swordsman. Warning the youth not to speak to anyone about the assault on Thorold's manor, he instructed him to wait for them at the abbey.

Despite the initial setback, the company was much cheered when the men promised by the abbess joined them. Thomas was pleased that she had kept her word and, by God, she had moved fast. The two men at arms, Berner and Tancred, were waiting with several extra mounts and an assortment of weapons. Thomas, wondering how the abbess had acquired such a deadly armoury, could not resist a smile of admiration.

Though the weapons might be welcome, he was not confident that his five outlaw recruits would be able to handle much more than a knife or club. Three of them, Masters Will, Galt and Pain wore permanent looks of apprehension and only one, the muscular Master Turstin, confessed to having any military experience. Since he had, however, been outlawed for desertion, that did not augur well either. The remaining fellow, Geoffrey, was as thin as a wraith but claimed to have wielded a spear in anger.

"Against what?" enquired Enric. "Boar, stag or man?"

"Er, sheep…" murmured Geoffrey. "It was a fierce beast though…"

"God save us from fartwits," muttered Enric. "We're doomed."

Now that they had arrived, the weight of the task ahead grew ever heavier upon Thomas; but, though he shared some of his uncle's doubts, he thrust them from his mind. The last thing his nervous men needed was a hesitant leader; hence, he concentrated on planning how they would take Thorold's manor house. It had to be a swift, deadly raid; for, with the men at his disposal, any prolonged skirmish was likely to end in disaster. But, of course, however well-planned the attack, there was always the chance that something would go wrong.

Edwin and Eadwulf returned to report that Thorold's manor house was alive with wild celebration – no doubt the new lord of the manor was still celebrating his wedding and the good fortune of being newly-made a knight. Well, that suited Thomas perfectly for, under cover of darkness, he was able to move his company close to the manor hall. With the night resounding with loud cheers and raucous carousing, they had no need to be especially quiet.

With any luck, by the small hours, Thorold and the rest of his household would be snoring soundly. Since there were no guards posted outside at all, it appeared that the Breton did not fear an attack from anyone - but then, that was Thorold: brutal, confident and very, very dangerous.

"We go in at dawn," Thomas said to his uncle. "Yes?"

"Aye, we'll catch the pissmaggots asleep," agreed Enric.

"But… what if the door to the hall's barred?" asked Thomas. "Our surprise attack will fail at the outset."

"Another reason to attack at dawn," explained Enric, "'cos there's always some poor bastard who needs to go out for a piss at first light. So, when the first one opens the door, we take the arsewipe down and then slip in - quietly…"

Thomas, however, was far more concerned about what would ensue after they 'slipped' in. He doubted Thorold would simply hand over the captive girls and, any fight with that butcher could only be a fight to the death. With his mind clouded by endless doubts, Thomas found even a brief dozing sleep came as a relief.

When Enric nudged his arm to wake him, he knew that dawn must be close and, once the others were roused, he led them to the perimeter of the manor house. Lying there on the dew-sodden ground behind the low earth rampart that ringed the modest hall, Thomas waited with growing impatience for the sun's first rays. When they flickered through the woodland to the east and glistened upon the nearby river, Thomas clasped hands with Enric and readied himself to launch the attack.

What he needed now was a man who desperately needed to relieve himself; but what if no-one came out, thought Thomas? Perhaps they all just pissed in a pot. What if all those heavy-lidded men waited until the full glow of dawn was long past before they unbarred the heavy oak door to venture out? By then most of the household would be awake and any chance of surprise would be utterly lost.

His fears though proved groundless for, shortly after dawn broke, his uncle wore a broad smile of satisfaction. Unfortunately, it was not just a lone bleary-eyed fellow who emerged from the hall, but three at once.

Crouched beside him, Enric cursed: "Shit of a priest, three of the damned sowswivers. God's nails, are they going to hold hands?"

With only two bows in the company, they could not take out all three men at once; and it only needed one to raise the alarm. Thomas cursed his folly; why had he not foreseen that several comrades might want to piss in the face of dawn together? Yet, since the moment could only come once, it simply had to be seized.

Flanked by the two archers, Enric and Edwin, Thomas whispered: "As soon as I'm close to one of those fellows, take out the other two."

Before either man could react, let alone reply, Thomas was clambering over the earth mound. Tumbling clumsily over the heap of crumbling earth, he stumbled, groaning, towards the three soldiers. All he had to do was get their attention without causing them to panic; so, drunkenly mumbling a song, he staggered several yards further before falling down on his face. Their piss steaming in the cool dawn air, the three men stared blankly at him for a few moments and then, to his annoyance, ignored him.

"Morning, good fellows," slurred Thomas, desperate to get their interest without raising the whole house. "Have you left me a drop of ale?"

"Where'd you spring from?" demanded one of them.

"You one of the king's men?" asked another whose expression betrayed his suspicion.

Wondering vaguely why the fellow would even think that, Thomas shambled closer to the trio and retorted: "I've been out here all night."

The third man at arms, nearest to Thomas, merely stared at him, slack-mouthed, and proceeded to empty the rest of his bladder over his own boots. A sudden, inadvertent guffaw from Thomas broke the tension of the moment, though it did little to allay the men's growing unease.

"I don't know you," grumbled the one who had spoken first, reaching for the knife at his belt.

"Nor I," declared damp boots. "You're not-" but he stopped mid-sentence when his two comrades were hurled wordlessly backwards. Too late, he hauled out a barbarous looking blade which might well have carved open flesh to the bone, had Thomas's seax not swiftly sliced across his throat.

With regret, Thomas watched the fellow crumple at the knees to stain his boots for a second time. Before the final victim even struck the ground, Enric was leading the men in and they moved swiftly to cluster around Thomas beside the half-open timber door of the manor house.

"Make ready," breathed Thomas, carefully easing out his sword. To Enric and Edwin, he murmured: "When the fighting starts, be busy with those bows – and try not to kill our own men..."

Then, in two strides Thomas crossed the small entrance porch and crept into Thorold's Hall. In the gloomy interior, a dying fire at the hearth exhaled a lazy wisp of smoke but no trace of warmth. Several long oak tables filled the chamber, with an assortment of sleeping bodies draped over them. But Thomas could not see Thorold among them.

Even as he peered into the furthest recesses of the beamed hall seeking the knight, he realised with a sickening feeling that it housed more men there than he had anticipated. Just as well then that they had already accounted for three of them. Nonetheless, the remainder, by the look of their muscled arms, were men of war though some lay half-naked in the arms of a woman. Perhaps one or two of those were wives; but a glance at several of their young faces confirmed to Thomas that he had found some of the abducted girls.

For a few moments all slumbered on but, of course, it was not long before the dogs smelt trouble. One great, black beast was the first to lever itself to its feet and fix Thomas with a quizzical stare. At first it gave only a low, hesitant growl; but if it decided to start barking, hell would surely be unleashed – and he still had to locate Thorold. Thomas had a feeling that if he approached the animal, soon flanked by another, sleeker beast, he might only provoke it. So, crouching down onto his knees, he held out an open palm to the animal while holding his weapon ready behind him in case the dog attacked.

For a moment there was an awkward stand-off during which Thomas prayed that no-one would wake up. No-one did and perhaps that allayed the dog's suspicions for it finally walked towards Thomas and sniffed at the proffered hand. Though perhaps still not entirely reassured, the animal gave a cursory grunt and returned to flop down in its place on the rush-covered floor.

With a sigh of relief, Thomas motioned the others further inside and went to investigate a heavily-curtained area at the far end of the hall where he expected to find Sir Thorold and Lady Isabel. Waiting there, he glanced back at his comrades to ensure that they were all in position and his bowmen had arrows nocked. Then, sweeping the curtain aside he stepped into the alcove where indeed he found a startled Thorold. While the naked girl beside him, who wasn't Lady Isabel, slept on, a smiling Thorold levered himself up to a sitting position on the low straw bed, with a knife already in his hand.

"My hound doesn't need to bark, Saxon," he chuckled. "One little groan is enough to wake his master. Pity about Roland – last night's feast was in his honour – so I hoped you'd come for me."

Their conversation caused most others in the hall to stir and at once there were shouts of outrage as the men at arms realised that they were surrounded.

"Peace!" snarled Thomas and a hush descended. "I want only the women you've taken."

"God's wounds, Saxon, how many women do you need?" enquired Thorold. "I'm told you've already lain with one maid; do you now come to steal even my household servants away?"

"Where are the rest?" growled Thomas.

"Safe," replied Thorold. "And God knows, boy, they're safer than you."

"I swear I'll kill every man here to find those girls," warned Thomas, "starting with you, Thorold."

"It's *Sir* Thorold now – but I'm sure you've heard I'm a knight," said Thorold with a broad grin. "But, no matter, for there's already an account to be settled between the two of us."

"You see that man with his bow pointed at you, *knight*? That's my cousin, who knows that I detest you. So, where are the girls?"

The moment Thorold's grin faded; Thomas believed that he would comply – at least for a time. He might be brutal, but Thorold was no fool. He would know that, as long as a bow was pointed at him, he must bide his time.

"The young… *ladies* have their own chamber," announced Thorold affably. "One they share with my lady wife…"

"Where?" rasped Thomas.

"I'll have to show you," said Thorold, indicating a key looped around his neck, "because you'll need this."

"Toss it to that youth," ordered Thomas, pointing at a servant cowering on the ale-sodden rushes under a nearby table.

"As you please," replied Thorold, lobbing the key to the servant.

"Release the girls," Thomas instructed the servant, without taking his eyes off Thorold. "Tancred, go with him."

With every passing moment, the silent hostility in the hall was mounting, for Thorold's men at arms were waiting only for their lord to make his move. Being trained men at arms, each would have noted where his weapons were and marked his closest opponent. By contrast, Thomas was acutely aware that his own much less skilled comrades would act only on instinct or perhaps, self-preservation.

Opening the door to release the women must have taken only a few minutes but the wait seemed unbearable. The grating of the key in its lock sounded astonishingly loud and Thomas, breathing out long and slow, felt the beads of sweat dribbling down his chin. A sudden cry from Tancred tightened even further the tension in his limbs. Still watching Thorold like a hawk, Thomas shouted: "Are they there?"

"Oh, aye, they're here," groaned Tancred, stepping back into the hall carrying an unconscious Lady Isabel.

Just for an instant, Thomas flicked his shocked eyes across to the thin, dishevelled creature in Tancred's arms. It was only a moment, but it was long enough for Thorold to leap off the bed bellowing: "Dogs!"

Edwin's arrow thudded harmlessly into the wall above the bed and Thomas roared: "Get the girls outside!"

The hall, so still only seconds before, turned at once to bloody chaos as every man moved to grapple with an opponent. In such a confined space cluttered with benches and tables - never mind the warm coals of the hearth - a melée was utter madness. Frantic shouts filled the air, punctuated by several piercing screams. Snatching up a sword, Thorold made straight for Thomas, who met his first blow with the sword in his right hand and seax in his left.

Though he had heard tales in Brystole about the might of Thorold's sword arm, Thomas had never fought the Breton and the first arcing slash forced him back at once. Relentless in its intensity, Thorold's fury surged over Thomas until he was pinned against one of the long tables. Had Thorold not been momentarily distracted by one of his men at arms being hurled bodily across the very same table by Turstin, he might already have hacked Thomas apart. As it was, thanks to the outlaw's efforts, Thomas seized the chance to slide out from beneath his adversary's blade and, for good measure, rake his seax across Thorold's exposed belly. To his immense regret, the wound scarcely yielded more than a few drops of blood; but it further enraged his powerful opponent and soon Thomas was retreating again.

In the rare, frantic moments he could spare to scan the hall, he saw only grappling, snarling bodies and, in the midst of it all, he glimpsed Tancred doing his utmost to guide the gaggle of shrieking women to safety. Even so, among the fallen men at arms, there was more than one woman bleeding out onto the stone flags. This was not at all how he had planned it because, by now, Edwin should have put several shafts in Thorold's breast - so, what in God's name had happened to his cousin?

So much for his swift, well-planned attack. As far as he could judge, there were a dozen or so men still fighting – though perhaps only five were his. But Turstin and the abbey man, Berner, were proving to be an inspiration to the others; so, the struggle appeared evenly poised. Yet, if he succumbed to Thorold's thunderous blows, it would all be over very swiftly. Feinting left, Thomas stabbed his sword at his opponent's right thigh; but Thorold, quicker in both thought and movement, saw the blade coming and turned it deftly aside.

"Still a novice, Saxon," growled the Breton, before unleashing a succession of rapid sword thrusts with a final great lunge piercing the mail on Thomas's left side. The sword point punched an inch or two into flesh. Thorold, sensing victory, bludgeoned Thomas back towards the hall door where he skidded on a slick of blood. The slip allowed Thorold's sword to evade his flailing blades and scrape across his mailed chest. Though the iron mail held, Thomas was driven backwards again and it was then that he discovered his cousin lying motionless upon the floor beside a groaning Geoffrey.

Whatever Thomas attempted to counter his adversary's belligerent strength seemed to have little discernible effect. Eyes, stung by the sweat from his brow, searched in vain to pick out any of his comrades in the tangle of writhing bloodied bodies. And despair loomed for, having defeated Roland de Burgh, it seemed that Thomas was destined to fall to the dead man's closest friend.

28

17th June at Schaftesberia Castle

Ralph de Sarne was surprised how easily he had hoodwinked Thomas into thinking that he was badly hurt. How his spirits soared at that moment when he looked Thomas in the eye and lied. As soon as Thomas and the others were out of sight, he set off for Schaftesberia Castle. Of course, he did not want to prevent Thomas from crushing the monstrous Thorold Le Breton – indeed he prayed the Saxon would free his sister, Isabel, from her cruel marriage. But, if Thomas somehow succeeded and survived the encounter then, for Adeline's sake, he would have to be sacrificed.

Thomas was a traitor and an outlaw who would bring only ruin to those close to him and Ralph grieved that his sister could not yet see the truth of it. However, with luck, Sir Roger would waylay Thomas on his return along the Sturministra road and Adeline need never know the part her brother had played in the ambush. It was all for the best, he assured himself and he was certain that, as time passed, Adeline would come to understand.

Yet, even during the short ride to the castle, the first doubts began to creep into his head; and, only by focussing upon Adeline's redemption, could he justify his betrayal. At the castle gates, he pounded on the timbers, desperate to report where Thomas was before his nerve failed. When the gate was opened, Ralph rode straight in ignoring, on this occasion, the half-hearted protests of the gatekeepers. In his frantic haste, he vaulted from his horse only to land heavily upon his slightly injured leg. Hence, when Sir Roger emerged from the hall, flanked by two men at arms, Ralph was limping across the castle yard towards him.

"Well?" enquired Sir Roger gruffly. "I take it your careless haste means you've something for me."

Perhaps Ralph's face betrayed his growing reservations, for the knight suddenly gripped his arm and demanded: "Do you have something for me, or not?"

Aye, thought Ralph, betrayal of a friend is what I've brought you. When he did not immediately respond, Sir Roger snarled at him: "Out with it then, boy!"

"Ralph?" cried a voice from the tower above.

Adeline's cry sliced through Ralph's fragile resolve and, burning with shame, he pleaded with Sir Roger: "Not out here, I beg you.."

After a glance up to the rampart where Adeline stood, Sir Roger darted Ralph a sharp nod of agreement before hauling him away into the hall. The moment they were inside, he pressed the youth harder.

"You came to tell me something," he growled. "So, you'd better get it off your chest, lad."

Ralph gave a rueful shake of the head. "It's about Thomas FitzRobert…"

"I should damn well hope it is," retorted Sir Roger, "else why would I be wasting my time with a fool like you? Have you seen the renegade, or not?"

"Aye, he's on the road south to Sturministra," stammered Ralph.

"Truly? You're certain?"

"Aye."

"He's fleeing south then?"

"Not fleeing; he goes to free my sister, Lady Isabel from Sir Thorold…"

"Pah! Sir Thorold is her lawful husband."

"It seems that her husband has taken other girls to his manor…" murmured Ralph.

"Yes, the abbess did come moaning to me about that," acknowledged Sir Roger. "Very regrettable… but what has it to do with FitzRobert?"

"Well, Thorold is his enemy and Isabel… well she, of course, is Adeline's sister too…"

"So, he hopes to remove a foe and please his lover at one stroke," scoffed Sir Roger. "But how can he hope to do that on his own?"

"He's not alone; he's got six or seven others with him now – all outlaws."

"And you're certain they've taken the Sturministra road?"

"Aye."

"Well, if any survive an encounter with Sir Thorold, I'll be surprised," mused Sir Roger. "And yet, the Saxon did kill Roland and his escort on his own – no mean feat. Will they return on the same road, do you know?"

"I believe so," replied Ralph, "for they intend to take the abducted girls to the abbey."

"Excellent," said Sir Roger. "So, either Thorold kills him or he falls into my hands - perfect."

"Can I see my sister now?" asked Ralph.

"What, see your sister and blurt out to her all you've just told me? I think not, lad."

Turning to the two men at arms, he said: "Take his weapons and lock him up in the stockade with the other felons."

"But I've done all you asked of me," protested Ralph.

"What exactly have you done, Ralph?" From the stair, Adeline's ice-cold voice impaled him.

He had no need to reply for he could see by the disgust etched across her face that Adeline had heard enough. Next moment she flew down the steps and hurled herself at him, shrieking and scratching at his face with her nails. And the bewildered Ralph just stood there and let her do so; for, at last, he understood that, however good his intentions, it no longer mattered because his sister would revile him till the day she died.

After a few moments, Sir Roger, tiring of her assault, seized her by the shoulders, thrust her at the stair and ordered her back to her chamber. Rigid with frustrated fury, she complied but not before she fired a last withering look at her half-brother. When the guards dragged him stumbling from the hall, Ralph realised, from the satisfied grin upon Sir Roger's face, that the knight had utterly deceived him.

On his previous visit, Ralph had scarcely noticed the castle stockade, but he became uncomfortably aware of it when he was bundled inside by the guards. Tossed onto the muddied ground on his knees, only when he raised his head, did he realise that all eyes were fixed upon him.

"I've seen you here before," remarked one of the prisoners - older than the rest and built like a stack of barrel staves. "Who are you?"

"A fool, it seems, whose sister is held here by Sir Roger," muttered Ralph, unwilling to meet the eyes of his fellow inmate. "And I've betrayed her…"

"How betrayed her?"

The prisoner's aggressive tone only registered with Ralph when he realised that a ring of solemn faces had closed in around him. Suddenly every man seemed very interested in what he was saying. Their grim countenances suggested that he might already have said too much for his own safety; but he suspected they would not leave the matter there.

"I… I betrayed the youth she loves," Ralph blustered. "Though the wretch is certainly not worth such devotion…"

"Thomas FitzRobert?" enquired their spokesman softly.

Ralph trembled and said nothing more.

"Was it Thomas FitzRobert that you betrayed?" snarled the fellow, taking a step towards Ralph.

"Aye, it was," he confessed. "It was…"

"Well, that's a great pity," said his inquisitor, "because Fitz – and his young lady – are dear to us… very dear indeed."

Adeline's earlier attack paled beside the murderous flurry of blows that rained in upon him from the circle of inmates.

"Stop!" he yelled. "Help, help!"

But the blows kept coming and, though Ralph curled up his battered body to protect himself, every now and then a boot landed in his belly. He was certain he would die there, a bloodied mass of torn flesh and broken bone – and he might have done had the guards not hauled him out and thrown him down outside the stockade in disgust.

"Stay right there, you weak-willed tosspot," ordered the gatekeeper, "or we'll put you back in with those wolves."

Since dire threats had pursued him out of the stockade, Ralph had no inclination to return to that bearpit again. Hence, he remained exactly where they left him until the middle of the afternoon, when Sir Roger led a heavily armed, mounted party out of the gates and insisted that Ralph went with him.

As Ralph was bundled up onto his mount, he protested: "Why are you taking me?"

With a smile, Sir Roger replied: "I thought you'd like to be there when we capture the Saxon when – or if - he returns from Sturministra."

"And if he doesn't survive, what of me?" asked Ralph.

"I don't know," replied Sir Roger, "for what is to be done with a wretched coward like you?"

29

17th June in Sir Thorold's Manor at Sturministra

Thorold just kept on coming, battering Thomas with his heavy sword and, though armed with Roland's magnificent blade, Thomas struggled to match the raw strength of his opponent. Driven back to the great oak-framed doorway, Thomas stared back into the hall, where the savagery of the contest was manifested by the upturned table boards, blood-smeared tapestries, and torn banners.

Yet, despite all, Thomas took heart at the sight of young Galt, the tanner, hoisting up a brazier to crash it down onto an opponent's skull. Elsewhere his few men were hanging on; what they needed was a spark of inspiration from their new lord. But Thomas was overmatched and, moments later, Thorold drove him out of the house and into the small yard outside. At once there were screams from the girls left there by Tancred and, at the sight of the miserable huddle of young womanhood, Thorold roared at them: "Don't worry girls, you'll soon be back in my bed again."

As the terrified girls cowered behind the wretched Lady Isabel, the sight of her bruised and bloodied visage, devoid of all hope, burrowed deep into Thomas's soul. It wrought a sudden, dread change in him. A righteous zeal, born of despair, coursed through him and, fuelled by outrage, it induced a murderous fervour he had known only once before… in Osbert's tavern.

Thorold was unaware of the change until Thomas charged at him, bull-like, wielding both his blades with every fibre of his body. Such was the force when the two warriors collided that Thomas's seax was torn from his grasp. All the same, he screamed in triumph when his sword plunged into Thorold's midriff; for, without a mail shirt, Thorold was mortally vulnerable. But, though his opponent staggered backwards, bellowing with rage, Thomas had celebrated too soon; for both combatants soon realised that the wound under Thorold's ribs was not going to kill him.

Once more, the broad, infuriating grin flowed across Thorold's face. "It'll take more than that child's scratch, Saxon," he snarled.

But Thomas, thirsting for blood and far beyond reason, scarcely heard the taunt. When he flung himself at Thorold again, their swords met with such a steel-shuddering crash that Thomas's whole body trembled from the impact upon his right shoulder. But the collision rocked Thorold back too and, all the while, blood still trickled from the wound on his torso. Hence, it was very much in his interest to bring the fight to a swift end.

A clear-thinking Thomas would have realised that he need only fend off his adversary until blood loss fatally weakened him. But Thomas was beyond waiting, indeed beyond any control at all, so that when the two grim-faced men slammed into each other again, the impact caused the young girls to shriek anew. With swords pressed hard against each other, neither man could force the other back. Thorold reached for his dagger. Thomas's seax was only a yard away; but it might as well have been half a mile. With Thorold gripping him in a deadly embrace, Thomas glimpsed the flash of a blade in the early morning sunshine and lost hope.

Only when the Breton uttered a scream of agony, did Thomas recognise his own seax buried up to the hilt in his opponent's bloody groin. One of the serving girls had darted forward to retrieve it; and now she stood, eyes riveted upon her own crimson-stained hands. Her moment of courage was spent but Thorold was still on his feet and, despite his terrible wound, he clubbed the girl aside as if she were made of straw.

"You'll pay for that later, you little bitch," he croaked, but Thomas could see that his strength was ebbing away as fast as the blood dripping from the fresh wound. All that remained of Thorold Le Breton was the husk of a mighty warrior; so that when he raised his sword to strike, Thomas knocked it easily from his grasp.

Dropping to his knees, the knight mumbled: "I yield, I yield…"

But Thomas, his blood still boiling, swept his sword down to sever the Breton's head with a single blow. Then, snatching up the grisly trophy, he bore it into the manor house, roaring: "Your murdering lord is dead!"

Those of Thorold's men left standing exchanged a swift glance and then charged at Thomas together. The first was buffeted back by a blow from Thorold's chin, while the second's skull was split by Berner's sword. The last man might have gutted Thomas with a spear had a sword thrust from Enric not gutted him so that he went down thrashing like a dying boar.

Only when all his enemies lay still, did Thomas gasp and fall upon his knees, his rampant bloodlust finally sated. Pausing then to catch his breath, he nodded his thanks to his uncle and joined his surviving men as they staggered out of the manor house into the welcome sunshine. Going to each in turn Thomas clasped a hand or, in the case of Tancred, whose hand dripped blood, patted him gently on the shoulder.

The young girl who had attacked Thorold with the seax held out the blood-stained weapon to Thomas.

"I don't need this now, lord," she said simply. Then, realising that he was still holding Thorold's dripping head in one hand and his sword in the other, she leant forward to sheathe the seax for him.

"You were brave," he told her.

She pulled a face and retreated in haste at the approach of Enric, whose face was spattered with blood.

"You're hurt, nephew," he observed.

In response, Thomas held up the severed head and murmured. "Aye, but not as bad as he…"

"The fighting's done," reported Enric.

"So, how do we stand?" asked Thomas, though he hardly dared to ask.

"We lost Master Pain, the older one-"

"I know well enough who he was," grumbled Thomas, idly tossing his enemy's head into the yard. "Who else?"

"Turstin's bad," replied Enric. "Spear in the gut - so, he likely has only a few hours…"

"Let's pray he pulls through, for he fought well," said Thomas, though Enric's answering grunt suggested he would not; for both men knew that a deep belly wound was nearly always fatal.

"And the rest?"

"By God, or blind luck, Will, Geoffrey and Galt came through with only a few minor wounds. Edwin's got a cracked head, Berner's alright too but young Tancred – well, his hand's carved up bad."

Thomas gave a weary nod of acknowledgement, knowing it could have been very much worse.

"And Thorold's men?" he enquired. "How many wounded?"

"None," muttered Enric flatly.

"None?" gasped Thomas. "How's that possible?"

His uncle, clearly reluctant to go into detail, said only: "Several of our comrades, like you, decided that dead men can't rise to fight again…"

"Christ forgive me," muttered Thomas, knowing that he had not set the example a true lord should.

"I'll get everyone doing something," said Enric. "That always helps."

Doing something did sound like a good idea, but Thomas struggled to drag his eyes away from the butchered bodies. None of it seemed to trouble his uncle but then it occurred to him that Enric must have seen far worse slaughter in the Holy Land.

While Enric set off to find work for bloody hands, Thomas sought out Lady Isabel, who was still surrounded by most of the freed girls. One, he observed, still appeared to be wearing the remains of a nun's habit. She looked young so was very likely the missing novice; though what she was now was quite another matter. All of the girls cowered away from him, some wailing, some silent. Most seemed unhurt – at least compared to those who lay in the hall; but Thomas suspected that their worst wounds lay deep inside.

"Girls," he told them, "I am Thomas FitzRobert and you are now under my protection. The Abbess of Schaftesberia sent me to find you and bring you back home, so you need no longer fear for your lives."

"Our lives, lord," muttered one. "What lives? What are we fit for now?"

"Aye, what will we do?" cried another.

"For now, be thankful you're alive," he told them. "And I beg you, help the wounded."

The slight young novice, he noted, responded at once while others looked first to Lady Isabel and, only when she nodded her assent, did they stumble away to help.

Wearily, Thomas ushered them into a hall that more closely resembled a shambles. Sensing their reluctance, he assured them: "It's just blood, girls; and it'll wash away. There's no-one here now to hurt you."

Once again, it was the young nun, with resolute countenance, who stepped forward first and Thomas could not help but admire the girl's courage. His surviving men at arms were already beginning the grisly work of clearing the dead from the hall. Thomas could not help flinching when he saw among them two of the serving girls. Galt and a dazed-looking Edwin carried one of the corpses past him and in his uncle's arms lay the ruptured body of the other abducted nun.

"One arsewipe used her as a shield," Enric muttered bleakly.

Though Thomas had warned the abbess at the outset that the proud Thorold was unlikely to surrender his captives meekly, to see them now so bloodied and torn, was something he never expected to forget. Yet, the whole struggle, from the moment Thorold launched his first unrepentant blow, was only a blur now to Thomas… random half-formed scraps in his memory. Indeed, all he remembered clearly was standing over a dead, headless Thorold, with a handful of the knight's hair clenched in his fist.

The remainder of the morning was spent on the grim tasks of treating wounds and burying the dead; though, in all conscience, Thomas would rather have abandoned the bodies of Thorold and his brutal comrades to the crows and other scavengers. Yet, even at such dark moments, he knew that a lord must try to keep his faith and do what should be done. So, to the astonishment of the priest, they buried the villains' bodies in the church yard of St Mary's and left the fate of their souls to God.

By midday, Thomas accepted that they could not leave Sturministra for at least another day; for the survivors, both the girls and those who had fought so well, needed more time to recover. He resolved to remain at the manor house for the rest of the day and night and then set off early the next morning. It would be a slow journey back and, since he needed all the mounts to carry the wounded, some would have to walk back to Schaftesberia.

During the morning some of the late Sir Thorold's tenants, curious to know what had happened, had turned up sheepishly at the manor house. When they saw the row of bodies laid out in the courtyard, they simply stared dumbfounded. Thomas knew exactly what they were thinking: their new lord of the manor was dead so, what did that mean for them? During the afternoon word must have spread more widely for several more tenants arrived and, by evening, when the labourers returned from the fields, a small, murmuring crowd had gathered, though no-one dared to ask the heavily-armed victors what was to happen at Sturministra now.

Silencing the muttering assembly, Thomas announced: "The Abbess of Schaftesberia asked me, Thomas FitzRobert, to bring back half a dozen young girls stolen away from their homes by Thorold le Breton - and I have done so. Perhaps he also took some of your own; but all now are free, while Thorold and all his men at arms are dead."

When it appeared that Thomas had finished, a lone figure stepped hesitantly forward and removed his cap. "Are you now our lord then?" he enquired.

"That's for the king to decide," replied Thomas.

"But what will become of us?" asked the fellow.

Thomas, his head still crammed with stark images of blood and fury, retorted crossly:

"Do you need a cruel lord to tell you how to till, to sow or to harvest? Just go about your work as you always have and soon a new lord will come."

His response led to a great deal of discussion, though muted; and, soon after, the crowd dispersed to their homes, leaving only one soul: a young, slim, olive-skinned girl in a grease-stained tunic. It was the girl who had wielded his seax so effectively against Thorold.

"What about me, lord?" she asked. "I worked in the lord's kitchen each day. If there's no lord, I don't eat."

"What's your name?" he asked.

"Selima."

"You're a cook?"

"I learned cook," she explained, "And I learned well, I think."

"But this morning you took up arms against your lord," he remarked.

For a moment Selima appeared decidedly uncomfortable, but then she looked him in the eye and replied: "One blade cut same as another, lord – on any beast."

Thomas nodded and then a thought struck him. "If you're the cook, why were you locked up?"

Selima's eyes wandered and she made no reply.

"Well?" persisted Thomas.

"I… I spit in lord's food," she confessed.

Struggling to suppress a smile, he murmured: "Very… bold. Do you often spit in the food you cook?"

"Never before, lord," she replied, flushing with anger, "but, in the night, he… took me and I… I was angry."

"We've not eaten all day, Selima. I'd like you to stay and cook for us."

Eyeing him with hooded eyes, she enquired: "And on the morrow?"

"Let's see if you can cook first," replied Thomas. "And don't spit in our food…"

With a shrug that hinted at compliance, Selima set off towards the hall, so he took that as an acceptance. She seemed to acquit herself well in preparing the meal for, by the end of the evening, thanks to the riches discovered in Thorold's larder, all were well fed and, if Selima spat in their food, no-one noticed.

30

Dawn on 18th June at Sturministra

Thomas drew some solace from the bright, shimmering dawn; for somehow, troubles seemed less daunting when the sun was shining. It was a welcome respite for a youth who felt as if he had been hurtling headlong since the moment he fled from Brystole. If there was one lesson his recent experience had taught him it was that decisions made in haste could have calamitous consequences.

Though uplifted by the splendour of the sunrise, Thomas was obliged to address a concern his uncle had raised the previous evening. Enric feared that, if someone from the abbey let slip that Thomas FitzRobert had ridden for Sturministra, then Sir Roger might hear of it. Given his new notoriety, Thomas imagined that knowledge of his movements could well earn a man a little coin. Thus, Thomas had eschewed some much-needed sleep and instead asked among the outlaws whether any were local men. If the company needed somewhere close by to take refuge, Thomas would need the help of someone who knew the area well. It emerged that one of the newly-sworn outlaws, Will, was a Blaneford man – born a stone's throw from Sturministra.

So, even as Thomas basked in the early morning sun, he was reflecting upon what Will had told him. If he judged the mood of his small band correctly, no-one would care to remain another hour in a place where the stench of death still lingered. Whatever lay in store for them on their journey, they looked eager to be on their way. Thomas, who had despatched Edwin and Eadwulf to scout the road north, now anxiously awaited their return.

Already, the horses, which had been saddled for some time, were champing and snorting restlessly, while the first of the wounded were being lifted up onto their backs. Since there was still no sign of his kinsmen, Thomas instructed the helpers to take their time with their comrades and was pleased to note that every care was being shown. Even so, very soon, many would begin to wonder why the company had not yet left.

Since it was unlike his uncle to leave any important matter unresolved, it was no surprise when Enric sidled across to him to murmur: "Did you think on what I said? 'Cos it would only take one fartwit from the abbey – a stable lad, or anyone…"

"Aye, but would Sir Roger ride all the way down here on the word of a stable lad?" mused Thomas.

"He doesn't have to ride here, nephew," said Enric, "for there's only one road we can take back to Schaftesberia…"

"Perhaps not," murmured Thomas. "Because you'll be surprised to hear that I did act upon your advice last night."

Beckoning Will over to them, he said: "Tell Master Enric what you told me, Will."

"Which bit, lord?" enquired Will.

"The bit about the way north," grumbled Thomas, who couldn't think what else of note they had discussed.

"Oh, aye," agreed Will, "I can take us back another way - west from Blaneford along the Stur valley, then cut north-east to Schaftesberia."

"You sure about that?" challenged Enric. "This isn't the time to make idle boasts to impress the lasses."

"No, I'm sure," declared Will, "I swear it."

"Riders coming!" announced young Tancred abruptly.

Thomas's hand reached for his sword hilt until he saw, with relief, that it was his two Saxon kinsmen splashing across the grey river towards the manor hall. Cantering into the yard, Edwin and Eadwulf dismounted at once and relinquished their mounts to several of the girls.

"Well?" grunted Enric.

"No sign of riders on the road anywhere near here," reported Edwin.

"Excellent," said Thomas, knowing that the road due north would be much faster.

"But," added Edwin, "when we rode a few miles further, we passed two traders who told us that messengers had been sent out, seeking news of a company of vagabonds led by the outlaw, Thomas FitzRobert…"

"Damn me; he knows," cursed Enric.

It was a blow but at least Thomas knew that taking the quickest route north to Schaftesberia was now out of the question. Turning to Will, he said: "We're in your hands now, lad… lead on."

When the column finally set off, the horses carried not only the wounded and several of the weaker girls, but also a considerable load of confiscated goods and weapons. Thomas reckoned that, since their pace would, in any case, be painfully slow, the mounts ought to cope with the additional baggage.

Leading the group on foot with Will, Thomas forded the Stur, grateful that the spring rains had abated in recent days. Though they set off on the north road to Schaftesberia, he had no intention of remaining upon it beyond Blaneford. As the morning wore on, however, Thomas feared it might take all day just to cover the seven or so miles to where they would leave the road.

A pallid-faced Turstin, his wound bound tight, had insisted upon riding; yet, though he was uncomplaining, it was plain to all that the fellow was suffering greatly. And he was not the only one, for Thomas had only to look at the dull-eyed faces of some of the young girls to see wounds of a different sort. Some, he knew, fretted that they could never resume their old lives; but, whatever dolorous fears haunted them, all Thomas could do was try to keep them safe while they were in his care.

It was a mighty relief when, just before they reached the village of Blaneford, Will pulled up where a narrow track left the road to the west.

"We'll follow the river from 'ere," he announced.

"And you're certain you know the way?" Enric pressed him again.

"Oh, aye," replied Will. "Have no worries about that, Master Enric."

"Well, why don't you lead the way," said Enric, "and I'll do the worrying…"

"And you can lead us all the way to Schaftesberia?" added Thomas.

"Aye, lord," insisted Will, clearly irked by their doubts. "Why don't you trust me?"

"Just remind me why you were outlawed, Will."

Will's ebullience appeared to diminish as he mumbled: "It was all a mistake, lord…"

"Ah, and what was the charge against you?"

"Er, bearin' false witness, lord..."

"How God doth truly love a sinner," muttered Enric.

"Let's hope it's a mistake you've learned from," growled Thomas but, since he had little choice, he gave Will a nod and the outlaw led the straggling column off the road to the west.

"Follow Will's lead," Thomas ordered his bewildered companions, hoping he sounded more confident than he felt.

As they followed the track along the Stur valley, Thomas reckoned that, earlier in the year, the winding river must have overflowed its low banks. The path they were following now might then have been close to impassable but, after some early summer sun, the river margins were a little drier and it was easy going both for the horses and those trudging along on foot.

Only when they reached a great bend in the river, did Will come to a halt and prod his finger northward. Though Thomas expected that to reach Schaftesberia they would, at some point, need to abandon the valley floor, he eyed the terrain around them without enthusiasm for, in all directions, the ground appeared to slope steeply upwards.

Pointing to the nearest hill, Will announced cheerfully: "They say that long ago the ancients used to take refuge up there, lord."

"Aye, perhaps they did," replied Thomas, "but we're not going up there."

"No lord," Will promised, with a grin. "We'll be goin' round the hills, eh?"

Since Thomas had only a vague idea exactly where they were, he had no choice but to put his faith in Will in the hope that the youth truly knew where he was going.

"Carry on," he ordered. "But keep clear of villages - however small. The less we're seen, the better for all."

Despite Will's assurances, they were obliged almost immediately to follow an overgrown path which led slightly upward; but, after more than a mile of gentle climbing, they reached a broad plain. Though Thomas feared his company would probably be visible from miles around, he decided that there were only so many threats he could control. As the afternoon wore on, his hopes of shepherding his charges as far as Schaftesberia that day slowly evaporated. At the same time, he still had to work out how they could reach the abbey in safety, if all the chief roads into the town were being watched by Sir Roger's men. Gradually, mile by mile, a ludicrous idea took root in his troubled mind.

Lowering his voice, he confided to his guide: "We can't go straight to Schaftesberia, Will."

"Where then, lord?" asked the outlaw.

"You know Duncliffe Forest?"

"Aye," agreed Will. "As well as any man from round 'ere."

"Good. Then lead us there instead."

"Are you sure, lord," said Will doubtfully. "It's a very great forest and many a man's got lost in it."

"I know enough about the forest," replied Thomas. "You just get us to the edge of it and let me worry about what we do next."

"But we won't get there today, lord," declared Will.

"No, but we wouldn't get to Schaftesberia before nightfall either," said Thomas.

"Schaftesberia would be quicker though, lord," persisted Will.

"Aye, if you want an early death," growled Thomas. "Now, lead on; and start looking for somewhere to camp for the night."

Will gave a heavy sigh. "There won't be many places," he lamented. "But if we're goin' to stop, best we do it on higher ground 'fore we get to the marshlands. There's a place I know, just east of Archet, lord."

"Ideal," agreed Thomas, who had never heard of Archet.

"Hardly anyone lives in Archet," explained Will.

"Hardly anyone's still too many," grumbled Thomas, though it seemed they had no choice.

Archet turned out to be a settlement in two parts. Its west end comprised a row of ramshackle cottages which were clearly inhabited and therefore offered no secluded sanctuary for a company trying to attract the least possible attention. But Will, undeterred, led them across a small stream onto rising ground on the eastern side of the village which boasted more woodland than buildings. A huddle of small derelict dwellings shrouded by the trees were flanked by disused animal pens.

"Well found, Will," approved Thomas. "This will do us well enough for one night."

So, exhausted after the trials of the past few days, they made camp among the dilapidated stock pens adjacent to one of the ancient, half-ruined hovels.

"Get a fire going," Thomas ordered Eadwulf.

"A fire will tell folk we're here," Edwin warned.

With a shrug, Thomas replied: "The folk who live in Archet already know we're here; so, a fire isn't going to tell them much. Go and see if your bow can find us some game, eh?"

Thomas worried about the girls who, he imagined, would be struggling to banish the dread memories of Sturministra – indeed, perhaps some never would. When Lady Isabel sought him out, he was surprised for she had scarcely addressed a word to him since her release from Thorold's locked cell. Nonetheless, during the day's journey, he had noticed a subtle change in her; facing him now, she appeared more composed than the crumpled, whimpering wretch he had freed. From her cool manner, however, he could tell that she had not yet forgiven him for lying with her sister – and he feared that perhaps she never would.

"I should have thanked you," she murmured.

"You don't have to," he said, perhaps a little terser than he intended.

"I may not approve of you, Thomas - or what you've done to my sister – but I'm not a fool. I know well enough what fate awaited me had you not risked all to free us and… I shall ever be grateful for that…"

"I was glad I could help you," he replied but her hesitant manner suggested she sought something more from him. "Is there anything else I can do for you, my lady?"

For a few moments she offered him no more than a frown then muttered: "These other girls… I know just how they feel… soiled and beyond God's mercy. I am there with them, but I don't know how to help them."

"Just be their champion," he advised.

"Their champion?" she hissed. "How can I be when, before their very eyes, I was debased and violated in every way…"

"I'm sure you were, my lady, but so were they," he said softly. "You've all suffered the same undeserved torture but, if it's plain to me that you're no broken reed, I'm certain God sees it too. Those girls need to see it as well; so, show them your courage and your faith. Be their lady; for hope is all you can offer them now."

How empty his words felt for, if he was already weary of the burden of leadership, how could he wish it upon so young a lady? But, to his surprise, she clasped his hand before returning to her charges with head held a little higher and shoulders pressed back. He was pleased to see her passing among them, speaking to each in turn; it was a promising start, thought Thomas. He could not help chortling when, only a few moments later, he heard her berating Enric for not allotting the girls their own space to sleep - separate from the men. Thomas smiled in admiration, acknowledging that perhaps there was much more to young Lady Isabel than he at first thought.

Edwin's hunting skills proved their worth and Selima, aided by several others, prepared a meal which, though it did not fill any bellies, certainly warmed a few hearts. Later in the evening when the camp was quiet, Selima came unbidden to sit beside him - so close that he was aware of the scent of her.

"Thank you, lord," she murmured, "for taking me with you."

"I needed a cook," he said simply.

"What will happen to me when we get to Schaftesberia?" she asked.

"Were you Thorold's slave?"

"All were slaves in that devil's place," she retorted.

"Well, he's dead now," said Thomas, "so I suppose I must decide what to do with you. Were you a servant to the last lord of Sturministra?"

"I'm not sure."

"But you must know," he argued. "Everyone knows their place – even if they don't much like it."

"My place was not so… clear."

All Thomas wanted to do was plan for the morrow and then catch up on a little sleep. What he did not want to do was listen to a stray girl's troubles all night. Yet, since her fate now lay entirely in his hands, he was obliged to listen and then decide.

"How came you to Sturministra?" he enquired, hoping for a brief account.

"The mother of my mother… was a servant brought here from Antioch," Selima told him.

"Then you're a servant," said Thomas simply.

"My mother was a servant," explained Selima, "but she did not die a servant."

"Well, what was she when she died?" asked Thomas, wishing he had never started the conversation.

"She died giving life to me," said Selima softly.

"Ah."

"My father was the lord of Sturministra; and I… I'm his dark-skinned bastard…"

That, thought Thomas, was something at least of which he had some understanding. "A bastard is what you were born, not what you are," he observed, wondering briefly if he was talking about himself or Selima.

"My father had no other children and his wife died long ago," continued Selima. "He gave me much, but he never made me his heir."

"Then it seems no man has claim over you; so, what do you want to do?"

"I could be your cook at Schaftesberia," she suggested.

"My cook?" he said, non-committal, because he could see little use for a cook on their journey to Normandy. "You'd be more welcome if you were a warrior."

"Or I could just serve you…"

"As a cook."

"In any way you please." she murmured, resting a hand upon his shoulder.

Shrugging off her hand, he growled: "Just because you were a whore to Thorold, doesn't mean you have to stay a whore."

Stung by his sharp reproach, she pulled away, gasping: "Forgive me, lord; I beg you. Forgive me. Some men…"

"I'm not some men," he snapped. "Perhaps you should go to the nunnery at Schaftesberia."

"But I'm not a Christian, lord."

"Ah, I thought perhaps your father…"

"He tried, but my faith was all my mother left me."

"I see," said Thomas, though he did not see at all why anyone wouldn't want to worship Christ. But then, nothing about this sultry young girl fitted into the narrow confines of his world.

"If you take me in your service," she pleaded. "I'll be loyal and I'll work hard."

"My service?" he laughed. "You'd be serving an outlaw and a traitor on the run. God's breath, lass, I don't know where I'll be from one day to the next."

"Then I shall go where you go, lord."

Puffing out his cheeks, he shook his head.

"You know I can fight too, lord," Selima beseeched him. "I will fight your enemies and be a friend to those you love."

Studying her earnest countenance for a few moments, he conceded finally: "Perhaps, in time, I might have use for such a servant. Do you swear by… all that you hold dear… that you will answer only to me?"

"I swear, lord," she replied fiercely, clasping his hand to emphasise her allegiance. "And if I fail you, it will be because I'm dead."

"Then I shall have your service," he agreed, "and you will have my protection."

"What do you want of me, lord?" she murmured. "Shall I stay here with you?"

With a brusque shake of the head, he told her: "No, go and get some sleep."

Yet, as she walked away, his eyes followed her movement, lithe and sinuous, against the flickering firelight.

31

19th June near Archet, south of Schaftesberia

Since leaving Archet just after dawn, they had been crossing an expanse of marshland, which their guide, Will professed to know better than anyone. But, as the ground became ever boggier, Thomas winced every time a horse stumbled - certain that it was only a matter of time before one plunged into the mire and broke a leg. Hence, he was greatly relieved when he saw the land ahead gradually rising towards the distant, but familiar, forested hill top of Duncliffe.

As they rode ever nearer to the forest, Thomas sought Enric's counsel in resolving the thorny task of conveying their charges safely to the abbey. Yet, by the time they reached the margins of the woodland, they had barely put together anything resembling a plan. To fulfil his obligation to the abbess Thomas had to return the abducted girls but, with Sir Roger actively searching for him, it seemed an impossible task.

"Let's look at this another way," suggested his uncle. "It's you, Sir Roger wants, not these lasses; but it doesn't have to be you that takes them to the abbey, does it?"

"But who else?" argued Thomas. "The abbess only knows you and… perhaps Edwin."

"Has to be me then," concluded Enric. "'Cos you daren't lose both your archers."

"But I should be doing it," protested Thomas.

"Listen, Thomas, if you're with them it only makes it riskier for those girls," said Enric. "You've done your part, lad – and well done it was too. So, don't ruin it by getting us all killed at the last."

Thomas finally acquiesced so that, when he pulled up at the forest's edge, he split his company into two. He was not surprised to see consternation on the faces of many;

nor did their fears diminish when he announced that Enric would escort the women and wounded to the abbey, while Thomas would go on to Wilflaed's cottage. There were cries of alarm from some of the girls for it was Thomas, not Enric, who had given his solemn oath to protect them.

Since Enric would have to time his arrival at the abbey around the hour of Vespers, there was no time for delay. But, it was clear that some of the girls were worried about going with his uncle. Indeed, some might well have refused to do so, had Lady Isabel not intervened and taken the lead.

"Come," she ordered, riding across to join Enric. "We are close to the end of our journey; let us not lose heart now."

When Edith joined her with Tancred, the rest followed, albeit with some lingering reluctance. Only Selima flatly refused to leave Thomas; but, as he knew very well, Selima, unlike all the other girls, did not see the abbey as a place of refuge. She would be worried what might happen to a heathen girl in such an austere Christian institution, yet Thomas did not want her with him that night.

"I am bound to *you*," she protested.

"Aye, you are," growled Thomas, "so you will do as I bid you… or be forsworn."

Selima did not take his stern rebuff well and, when his uncle departed, Thomas found her resentful eyes still glaring back at him. It was a long, challenging look until he broke the connection and turned away to lead the remaining outlaws into Duncliffe forest. At first, coming in from the south, he struggled to find his way to Wilflaed's cottage and only found it after following half a dozen false trails.

Arriving at the cottage, there was clear evidence that Sir Roger's men had been there: not least, a table overturned and many of Wilflaed's potions and herbs scattered across the floor. A thorough search of the surrounding woodland, however, turned up no watchers lurking in the shadows and Thomas was granted what he desperately needed: an hour or so of calm reflection.

During the long journey from Sturministra, Thomas had done little else but ponder upon what he should do when he returned to Schaftesberia. The fact was that, though he had led his uncle to believe that he would flee to Normandy, he just couldn't do it; he couldn't leave Adeline. His vows to her were not to be taken so lightly and, having risked all to save Isabel, how could he do less for her sister - his own wife? Of course, he had not discussed his fledgling plan with Enric, knowing that his uncle would certainly have tried to dissuade him from even attempting it.

But, in the late afternoon, Thomas felt confident enough to gather his outlaws about him to explain what they were going to do.

∞ ∞ ∞ ∞

His small column joined the familiar road from Scireburne to Schaftesberia moving only at a slow walking pace since half their number had no mounts. As soon as they drew close to the town, they left the road and crossed an open stretch of ground to come at the fort from its northern slope – using the same narrow track that Thomas had descended with Roland only a few days earlier. He aimed to arrive at the castle just as darkness was descending when the castle guards might least expect an incursion.

In a lightly-wooded glen at the foot of the path, they hobbled their horses and prepared for what was to come. The northern slope was far steeper than its southern counterpart, but it offered much more tree cover – helpful as long as a little daylight lingered. Thus, in the twilight they had to complete the treacherous ascent up to the castle ditch; because, once it was fully dark, such a climb would be near impossible.

At a signal from Thomas the outlaws moved forward and, leaving the base of the slope, began to mount the hill. Almost at once, Thomas realised that it was going to be slower than he anticipated since the hillside was still a little slippery. Despite the conditions underfoot, he was reassured to find that the men were following him up doggedly, though there were occasional slips and muttered curses. They were only halfway up when Thomas, like most of his comrades, was breathing hard. Only the prospect of seeing Adeline again drove him on, one aching step after another. It was a great relief when he glimpsed the small tower on the north rampart looming above him and he could finally come to a halt.

Breaking through the wooden palisade would, he expected, be straightforward enough since he and Edgar had deliberately left several adjacent poles only loosely embedded in the damp soil. But, though entry to the castle might not be too difficult, what happened once they were inside was far less certain. He did not ask himself whether his barely trained outlaws were ready for such a challenge, for he knew they were not.

While they had scrapped with courage and spirit at Sturministra, they were not even close to being ready for an assault that required stealth and ice-cold determination. In some though, he had noticed a difference in their bearing and confidence; he could only pray that they would be able to steady their comrades. His instructions had been most explicit so, as long as they carried them out, there was a good chance of success. Of course, if they ignored his orders, they would all be in deep shit.

"Why aren't we attacking at dawn?" whispered Galt abruptly. "It worked at Sturministra."

"It did," agreed Thomas, "but this time we have to get in and out quick. That should give us the rest of the night to put some distance between us and our pursuers."

Galt nodded, though he looked far from convinced.

More worried than ever, Thomas gathered them around him one more time to go through yet again what needed to be done. "Once we're in," he reminded them, "Will stays by the gap in the palisade, lest a passing guard chooses that very moment to walk the fence. Eadwulf, Galt and Geoffrey will go to the stockade, free the prisoners and take them out of the fort. While you're all doing that, I'll be going into the tower with Edwin to find Lady Adeline. And remember, all must be done in silence."

Once the castle garrison was alerted, their cause would be lost. The outlaws might be better-equipped to fight than they had once been but, against experienced men at arms wearing mail, a full-scale melée could only have one outcome: a stack of corpses and a few more outlaws lodged in Sir Roger's stockade. Added to which, the released prisoners would have no weapons at all.

Only when no glimmer of the setting sun remained did Thomas whisper to his men to make ready. This time, he would not be taken; this time, he would free her and, either she would leave with him, or she'd be widowed and free to marry someone else.

32

Early evening on 19th June, south of Schaftesberia

"We're getting close to St James, Master Enric," announced Tancred.

With a nod, Enric came to halt and told the others: "Close up and stay together. If any man tries to stop us, we'll answer that we're under the protection of the abbess - which is true, Master Berner, is it not?"

"Aye, it most certainly is," agreed Berner.

"Best you walk with me up front," Enric told him. "Your comrade Tancred can watch our backs."

Though Enric was relieved to have brought his charges so close to their destination without any hindrance, he was well aware that far greater risk would arise as they drew near to the abbey where Sir Roger had very likely posted men on watch. Just as he was about to lead the column onward through St. James, Lady Isabel rode up alongside him.

"What is it now, my lady?" enquired Enric, thoroughly weary of women's company.

"I have something to tell you, Master Enric." she said, bending down to speak to him.

"This, lady," he hissed, "is hardly the place to stand jabbering."

Though Lady Isabel raised her eyebrows at his complaint, she persevered nonetheless.

"Your nephew instructed me to give you a message when you reached St. James."

"What do you mean instructed?" groaned Enric. "Why didn't he tell me before we left?"

"Do you want to hear his message, or not?" enquired Lady Isabel.

"Aye, you'd best spit it out, my lady."

"Lord Thomas intends to free my sister…"

"What?" snarled Enric. "The fool – but when?"

With a glance at the darkening sky, Isabel replied: "About now, I should think."

"Damned arsewit," cried Enric, whose sudden outburst caused immediate alarm among the women.

"Master Enric," chided Lady Isabel, "I am also instructed to remind you that you still have a task to finish…"

"Aye, Thomas knew it," he growled, furious that his nephew was going to the castle without him. Since he recalled only too well what happened the last time Thomas tried to sneak into the castle, he feared a second attempt would end very badly.

"You appear to lack confidence in your nephew," observed Lady Isabel. "Don't you believe he can rescue my sister?"

"I believe he'll do all he can, my lady and… well, perhaps, if any half-witted youth could free her, I suppose it would be him."

A wry smile crossed her lips before she said: "I had no faith in him once, Master Enric; but now I do. So, shall we continue?"

Making no attempt to hide his chagrin at being reminded of his duty by such a slip of a girl, Enric led the party on once more. Tancred dropped to the back of the column but, Enric noticed, he was soon joined by a certain young novice nun. Good for them, he thought, with a sly grin. But soon the old Saxon thrust such trivial matters from his head; for he would need his wits at their sharpest when they travelled the last mile to the abbey.

If the abbess kept to her promise, then, at Vespers, someone should be at the small abbey gate to receive the abducted girls. All Enric had to do was get them there but the sound of the abbey bell tolling told him that time was running out for it must be Vespers already. The moment they reached the small crossroads beyond the church of St.

James, his hopes of an unhindered journey were dashed. Several men were lounging there but, the moment Enric's column drew close, their hands reached for their weapons. One of their number scrambled onto his mount and rode off to the south at a canter, while the others spread out to block the lane.

"Halt!" ordered the leading man at arms.

Enric, not willing to be overawed by a mere soldier, continued striding towards the fellow and only stopped when he was scarcely an arm's reach away.

"Who dares interfere in the business of the Abbess of Schaftesberia?" he demanded, with what he prayed was the right amount of outrage.

Clearly the guard was not expecting such a challenge for he hesitated before enquiring: "Who are you then?"

"I and my comrades," replied Enric, indicating Berner and Tancred, "have been charged by the abbess to return these young ladies to her care. So, step aside, fellow, if you please."

"I don't know anything about that," mumbled the soldier.

"Of course, you don't, you dull-witted blood-spittle," retorted Enric. "The Reverend Mother doesn't share matters of importance with every pox-ridden knave in the town. Now move aside, for we've wounded among us."

The man at arms glanced at each of his comrades in turn but found little support in their blank stares. Even so, he still appeared reluctant to move.

"My lord, Sir Roger of Schaftesberia, has charged me to stop you for there are outlaws among you."

"Do I look like an outlaw?" interrupted Lady Isabel fiercely, thrusting her mount forward to force the man at arms to retreat a pace. "I am Lady Isabel de Sarne, wife of Sir Thorold Le Breton and neither I, nor the abbess, answer to your lord. So, move aside fellow, now."

Enric, who had to admit that he was impressed by the young girl's confident demeanour, could not suppress a smile at the thought that Thorold was far more helpful to his wife dead than he had ever been alive. In the face of Lady Isabel's challenge, the man at arms backed down and waved his companions aside to clear a path along the lane. Enric's relief as the company crept ever closer to the sanctuary of the abbey, was tempered by the thunder of horses' hooves approaching from the south. At once, he dropped back and reached for his bow.

"Take the lead," he told Berner. "And don't stop for anyone until you're inside that abbey gate."

Joining Tancred, Edith and Selima at the rear, he ordered: "Tancred, stay with me. Edith, you go on ahead with Selima."

The novice, whose bright blue eyes rarely left Tancred's face, would certainly have stopped there, had Tancred not insisted that she went on. So, while their companions continued on their way up the sloping Laundry Lane towards the abbey, Enric and Tancred stood blocking the narrow lane against the oncoming horsemen.

As Enric expected, Sir Roger led the riders but, to his astonishment, he saw Ralph de Sarne among them.

"Stop!" shouted Sir Roger. "Stop where you are!"

"We're already stopped," retorted Enric. "Not that it's any business of yours."

"I mean the others, God damn you!" railed Sir Roger pointing to the girls a dozen yards further on.

"The Abbess of Schaftesberia doesn't need your permission to act," Enric told the angry knight.

"And I don't need to explain myself to an outlaw," stormed Sir Roger.

"My nephew might be an outlaw," replied Enric, with a smile, "but I'm not; and, just now, I serve the abbess, as does my comrade here. We are escorting the recently-widowed Lady Isabel de Sarne and some other young girls to the abbey – and you have no power to stop us."

Enric was feeling confident until a stern-faced Lady Isabel trotted back down the lane to join them.

"God's nails! Why have you come back, lady?" grumbled Enric.

"Because of him," replied Isabel, jabbing an accusing finger at her half-brother.

"Isabel?" cried Ralph. "Can it be you, safe and well?"

Glaring at him, she cried: "How is it you ride with Sir Roger now, Ralph?"

It was Sir Roger who replied: "Because your brother has shunned the company of outlaws, my lady and now he's helping me to apprehend the killer, Thomas FitzRobert."

"Is that true, Ralph?" demanded Isabel.

Ralph, transfixed by his predicament, struggled to utter a word.

"Tell her then, boy," goaded Sir Roger.

"I – I thought you at least would be pleased," muttered Ralph.

"Aye, I suppose that once, I would have," said Isabel, "but I've had reason to change my opinion of Thomas FitzRobert…"

"Your husband, Sir Thorold, would be angered to hear you speak so, my lady," warned Sir Roger.

"Aye, well, what Thorold thinks about me no longer matters," replied Isabel stonily. "My late husband lies with the worms; and, for that, I have Thomas FitzRobert to thank."

"We heard rumours," murmured Sir Roger. "But… is Sir Thorold truly dead then, lady?"

"Aye, he is," confirmed Enric, "and he's shorter by a head too."

"Another brutal murder then by Thomas FitzRobert," declared Sir Roger. "And I charge all of you as his accomplices."

Enric, fearing Sir Roger would move swiftly, nocked an arrow to his bow and levelled it at the knight's chest.

"Allow us to pass on unhindered to the abbey, Sir Roger, or we shall be forced to defend these women."

For the first time Sir Roger, seeing the arrow pointed at him, hesitated and, while he delayed, Isabel followed the women up the lane leaving only Enric and Tancred once more facing close to a dozen mounted men. Enric cursed under his breath for a steely glint in Sir Roger's eyes suggested that he was about to order the assault.

"Follow Lady Isabel," Enric murmured to Tancred, fearing the youth would get himself killed if he stayed.

But Tancred gave a determined shake of the head; so, together, the two men began to back away slowly up the hill, while Sir Roger's far more numerous assembly awaited his command. The knight feigned to turn his mount away but then darted into the midst of his men, shouting: "Take them! Take them!"

Enric broke into a run, hauling young Tancred with him up the lane.

"We'll never make it," gasped Tancred.

"By God, if we don't," snarled Enric, "I swear I'll be taking that sowswiving knight with me."

When he stopped for an instant to raise his bow, he saw, with regret, that it was Ralph de Sarne leading the chase. He'd intended to loose an arrow at the pack of them; but he was reluctant to kill the youth – however, misguided he might be. Ah, well, he thought, what must be, will be.

But, just as Enric was about to let fly, Ralph cajoled his mount to veer across the front of the chasing pack, bringing them to a chaotic halt. In the confusion, Ralph himself was unhorsed and another animal fell, screaming with pain. The diversion, as the youth no doubt intended, allowed Enric and Tancred ample time to escape to the abbey gate.

Yet, Enric did not run.

"God's nails!" he cursed, for he could hardly leave the ladies' half-brother lying in the middle of the lane at the mercy of Sir Roger's baying men at arms. While Enric stood still, however, Tancred sprinted back past him down the lane to help Ralph up.

"Foolish young pissweeds," growled Enric, raising his bow to cover the pair as they retreated towards him. When one rider finally broke free from the tangle to pursue them, Enric took aim and let fly. At such close range, the arrow sped to its target and punched deep through the fellow's mail coat. After the first horseman fell, Enric did not linger but hurried after Ralph and Tancred.

Catching up with the pair at the small abbey gate, all three hurtled through it before it was slammed shut behind them. Dusk was already giving way to night for the torches by the gate burned brightly enough for Enric to make out a frowning abbess standing beside Lady Isabel.

"Master Enric," she enquired frostily, "have you just killed a man in my name?"

33

19th June after dusk at Schaftesberia Castle

Leading the outlaws in a slithering crawl across the freshly-dug ditch, Thomas then began to examine the adjacent palisade to locate the timbers which were not properly seated. While he plied the soft, wet earth with his fingers, Edwin strung his bow and nocked an arrow to it.

"I pray you won't need that," murmured Thomas.

"Aye," agreed Edwin, "better to be ready though, eh?"

Soon the men were straining to lever out several of the loose wooden stakes that Thomas had located. But his cousin Edwin fixed his attention only upon the guard tower above them. Though Thomas had only ever seen one man posted there before, Edwin's task was to ensure that no watchful sentry raised the alarm. By the time three of the thick timber poles had been prised out of the ground, the men were left plastered in mud. A grinning Master Galt slid down the slope a yard or two until he collided with one of the discarded stakes.

When he couldn't stifle a yelp of pain, at once, a guard atop the nearby tower loomed forward to peer down at the gloomy slope.

"Who's there?" he called.

The outlaws, keeping still and silent, prayed that the sentry would lose interest – and, soon enough, he did. Unwilling to risk any further delay, Thomas led the small group swiftly through the gap and into the fort. At the stockade, he left the others and crept across the yard, seax in hand, with Edwin close behind. It was so dark that he was obliged to feel his way to the great central tower; but there he stopped at the steps leading up to the hall, because he was puzzled.

He had expected to find at least one man at arms at the foot of the steps yet, to his surprise, there was no-one there at all.

"Where is everyone?" he hissed at Edwin, who could offer only a shrug in response.

Once more Thomas scanned the courtyard but the only guard he could make out was one at the gate. Warily, the two men mounted the steps and, finding the door also unguarded, shuffled across the threshold. Keeping the door ajar, Thomas peered yet again across the yard to the gate against which a solitary sentry leaned.

"It's too damned quiet," he whispered.

As they entered the hall, he realised that there were several figures lying asleep on the hall floor, illuminated only by rush lights. One or two sat up in alarm when they saw the two men creep in with their weapons unsheathed. From the tone of their frightened whispers, he was certain that all were women.

"None shall be hurt," he told them, "as long as you remain here, still and quiet." Turning to Edwin, he said: "You'd better stay here and watch them."

Thus, while Edwin remained below, Thomas began to ascend the stairs with the utmost care, recalling the grim outcome of his previous clandestine visit. It was near impossible to mount the wooden steps without making some noise; and, the more he lingered, the more chance there was of discovery. As he crossed the landing outside Sir Roger's chamber, the floor seemed to creak louder with every step he took, but all he could do was pray that the knight had retired to his bed. At the end of the landing, he realised he was holding his breath and released it, slow and silent.

Climbing the rough-hewn steps to the next landing where Adeline's chamber lay, he reached her door and then listened for any sound within.

"Adeline," he hissed but there was no reaction.

Should he just open the door and slip in, he wondered; or knock gently so as to avoid alarming her? The decision was snatched from him when the door suddenly swung open to reveal Adeline, barely-dressed and with hair hanging loose. For a long and agonising moment, he simply stared at her, hardly daring to breathe lest perhaps he should wake from a dream.

Then they flew into each other's arms and he lifted her up, crushing her to his breast until she whimpered in protest for, while he was clad in mail and helm, she wore only her thin linen undertunic.

"I knew you'd come," she murmured into his neck.

"I am your husband after all," he whispered.

"Aye, and a great fool," she breathed. "You can put me down now."

"Why did you pull open the door?" he asked. "I could have been anyone."

But she answered his concern with a broad smile. "My hearing's sharp," she said. "I'd just undressed when I heard the boards creak outside my door. At first, I thought it might be Folcard but I know your voice. I'd know it in the raging fires of hell…"

"Aye, well, if we don't make haste, you might need just such a skill," he said grimly. "So, dress quickly."

With a dark grin, she replied: "That's not your usual greeting…"

"You're a wicked wife," he said, stroking her wayward hair. "But I'll not be trapped here again."

As she began to dress, he tried to help her until finally she pushed him away. "It'll be quicker with only one pair of hands wandering over me," she scolded. "Now, hand me my boots."

Once she was ready, he opened the door and glanced out onto the small landing.

"Keep behind me," he ordered, taking out his seax. "Sir Roger may wake at any moment and summon the whole garrison against us."

"I doubt it," she replied. "He's not here."

Stopping mid-stride, he said: "He's not here?"

"No, he left yesterday to trap you on the road from Sturministra," she said. "He'll be so… disappointed to have missed you."

"But that's excellent," he told her. "Escape will be much easier without him here. But wait… how did he know to look for me in Sturministra?"

Adeline looked away, unwilling to meet his eyes.

Brushing a tear from her cheek, he whispered: "What is it? What's wrong?"

With a shake of the head, she groaned: "It was Ralph who betrayed you…"

"Ralph? But why?"

"Because he wasn't thinking straight," she hissed.

"Well, never mind that now," he said softly, clasping her hand to lead her down the steps. "At least it'll help us get out of here."

They were half way down to the hall when Thomas suddenly came to a dead stop once more.

"What is it?" gasped Adeline, darting him a worried look.

"How many of the garrison did Sir Roger take with him?" he enquired.

"I don't know for certain; but a lot, I think - perhaps a dozen?"

"All mounted?"

"Aye," she muttered.

"Who commands here then?"

"Master Folcard."

For a few more moments, Thomas did not move.

"That's better for us, isn't it?" she whispered anxiously.

"Not just better, my dear; it's perfect," he told her, turning to go back up the stairs. "Come on."

"But where are we going?" she said.

"Do you trust me?" he asked her.

"If I didn't, I'd be a novice nun by now," she retorted, "or married to a knight..."

Chuckling, he sent her back up to her chamber, while he remained on the floor below and crept to Folcard's chamber door. Perhaps Folcard was disturbed by the footsteps on the stair, for he was already on his feet when Thomas entered. For a split second, the fellow must have considered resistance, but he was unarmed and the point of a seax was at his throat before he could lay his hand upon any weapon.

Pressing his blade to the man's throat, Thomas warned: "Be very careful, Master Folcard, lest my blade should slip. I really don't care for you much so, God knows, I'm labouring to think of a reason to keep you alive."

Forcing Folcard's arm up behind his back, he pushed him out of the door with the seax still hard against the flesh of his neck.

"Down the steps," he ordered. "And this blade is well-honed, my friend so, do or say anything I dislike and it'll slice through you before you can catch another breath."

Locked together, the two men descended awkwardly down to the hall where Thomas guided Folcard past Edwin towards the hall door before cracking his head against the timber of the door post. The man at arms groaned, crumpled onto the stone flags and lay still but his demise brought a gasp from those still on the hall floor.

"A few men are here too, lord," reported Edwin, "but only the servants."

"Aye, it appears that Sir Roger and most of his garrison are out for the night."

"Out?" grinned Edwin.

"Aye, but they may return at any moment so, before they do, we're going to take the castle."

"I thought we were going to Normandy," said Edwin.

"Only because we had nowhere else to go," said Thomas. "Now we do."

"But, cousin, Enric said-"

"Never mind what your father said; get up to the tower rampart and watch my back. I'm going to tell the others but, when you hear my signal, take out the guards on the two towers for I think they might have crossbows."

"What about those at the gates?"

"There's only one, so you can leave him to me."

As Thomas turned to go, Edwin hissed: "But, lord, I've only three arrows."

"Better not miss then," advised Thomas, hurrying down the steps.

Waiting until the guard at the gate was looking elsewhere, Thomas sped back across the yard to his comrades at the palisade.

Just outside the gap in the fence, they were all waiting.

"By God, lord, you had us all worried," gasped Eadwulf. "But where's the lady – and my uncle?"

Before Thomas could reply, a familiar gravel voice muttered: "So, you came back for us after all, Fitz."

"Aye, Edgar," said Thomas, clasping his hand, "as I swore I would."

"Are we ready to leave?" enquired the smiling Edgar.

"No, we're not going anywhere," explained Thomas. "We're taking this castle."

"Shit of a dog! I marked you out for a mad bastard the moment I set eyes on you," grumbled Edgar.

"You're free; so, you're welcome to take your chances outside," said Thomas.

"Can we truly take this place, do you think?" asked Edgar.

"With Sir Roger and most of the garrison absent... yes, we can; but only if we act fast."

Edgar wasted no time in idle argument. "What can we do to help?"

"Split up your fellows – Jonas and Will can help Galt here put the stakes back in to secure the palisade. Take the rest to the nearer of the guard towers and await my signal."

"What's the signal?" enquired Edgar.

"You'll know it well enough. Now, go. Eadwulf, take the far tower with Will."

"What about the gate?" said Eadwulf.

"Geoffrey and I will go there."

"But isn't there a guard house beside the gate," said Eadwulf.

"Act fast, I said," snapped Thomas, "and yet, you're all still here."

Eadwulf took the hint and hurried off with Will.

It was fully dark when Thomas and Geoffrey, making no attempt to keep out of sight, strode purposefully through the courtyard towards the gateway. Thomas suspected that, in addition to the lone gatekeeper, there would be several men taking their ease in the guard house but he hoped not to draw them out until it was too late. Success would hinge upon the defenders believing that they had already lost control of the castle.

"Halt!" cried the gatekeeper, raising his spear.

Though his shout might well have alerted every one of the few fighting men left in the castle, sadly, it would not save him. The gatekeeper had to die – and very noisily – if it was to have the desired effect. Thomas feared he might have to kill two or three more men, but he prayed that a demonstration would be enough to discourage the others.

"To arms!" cried a voice from one of the towers.

In response, Thomas drew out both sword and seax, roared out a single word: "Edwin!" and carried on walking towards the gate.

The keeper's desperate spear thrust was too slow and Thomas swept aside the point with his sword before burying his seax into the unfortunate fellow's throat. A yelp from one of the towers told him that Edwin too had struck. However, when a crossbolt blow thudded into the gate beside his head, Thomas frowned. He prayed that Edwin would not delay his second arrow for too long, but he heard no cry from the other tower.

Then to his relief, Edwin called down: "Done, lord."

That instant two men at arms emerged from the guard house and, though neither wore any mail, both carried swords and shields.

"Keep the gate shut, Geoffrey," ordered Thomas, as the pair approached.

Raising his voice loud enough for everyone in the small castle to hear, he bellowed: "I am Thomas FitzRobert and this castle is now mine. If any man wishes to contest that, he can do so; but three of your comrades already lie dead. Yield and live; or fight and die, as you will. I offer you this one chance; refuse it and no quarter will be given."

Hardly had he finished his ultimatum before the two men at arms exchanged a resolute look and charged at him.

"So be it," he muttered, with a heavy sigh.

Though they sought to attack him together and trap him between them, Thomas saw that, as ever, one would strike fractionally before the other. Sweeping down his heavy sword – so recently the property of Roland de Burgh – he splintered the shield of his first adversary. Moreover, the blade cracked through the shield to hack into bare flesh. With a scream the man fell and his comrade, though his sword was raised, came to a sudden halt.

"I warned you," Thomas snarled, glaring at the fellow and fighting the urge to slice down his seax from throat to crotch.

At once his opponent, dropping both sword and shield, fell to his knees beside the spreading pool of his comrade's blood. Another man at arms peered out of the guard house door before trudging out unarmed.

"Take a look in there, Geoffrey," commanded Thomas.

When Geoffrey reported the guard house to be empty, Thomas shouted: "Clear the towers!"

After a few minutes, several more members of the garrison were shepherded down into the yard by Edgar, Eadwulf and the others so that, in only a few moments, the capture of Schaftesberia Castle was over. The remaining men at arms surrendered their weapons – though some exhibited a bullish show of reluctance - and followed their comrades out of the gate towards the town gate opposite, bearing their dead and wounded with them.

"Edgar, take some friends and bring out Master Folcard. He's having a little sleep in the hall doorway just now – you may need to revive him; no need to be too gentle...."

When a dazed Folcard was eventually led outside, he scarcely understood what had happened; but his ashen face suggested that he was already wondering how he could possibly explain such an unimaginable disaster to a livid Sir Roger.

Looking Folcard in the eye, Thomas announced: "Tell your master that this castle is now held for Robert, Earl of Gloucester and the Empress Matilda. Now, get out."

Once all the garrison had filed out, the gates were firmly shut behind them and the new occupants gave an exultant shout. Like his fellows, Thomas could scarcely believe how easily the castle had been taken and went immediately to Adeline who had come down with Edwin.

"The castle is ours, my lady," he told her.

The pair embraced unashamedly in the courtyard but, though he was desperate to savour the next few hours with her, he knew that first he must ensure that his new acquisition was secure.

"We may have the castle, Thomas," she murmured, "but for how long? Will not the Earl of Leicester bring all his power against us - the king even, too?"

"Aye, my love, but we've only to hold out until my father arrives with his army," replied Thomas. "He'll raise the south-west against the king and the Earl of Leicester will flee like a whipped dog. We just have to hold onto this place until then."

"But we are so few…"

"Aye, so we'll need others - but first we must bring in my uncle and your sister."

"Isabel?"

"Aye, the recently-widowed Isabel," confirmed Thomas.

34

Late evening on 19th June, at Schaftesberia Abbey.

Enric was itching to escape from the abbey. Originally, he had intended simply to leave his charges at the abbey gate and head straight back to meet Thomas at Wilflaed's. Sir Roger's intervention, however, had forced caution upon him and Avice had urged him not to risk capture by rushing out recklessly into the night. Such prudence was all very well but, after Lady Isabel's revelation that Thomas had decided to make another visit to the fort, Enric wasn't even sure where he should go. If he could have spoken further to Avice, it might have eased his anxiety, but she was fully occupied tending to the injured, especially brave Turstin, who was still as pale now as he had been two days earlier. Only God knew how the fellow still breathed.

Of the abbess, Enric had seen nothing since her terse greeting at the gate; though Tancred told him that she had refused to admit Sir Roger so, clearly, she was not a woman to be taken lightly. A restless Tancred remained with Enric for a while but disappeared soon enough – no doubt in search of Edith. Something was certainly developing there, Enric reckoned, for the pair had been almost inseparable since the moment Edith had been freed. He could only guess what the poor lass had suffered at Sturministra but, whatever it was, the nunnery had clearly not prepared her for it. At first, Enric supposed that she was wisely keeping close to a man who might protect her. But he had seen the bond between the two grow tighter by the hour and every glance they exchanged and every casual touch of their hands only reinforced it. It reminded him of his own first love, with Avice; but, of course, as he knew to his cost, even such powerful love could be rent asunder by the pitiless forces at work in the world.

His idle musing upon the two young people caused him to drift into a shallow slumber, until a hand rested lightly upon his shoulder. When he looked up, he saw Avice standing over him; she looked utterly exhausted and her cheeks were stained from weeping.

"Turstin?" he enquired.

Sniffing away her tears, she clasped his hand and replied: "He fought well… to the end; but now, he's at peace."

Enric, who had only known the dead man for a matter of days, was surprised how his spirits sank at the news. Turstin's survival had been a symbol of their successful rescue and, with every mile they carried him, their hopes had grown – only now to be cruelly dashed at their journey's end. He was still holding Avice's hand and thinking about the dead soldier when the abbess finally paid him a visit.

"So, Reverend Mother," said Enric, "how are the girls now?"

Abbess Bella gave a sad shake of the head. "I will see them taken back to their families on the morrow but… I fear none will ever be the same again."

Enric nodded, for it was not the first time he had seen innocent girls torn from their families and treated brutally by warlike men. Few, he expected, would find the strength to live their lives without dark memories plaguing them for the rest of their days.

"And my two poor nuns," murmured the abbess, "one butchered by those cruel men – God help her – and the other, Edith, so greatly changed I fear she will never fulfil her vows. Her faith has been so sorely tested that all she speaks of now is her young rescuer, Tancred."

Enric gave a non-committal grunt, for his limited experience of nunneries suggested that the girl might be a great deal better off with Tancred.

"And Sir Roger?" asked Enric. "Is he gone?"

"Aye, I sent him away with angry words… for which I must repent later," replied the abbess, cheeks flushed with emotion. "But until I railed at him, he just would not leave. He accused me of aiding outlaws – you're not an outlaw are you, Master Enric?"

"No, I'm not, Reverend Mother," said Enric. "Not yet, at least; though I fear you've made an enemy there."

The abbess gave him a grim smile. "And I swore an oath to help your nephew, who we both know is most definitely an outlaw."

"So, will you honour that promise?" enquired Enric.

"I will try," replied the abbess, with a sigh, "but only God knows where that will lead me."

"My nephew will likely not be here much longer," remarked Enric.

"Don't tell me anymore," protested the abbess. "It's better I don't know…"

"I suppose I should go and find him," groaned Enric. "If he's still living after his latest mischief…"

"Well, he has my thanks for what he has done – for what you've all done… though lives were lost..."

As if trying to convince herself, she added: "Our cause was just, Master Enric, was it not?"

"It was, Reverend Mother," he assured her.

"Perhaps, but I must pray further upon it," she muttered and left him alone again with Avice.

For a time, the pair just stood there, glancing occasionally at each other; but, for Enric, it could only ever be a bittersweet moment. Though once they had been lovers, too many years had passed to rekindle that cold fire. God had only brought them together again for the sake of Thorold's victims; and the Lord, Enric suspected, probably knew best.

"I have to go while it's still dark," he told her. "My fool of a nephew will need me. If he's not managed to get himself killed, in a week's time, God willing, we'll be in Normandy."

Even as he told her, the thought distressed him; as if he carried an old wound that had never healed. When Avice made no reply, he walked out of the chamber without another word or backward glance, with only his boots echoing along the stone-paved passage. At the gate he found Berner and Tancred who bade him farewell as if they were old comrades in arms. Perhaps they were, he thought, having survived such a bloody struggle together.

Tancred held a horse for him to mount while Berner said: "God speed you, Master Enric, wherever you may go."

By riding out through the postern gate he had come in, Enric hoped to avoid being seen by the watchmen at the town's east gate; though of course the gate no longer provided much of a barrier to entry. Passing below the old hilltop town, he kept his distance from the castle and remained ever watchful. If Thomas had succeeded in freeing Lady Adeline, then he would be waiting either on the lower slopes below the fort or back at Wilflaed's in the forest of Duncliffe. If he was in neither place then he was very likely dead.

Leaving the road, Enric followed the rough track which skirted beneath the west flank of the castle. After a while, since there was no hint of a moon, he dismounted to walk the horse in the darkness. The night, as ever, was both his dearest friend and worst enemy. He was scanning the sloping heathland for the stand of trees where he had previously awaited his nephew when he picked out a lone figure under the woodland canopy. Only when he ventured closer, did he recognise his son.

"Edwin?" he whispered. "What's happened? Why are you here alone?"

"A change of plan," Edwin advised him.

"Oh, shit," muttered Enric. "Not another one…"

As he followed Edwin up to the castle, Enric could not believe what his son was telling him.

"How?" he gasped. "No, forget how – why? What in God's name was Thomas thinking?"

"You'll have to ask him that yourself, father," replied Edwin.

Part Four: Under Siege

35

8th August at Schaftesberia Castle

It would be a fine dawn, Thomas reckoned, for already a raw glow was illuminating the lofty tower chamber. He smiled at the tiny shards of light creeping steadily across the bed to illuminate Adeline's bare arse. Wherever that girl slept, she seemed incapable of keeping herself covered – not that he was complaining. Every moment he spent with her was one more than he ever expected - and every day he thanked the Lord for it.

Despite the powerful storm gathering all around them, for the first time in his young life, Thomas felt at peace. For as long as he could recall, his time had been spent cleaning the mail and weapons of his elders, or training in the yard to become one of them. When he tired of trying to catch his father's eye in the yard, he spent his free hours in such a drunken stupor that, before he found some willing company for the night, he usually passed out.

Whilst, during those years, he had undoubtedly honed his fighting skills, he was judged by many to be too reckless since it took only the smallest incident to unleash his savage temper. But he cared nothing for what the other men at arms thought until, of course, the fatal stabbing which turned his life upside down. It took the death of William de Burgh to compel him to confront the dark shadows that lurked deep in his soul. During the long wait for Enric, he had time for an ocean of reflection; yet, acknowledging his demons was not the same as extirpating them. Thus, he was still set upon a path to oblivion – until he met Adeline.

Entranced from the first moment by her beauty, he had thought of little else since that night. Somehow, in spite of their unpropitious first meeting, the two were steadily drawn to each other until, here they were, lying together in handfasted wedlock. Though he could not explain how, Thomas knew that she soothed his restless demons. Aye, she had subdued them; but they were still there….

Bending over her, he kissed the back of her neck and did not stop until she began to stir.

Opening a reluctant eye, she complained: "I was asleep…"

"Even while you sleep, you arouse me," he murmured, resting a hand casually upon her upper thigh. "Your skin is so smooth…"

"But your hands are so rough," she moaned. "Perhaps I should have married Sir Roger after all."

"Just the scars of battle," he replied, but his attempt at humour was half-hearted for her casual mention of the knight's name was enough to remind him of their dire predicament.

Adeline, no doubt sensing the change in him, reached up to cradle his face in her hands and draw him close. But the kiss she pressed against his lips was not one born of unbridled passion; it was soft, gentle and long. It was her way of saying that she had abandoned all else for him and would remain with him no matter where or how their journey ended. For a while longer, the pair lay there in each other's arms, until the noise of folk stirring elsewhere in the castle finally obliged them to abandon the sanctuary of their bed.

Much had happened in the six weeks since Thomas snatched Schaftesberia Castle from Sir Roger's grasp and every day seemed to bring ever more testing challenges. He feared his shortcomings as a castellan must, by now, be obvious to all; for what did he know of managing a castle –

even such a small one? Preparing for Sir Roger's inevitable retaliation meant being ready for a siege which they would struggle to withstand.

Enric had been quick to point out that, aside from the other dire problems they faced, they simply did not have enough men. His uncle, of course, was right because, in those first few days of their occupation, his small company had rattled around the castle. Yet, after a week or so, that changed. It appeared that, by attacking Sturministra and killing Thorold Le Breton, Thomas had drawn attention to himself. Somehow word spread that Gloucester's bastard son, Thomas FitzRobert, had raised his father's standard at Schaftesberia. Though, as Adeline gently pointed out, he did not actually have one to raise.

The earliest recruits to his cause came from further west with startling news of other pockets of rebellion against King Stephen. Though at first, Thomas doubted much of what the newcomers told him, it was clear that his was not the only act of rebellion. The moment Earl Robert of Gloucester declared for Matilda, several of his allies rose up in revolt and the early tidings were encouraging. Thomas learned that, though King Stephen was attempting to seize his father's mighty castle at Brystole, it was still held securely by his half-brother, William. Elsewhere, he heard that, further north, Schrosberie Castle too was bravely holding out against a royal siege.

As the weeks passed, however, word reached him that two other rebel castles in the south-west at Richmont and Castle Cary had succumbed to the siege engines of the king. Thus, any solace he derived from knowing that he was not alone in defying the king, was tempered by such defeats. Worse still, it was clear that Thomas could expect no help from any other rebel strongholds for they were either too far away or already under siege themselves. Hence, he had no choice but to await his father's return; which is why, the day after he took possession of the castle, he despatched an urgent messenger to Normandy.

All the while, a continuous trickle of rebel refugees arrived until he had close to three score fighting men. Such support, however welcome, created its own problems for some men brought wives and even children to the safety of Schaftesberia. Since Thomas could not possibly feed them all, the elation and blind optimism of the first few weeks were gradually eroded by harsh reality.

That morning, leaving Adeline to finish dressing, Thomas went to find his uncle, upon whom he now relied very heavily for advice. Together they had spent many hours trying to mould their recruits into an effective fighting force. But though some showed promise, it was clear that many had come to Schaftesberia only because they were better at fleeing than fighting. The weapons confiscated from Sir Roger's men at arms and his small armoury were distributed to some of the new arrivals but it was by no means enough. Enric was supervising the making of more Welsh bows, but they had few arrows and no skilled fletcher to make more. In short, their men were poorly equipped and wholly unprepared.

In expectation of an imminent assault, Enric had strengthened their defences by excavating a deeper ditch below the palisade and lodging sharpened stakes within it. The gates too were reinforced with heavier timbers and where the stockade once stood, several lean-to quarters were constructed to house the influx of fugitives. Food though, was the main concern; for, while the harvest was now very close, Thomas doubted they could procure enough grain. Enric insisted that they must cram in ever more livestock, but the castle was already so overrun with animals that their stench pervaded the air – and, in any case, fodder too was scarce. Since there was no castle well, rainwater was collected in large barrels but, as with everything else, it was not enough.

"So many people," groaned Enric.

"They come to our aid, uncle."

"They come for safety which we can't provide," argued Enric. "We can't take any more, Thomas. God's nails, we can't cope with those we have. I can only see one end to this…"

"The end will come when my father arrives," declared Thomas.

"If we don't die of thirst before that," scoffed Enric. "There's not a drop of water on this hill - aside from what's in our barrels and cisterns. We'll have to bring more up in wagons 'cos, once the siege starts, we won't be able to."

"I think it's time I called upon my… ally," murmured Thomas.

"You think she'll help?" grumbled Enric. "She's done nothing so far."

"In return for freeing those girls, the abbess swore to help us."

"Aye, but that was before you decided to steal a castle," retorted Enric. "You can't expect her to honour that oath now."

"Well, I do," insisted Thomas.

"With Sir Roger's goatswivers watching the abbey day and night, I don't see what she can do anyway," said Enric.

"I'll have to go to the abbess and press her to keep that oath," said Thomas.

"Can't happen," said Enric. "Even if we could sneak out of here, we'd never get into the abbey."

"I wasn't thinking of sneaking out," said Thomas.

"Go at night, you mean?" said Enric.

"No, I mean it's time we moved against Sir Roger."

In the past few days, Thomas had been devising a plan to dislodge Sir Roger from the camp he had established south of the castle. But, until now, he had not been ready to put it before his uncle for it was a gamble – a gamble of which his uncle would not approve.

"We ride out of here in broad daylight," said Thomas, "so that all – including Sir Roger - can see that we don't fear anyone."

"But we do," muttered Enric.

"I don't," declared Thomas.

"Aye, well you should because you're an outlaw; so any man's free to take your-"

But Thomas cut short his uncle's protest

"I'm only an outlaw if I acknowledge Stephen as my lawful king," replied Thomas. "And, since I don't, why am I hiding?"

"Because you'd die out there," snapped Enric. "Even for a fartwit like you, it's a damned foolish idea."

"Sir Roger thinks he's got us trapped here," said Thomas.

"Aye, because the sowsarding arsewipe has," growled Enric.

"How can we be trapped when he's only got a handful of men?"

"Aye, but trained, well-armed men." persisted Enric. "While all we have is a piss-poor rabble – which is why we agreed to lie low and wait for your father."

"But, as you never stop telling me, uncle, without more food and water, we'll be lucky to last even that long."

"So we attack – is that what you're saying?" groaned Enric. "Risk all in some wild assault?"

"Just hear what I have to say," said Thomas.

Enric heard him out with little show of enthusiasm and afterwards, as Thomas feared, he fired question after question at his nephew until finally, he pointed out one or two fatal flaws. For a few minutes neither man spoke until, to the astonishment of Thomas, Enric suggested a solution to one of the problems he had picked out. One by one, his suggestions shaped the scheme and it was not long before he appeared to regard the entire plan as his own creation.

"This might just be bold enough to work," he concluded. "And it's best if our new pissmaggots have something to do - no matter how bloody it could be…"

It was true enough, thought Thomas, that since work on the castle improvements had been completed, many of the menfolk were growing visibly bored – a situation which never augured well. The enterprise that he and Enric intended would give the men a purpose, even if it was one that might also get them killed.

Once their preparations began, the whole castle was soon afire with excitement and also much trepidation. Indeed, as the decisive moment approached, even Thomas began to voice some doubts.

"By Christ, uncle, this will take some doing," he said. "We could lose all our horses and half our men…"

"Don't start hurling shit at the plan now," snapped Enric. "This is what you wanted, remember."

"Aye, because we have to buy just a few more weeks," murmured Thomas, "until my father comes."

"I'll settle for one more week," replied his uncle.

"Perhaps it should be you that goes to the abbey," suggested Thomas.

"We've talked over this a dozen times," growled Enric wearily. "It has to be you that talks to the abbess. You're the one she swore the oath to."

"Aye, I suppose… but you will be at most risk…"

"Make no mistake, Thomas, we could both die out there," grumbled Enric. "So, are we doing it, or not? Because, God's nails, lad, you need to make up your mind."

36

10th August, Schaftesberia Castle

Just after dawn, every horse they possessed was ready in the castle yard and, among the riders, there was a murmur of anticipation. However, when Thomas scanned the faces of those watching from the ramparts, he saw only apprehension and doubt. From the tower, he looked out over the whole of the town, even as far as the abbey. Beyond St. John's church, below the castle to the south, he could see Sir Roger's small camp which looked almost deserted. That was probably because most of the knight's few mounted men at arms were patrolling the area around the castle hoping to prevent any more folk from joining the renegades. Though Sir Roger's tactic had drastically reduced the number of recruits entering the castle, Thomas had learned from several outlaws that many of those turned away had taken refuge in nearby Duncliffe Forest.

Focusing his attention for a moment upon the abbey, Thomas observed five or six of Sir Roger's men posted, as every day, outside the town's east gate. There, they were close enough to control access to the main Abbey entrance. As he transferred his attention once more to the yard below, he felt Adeline's hand grasp his before she reached up to kiss him on the cheek.

"Am I doing the right thing?" he whispered. "What if-"

But her fingers pressed against his lips to silence him. "Our lives rest in God's hands, my love, as they ever have," she murmured. "And He's brought us this far so, let's not ask 'what-if.'"

Feeling the strength of her belief coursing through him, Thomas felt ready to take on an entire army.

"Well then, it's time," he said and raised an arm to Enric, who was waiting at the castle gate.

At once the gates were flung open and Enric rode across the short distance to the west gate of the old town with more than half of the castle's horsemen following him. Still watching from above, Thomas grimaced as the company cantered through the town towards the opposite east gate, scattering folk in all directions. That would not help endear him to the town's merchants, thought Thomas, for they were already disgruntled by the effect upon their trade of his seizure of the castle.

The moment Enric's party hurtled on through the old burh's east gateway, Sir Roger's loitering men at arms scrambled onto their mounts to intercept them. After weeks of waiting around, they were so eager to take up the chase they failed to notice that a lone rider was hanging back from the rest. Hence, once the pursuers had ridden off, Edwin was able to casually walk his horse up to the abbey gate.

"My turn now," muttered Thomas.

"Aye, but… just come back, husband," Adeline entreated. "Please…"

With a final grin to reassure her, he walked briskly away to descend the tower steps to the hall, now stripped of Sir Roger's banners. In the yard, the remaining riders awaited him; some restless, most terrified. When he finally led them out of the gates at a steady walk, he knew that Sir Roger would be aware of his departure but, with most of his men following Enric's larger force, there was very little the knight could do about it.

Taking his horsemen through the ramshackle west gate, Thomas noted how shabby the buildings were - almost derelict in places. The town was growing eastwards now beyond the abbey, where footsore pilgrims gathered like sheep to be fleeced. Some folk travelled many a mile for a glimpse of poor old St Edward's bones.

By the time Thomas reached the abbey gate, it already lay open to receive him and he led his small party through unhindered to dismount in the inner courtyard. He smiled to see the familiar figure of Berner there to meet him, along with Edwin and Avice. Within moments, young Tancred also ran up to pay his respects to Thomas.

"You were not pursued then, lord," he remarked, clearly a little surprised.

"No, because Sir Roger now has fewer mounts than I do," he replied with a grin.

Avice, he observed, wore a worried frown so perhaps Edwin had told her of Enric's task. However, she recovered her composure sufficiently to invite Thomas to follow her deep into the heart of the abbey. With a rueful smile, Thomas acknowledged that, while the abbess was prepared to let him enter by the main gate, she intended their meeting to be a clandestine one. Thus, in a privy and pleasantly cool chamber, the Abbess Bella received him with a welcome which was also pleasantly cool.

"I am pleased at last to be able to thank you myself, Thomas FitzRobert, for what you did at Sturministra," she began.

Irked by her rather formal tone, he couldn't resist replying: "You mean for killing Thorold Le Breton?"

"You know very well for what I give my thanks," scolded the abbess. Her response was measured and her manner, most definitely, aloof.

"Aye, but you also know very well that what you wanted couldn't have been achieved without the death of that knight and his creatures," replied Thomas. "Because, sometimes, Reverend Mother, you must spill some blood to do what's right."

"Well, an outlaw would say that," she conceded. "But however it was achieved, all the girls have now either returned to their homes or found a place here in the abbey."

Thomas was in no doubt that those girls who had 'found a place' were the ones whose families had rejected them as sullied goods. Such girls, through no fault of their own, would be judged poor material for a good marriage. Their abductor might be dead, but he had still ruined their lives.

"The girls suffered much," he told the abbess, "As did Lady Isabel."

"A wife must often endure," said the abbess, as if reciting from the scriptures.

"Must she?" replied Thomas sharply. "Do you speak from personal experience, Reverend Mother?"

Ignoring his thinly-veiled barb, she said: "You may tell Lady Adeline that her sister is much recovered from her ordeal and her half-brother is also well."

"She'll be most heartened to know that," said Thomas.

"I must admit, Thomas, that I am most surprised you've dared come here, after your shocking attack upon Sir Roger's castle."

"Shocking, Reverend Mother?" scoffed Thomas. "Well, I'm sure Sir Roger found it so; but you might recall that it took place at the very same moment that Sir Roger was doing all he could to prevent my uncle from delivering Lady Isabel and the other women safely to you."

"I confess that his attempted… intervention did disappoint me," admitted the abbess.

"Sir Roger is not your ally, Reverend Mother," warned Thomas. "If you rely upon him, you'll tread a dangerous path."

"But I must," she replied. "This is a royal abbey, Thomas; I answer to the Bishop of Salesberie and the king himself."

"Aye, a bishop who also, like Sir Roger, refused your plea for help," retorted Thomas bitterly. "I am your only true friend here."

"You?" scorned the abbess. "Tell me how I can possibly be a friend to the outlawed bastard son of a traitorous earl?"

"Because," said Thomas, "I recall exactly what you promised me: 'Fight well and I swear I shall do all I can to help you.' Your words, Reverend Mother - when you wanted my help - your solemn, sworn oath to help me."

As the significance of his challenge struck home, the white face of the abbess turned almost grey. Of course, she had never anticipated that her oath would need to be honoured; for, even if Thomas survived his dangerous assault on Sturministra, he was likely to be on the run and, as his uncle had implied, very far from Schaftesberia Abbey.

Several moments passed during which the abbess said nothing but stared long and hard at Thomas.

"Well?" he prompted.

"I swore an oath to a traitor outside the law," she murmured, "and, 'tis oft said that an oath to an outlaw need not be honoured..."

"Let me help you to fulfil that oath," offered Thomas. "I shall never ask you for arms or men to wield them. But, at the castle I have many women and children. So, the help I require is for them, not me; food and water, for the most part."

"I see…" breathed the abbess.

"I hope you do see," said Thomas, stern-faced, "because this is the price of my help at Sturministra. You will ensure that, no matter what happens to me or my fighting men, their families will not starve, nor be enslaved or mistreated. You will provide for them as long as the castle is under siege and - if it comes to it – you will take the families into the sanctuary of the abbey."

"You ask a great deal," said the abbess. "I must pray upon this, before giving you an answer."

"By all means pray on it, Reverend Mother," replied Thomas, "but don't pray for too long. And you might care to ask the Lord whether an oath before Him, to a man who was willing to give his life in your service, can be denied? I shall expect your answer tomorrow without fail."

A wan smile ghosted across the face of the abbess. "Or what?" she said.

Though her mocking expression provoked him just for a moment, he tempered the dark fire rising within him.

"Since I claim lordship over Schaftesberia," he said gravely, "You would surely rather be my ally than my enemy."

Ignoring his threat, the abbess smiled and said: "You may claim lordship, but it's still Sir Roger who controls this town."

"Let's see, shall we, Reverend Mother, whether, by the morrow, that still holds true."

After a slight nod of assent, she said: "I shall arrange refreshment for you and your comrades."

"Thank you, but that won't be necessary for we have other – rather urgent - matters to attend to."

"Very well," she said, "but there is some other business we must discuss."

"And what's that?" asked Thomas briskly, unwilling to delay his departure any further.

"Several of those who returned from Sturministra have asked to leave the abbey precinct and, God help them, they wish to take refuge with you in the castle. Though I've warned them of the dangers, they seem determined."

"How many?" enquired Thomas.

"Five. The healer, Wilflaed, would be very useful here, but she seems to have acquired some misguided loyalty to you. Ralph de Sarne begs you to allow him to see his sister – which I think you should. Young Tancred also wants to join you and, I fear that the novice, Edith, will go wherever he goes. And, after what she has endured, I can hardly condemn the girl. Oh, and there is that infidel girl who simply cannot stay here."

"Ah, Selima; aye, she is sworn in my service," he said, with a sigh and caught the strange look the abbess gave him.

"All are welcome under my roof," agreed Thomas, wondering how he could possibly find room for yet more recruits. "But they must be ready to leave at once and," he added slyly, "you'll need to provide a mount for each one."

"A horse for each of them?" protested the abbess. "Why, they've only a few yards to walk – and I cannot lend you five horses."

"It isn't a loan, Reverend Mother," said Thomas, knowing that the abbess would be only too pleased to rid herself of a truculent non-believer and a novice who was infatuated with one of her own men at arms.

"Oh, very well," she agreed.

"Swiftly then, if you please," he ordered, before leaving her to wait with Edwin and the others at the abbey gate. To his relief, Tancred soon appeared leading two horses – one with both Edith and Selima already mounted upon it. With a wry grin, he acknowledged that the abbess had managed to save herself at least one horse.

As soon as Wilflaed rode up with a sheepish Ralph, Edwin led the way out of the gate back through the town to the castle where the new arrivals faced a rather mixed reception. While everyone was pleased to have the skills of Wilflaed at the castle, no-one seemed quite sure what they thought about the others.

Adeline greeted her feckless brother with cool reserve; for, Thomas suspected that, though she had learned of Ralph's heroic part in helping Enric to evade capture at the abbey, it might be a long time before she truly forgave him.

When Thomas finally dismounted to greet Adeline, her face wore a puzzled frown as she eyed Selima.

"Who is that?" she asked.

"Er, she's a cook who fought bravely for us at Thorold's house," replied Thomas airily. "She even wounded Thorold with my seax."

"I see," said Adeline, whose cheeks, Thomas noted, appeared a little flushed. "And how was it that she had your weapon in her hands?"

"I'll have to explain all that later," he told her. "All you need to know is that her actions saved my life and she's now my sworn servant."

"Then she will forever have my thanks," said Adeline, giving him a curt nod.

Thomas, praying for divine intervention, was rewarded by a shout from Eadwulf on the rampart above: "Riders!"

"Where from?" demanded Thomas.

"The west," Eadwulf called down.

"Is it Enric?"

"No, lord," reported Eadwulf. "Not him but, whoever they are, there's only three or four…"

Thomas turned away in frustration for, though such petty numbers might not seem important to Eadwulf, they could mean the difference between victory and annihilation.

"Are they making for Sir Roger's camp?" he cried up to Eadwulf.

"Aye, lord."

Very soon Thomas would ride out of the castle with all the fighting men he could muster, hoping to combine forces with Enric and launch a decisive attack upon Sir Roger's camp. Yet, while Sir Roger's ranks appeared to be increasing before his very eyes, he did not even know if Enric's men were still alive.

37

10th August at Schaftesberia

As Enric sped past the abbey gateway with his small company, a swift glance behind told him that Sir Roger's watchers had taken the bait. Indeed, with Folcard at their head, they were closing up much faster than Enric had anticipated. Cursing aloud, the Saxon veered sharply down a lane to his right, which descended the steep hill beside the abbey's high east wall. At breakneck speed, it was a dangerous manoeuvre and he was much relieved to arrive at the foot of the slope in one piece. With no time to linger, he cantered on towards St James, praying that the rest of his comrades had survived the downhill charge.

Racing past the church, he followed the reverse of the route he took when escorting the girls from Duncliffe to the abbey. Though the leading pursuers were still worryingly close behind, he reckoned that, if he could keep ahead of them on the road, he could shake them off through the woodland. It was the forest that held the key to his success; or at least, he prayed it did. First, he must make contact with those fugitives Sir Roger had turned away from Schaftesberia Castle. Once he had done so, he had to return, with as many additional men as he could muster, to meet Thomas at midday at Sir Roger's camp. Together they would then launch what they hoped would be a decisive assault.

Before dawn, Thomas had despatched to Duncliffe Forest two of his most reliable outlaw recruits, Geoffrey and Will, to rally men to join the fight. All the rumours suggested a large rebel camp in the forest but, to Enric, it still sounded far-fetched. Privately, he feared they would find few men willing to fight. Folk who had already fled from the rebellions in the west would, he reasoned, be very likely to keep running. A strategy that relied upon phantom warriors would surely be doomed to fail.

Though Enric was supposed to meet Geoffrey and Will at Wilflaed's cottage, neither he nor Thomas had expected Folcard's horsemen to be so determined in their pursuit. Enric used all the forest trails he knew, but he simply could not lose them. As the morning wore on, he was acutely aware of time slipping fast through his fingers. If he failed to join Thomas by the appointed hour, he shuddered to think what the reckless youth might do.

"God's nails," he muttered, as he felt his mount tiring beneath him, for their horses couldn't run forever. His nephew had insisted that, on no account, was he to get drawn into a mêlée and, for once, Enric wholeheartedly agreed with him. But, clearly, God had other ideas.

Since there was no alternative now, all he could do was pray that the Lord's great plan didn't include the annihilation of his dozen men. Having decided they must fight, Enric headed for the cottage, knowing that, in a close struggle, having Geoffrey and Will might make all the difference. Indeed, they might well have done except that, when Enric burst out into the clearing around Wilflaed's cottage, his two comrades were nowhere to be seen. In desperation, Enric was forced to wheel his column around to face Folcard, who was a mere forty yards behind them.

Every ageing muscle in his body quailed at the mere thought of imminent combat, yet oddly, at the same time, he still felt a keen stab of excitement. Enric had learned his bloody trade at an early age in the searing heat of a squalid town in the Holy Land. When he expected every day to be his last, cheating death became a way of life; but this green and leafy clearing was a very long way from the Holy Land.

More in hope than expectation, he roared at his half-trained comrades: "Form a line!"

But, as he feared, several of his men were still wrestling to turn their mounts long after the rest had lined up to face their opponents. With Folcard's snarling men at arms racing towards them, Enric composed himself; for sometimes all a fighting man could do was draw his weapon and pray for deliverance.

Raising his blade aloft, he bellowed: "Go at the devils!" and charged.

To his great relief, he found that his stout-hearted comrades were trying their best to follow his lead. That first collision was, as ever, loud and brutal – no doubt louder than any of his men expected and far more brutal than they could imagine. Two of his men were unhorsed at once, but Enric's eyes sought only Folcard. In the rolling skirmish that ensued, it appeared that his opponent had a similar aim - each man reckoning that, if he could cut down the other, it might end the contest in an instant.

Feeling the thrill of battle coursing through him, Enric crashed his sword onto Folcard's shield, grinning to hear the crack of splintering wood. Yet the shield held and his adversary delivered two punishing blows of his own. Hauling his mount around to attack again, Enric battered Folcard's shield for a second time but without inflicting further damage. Cursing, he knew that trying to kill Folcard was already taking too long. His comrades needed him for, though they were resisting bravely, all the courage in Christendom could not make up for their lack of training. Enric marked how their more experienced opponents were trying to split them up and pick them off one by one.

Fuming with frustration, Enric broke away from Folcard and bellowed: "Regroup at the house!"

Even as the old warrior rode for Wilflaed's cottage, he knew that, while the building would give his men a wall at their backs, its protection was largely illusory. By the time Enric arrived, the giant Garth - never much of a horseman -

had fallen as he tried to dismount beside the cottage wall. Two mounted pursuers sought to skewer him there with their spears, but Garth was strong and quick for his size. Scrambling out from under the flailing hooves, he rolled swiftly onto his knees, with his fearsome great axe in hand.

While still on his haunches, he swung his axe wildly at his mounted assailants, hacking one rider's foot off with his first blow. Drenched by the resulting spray of blood, he stood tall and carved down both man and beast. By then, his friend Jonas, encouraged by the bullish show of resistance, dismounted to join him. When a thrust from Jonas' long spear impaled another mount, their opponents sheered away. Indeed, the sight of the two huge men fighting shoulder to shoulder with such brutal effect seemed to unnerve Folcard's men more than a little.

As more of his comrades leapt – or fell – from their horses, Enric bellowed: "Spears! Just hold your ground!"

The command, of course, was rather superfluous since they already had their backs up against the cottage wall. Soon the company was completely encircled, but managed to present enough well-honed spear points to deter the enemy horsemen for the time being.

Enric, breathing hard from the effort of making repeated spear thrusts, was astonished his comrades had lasted this long – and, in truth, he was rather proud of them. Fixing Folcard with a murderous glare, he grinned with teeth bared, in the certain knowledge that, if the turdsucker wanted to finish them, he would have to come at them on foot. So, let him come, thought Enric, for Folcard, with far better horsemen, would be forced to surrender his greatest advantage.

"Come on, arsewipe," muttered Enric, as he gripped his spear shaft ever tighter in anticipation of impaling his opponent upon its point.

As their opponents abandoned their mounts and arrayed to make their assault on foot, Enric reflected that now would be an excellent time for a horde of spirit warriors to swarm out of the forest and deliver the outlaws from their impending annihilation. But, as Folcard's line of men trudged forward with the sun glinting upon their spear points and sword blades, Enric peered across the clearing in vain. No-one was coming; and why would they? Only a fool would join such a one-sided fight.

For a short time, Enric and his comrades, working their spears like wild men, kept Folcard's men at arms at bay. But soon, inevitably, some spear shafts were broken and others were carved aside. The moment a gap appeared, a sword or axe swept through it to split a shield or bite into flesh. Triumphant shouts and wailing cries of agony fused into an ever-greater clamour and Enric, driven back by Folcard himself, needed every fibre of his strength just to stay alive.

On the blood-soaked ground outside the cottage, he watched his comrades fall, one by one. When a spear point pierced his calf, a despairing Enric snarled both in pain and regret; for he had failed Thomas… and failed the earl, his father, too.

38

10th August, late morning at Schaftesberia Castle

Men and horses shuffled impatiently in the castle yard, while Thomas pondered what to do. The sun was already high so, to keep to the plan agreed with Enric, he should be attacking Sir Roger's camp now. But there had been no word from Enric and, if his uncle was not in position near the knight's camp, Thomas simply did not have enough men to launch an assault. True, he could strip the castle bare and leave it utterly defenceless; but such a gamble would put at mortal risk the very people he sought to protect.

Among the anxious crowd in the yard, Thomas spied young Tancred with his arm around a tearful Edith. Not only could Tancred fight better than most young men, but he was also the most capable horseman in the castle.

"Tancred," called Thomas, beckoning the youth to him.

"Yes, lord," said Tancred.

"I need you to find Master Enric for me," said Thomas.

"Of course, lord, but… where will he be?"

"That's what I need you to find out," explained Thomas. "If he's close to Sir Roger's camp, all well and good. Tell him I'm coming with all speed."

Tancred frowned as he considered the alternative. "What if he's not there, lord?" he breathed.

"Then you must ride hard to Wilflaed's cottage and find him," instructed Thomas. "He was to meet Geoffrey and Will there. So, if you find him, tell him I'll be at Sir Roger's camp – living or dead, as it pleases God."

Tancred paled at his response, but Thomas had not yet finished.

"If Enric is… lost, go to the knight's camp; but, if you see my attempt has failed, then return to the castle at once. You understand?"

"But…"

"You will come back here and you will take my Lady Adeline - and Edith if you wish - – to Normandy. There you must seek out my father, the Earl of Gloucester, and tell him all."

"But lord-"

"Swear it," snarled Thomas. "I need to know that she'll be safe. You understand me?"

"I swear, lord," agreed Tancred miserably.

"Now go – as fast as you can ride," ordered Thomas, raising his voice to shout: "Open the gates!"

Acutely aware of the need for haste, Tancred paused only to gently press Edith's shoulder before swinging up onto his mount to ride straight out of the half-opened gate.

"Make ready to leave!" Thomas told his remaining horsemen and watched them mount their horses with varying degrees of competence.

Drawing Adeline aside, he drank in the sight of her as if he might never see her again and murmured: "I have to go now, my love. And, if the worst happens, you must put your trust in Tancred. He'll take you to my father-"

She stopped his words with a long kiss – hard and fierce; and when they drew apart, he pulled away from her, their fingers sliding slowly apart until only the tips still touched.

"No more words, Thomas," she whispered, with a radiant smile, "Till we touch again."

If he didn't leave at once, he feared he never would, so he strode away across the courtyard where the riders were gathered around his mount. Drawing in a long breath, he tried to steady himself for it would be the first time he'd led men into battle. And, if this was to be the only time he did so, he was determined to make his father proud.

Though he was vaguely aware that a commander ought to encourage his men before a fight, he sensed that empty promises would win him few friends. So, as the horsemen formed up by the gates, he told them: "We go to fight, certainly to bleed and, perhaps to die; but why not, since we fight for those we love? Now we must ride out in silence; because, by God, without the advantage of surprise, we're all dead men."

What they made of his blunt warning, he had no idea; but, if they were scared, they should be because he certainly was. After a last glance back to Adeline, he walked his horse out of the gate with measured step in an attempt to radiate calm confidence. Flanked by Edwin and Edgar, he wheeled right onto the steep downhill lane towards St John's.

It was a quiet, though tense descent, hugging the line of trees beside the road until, a little after the church, Thomas swung right again towards the small copse beyond which Sir Roger's makeshift camp lay. He could only pray that the knot of trees and bushes would cloak his small company for, if not, they might never reach the camp at all. When, a few moments later, he pulled up among the trees, he nodded to Edwin, who dropped from his mount, swiftly strung his bow and disappeared into a thicket.

The knight's camp was so close that the sound of the soldiers' laughter carried on the west wind to the waiting riders. His men seemed bullish enough but only because they knew nothing of the carnage that was hurtling towards them. While Thomas waited for Edwin, his stomach crawled with doubts and he was much relieved when a soft rustling in the bushes announced his cousin's return.

Edwin's face, however, told its own tale of woe.

"Well?" asked Thomas.

"I had to take down two sentries," reported Edwin. "So, two less opponents, which is just as well…but we can't delay long."

"And Enric?" enquired Thomas, fearing the answer.

"Not here yet," murmured Edwin.

Thomas took the crushing blow with only a flicker of concern and enquired simply: "How many men at arms did you count?"

Edwin, perhaps still pondering his father's fate, made no reply.

"Edwin?" urged Thomas. "What are their numbers?"

"Ah, some good news there, for I counted only nine."

Thomas, not sure how nine amounted to good news, pressed his cousin further: "And how are they arrayed?"

"Just taking their ease mostly," replied Edwin.

"Was Folcard there?"

"Didn't see him…"

As long as they maintained the advantage of surprise, Thomas reckoned they might be able to take nine, even without Enric. Yet always there were doubts – such as what had become of Folcard and those others who had followed his uncle? God's breath… every decision felt like a reckless gamble since, in combat, death was only ever a sword thrust away.

"It's well past midday," Edwin reminded him.

"I know that," snapped Thomas.

"What are we going to do then?"

"I'm going to attack Sir Roger's camp. But you will make your way on foot to the north side of the camp. Take Ranulf and Long Tom with you. When we charge in, strike at them from the flank; with luck, they'll think our numbers are greater..."

"Aye," agreed Edwin, "just give us time to work our way around."

"Make haste then," said Thomas. "The longer we sit here, the more chance someone's going to find us."

Thomas kept with him the eight men whom he thought were best equipped to fight on horseback, though few possessed any combat experience. So, he would use them as the very bluntest of weapons and thus his instructions were brief and bloody.

"Ride fast and try to kill every man who stands before you," he told them. "Don't stop and don't even think of mercy; for, have no doubt, if you don't kill, you will be killed."

Turning away from their ashen faces, he winced at the thought that not all of them would reach the far side of the camp. And that was just the start, because those who survived the first charge, however few, would need to canter back through the camp a second time. Even then, two passes might not be enough...

"Spread out," he whispered. "Use your spears and… stay on your damned horses."

He wanted to say more, but knew that fine words washed unheeded over men primed to fight. And, in any case, nothing he said would help the poor bastards live through the next few minutes. Worried that their fragile resolve might soon evaporate, he reckoned he'd given Edwin as long as he dared. Nudging his horse into a walk, he led the riders out, between the clumps of trees, towards the east flank of Sir Roger's camp.

Without a glance behind, he urged his mount to a trot and made a show of levelling his spear in the hope that it would remind the rest to do the same. By the time he broke out of the trees, trembling with anticipation, his horse was at a canter. He crossed the ten yards of open ground in seconds and time seemed to run even faster as he leapt the shallow bank marking the camp's edge.

Before him, he glimpsed the astonished faces of men at arms. Roaring at those in his path, he lunged with his spear. Though its point pierced a soldier's breast, the weapon was instantly torn from his grasp. A man raising an axe appeared abruptly in front of him only to be plucked aside by an arrow. Thomas gave silent thanks to Edwin, but was then engulfed by the snarling cries of fighting men.

Wrenching out Roland's fine blade, he hurtled onward through the growing clamour. His mount swept aside a half-raised spear before thundering over its bearer. When Thomas slashed down at another, feeling the bite of steel into flesh and bone, he knew that his war had truly begun. Scanning panic-stricken faces, he searched for Sir Roger but, by the time he picked out the knight, he was already past him. So, he surged on, careless of those he carved aside and, only when he leapt across the western boundary of the camp, did he dare to slow and look about him.

With a groan, he saw that his losses were even worse than he feared. Half his company were gone and, of the four riders who came to a ragged halt beside him, not all had escaped injury. The amiable and self-avowed thief, Peter, sat lopsided on his mount, shivering in shock at the sight of his blood-soaked leg.

Grim-faced, Thomas cried: "Help the lad from his horse before he falls."

"No, lord," protested Peter, forcing a grin. "I'm going back with you…"

"No, you're not," said Thomas.

Peter was still arguing his fitness to continue when he slid, cursing, from his mount and landed with a grunt of pain. Thomas could only wonder at the embarrassed smirk on the wounded youth's face.

"Bind that leg fast," he ordered, as a breathless and bloodied Edwin ran up to join them with Long Tom beside him.

"Ranulf?" muttered Thomas, but his enquiry brought only a glum shake of the head from Edwin.

The bleak knowledge that he had sacrificed half his men with the task still far from done caused Thomas a stab of guilt. How would he look their loved ones in the eye? Yet, if he gave up now, he would surrender control of Schaftesberia to Sir Roger. All help would be denied to the folk at the castle, spelling doom for those who had sought refuge there.

Sir Roger's remaining men at arms would be ready when they attacked for the second time, so any further delay simply afforded his opponent more time to plan a bloody reception.

"No sign of your father?" he asked Edwin.

Before his cousin could reply, Thomas heard the sound of fast-approaching horses, crashing through the forest from the west – and hope stirred in his heart. But it was not Enric who burst out of the trees but Folcard, Sir Roger's second in command, accompanied by two other mounted men at arms. The three riders, no doubt as surprised as those with Thomas, just charged on through. Though, at the last moment, Thomas attempted to block Folcard's path, his adversary was a skilled rider and evaded him easily. A few cursory blows were exchanged but no wounds were inflicted and an instant later they were gone.

Their arrival spelt disaster for Thomas and his surviving men for, if he launched a second assault now, they would certainly be heavily outnumbered.

"If Folcard's here, then my father's likely dead," muttered Edwin miserably. "And I never truly knew him."

The two men exchanged a bleak look.

"If we're going to do this, lord, we'd best do it quick," advised Edwin. "We took down a lot of them and I've still four shafts left. I could cull the pack a little more, eh?"

Thomas gave a sigh. "Very well Edwin… mark Sir Roger, if you can. And Tom, try to keep my cousin alive, eh?"

"I'll do me best, lord," promised Tom.

"We'll come at them from the north this time," Thomas told Edwin. "So, you move in from the west side."

"I'm ready, lord," cried Peter.

"God's blood, Peter, you'd best keep out of sight."

"Bugger that," groaned Peter. "Just get me up on that damned horse."

Conceding defeat, Thomas waved an arm to his comrades who helped Peter to remount.

"One last charge then, lads, to get it done," Thomas told them, walking his horse through the trees that surrounded Sir Roger's camp.

"Remember, be swift and merciless," he reminded his comrades, as he tapped the top of his helm with the hilt of his sword and trotted his horse towards the northern boundary of the camp. Picking up pace fast, he crossed the earth bank with all his attention focussed upon the defenders ahead of him, most of whom were still on foot. But, far too slowly, he noticed a figure rise to his feet and take aim with his crossbow…

"Crossbows!" he screamed, but by then, his mount, with blood pouring from a wound in its chest, was crashing down, mortally wounded. A triumphant roar from Sir Roger suddenly filled the air: "No quarter!" cried the knight, "give no quarter!"

Hurled forward, Thomas thudded heavily into an opponent so that both men were sent tumbling and snarling to the ground. Though he was winded, Thomas somehow contrived to find his feet. The attack, of course, had stalled and, trapped in a maelstrom of shrieking horses and roaring men, Thomas couldn't tell whether any of his comrades still lived.

When his shield disintegrated after several pounding blows from the fellow who had inadvertently broken his fall, Thomas tossed aside the useless remnant. Then, drawing out his seax, he faced his adversary with a blade in each hand. Battering the fellow backwards with his sword, he rammed the seax at his neck several times until the wretch dropped to the turf with his throat torn open.

A spear point grazed across his mail shirt but Thomas hacked it in two, only to be stunned by a weapon clanging against the side of his helm. Dizzily, he swung around to confront his new opponent with a hopeful slash of his sword, but almost overbalanced as he found himself face to face with Folcard. When the latter's blade rang against his hastily raised parry, it jarred his entire arm. Suddenly, his sword seemed heavier than a great boulder and instinctively he stepped back and almost stumbled over a fallen body. Glancing down at his feet, he realised it was Long Tom.

Folcard came at him again with Sir Roger, only a few yards away, exhorting his man to finish Thomas while he could. Cursing in frustration, he dropped the seax and clasped his sword hilt in both hands as he braced himself to parry another hammer blow. But a strangled cry from Sir Roger distracted both combatants. Seeing the arrow lodged in the knight's calf, Thomas took heart from the knowledge that Edwin, at least, was still in the fight.

The brief moment that Folcard squandered staring at his crippled lord, gave Thomas a slim chance and he seized it. Driving his sword at Folcard's breast, he grimaced when the point was turned aside by the chain mail. But perhaps, in that instant, God favoured Thomas for the blade slid up to chop through the mail at his opponent's shoulder. Though he took a pace back, Folcard assessed the wound and swiftly dismissed it.

Wiping a smear of blood from his neck, he cried: "Try again, Saxon!" and rushed at Thomas like a snorting, wounded boar.

Feinting to lunge, the tiring Thomas swayed, narrowly evaded Folcard's murderous blade, and brought his own sword crashing down on the back of Folcard's helm. The latter turned, but was clearly dazed, and failed in his desperate attempt to turn aside a thrust at his groin. Yet Thomas cursed when his sword missed its target and, instead, the point gouged down Folcard's thigh. The immediate spurt of blood told both men that it was a mortal wound and, only seconds later, with his face a deathly pale, Folcard's legs gave way under him.

Thomas took little satisfaction from the kill for, casting his eyes about him, he found none of his own men still standing and Sir Roger, having snapped off the arrow protruding from his leg, railed at his remaining men at arms to surround Thomas.

39

10th August, early afternoon at Sir Roger's camp south of Schaftesberia

When Thomas bent down to retrieve his discarded seax, he was seething with guilt-fuelled rage. A cluster of Folcard's comrades came at him baying for blood, but every sinew in Thomas's body seemed afire. Blood, they crave, thought Thomas; so, he vowed silently, blood they shall have. Without even waiting for his enemies to close in, he surged forward and carved a savage swathe into their midst. With raging hands, ever more bloodied, he wielded his two blades like the reaper's scythe. Seeing not a man but a demon facing them, Sir Roger's men at arms scattered before him but few escaped his flesh-seeking steel.

With his eyes fixed next upon Sir Roger, Thomas was careless how many he bludgeoned aside in pursuit of his quarry. Shouting for a horse, Sir Roger hobbled away from him, clearly bent only on survival. Elated that his enemy was within his grasp, Thomas attempted to take another pace forward but, at that moment, as if God Himself stood in his path, he stumbled to a halt. Too exhausted to continue, he could only mutter dire curses and watch, powerless, as Sir Roger snatched at a passing mount and clambered upon it. He scarcely noticed when other warriors joined the fray and slaughtered the rest of Sir Roger's men at arms.

When his cousin, Edwin hurried to his side, Thomas pleaded: "Take the fleeing bastard down, Edwin."

But Edwin, staring in bewilderment at the trail of wounded and dying men in his cousin's wake, simply murmured: "I've no arrows left…"

So, with a despairing groan, the bone-weary Thomas dropped to his knees watching Sir Roger ride away to the north. However, the knight rode alone for the rest of his men at arms lay dead in the camp. Only when Thomas saw Enric walking towards him did he understand that it was his uncle's arrival that had put such an abrupt end to the struggle.

"So, you're not dead, after all," croaked Thomas, his throat as dry as old leather.

"Nor you," replied Enric, "though, by the look of you, not for want of trying."

"It's not over, uncle," murmured Thomas.

Enric nodded. "Aye, I know…"

"They're all dead," wept Thomas. "My brave lads…"

It was Edwin who clasped his bloodied hand and assured him: "Some lord, but not all; and others will wear their wounds with pride."

Once he recovered a little strength in his legs, Thomas wandered around the bloody camp and saw that, whilst some were beyond help – among them, Long Tom and Ranulf – there were several walking wounded. Others too would live, though not as they once had; and there were also those who still breathed now, but whose wounds would turn bitter by nightfall.

He was staring at the untidy mound of corpses when his uncle came to embrace him.

"Sir Roger's men… they're all dead," muttered Thomas. "Every last one."

"Aye, when we got here and saw just you and Edwin standing, I fear the lads – well, all of us - got a bit… well, let's say that you're not the only one whose blood was up," he confessed. "And we'd lost men earlier to Folcard so…"

"So, we've butchered a dozen men who served their lord well and left free the one man we truly needed to kill," whispered Thomas.

Enric put a hand on his nephew's arm. "Would you rather we were all dead then?" he argued. "God's nails,

Thomas, this is a victory – and a damned unlikely one - so, take it."

Gazing around the grassy clearing that now resembled a shambles, Thomas muttered: "Doesn't seem like one… why didn't you come to our aid sooner, uncle?"

"Folcard had us penned in until Geoffrey and Will turned up with a dozen more recruits."

"New recruits," scoffed Thomas morosely, "who'll soon be dead recruits…"

Enric continued: "Then Folcard got away from us-"

"I noticed," growled Thomas.

"-so we rode here in haste, lad. It was all we could do…"

"Aye," acknowledged Thomas. "But come, for those at the castle deserve to know the outcome swiftly."

"You go ahead," said Enric, "I'll see to the dead and wounded."

Edwin came up with a horse but Thomas waved it away. "Use the horses for the wounded," he said, knowing that many mounts would have been lost in the carnage.

As he trudged up the hill, he soon found Peter, the thief, limping along silently beside him and the sight brought a grim smile to his lips. To see that Peter had, after all, survived, raised his spirits more than he could have imagined.

When he entered the castle, cheers rang out but they soon faltered when it became clear how few men had returned. Willing hands, nonetheless, hastened to give succour to the walking wounded.

Adeline ran to Thomas to embrace him, but stopped short at the sight of his blood-soaked mail; her pale countenance no doubt contemplating what might have been.

"Is it… over?" she gasped.

"For now," he replied. "We have Schaftesberia but we've paid a high price for it; and Sir Roger escaped. So, all we've won is a little time; let's pray we've won enough of it."

Wrapping her arms around him, despite the blood, she said: "Come, let me bathe your wounds."

"See to others," he said, dismissing her concern, "for I've nothing worth calling a wound."

Sensing his mood, Adeline left him to help Wilflaed and others tend the wounded and comfort the bereaved. During a long afternoon and evening, the castle inhabitants, having cared for the wounded, began to mourn and honour their dead. Thomas, his nerve all but shattered by the day's events, presided over all and his brooding presence did nothing to raise the spirits of his retainers. Despite the frequent reassurances of Enric, Thomas had yet to convince himself that what he had gained was worth the terrible price in blood.

Later that evening, as if guided by God's relentless hand, the long-awaited messenger arrived from his father in Normandy. Debilitated by the trials of the day, Thomas received the utterly spent envoy in his chamber with only Enric and Adeline present.

"So, my friend," he said, "first, tell me: is my father well?"

"He is very well, lord," gasped the messenger, "but he was… surprised to hear of your capture of Schaftesberia Castle."

"Speak freely, man," urged Thomas, too fatigued to suffer idle words. "Was he displeased?"

"No, lord – indeed, the opposite, but-"

"But what?" grumbled Thomas.

"He fears for you," replied the messenger, "because…"

"I see your report has a bitter taste," murmured Thomas, "so pray, just spit it out."

Taking a deep breath, the message-bearer told him: "Lord, your father regrets that he cannot take ship to England with the Empress Matilda before winter."

"What?" snarled Enric.

"You're certain that's what he said," asked Thomas.

"Yes, lord, I fear so; for Waleran de Beaumont has your father trapped."

Thomas nodded, momentarily lost for words.

"We thank you for your service," Adeline told the messenger. "Go now, get some food and find a place in our hall to rest."

But before the fellow left, Thomas muttered: "We'll speak again tomorrow; until then, tell no-one else what you've told us – you hear me, no-one."

"Very well, lord," agreed the messenger.

"You understand?" insisted Thomas.

"Aye."

"On pain of death…" warned Enric.

40

11th August 1138, in the early morning at Schaftesberia Castle

Thomas lay wide awake with Adeline's head weighing heavily upon his badly-bruised shoulder; but it was a far greater burden which was robbing him of sleep. He implored the sun not to rise; for, however glorious the dawn might be, it would be far from welcome. Daybreak meant the opportunity to make yet more mistakes – as if he hadn't made enough.

Lives had been sacrificed and a sea of blood spilled simply to gain time for Robert, Earl of Gloucester to arrive from Normandy. Now Thomas was exposed as a fraud, whose hollow promise of sanctuary at Schaftesberia was worth no more than his uncle's offer of pardons for his outlaw recruits.

"What will you do?" murmured Adeline, who it appeared was not asleep either.

"I don't know," confided Thomas. "I've been found out, haven't I? What do I know about war, castles or sieges? As I'm sure my uncle will gladly tell you, I'm too young to know anything..."

Abruptly, Adeline sat up beside him. "But it's not up to your uncle," she told him. "You're the earl's son-"

"Aye, the earl's half-Saxon bastard..."

"Well, the folk in this castle have been trusting that half-Saxon bastard for many weeks," she declared.

"Aye, and that trust has already killed more than a dozen of them," he groaned, easing Adeline aside to slide off the narrow straw bed.

"They had faith to follow you in life... and in death," insisted Adeline, her cheeks glowing. "It's you, Thomas FitzRobert, that decides our fate – and only you. You can call upon your uncle's advice - or that of Edwin, or Edgar; but I trust in you and I believe the folk here do as well."

But Thomas could only think that her love was blinding her to his shortcomings. About one thing, however, she was right: he had a decision to make and he would need advice to make it. He could not hide from all his comrades the dread news the messenger had carried – indeed some may already have guessed its import.

Kissing Adeline on the cheek, he murmured: "I pray God that I can live up to your faith. But come, you must dress, for I'll need your advice too."

Walking down the stairs with Adeline, he found that folk were already setting aside their bedding to prepare the hall for its daily use. At once, he summoned Enric, Edwin, Edgar and Eadwulf and they sat down to discuss what they should do. He had little doubt that, like him, the others had spent at least part of the night absorbing the dread news that the rebels at Schaftesberia must fend for themselves.

As ever, it was Enric, who was the first to offer his opinion. "A siege is certain now," he declared. "And, we won't survive it, Thomas."

"I will not surrender this castle to Sir Roger," retorted Thomas.

"Pah, it's too late for that anyway," said Enric. "Because now the Earl of Leicester will come – and perhaps even King Stephen himself. We can't fight such power."

"And, if we try to," added Edwin, "a lot more folk here will die."

"Listen to me," snapped Enric. "We can't *try* to 'fight it out' with the entire sowsarding royal army."

"So we've no choice: we have to leave," said Edwin.

"Leave?" enquired Thomas. "And go where?"

"Normandy – where we should've gone in the first place," muttered Enric. "It's simple enough, Thomas: if we stay here, we all die."

"It would be hard to go on the run though," Edgar pointed out and, glancing at Adeline, added: "Harder still for… your lady."

Though Adeline said nothing in response, Thomas, seeing her lips press together in a tight, thin line, recalled how stubborn his new bride could be.

"Edgar's right. I couldn't ask you to live like an outlaw," he told her. "But perhaps the nuns at the abbey might be persuaded to take you in."

Enric shook his head. "If the abbess wouldn't take her before, why would she now?"

"Because the abbess owes me a debt that can never fully be repaid," said Thomas. "This is the very least she could do."

When Adeline stood up, Thomas winced, knowing it was not a good sign and the furrows of thunder across her brow told him what she thought of his suggestion. In case he was in any doubt, she railed at him: "You are not sending me to that nunnery. After all I've endured to be here with you - you would now send me away?"

"To keep you alive," he protested, "only to keep you alive..."

When Thomas sought moral support from his comrades, they all seemed, at that particular moment, to find much of interest in the wooden floor boards.

Enric ventured: "Perhaps…"

"Get out – all of you!" screamed Adeline and they seemed only too willing to comply.

Left alone with his lover glaring at him, Thomas decided to say nothing.

Snatching up his hand, she cried: "Am I worth so little to you?"

"You're worth everything to me," he replied. "That's why I strive to keep you safe."

"If all I wanted was to be 'safe', do you think I would have come to your bed at Wilflaed's?" she demanded crossly. "Or chosen to wed you and stay here with you against all reason?"

"Aye, when I believed my father would come," he argued, "this place seemed to offer us the best chance. But to be an outlaw on the run - I don't want that life for you."

"Well then, you're going to be very disappointed, Thomas," she breathed, "because I'm in this fight with you to the very end - whatever that end may be…"

"But if we leave here, it'll be a rough life."

"Then don't leave," she replied. "This castle is surely your one great strength, isn't it?"

"It could be, but with no help from Normandy, I'd just be condemning to death all those who've come here. They came seeking sanctuary and-"

"They came because they'd nowhere else to go," retorted Adeline. "And they still don't. Like us, they were desperate and prayed for one last chance to survive."

"But if the castle's taken, the fighting men will be killed and the women…"

"So, they have every reason to defend this place with their lives, as do we."

"You just don't understand," groaned Thomas. "Even if we could defend the castle, we'll run out of food and water soon enough. I can't tell people to stay and die here… for nothing."

"Fine, then don't tell them," said Adeline.

"What?"

"If you care so much about them, let them decide their own fate. Lay bare the worst that may happen and see what they say."

With a slow nod, he murmured: "Just tell them the plain truth of it."

"Aye," she agreed. "It's the only way, Thomas. And you must speak to them in the hall this very night because, by then, rumours will be running apace through the castle."

"But, when they know what they face," he breathed, "they'll surely lose all hope."

Adeline smiled, kissed his cheek and replied: "Hope lies in the heart, Thomas, not the head."

∞ ∞ ∞ ∞

That evening, Thomas summoned the castle inhabitants to gather in the cramped and smoke-filled hall. Fresh-faced youths squatted on the rush-strewn floor and small children squirmed on their mother's laps while most stood further back with worry etched upon every countenance. Sending Edwin and Eadwulf to keep watch on the ramparts, Thomas also called in all the sentries. By then, it was clear to all that this was no casual evening assembly. When he mounted the dais with Adeline at his side, a hush descended over the company, save for the mewling of babes and dogs gnawing at their bones.

"I bear grave news," announced Thomas, but he saw at once, from the expressions on several faces, that he would only be confirming what many already feared. Even so, he thought, it was better they heard it from him. Thus, in a few blunt, doom-laden words, he explained their perilous situation.

For a few moments, his simple declaration subdued them all; but, as is the way of people, it was not long before a low murmur of discussion began, as husbands turned to ashen-faced wives and men conferred with their closest comrades. Unable to offer them any reassurance, Thomas let them talk out their fears until, eventually, an uneasy silence reigned once more in the hall.

"Well then, what say you?" asked Thomas, anticipating a flood of terse observations and complaints. Yet, when no-one said a word, he realised that they were sitting there, waiting for him to offer a solution. Christ's bones, how downcast they would be when they learned that he had none.

"I can't ask you to stay here against such overwhelming power," he told them, "And any who have sworn fealty to me, I will gladly free from their oaths. For your own sakes, the sooner you leave, the safer you'll be."

The prolonged quiet was beginning to unnerve him, for it seemed that no-one was especially keen to voice their thoughts until finally someone called out: "What will you do, lord?"

"I will stay here," he replied and realised, for the first time, that it was what he always intended to do, whether his father came or not. "And," he added, "I shall try to hold this castle until my last breath."

The moment his words were out, Adeline squeezed his hand and he saw, to his surprise, that she was smiling at him. While he was still pondering how little he understood the mind of a woman, another one stood up only a few yards from him. He recalled her well for she had arrived with no husband but two young boys who now sat at her feet.

"So, lord," she began hesitantly, unused to speaking her mind before so many others. "See these two lads 'ere – they're the sons of an outlaw. They've been dragged from hedge to barn, half-starvin' for the past year – almost died last winter along with their poor sister... But, since they've been 'ere, they've been fed – not much, but enough. And they've been safe…"

"Aye, but what I'm telling you is that they'll be safe here no longer," declared Thomas.

Her face twisted into a grim smile before she replied: "You tell us there's a good chance we'll die 'ere, or starve come winter. But I tell you I'd sooner we died 'ere among friends than froze to death in some chill forest glade on our own."

Looking around the crowded hall, Thomas saw a good many heads nodding in agreement and could not help noticing that Adeline was still wearing that wry smile upon her face.

"I urge you all to think hard upon this," he persisted. "If you're in this castle when it's taken, it will go badly for you all – worse than you could ever imagine..."

Another voice then spoke up, one of those wounded badly in the assault on Sir Roger's camp. "We faced the same threat at Castle Cary, lord, and I admit... that I fled; but there's nowhere else to flee to now, is there? We're better off in here than outside."

In desperation, Thomas looked across to Enric but his uncle - as unhelpful as ever - simply spread his hands out in resignation.

"So be it," concluded Thomas. "I will assume that anyone who is still here at noon tomorrow intends to stay to the bitter end. And may God help us all, for our fate lies now in His hands."

When Thomas slumped down beside Adeline, he felt numb.

"I tried to tell them plainly," he whispered miserably. "What more can I do?"

Adeline simply kissed his cheek and murmured: "You can put your faith in them."

But he still shook his head because, though his sweet lady's heart might be filled with hope, she had no idea how ill-prepared they were for what was to come.

Joining the pair at the table, a glum Enric remarked: "Well, Thomas, you certainly know how to lift the mood."

"A song," cried Edgar. "That's what we need. Where's young Peter? He reckons he wants to be a gleeman. So, come up here, Peter and give us a poem, or a song. And Jonah, find that pipe of yours to play."

"The youth's wounded," protested Wilflaed.

Edgar chortled in response. "He don't use his leg for this."

So Peter limped up to the dais, looking far from confident. "I've never – I mean, I s'pose I could do… The Poor Maiden Lost." he suggested.

"God's nails," grumbled Enric. "That sounds cheerful."

"Do the one about the harlot and the devil," urged Edgar. "That always gets a few laughs."

With a glance at Adeline, Peter hissed: "Can't do that one, Edgar; it's about you know, a… whore so it's, you know, a bit… ripe."

The red-faced gleeman was rescued by Adeline who assured him: "Go on, Master Gleeman, see if you can bring a flush to my cheeks."

Peter's own cheeks turned pale as he stared at the company crammed into the hall before him.

"They're all still talking…" he muttered. "And some are leaving."

But Edgar put a hand on the youth's shoulder. "Once you start, lad, they'll stop – I promise you."

Thomas feared the worst when Peter began to recite the poem for his hesitant voice could scarcely be heard above the crowd. But after the first few lines, most folk in the hall stopped to listen which appeared to give him a little more confidence. By the time he reached the first refrain, Jonah's pipe was accompanying his words and, when the rousing chorus began a second time, some of his audience joined in. Much encouraged, Peter almost seemed to grow in stature as he performed the rest of his tale, some in verse and some in song but all with good humour.

Thomas, astonished how the gleeman was casting a spell over the whole company, grinned at his lady. Peter finished to a round of cheers and calls for more; so, he looked to Thomas for approval. Enric glared at Thomas and drew a finger across his throat; but Thomas ignored him and nodded to his new gleeman. Jonah and Peter performed for another hour or so until the latter's croaking voice gave out.

That evening, those who slept in the hall took a long while to settle down for the night and some whispered conversations continued well after the last rush lights sputtered out.

When, next morning, Thomas gathered his closest advisers once again, it was clear that Enric was appalled by what he had done.

"You've let these folk think we can actually defend this place, Thomas," he complained.

"I could hardly have made the tale any darker," argued Thomas.

"But we can't survive a siege," insisted Enric. "If we stay here, we'll die; that's certain."

"As I recall, uncle, that's more or less what I told them – and I don't recall hearing a murmur out of you."

"Well, you'd already said more than enough," said Enric, "but don't you see: those poor fartwits still think you're going to come up with some miracle."

"Well, not a miracle exactly," said Thomas, "but I do have an idea about getting some more men,"

"That's just a dream, boy!" cried Enric. "Get it into your head, will you? No other lord will dare help you."

"There's one who might," murmured Thomas.

"Who?" snapped Enric.

"My brother, William."

His uncle gave a weary shake of the head. "God's breath, every time I start to think you might have learned some sense, you find a way to remind me that you haven't. Brystole is surrounded for every man who's come here from the west has told us that. So, you can't even get to your brother. God's nails! That's the worst idea you've ever had – and that's saying something."

"I can get into Brystole castle," declared Thomas.

"Alright, let's say you can," said Enric. "But you'll never get out again."

"And it's not that far away," said Thomas, ignoring his uncle's objection. "I can be there and back in a few days."

"You're not listening to me, you fool," snarled Enric.

Though he was used to being berated by his uncle, Thomas noticed the shocked reaction of the others present. Thus, he paused for a moment and looked Enric in the eye.

"You'll call me either nephew or lord," he enjoined his uncle. "Not boy, or lad, or fool, or fartwit or anything else you please. Is that clear?"

Enric, clearly stunned by the firm rebuke, said nothing but gave a sullen nod, so Thomas continued: "I value your advice, uncle; but whether I live or die here, it will be my decision, not yours."

Unusually, Enric seemed lost for words; probably, Thomas reckoned, because he was too livid to trust what he might say. Undaunted, Thomas continued to outline his plan without further interruption.

"We've earned a brief respite; so, this might be the only time I can reach Brystole," he explained, "before our enemies gather around Schaftesberia again. My brother's men sit idly, bottled up in Brystole; if he releases some of those men at arms to me to hold Schaftesberia, we can ensure that my father will have two strongholds when he arrives in the spring."

Enric, not one to keep silent for long, enquired testily: "And what, *lord*, makes you think your young half-brother will trust you with any of his men at arms? You're hardly on the best of terms, are you?"

"I believe he will," argued Thomas, "because it's what our father would do."

Enric gave a sigh of resignation and raised no more objections which was a relief because, now that Thomas had decided upon his course of action, he needed to arrange how the castle would be managed in his absence.

"I suppose you want me to come with you," remarked Enric grudgingly.

"No, I don't," replied Thomas. "I want you to prepare this place for a long siege. And, without Sir Roger watching our every move, I expect the abbess to help us with water and provisions. While I'm gone, uncle, it'll be your task to win her over with your usual charm and wit…"

The look of disgust upon Enric's face suggested to Thomas that he would be missing an interesting exchange. But his uncle replied: "I gladly accept command in your absence, lord."

"I'm not offering you command," said Thomas brusquely. "Lady Adeline, as my wife, will have command. But I require the pair of you to work together to strengthen the castle while I'm away."

Enric stared at him, open-mouthed – but so did Adeline.

"Will you two hold this place until I return?" he asked, offering a hand to both of them.

"Aye, husband, I will," pledged Adeline, clasping his hand to kiss it.

Thomas looked to Enric. "Uncle?"

"Aye," agreed Enric, grasping his hand firmly. "'cos God's nails, *lord*, what else would I do?"

Part Five: Castellan

41

16th August, dawn at Schaftesberia Castle

It had been three whole days since Thomas left yet, around the castle, no-one spoke of his absence. Perhaps they feared that if Thomas did not return, all was truly lost. Just as the first hint of dawn coloured the sky, Adeline walked up the few steps to the tower rampart to gaze out to the west. Though she knew that he might not come back for several more days, she could always hope; and, standing there in the cool dawn to pray for his safe return, seemed to subdue her doubts – at least a little.

Shivering at the prospect of losing him, she tried instead to concentrate on what she was supposed to be doing in his absence. The arrival of Enric on the rampart, however, reminded her that, as far as he was concerned, she could do very little. Thomas had made it plain that Adeline, as the lady of the castle, would have command, aided by Enric's advice. But, in practice, the old Saxon had simply assumed control of the castle and paid no heed to her protests. Every decision, however small, went through him, leaving her as a… well, she was not entirely sure what she was.

In the chill morning air, he nodded to her as one might a stranger and though, for Thomas' sake, he was unfailingly polite, she had no doubt that he blamed her for every one of their many troubles. It had become an effort to exchange even a few words with him; but always, she tried….

"Will the abbess help us, do you think?" she enquired.

"I've got that in hand," replied Enric shortly.

"But it's been three days now…"

"You know nothing of such matters, lady," groaned Enric. "It's far too complicated for you to worry about."

Used to his thinly-veiled insults, she took it on the chin, for his curmudgeonly remarks only reflected what every other man in the castle thought of her competence.

"Perhaps I could speak to the abbess?" she ventured.

"No, you should keep out of it," ordered Enric.

"But why?" she demanded.

"'Cos we're only trapped in this shithole because of you."

"None of this was my doing," she cried, stung by his savage reproach.

"Come, you must know that you're the only one with any real sway over Thomas now," he argued. "I swear, if you told the lad to cut his own throat, he would. Aye, and, if you'd told him not to go to Brystole – as I did - he'd still be here."

"That's not true," she protested, "and certainly not fair."

"Fair?" scoffed Enric. "Was it fair to tangle him in your troubles when he'd enough of his own?"

"From the very start, I warned him off," she said.

"Aye, you warned him off - till you lay with him."

"That was later," she protested.

"Hah! It was a few paltry days later you spread your legs for him," sneered Enric. "And you think you're still a lady? I've known whores take longer to snare a man."

Mortified by his brutal accusations, Adeline stalked away, only now grasping the depth of his resentment. If Thomas's uncle could call her a whore to her face, what must everyone else in the castle think of her? She was still in shock as she descended the stairs to the ground floor, where she found Wilflaed laying out her healing salves and surgical blades in the hall.

"Have you heard something?" gasped Adeline. "Are there wounded men coming?"

With a frown, Wilflaed shook her head. "I do this every morning," she replied, "which you would know if you stepped more often out of your lofty chamber."

The healer's sharp tone seemed yet another slap in the face; but, while Adeline expected Enric's censure, she regarded Wilflaed as a friend.

Miserably, she muttered: "What will I do if he doesn't come back?"

"Spare me your mewling," grumbled Wilflaed. "You're not the only one here who's afraid; but the rest of us can't just sit on our arses all day doing nothing."

"Why do you chide me so?" wept Adeline. "What have I done?"

"Nothing," snapped Wilflaed. "Nothing - and I thought better of you than that. You've a part to play here, you know."

"Aye, the whore's part, according to Enric," moaned Adeline. "And I dare say you, along with everyone else here, thinks the same."

Wilflaed stopped rolling a length of linen cloth and focused her attention upon Adeline.

"Everyone else here does something for the whole company," explained Wilflaed. "Some feed us, or tend the stock, or guard the rampart, or care for the children. Yet you, my lady, do nothing… I've talked to most folk here and I've never known anyone use the word 'whore'; but I have heard folk wonder what you do here apart from warm their lord's bed."

"But, I'm his… lady," cried Adeline. "You know that. We're married."

"Aye, but though handfasting is good enough for an old Saxon like me, there'll be some who say your marriage hasn't been blessed by the church."

"Thomas has sworn that it will be; I don't know what else I can do."

"About that, nothing," agreed Wilflaed. "But if you want to be treated as Thomas's lady, you need to start acting as if you're his lady."

Swallowing down the last of her pride, Adeline muttered: "In truth, I don't even know how to be a lady. I was raised by Ralph's mother, my father's housekeeper. She was kind but I doubt she knew how to be a lady either."

"Hah!" scorned Wilflaed. "By Christ, you're a woman, aren't you? You already have all the skills you need. Look around you: how many of the women here were raised to live as outlaws, on the run and living off scraps? Not many, I should think. But they manage; and so should you. If you don't want to be seen as a whore, then stop playing the whore and start being the lady - and don't blame others for your own weakness."

"I'm not weak," declared Adeline, stung by the charge.

"Then prove it. I told you once that if you chose Thomas, you'd need to walk through fire with him." Her expression softened into a smile. "I think, my dear, that it's long past time you thrust your hand into those flames."

Disturbed by Wilflaed's words, Adeline retreated to the stair but, before she even reached it, she was forced to accept that the healer was right. All those weeks ago she had faced a stark choice: marriage to a knight well-favoured at court, or a dangerous coupling with a half-Saxon bastard who offered only uncertainty. Her own decision had made her an outlaw, not Thomas; but perhaps it was the last true choice she had made. Since then, she had simply allowed all else to flow around her. The clothes on her back were worn and torn and she had allowed her hair to remain tangled and unkempt. In truth, she even looked a lot more like a whore than a lady.

Thomas was gone; and, whether he returned or not, she would have to carve out a life there in the beleaguered fort. She could not be the first lady to face such a mortal challenge; so, what should a lady do?

Taking several deep breaths, she ventured outside the hall into the yard for the first time since Thomas left and saw surprise written on every face she encountered. Though she forced herself to smile at folk, she found that some nodded a nervous greeting while others looked away. It was the men's eyes, she noted, that lingered longest upon her, whereas it was mostly the women who refused to meet her gaze. Aye, she acknowledged, definitely a whore then; and, for a few moments, her fragile resolve wavered. For a moment, she felt weak at the knees and leant her forehead against the rough-hewn timber of the gatepost, until she became aware of Wilflaed beside her.

"I didn't say you had to do it alone," murmured the healer, grasping her hand. "Come… lady, walk with me a while."

Taking Adeline's arm, she led her around the fort where they observed folk at work and Adeline could only wonder at how committed they seemed. Many of the women and girls were spinning, while men were continuing to strengthen the palisade. And young boys… well, they were just being young boys: rushing about to no apparent purpose while ignoring the complaints of their elders.

"Being a lady's simple enough," advised Wilflaed, with a mischievous grin. "Just walk tall, smile and give encouragement – and by Christ, do something with that hair…"

"Should I offer to help?" muttered Adeline.

"Ladies don't offer, they just do," remarked Wilflaed.

"But I don't know what to 'do'."

"The lady of the house does whatever she feels is right."

Having delivered that final piece of advice, the healer squeezed Adeline's hand and left her beside two very young girls attempting to spin a thread. One thing Adeline did know something about was spinning; so she crouched down beside them and, sensing one girl's frustration, she took her hands to steady the spindle and guide her fingers. When together they succeeded in spinning a short length of yarn, a broad smile lit up the girl's face.

"What's your name, child?" enquired Adeline.

"Alys," replied the girl. "And what should I call you?"

"I'm Lady… I'm Adeline."

She continued to sit on the damp ground with the girls for some time and others soon came to join them. Only when stiffness gripped Adeline's legs did she leave them. Struggling to her feet, she walked up to the rampart at the point where its lines of defensive wooden poles converged to meet above the steepest slope. For a time, she stared out over the lands to the north and west; for those were the directions, Thomas told her, from which a threat was most likely to come. Though they had heard that King Stephen was still in the west, other rumours reached them that the Scots had invaded and the king had taken his army north to meet the new danger. How hard it was, she thought, to know what was real and what was not.

Walking around to the east rampart above the gate, she studied the old burh adjacent to the castle and beyond it the tall tower of the abbey church. As she stared at it, an idea struck her. Though Enric had the castle well organised, she suspected that he had made little genuine attempt to persuade a reluctant abbess to supply the help they needed. She wondered if a woman might venture where a crusty old warrior feared to tread. Enric would never seek her help and he'd be livid if she interfered; but Thomas had charged her with command and, after all, a lady shouldn't have to ask…

From the rampart, she cast her eye over the castle yard until she saw one of the people she needed. Since Thomas had taken Tancred with him to Brystole, Edith, missing her young man, had wandered the castle like a lost lamb; so, it seemed that she too needed a distraction. Descending past the gate, Adeline hurried across the yard to intercept the girl, though she had scarcely spoken a word to her before.

"Edith," she blurted out. "I'd like to talk to you."

"As you will, my lady," replied Edith, unaware that her response almost prompted Adeline to hug her.

"What do you do here, Edith?" she asked.

"Er, I wash, I help Selima sometimes, and I watch the babes too," pleaded Edith. "I work hard, lady. I beg you not to turn me out."

"Turn you out?" laughed Adeline. "I wouldn't do that – no, I want you to serve me, if you will."

"Serve you, lady?" murmured Edith, as if unfamiliar with the concept.

"Work with me alone," explained Adeline. "Are you willing to do that?"

"I live here at our lord's will, lady," said Edith, "But I would gladly serve you. What would you have me do?"

"You will work with me on whatever I'm doing. But your first task is to tell me all you know about the abbey and Abbess Bella. And, while you're doing that, I need you to braid my hair..."

It turned out that Edith, though a naturally self-effacing girl, was a careful observer of people and there seemed to be nothing she didn't know about the abbey and its abbess. After a long discussion with Edith, Adeline decided that she knew enough to argue her case with the abbess. Moreover, after several faltering attempts, her new servant managed to braid her hair with what was now, admittedly, a rather faded green ribbon. Shortly after midday, wearing a simple linen cloth over her head, she felt ready to take on all Christendom.

Enlisting the help of Wilflaed, she set out to leave the castle; but, at the main gate, the three women were stopped by one of the gatekeepers.

"Are you going out on your own?" he enquired, wearing a look of puzzlement.

"I'm quite capable of walking alone," Adeline replied icily. "But, as you see, I'm accompanied."

The keeper still looked doubtful. "But it's just that…"

"It's just what?" asked Adeline, beginning to feel rather like a prisoner.

"Master Enric gave us strict instructions to keep you safe."

"Did he?" growled Adeline. "Well, I'll be quite safe, thank you."

"Perhaps I ought to fetch him though…"

But Enric must have observed her attempt to leave for he was already striding across to the gate.

"Where are you going?" he demanded, his tone brusque.

"Where are you going, *my lady*?" recited Adeline. "I'm going to the abbey, Master Enric."

"Why… my lady?" Enric pressed her.

"I thought I might become a nun," retorted Adeline. "Why do you think I'm going? To do what you've not been able to do – get us more help."

Ignoring her rebuke, Enric told her: "I can't see how you can do that but, in any case, you shouldn't be going out on your own."

"I shan't be on my own," replied Adeline, indicating Edith and Wilflaed. "And I'm sure I'll be quite safe at the abbey."

"No, I'll have to send two guards with you," blustered Enric, clearly wrongfooted by her sudden decision to visit the abbess.

"As you please," agreed Adeline. "But we're leaving now, so they'd better make haste."

Leaving the discomfited Enric in her wake, Adeline could not resist a tiny smile of triumph.

"Poor man," lamented Wilflaed. "He has no choice - for what would your lord say if he let you go out without any protection?"

While Adeline had to accept that her companion was right, she could not help celebrating a small victory over the grumpy, obstructive Saxon. Within a few moments, two breathless spearmen from the castle caught up with them. Adeline decided to go to the abbey on foot through the old town to see, first-hand, how the people of Schaftesberia lived. Having scarcely ever visited a town in her youth, she was determined to learn all she could about this one. But every step she took brought disappointment, for she understood very quickly that old Schaftesberia was in decay and had been for a long time.

Only when she passed through the far east gate, did she discover the new beating heart of the town: close to the abbey. There, in the market place, Adeline was fascinated, not only by the array of goods, but by the sheer number of people milling about.

"So many people," she muttered.

"It's not always like this," explained Wilflaed. "There's a lot more pilgrims today by the look of it."

A nervous-looking Edith interrupted. "Lady? We've gone past the abbey gate."

"Indeed," acknowledged Adeline, with a last wistful glance towards the market place.

At the abbey gate, she went to join the queue of pilgrims awaiting entry but Wilflaed hissed: "Ladies don't wait like penitents."

Looking down at her tattered clothing, Adeline felt a flush in her cheeks for she hardly resembled anyone to whom the average pilgrim would be willing to defer. Thus, she continued to hang back until, to her astonishment, the usually timid Edith announced: "Make way for Lady Adeline de Sarne! Make way."

A bewildered Adeline could not recall the girl ever speaking at anything above a whisper but, before she knew what was happening, Wilflaed took her arm to guide her through the crush at the gate. The gatekeeper, however, looked her up and down and greeted her with a shake of the head.

"What do you want here?" he enquired, in a voice dripping with distain.

At once, Wilflaed replied: "Lady de Sarne is here to see her sister, Lady Isabel, and the Abbess Bella - not that she needs to discuss her privy business with the likes of you. So, step aside."

Grudgingly, the gatekeeper opened the gate a little wider and Wilflaed pushed past him with Adeline, Edith and the two guards following.

"Being a lady seems to mean saying nothing," observed Adeline.

"You wanted help, girl; and now you're getting it," muttered Wilflaed. "So, be grateful."

"Do you even know where you're going?"

"Oh, yes, we're going to find Avice," replied Wilflaed.

"But I wanted to see the abbess," protested Adeline. "And my sister."

"Avice first," advised Wilflaed, "and then you'll be better received by the abbess. I suspect your sister will soon know you're here, because I imagine Edith's voice must have carried halfway to Duncliffe Forest."

Though Avice embraced her friend, Wilflaed warmly, she seemed less certain how to greet the would-be lady. Adeline, not wishing to be led any further by Wilflaed, however well-meaning her intentions, spoke briskly.

"I speak for Thomas, Lord of Schaftesberia and I wish to see the abbess," she declared.

"Do you, my dear?" smiled Avice. "But I thought Master Enric spoke for his nephew…"

Thinking it best not to become embroiled in a discussion about who ruled at Schaftesberia Castle in Thomas's absence, Adeline replied: "I've come to discuss with the abbess the help that she promised us."

"Ah," said Avice. "I believe the abbess has many matters to attend to today. Perhaps tomorrow-"

"So do I," interrupted Adeline, "So, please tell her that I'm here."

Avice, who appeared unusually flustered by Adeline's arrival, said only: "Wait here… my lady," before she bustled out of the chamber.

"I thought Avice was your friend," said Adeline, "but she didn't seem very welcoming."

"Avice has known the abbess a great deal longer than she's known you," remarked Wilflaed, adding with a sly smile. "And I think she fears you just a little."

"Me, but why?"

"Er…well, you've a spirit, a passion, about you, lady," explained Wilflaed. "And there's your close bond with Lord Thomas - your… very close bond. Have you forgotten that you lay with him even before your handfasted alliance," Wilflaed pointed out.

"Oh no, I remember that very well," retorted Adeline, with a dark grin. She reckoned her eyes were probably still sparkling from that particular memory when Avice returned with the welcome news that the abbess would see her.

"But just you," she told Adeline.

Wilflaed looked a little anxious at the idea of Adeline seeing anyone important on her own; but, clasping the healer's hand, Adeline reassured her: "Don't worry, dear friend, because I think, at last, I begin to see what the lady of Schaftesberia must do."

Yet, despite her bold words, Adeline was utterly daunted by the prospect of facing the abbess alone and her fears proved well-grounded for the abbess greeted her by focussing at once upon her liaison with Thomas.

"I'm told you call yourself the Lord of Schaftesberia's lady," observed the abbess.

"It's what Thomas calls me too, Reverend Mother," replied Adeline, "so I suppose it must be true."

"Yet you are not his wife."

"Indeed I am," she declared, "for we have made our vows."

"Perhaps, but such a handfasted union is neither blessed by God nor permitted by your guardian, Sir Roger," said the abbess. "So, without those endorsements, your vows mean very little."

"I suppose only God can judge our vows," replied Adeline, "but, believe me, Reverend Mother, my marriage is, just now, the least of my troubles."

"Very well, let us waste no more time contesting your title, my lady," agreed the abbess. "Please, tell me why you've come here."

"That's simple enough," said Adeline, though, of course it wasn't. "Speaking of vows, you swore an oath to give your aid to Lord Thomas and he told you what was needed. I believe you promised to seek God's guidance and yet still, we await your answer."

The abbess looked momentarily disconcerted. "But… I heard that soon you will be under siege so, I thought…"

"That we would give up and run away?" suggested Adeline.

"Well, yes."

"So, the reason you didn't send the supplies we asked for was that you thought we would be leaving?"

"Indeed."

"Then, let me be frank, Reverend Mother, we're not leaving. We will continue to hold the castle for the Empress Matilda."

"I see, but… how can you hope to win?"

Ignoring her question, Adeline continued: "So, you can see that what my lord asked you for, is still required. When can we expect it?"

"I… I shall need to pray upon it," answered the abbess quickly.

"Surely you must already have prayed more than enough about it," declared Adeline, surprising herself with the iron in her tone. "You said you didn't send help because you thought we were leaving, so God must have given His blessing. I doubt the Lord has changed His mind in a matter of days."

Clearly shocked by Adeline's forthright response, the abbess scolded: "Who are you to understand the will of God? I'd say that a lady who shunned a respectable marriage to Sir Roger to live in mortal sin with an outlaw, knows little of God."

Struggling to hold her nerve, Adeline cried: "In truth, Reverend Mother, I fell in love with Thomas before he was outlawed and do not challenge me about God; for I have faith – and God knows it!"

In the face of Adeline's vehement defiance, the abbess made no further protest and simply sank down, with a weary sigh, onto a nearby stool.

"I am in a very difficult position," she confessed.

"Aye, I don't doubt that, Reverend Mother," conceded Adeline. "But your 'position' is hardly as difficult as ours. I'm told the abbey has ample provisions and is collecting a very favourable harvest. So, you have the means to help us, if you have the will."

For the first time during the audience, the abbess met her eyes and, with a shake of the head, said: "Very well, I shall do all I can... but I expect I'll live to regret it."

"Thank you," beamed Adeline in relief, "I'll expect the first of your wagons tomorrow. Good day to you, Reverend Mother."

Sweeping out of the chamber into the stone-flagged passage outside, Adeline had to gulp in several deep breaths, but could not suppress a grin of satisfaction. Though, of course, she would only know whether she had truly convinced the abbess on the morrow, when a wagon arrived – or did not… as the Lord pleased.

"Will the abbess help you?" asked Avice, who had been waiting for her outside.

"She has said so."

Avice nodded and gave her a reassuring smile. "I've learned not to be surprised by what the Reverend Mother does, my lady. You've fought hard for your people and I'm sure she respects that. Let me take you now to your sister, who is lodged among the novices."

Isabel was waiting for her in a cell which looked even smaller than the chamber Sir Roger had bestowed upon Adeline at the castle. Uncertain what welcome she might receive from her sister; Adeline was quite overwhelmed when Isabel flew into her arms. For a long while, as they embraced each other, neither girl uttered a word and Adeline simply savoured an occasion she feared might never occur again.

When they eased apart, Isabel said: "The abbess has been kind, allowing me to stay here."

"Aye, but if - when our situation improves," said Adeline, "you could come to live with us at the castle."

"But I'm going to live here, sister," said Isabel. "Did the abbess not tell you?"

"I knew that she had offered places to those girls rejected by their families – but you are certainly not among those," declared Adeline, "for you are much loved…"

"But I've taken sanctuary here, Ade," explained Isabel. "If I do not, then my guardian lord, Robert of Leicester will marry me to whomever he wishes. Why, Sir Roger approached the abbess about marrying me almost as soon as Thomas brought me back from Sturministra."

"What?" cried Adeline in disgust. "So, if he couldn't have me, he would get our inheritance through you."

"Something like that," confirmed Isabel. "But I've no desire to marry anyone, ever again…"

"But you're still so young; you may find love, or at least a husband who'll treat you well."

Isabel took her sister's hands in hers. "I want to stay here; it's so… peaceful. You may have found love, Ade, but my path has never been the same as yours, has it? I am content to join the novices here."

Adeline was so stunned that she struggled to give voice to her thoughts and merely embraced her sister once again, wondering at the twisted irony of their fates. The disgraced heiress, bound for the nunnery, falls even further from grace while her sister, destined for marriage, chooses to serve God instead.

"I'm not certain when I'll see you again," murmured Adeline. "For all I know, I might be dead before the year's out…"

"Don't even think that; for God will look after you," whispered Isabel, "and I shall pray for you every day."

"Will you pray for Thomas too?" asked Adeline.

"Why wouldn't I?" replied Isabel, "He saved me from Thorold – and I have to believe that was God's work. I know that Thomas is a good man."

After bidding a tearful farewell to Isabel, Adeline joined her companions at the abbey gate. She ought to have felt optimistic that she had convinced the abbess to help them but, as she walked back to the castle, her mind dwelt only upon the knowledge that her sister was to remain in the nunnery forever. But it was more than that for, only when she confided her fears to Isabel, did she confront, for the first time, the possibility that she would live and die as the wife of a renegade lord.

42

Late afternoon on 16th August, 1138, south east of Brystole Castle

Before them stood the vast fortress city of Brystole and Thomas was mightily relieved to see it at last. A journey that should have taken one day, or two at most, had eaten up the best part of four. The distance from Schaftesberia might be small, but much had changed in the south-west since Thomas had left Brystole. Along their route, the raw scars of rebellion were visible in several places; which bore out what many of his own recruits had told him. Passing through Castle Cary had been a sobering experience… staring, solemn-faced, at the fire-scorched walls pock-marked by stones from the king's siege engines. In the coming weeks, Thomas reflected, Schaftesberia Castle might well meet the same fate as Castle Cary.

There were also, he noticed, more folk on the move than ever before: small family groups, very likely displaced by the troubles, but also bands of armed men. Just north of Castle Cary, they encountered one such company of a dozen or so horsemen, whose commander stopped the four riders to enquire who they were and whither they were bound.

Thomas, increasingly uncertain about whom he could trust, dared not identify himself as the son of England's most prominent traitor, so he offered a false name. His assertion that he served the Earl of Leicester and was heading to Brystole to join the siege was greeted with stony looks by his interrogators.

"You'll know who commands the siege then," remarked one of them.

Thomas, having no idea, was obliged to rely on a little vague bluster. Keep it simple and impossible to verify, he told himself.

"All I know," he had insisted, "is that we're ordered to join the men there to support the siege."

At that point he estimated that they were still at least fifteen miles south of Brystole – so, too far to cut and run. The uneasy standoff only ended when they were grudgingly permitted to continue on their way. At first, Thomas was greatly relieved, until he realised that a few of the riders were following them. Of course, the moment they reached Brystole, their subterfuge would be laid bare – along, no doubt, with their hides.

Though attempting to lose the troublesome men at arms trailing after them was sure to be seen as an admission of guilt, he could hardly wait until Brystole. Since it was late in the day, he decided to use the cloak of darkness to shake off their pursuers. By the time they set off again, long after dawn on the following day, it appeared they had been successful; but, in the course of their nocturnal detours, they had been obliged to abandon the Brystole road. Hence, Thomas had strayed into an area of forested slopes and valleys of which he had no knowledge at all.

In former times it would have been a simple matter to ask a local fellow the way but now, suspicion lurked in the countenance of every man he met. It was hard to blame those whose blackened fields still showed the devastation wrought during the king's punitive march from Castle Cary. With their villages torched and life-giving crops destroyed, such hapless communities would never recover from the consequences of his father's treason.

After wasting a further frustrating day trying to find their way north, they happened across Richmont Castle where the charred gateway told a familiar, and disheartening, story of another rebel stronghold subdued by the king. After Richmont they lost their way again attempting to cross yet another densely-forested valley. Thus, in desperation, Thomas struck out westwards along the valley floor and thence across a range of low hills until, after a further day's ride, they reached the coast. And now, having followed the shore until Thomas recognised where he was, they had arrived at Brystole.

Thomas could only stare blankly at the swathe of land to the south of the city, ravaged by the passing of King Stephen's army. Around now, there should have been a harvest but, whatever was ready to harvest was already cut and the rest was left to rot in the fields. With the land so barren, he feared how the great city would fare in the coming winter; though they might at least be supplied along the river. Every so often the breeze swirled around from the east carrying a smoky stench from the besiegers' camp.

Tancred and Eadwulf, young in years like Thomas, were bewildered not only by the extent of the devastation but also by the sheer size of the city and its castle.

"It goes on for miles," said the awestruck Tancred. "And look at that stone keep! I've never seen one that tall."

"And there's a moat all the way round," gasped Eadwulf.

"Aye, that's why the king can't take the place," said Thomas. "So, starving it out is all he can try to do. But it won't work because my father knew this was coming and the castle will be well provisioned. I reckon the king must withdraw come winter."

"Aye, but we can't wait till then," remarked Edgar. "And you lads better get used to the sight of land laid waste, 'cos the longer this rebellion goes on, the more of it there'll be."

Studying the city from the far side of the broad southern meadows, Thomas observed that there were royal companies posted outside the walls all around the city. Near the gates especially, even more men patrolled - perhaps to deter the restless occupants from venturing out. Of course, his half-brother William, though young, was not foolish enough to make pointless forays out of the city.

Eadwulf gave a grim shake of the head. "Perhaps Enric was right, lord, for I can't see how we can get in, because, well, it's… surrounded."

"Oh, we'll get in alright," Thomas assured him. "It's getting out again that might be more of a problem…"

"We could take a boat down the river to the port, lord," suggested Edgar.

Edgar's proposal was exactly what Thomas had originally planned to do; especially since that was how, months before, he had been spirited out of the city. However, now that he had observed the besieging forces more closely, he changed his mind.

"I'd rather not abandon the horses," he told them, "and I reckon we might just ride in through the nether gate."

"But… it's surrounded," repeated Eadwulf.

"Aye, it is," agreed Thomas, "but it's the nearest gate to us. Look at those idle fools; they're not expecting any trouble, are they? See, most aren't even wearing any mail. And, don't you think it might hearten the garrison if we go in with a bit of a show?"

"It'll be a show right enough if they hack us to pieces under the walls," grumbled Edgar. "I doubt your uncle would approve."

"Aye, but my uncle's not here," said Thomas.

"Maybe not, but he'd want me to tell you all the same," replied Edgar. "And we can't just ride down there, for it'd take only one crossbowman or archer to ruin your grand entrance, lord."

"Indeed, Edgar; which is why we'll need to create a little trouble somewhere else first."

"You think their commanders will fall for some ruse?" scoffed Edgar. "There's only four of us."

"We'll make for the Nether Gate," explained Thomas, "because the bridge is still intact. Now, do you see those three wagons on the hill south of the gate - all three of them are going to take a little journey down the hill towards the river Frome."

"I don't see how," said Edgar, "they look well-sited to me."

"I imagine they are now," replied Thomas, "but they won't be once you three remove the blocks holding them and give them a hefty push."

"What, with everyone watching us?" cried Edgar.

"Trust me, Edgar, no-one will be watching you," said Thomas. "They'll all be watching me on the road - until the wagons are on the move, when you'll shout to them for help. Once they are distracted, you'll run down to join me."

"Run?" queried Edgar.

"Aye, because I'll have all the horses with me," explained Thomas. "If they see you running towards them on foot, they'll assume you're their own comrades who've panicked. But, if the three of you were mounted, you'd be seen at once as a threat. Do you see?"

"It sounds like a big gamble to me," remarked Eadwulf.

"It'll be a quick way in," Thomas assured them. "And I suspect our arrival will draw more than a few watchers."

"Enric would most definitely not like this," said Edgar.

"No, he wouldn't," agreed Thomas, "but he'd carry out such a plan better than most."

"When do you want to do this?" enquired a resigned Edgar.

After a hurried glance at the western sky, Thomas replied: "About now, I should think. It's around dusk so you'd best get walking… and don't walk together… and try not to attract any attention before you reach the wagons."

"What do we do if we're challenged?" asked Tancred.

"Lie," said Thomas, with a grin. "Say you serve the Earl of Leicester."

"Aye," groaned Edgar, "'cos that worked so well last time."

For a time, Thomas watched the three men at arms go their separate ways and set off down the slope towards the castle. Then, after giving them what he hoped was enough time to make their way across the meadow, he mounted his horse and led out the other three beasts towards the road into the city. He dared not get too close before his companions were in place; so, when he joined the road, he took his horses along at a slow, dawdling walk.

From the road, he could not see his comrades but a glimpse of Edgar behind one of the wagons suggested that the younger pair were very likely in position as well. Continuing at a walk, he approached the bar across the road to Brystole, praying that his comrades were already busy working to release the wagons. Already, he was attracting some interest from the soldiers encamped nearby and soon he would be too close to flee. What in God's name were his comrades doing because the three wagons that should have been hurtling down the hill by now, were showing not the slightest tremor of movement.

"Halt!" cried one of the guards posted at the bar; but, Thomas, though he smiled and nodded politely, said nothing and simply carried on along the road until he pulled up at the bar itself.

"Come on, fellows," he complained, "I've had a long and tiring day, so just raise the barrier, eh?"

"What's your business?" asked the guard.

"My business?" groaned Thomas. "What do you think it is? I've brought up these spare mounts. Now let me pass so that I can get some hot food inside me."

"You'll be lucky," grinned the guard, lifting the bar. "Ain't seen hot food for days."

With another theatrical groan, Thomas waved his thanks and led the mounts on towards the castle.

"Don't get too close to the walls," warned another soldier. "They like to loose the odd arrow…"

"You need have no fear on that account," replied Thomas, who was beginning to think that the damned wagons must be staked to the ground. Then, at last, there was a shout from the mound, then another – Edgar's deep voice, he reckoned. Within a few moments, many of those guarding the roadway set off towards the wagons which were gaining ever more momentum as they descended the slope. With men running in all directions, Thomas simply continued along the road to meet his three comrades hurrying down to join him.

"You took your time," he complained. "Better mount fast because they'll not be confused for long."

His companions needed no encouragement and soon, the four riders were cantering towards the Nether Gate, urging their mounts on at the best pace they could. They had covered half the distance when an arrow from the castle battlements flew past Edgar's shoulder.

"Lord, they don't seem to know we're their allies," wailed Tancred.

Thomas bellowed up to the rampart: "I'm the earl's son, Thomas FitzRobert!"

The only response was a crossbow bolt which struck the ground just in front of Eadwulf's speeding horse.

"They can't hear you!" yelled Eadwulf, swerving to change his course.

Thomas tried once more for they were hardly more than a score of yards from the gate and sooner or later a missile would strike home. "It's Thomas!" he bellowed at the top of his voice. "William's brother, Thomas! Open the damned gate!"

To his relief, a sharp command echoed down from the battlements and no more arrows were loosed. The gate, however, remained firmly closed for the commander was clearly taking no chances. Thomas did not blame him for, in such unusual circumstances, it was right to be cautious. Sadly, all the shouting had captured the attention of some of the king's soldiers on the slope behind them. A swift glance told Thomas that the escaping wagons had been brought under control and when the next arrow flew, it came from the king's men.

Having come to a halt outside the Nether Gate, they were effectively trapped so Thomas shouted once more.

"Open the damned gate!" he roared, as an arrow thudded into the timber.

"Who are you?" a knight shouted back down to him.

"The earl's son, Thomas FitzRobert!" he snarled. "Open the gate before we're skewered to it!"

There was a pause during which several arrows narrowly missed the four men and one grazed the rump of Edgar's mount. More in shock than pain, the beast reared up and Edgar, not the most accomplished of horsemen, was thrown off. Perhaps it helped to convince the rampart commander, however, for, finally, Thomas heard the sound of the gates being opened. Even as they hurried inside, more arrows flew, with Edgar hauling his frightened horse in after the others.

Once they were safely inside with the gates firmly shut behind them, they dismounted to be greeted by the knight from the battlement. Clearly, he recognised Gloucester's bastard son, though Thomas could not recall the fellow's name. Thomas, still overcome with relief, nodded his thanks and asked: "Where's my brother, William?"

"At the keep," replied the knight.

Though his expression betrayed little of his thoughts, Thomas could imagine what was running through the knight's mind. The last time he had seen Thomas, would have been just after the killing of William de Burgh – and he would not be the only member of Brystole's garrison to regard the young man with thinly veiled hostility. But Thomas resolved to steel himself to anticipate and ignore such resentment. It was vital to his success at Brystole to prove to all that he was not the same callow drunkard from that fateful day in May.

"We've had a long journey," he said, "so, if you can find my comrades some food and a place to sleep, I'd be most grateful. I can find my own way to the keep."

The news of his dramatic arrival at the Nether Gate must have sped across the castle because his brother, William met him at the bottom of the long, steep flight of steps leading up to the keep.

"Brother," William cried aloud, embracing Thomas warmly; though as he did so, he hissed: "Why have you come back?"

Thomas grinned at his younger brother, appraising the youth. "You look older," he told him.

"Aye," agreed William, "I've had to grow up a lot over these past months, Fitz."

"They've wrought a great change in me too, Will," replied Thomas.

As they mounted the steps, William said: "I rather thought you'd be in Normandy long ago."

"And I would have been, but for a lass I met along the way…" confessed Thomas, unable to stop smiling when he thought of her.

William pulled a face. "Another girl, Fitz?"

"Aye, but this one's different – and I know that's what I always say; but she must be, for I've married her. But she's not the reason I'm here."

REBEL SWORD

"Marriage?" gasped his brother. "It's one surprise after another, Fitz. Come on then, tell me all while we find you some food."

That evening the pair spent several hours together while Thomas related all that had happened since his escape; and how it was that he had seized control of Schaftesberia Castle.

"I didn't even know there was a castle there," remarked William.

"There wasn't till this year," said Thomas. "Sir Roger of Schaftesberia has only just finished building it."

"So, I'm guessing that he wasn't well-pleased when you turned him out of it," laughed William, "and took his intended bride for good measure."

"Aye, some rough blows were exchanged and a good deal of blood was spilled," admitted Thomas.

"But where in God's name did you find so many men willing to serve you?" enquired William.

"Some, we recruited," explained Thomas. "Some we freed at the castle and others joined us from Castle Cary."

"Castle Cary?" said William sharply. "But why would they leave Ralph Lovell?"

"You didn't know?" said Thomas. "Lovell's castle was taken and the garrison fled - as at Richmont. We passed both on our way here."

"We'd heard the news of Richmont falling, but not Castle Cary," murmured William. "By God, that's a blow, Fitz. Our cause now rests only on a handful of forts along the Welsh Marches and upon Schrosberie – which still holds firm with a garrison of over a hundred."

"Aye, but I imagine that's not what our father hoped for," murmured Thomas.

"No, and there's still no news of his return," grumbled William bitterly.

"I can tell you that news," said Thomas.

"Has he landed then?" asked William.

"No. And he won't be coming now till next spring."

"Spring!" cried William. "But our cause already hangs upon a thread…"

When Thomas related what little he had heard from their father's messenger, William gave a sigh of resignation. "Then we are lost, Fitz…"

"No," argued Thomas, "by no means. Brystole cannot easily be taken and, if Schrosberie holds firm and I can last the winter at Schaftesberia, father will have at least three strongholds when he does arrive."

"If he were actually here, I believe the men of the south-west would flock to him in great numbers," said William. "But his absence hurts us badly. Schrosberie is already under siege – as, no doubt, you will soon be at Schaftesberia. And, from what you've told me, Fitz, I don't see how you can hold on to what you've taken."

"Aye, and that's the very reason I've come," said Thomas. "I need more trained men at arms; my men, though willing fighters, lack the skills to defend a siege. I also need crossbows and more arrows – indeed, a fletcher would help us greatly."

"So, you've only come here to take my men and arms," scoffed William.

"Without them, you're right: I can't hold Schaftesberia."

"But you're so isolated there, Fitz, that I'm not sure a few more men will make much difference. The king could bring hundreds against you; so, I'd be throwing away the lives of my men in a near hopeless cause. Why don't you stay here and help in the defence of Brystole?"

"Because I've given my word to the folk at Schaftesberia," declared Thomas.

"Then bring them here – with your new lady, of course."

"What? Bring those men with their women and children fifty miles to Brystole? I can't do that, Will."

"But, if your castle falls with those families inside, their fate will be even worse," William told him bluntly.

"Well, I have plans in place if that happens," claimed Thomas, though he was not at all sure that he did. "In any case, Will, how in God's name would I get them in here? And do you really want another fifty mouths to feed?"

William's long silence conceded the point.

"No, I thought not," murmured Thomas. "So, my only hope is to hold Schaftesberia until father comes."

"Till the spring, Fitz?" said William doubtfully.

"Aye, with the help of some of your men…"

"No, it's too great a risk," said William. "And I could make better use of them here."

"What, sitting on their arses doing nothing all day?" argued Thomas. "Here they're worth very little. I'm holding a castle with over two score of fighting men. If we're not to suffer the same fate as Richmont and Castle Cary, I need more trained men at arms."

"And how many do you think will be willing to follow you back to Schaftesberia, Fitz? The memory of what you did only a few months ago lives on here."

"Aye, well you better not tell them that since the death of William, I've killed his brother, Roland and his friend, Thorold le Breton."

"Truly? You've killed both Roland and Thorold?" cried William. "Well, that certainly won't make you any more popular with some of the folk here; though it might convince a few that you're no longer a weak-willed drunk."

"You could at least ask for volunteers," entreated Thomas.

"Volunteers," his brother's tone was dismissive. "If you got any, they'd be the worst sort of men, Fitz: cowards, thieves or men driven only by a thirst for fighting."

"Fair enough," agreed Thomas, "they'd have much in common with the rest of my company."

43

Just after dawn on 17th August at Schaftesberia Castle

Enric stalked the tower rampart, fuming a little more with every vexed step. Why couldn't the damned girl just stay in her chamber and leave the running of the castle to him? Suddenly, she wanted to be the 'lady' of the castle. Well, as far as he was concerned, she could call herself whatever she pleased, as long as she kept quiet and did as she was told. Her visit to the abbey was just the sort of foolishness he'd sought to avoid; God knew how much harm she'd done there.

This morning he must have it out with her; else there'd be no castle left by the time his nephew returned – assuming he ever did return. At once, he cast aside that dread thought; all he could do was hold the castle and pray.

It was Adeline's custom to rise early and join him on the rampart – a practice with which neither was especially comfortable. But at least today it would give him the opportunity to settle matters between them. Except, this morning the young lady had yet to emerge which, in itself, unsettled him a little. Why had she changed the pattern of her day? Was she scheming behind his back to flout his authority yet again?

If she had been a man, he could simply have stormed into her chamber to confront her; but he could hardly do that, so he would just have to wait – damn the girl. Patience was usually one of his strengths but, in this case, the longer he was obliged to wait, the more his resentment grew. When he could bear it no more, he took a purposeful step towards the door which led down from the rampart. And, naturally, that was the very moment she deigned to appear – but not alone. He groaned at the sight of Edith, for now he would have to reason with two empty-headed lasses.

"God give you good morning, Master Enric," Adeline greeted him brightly.

Enric, determined not to be distracted by her cheerful demeanour, replied: "Just now, *lady,* God's a little sparing with good mornings."

Adeline, offering a sympathetic smile, lamented: "Oh dear, something's made you grumpier than usual this morning, Master Enric."

"Aye, you."

"I see," said Adeline. "Well then, perhaps we need to talk."

"Upon that at least we're agreed," replied Enric. "So let's-"

"While a lord is away," interrupted Adeline, "his lady holds his castle, does she not?"

"Sometimes," blurted out Enric, confounded by her directness.

"And that's me, Thomas's lady."

"Aye, but-"

"You don't deny that I am his lady," said Adeline.

"No, he's made that clear enough," agreed Enric, "but you can't command a garrison."

"Why not?"

"Well because, you're not… a man."

"Clearly, but what of it?"

Enric, noting the smirk upon Edith's face, suggested: "Perhaps young Edith should leave us."

"No, Edith serves me," said Adeline bluntly, "so, she stays."

Again, taken aback by her obdurate manner, he struggled to marshal his thoughts.

Perhaps Adeline noticed his confusion for she said: "I believe you were pointing out that I'm not a man."

"Aye, indeed," said Enric. "I've nothing against you, lady, but the men just won't accept you."

"Well, I believe they will," insisted Adeline.

"No, they see you as a…"

"Whore?" suggested Adeline coldly.

"I've never said that, lady," declared Enric. "God's nails, I never have – and never would."

"You don't have to, Master Enric; you just have to keep ignoring me and everyone else will follow your lead."

"But you've no experience, lady," argued Enric, attempting to retrieve the initiative. "You simply don't know what to do, or say."

"How do you know that when you don't talk to me?" she enquired.

"It's just… plain to see," explained Enric. "Like yesterday, when you went to see the abbess."

"I only did so because you'd done nothing since Thomas left," complained Adeline.

"Such delicate negotiations can't be rushed, lady. I'll have to go there now and try to mend matters."

"I assure you that there's nothing needs mending," retorted Adeline.

With every argument she made, Enric's frustration grew and, the louder their voices sounded, the more desperate he became because surely everyone in the castle must be able to hear their dispute.

"I shall command and you will advise me, Master Enric," she declared, "as our lord decreed."

"But you don't know what you're doing," he railed at her.

Their escalating, and very public argument, was brought to an abrupt end by a loud cheer from down in the courtyard which prompted the two antagonists to peer down from the rampart to the gate. Enric could only stare, open-mouthed, as two heavily-laden ox carts trundled in through the gateway.

When he faced Adeline again, there was a broad smile upon her face.

"I think my discussion with the abbess must have borne fruit," she told him, "don't you?"

Enric, who felt as if he had just been cut off at the ankles, was utterly lost for words. Though he had never doubted Adeline's commitment to Thomas, he was forced now to consider that she might not be the empty vessel that he perceived her to be.

"The men respect you and nothing will change that," said Adeline. "But you and I must work together if we are to help and protect those who, like us, have committed themselves to our lord."

Strangely moved by her conciliatory tone, Enric could only nod in agreement for, in that moment, he had glimpsed a little of the strength Thomas must have seen in her.

"Are we agreed then," she asked, "that, until Thomas returns, I shall command, aided by your counsel.

"Aye, lady, as you wish," he agreed.

"Then, I believe your presence is required down in the yard," she said.

At once he bridled at being ordered about, until she smiled and added: "Someone accompanied the wagons and, I suspect that she is waiting to see you."

Darting a glance back down to the yard, he suddenly picked out Avice staring up at him and, muttering his apologies to Adeline, he hurried from the rampart.

The descent to the hall gave him a few moments at least to compose himself. Why was Avice here? Perhaps the abbess had asked her to accompany the wagons; but, if that was all, she had no need to exchange any words with him at all. God's nails, why had he not been to see her – if only as a friend? Except they weren't friends. Once they had been much more than friends, but now they were much less than friends. They were just strangers with a shared past.

Despite the time he had to prepare, his first words shot out like a flutter of startled pigeons.

"Avice… God's nails, why have you come here? No, I should say God give you good morning…Avice… It's been… I've not seen you for…"

His sentence came to a faltering halt as he struggled to recall how long it had been. Just the sight of her, however, persuaded him that it had been too long.

Slowly, it dawned upon him that she was replying to him and he had not taken in a word.

"I'm sorry," he mumbled, "I wasn't listening…"

Definitely the wrong response, he thought, for the deepest of frowns cast a shadow across her face.

"Of course," she said, sounding almost as flustered as he was. "You've many important matters to…attend to. I shouldn't have come. I'm sorry."

Unbidden, his hand reached out to grasp hers, as he murmured: "I'm glad you've come. So very glad."

"You are?" she said, bright eyes staring back at him.

"Aye," he breathed, "for it's been so long since Antioch…"

"We've already talked about that, Enric; and buried it," she told him.

"What if I don't want it buried?" he whispered.

Though she smiled, there was a tear in her eye and he feared that he was reopening an old wound.

"Our time has passed, Enric; there's no place in your life for me or my life for you," she said. "I have a place at the abbey and when I'm there, I know who I am and what I'm doing. But you… you're stranded on some great precipice, where there's no way down without falling… so, I've come to say: 'God be with you.'"

"Wagons are unloaded, Mistress Avice," announced one of the abbey's waggoners.

"A moment longer," she snapped at him and abruptly wrapped her arms around Enric.

"Seeing you again that first time at the abbey was a shock," she whispered. "But at least we've had the chance to talk about what happened in those old times. Rest assured that I'll always think of you fondly."

"I'm not dead yet," grumbled Enric, "nor do I intend to be anytime soon… if God's merciful."

"God is God, Enric," she murmured, "and He wasn't merciful in Antioch…"

When she strode away to climb up on the wagon, Enric felt bereft; and watching the cart rumble out of the castle gate seemed almost as painful as losing her that first time in the Holy Land. Perhaps she was right about God; for it appeared that He was minded to bring them together only to tear them asunder once again.

44

19th August 1138 at Brystole Castle

After three long days of promises and coercion, Thomas finally managed to persuade fourteen men at arms to accompany him out of Brystole. Getting them safely out of the city, however, was likely to prove more of a challenge than recruiting them in the first place.

"If you ride out the way you came in, Thomas, you'll soon be pursued and hunted down," advised William. "You know that; though you might not like to hear it. The only way out is by boat at night."

"I can't leave our horses," protested Thomas. "I risked all our lives to bring them in here. If anything, I need more mounts."

"I trust you don't expect any from me," said William. "Let's say your four are in exchange for all the men and arms I'm giving you. And, believe me, the river is your only way out – and even that will be dangerous."

Reluctantly, Thomas was obliged to accept defeat over the horses, though it would make the return to Schaftesberia much longer and even more arduous. Nonetheless, when he addressed his new men, he radiated confidence, knowing that if he didn't show belief then they were hardly likely to either. His recruits were, as his half-brother warned him, an unlikely collection of men.

Before they left, Thomas required all of them to swear an oath of fealty to him; though, of course, he had yet to learn whether any of their oaths could be trusted. At least two men were only there because it was a condition of their release from the castle gaol. Several others, Thomas suspected, might well turn their weapons upon him, if he showed the slightest hint of weakness. He was grateful to have at least three companions watching his back; for he might need them until he had the measure of the Brystole men.

In the small hours of the following day, three boats carrying the men, their weapons and enough provisions for the journey, set out along the river Avon towards the southern meadows. When Thomas set foot in the leading boat, he could not help but recall the last time he had made the same journey – in disgrace. All in all, he reckoned his situation had not changed much for the better and, if he was honest, only his love for Adeline gave him any cause for hope.

Just before dawn they were passing the curved wall of a building on the south bank enmeshed by wooden scaffold poles.

One of the men spat into the water and muttered: "Damned Templars…"

Thomas gave a taut smile, remembering that, when his father granted the land for the Knights Templar to build a church, the decision had not been universally popular. After the church, there was only the meadow land which bordered the river and Thomas could only pray that there were no royal sentries posted this far south. Any fears he might have harboured proved groundless, for they made landfall on the north bank without any alarms. The only sound was the swish of the wind through the tall meadow grass, still to be cut.

Without even the luxury of a pack horse, each man bore a heavy load of stores and weapons. The two crossbows, which he had insisted upon, proved to be the least popular item to carry. Low mutterings of complaint began shortly after they set off and seemed destined to continue throughout the day. Though they had started very early, Thomas was under no illusion that the journey to Schaftesberia would take them the best part of three days – assuming they encountered no trouble.

William had learned that the king's forces were occupied elsewhere and Thomas hoped that his information was accurate. As each passing day seemed to stretch out forever, his thoughts always strayed towards Adeline and the fear in his gut that he would arrive too late to protect her from the storm which was certain to come. The king might be preoccupied for the moment with Schrosberie, but soon he would surely turn his attention to Schaftesberia.

Yet, despite his constant worrying, they made good progress for the first two days and he was pleasantly surprised that his new recruits managed to maintain a brisk walking pace. When, on the third day, they drew ever closer to Schaftesberia, Thomas abandoned the road and put his faith in Edgar's local knowledge to guide them.

The forester led them through one of his previous haunts, the dense forest of Gyllengeham.

"The old king used to hunt here," he remarked. "And they say it wasn't just deer he had an eye for…"

"Aye, but I suppose it's just as well for me…" grinned Thomas, "since my father was one of his bastards." Then, anxious to banish any thoughts of the late King Henry's pursuit of the ladies of Gyllengeham, he added: "How far now?"

"A bit less than last time you asked," replied Edgar. "Five miles or so…"

That evening they camped in a small forest clearing, keeping well away from the nearby settlement of Gyllengeham, lest word of their imminent arrival should reach the ears of Sir Roger. This was the most dangerous stretch of their journey for, so close to their destination, the possibility of encountering a royal force was that much greater. Outlaws too were a constant threat though they were unlikely to take on a dozen or more heavily-armed men. Nonetheless, in an effort to remind his men that they were entering a hazardous area, Thomas doubled the watch that night.

Taking the first watch with three others, Thomas was relieved that, on his frequent circuits of the camp perimeter, he found no trace of outlaws – or indeed anyone else. When Edgar relieved him, he hoped to get some rest but, of course, it didn't happen. Despite the stillness of the night, his mind remained in turmoil because, in only a few hours' time, he would be with Adeline again. Yet their reunion would be bittersweet for it would herald the moment when their mortal struggle would begin in earnest.

As always, it was the lonely hours of the night when the doubts crept in. Even with the additional men he was bringing, it would be hard just to survive the storm of Sir Roger's wrath. The truth was that he had already been away far too long; so long that, for all he knew, the castle was already under siege. God's breath, what if it was already taken? It was such grim fears that dogged his waking moments, while listening with one ear for any jarring sound in the forest darkness which might warn of trouble.

He had just managed to drift off to sleep when Hawk, one of the new men on the second watch, shook him awake.

"What is it?" groaned Thomas.

"One of our lads seems to have gone missing," Hawk reported.

"Missing," said Thomas. "How can he be missing? He's been standing within a few yards of the camp."

"Well, lord, he told me he heard something and went to take a look," declared Hawk.

"Did you hear anything?"

"No, lord," confirmed Hawk.

"And the other sentries haven't noticed anything amiss?"

"No, lord. I think he's just… gone."

"Deserted, you mean?"

"Well, I suppose..."

"How long ago?"

"A while, I suppose..." muttered Hawk.

"Well, who is it?" asked Thomas wearily.

"Renold," replied Hawk. "Shall I rouse the camp?"

"No," grumbled Thomas. "Show me where he went and the pair of us will see if we can find him."

"Very well, lord," agreed Hawk.

Though Thomas was unwilling to wake the whole company on what might be a false alarm, Edgar had woken to take third watch and saw Thomas leaving the camp.

"Trouble, lord?" he enquired.

"Likely not," replied Thomas, "but we may have a deserter, Renold. I'll take a look with Hawk while you keep watch in the camp."

"Renold," Edgar murmured, thoughtfully, "wasn't he one of the pair released from the castle gaol?"

"Aye."

"Then perhaps we should wake everyone," suggested Edgar.

"No, let the poor beggars snatch a few more hours' sleep while they can," replied Thomas. "If this fellow's gone, he'll be a long way off by now. It's likely a fool's errand."

Edgar gave a shrug which suggested that he was not happy to leave the matter there; but Thomas murmured: "I know what I'm doing, Edgar."

Only when he left the clearing did Thomas fully appreciate how dark the tightly-packed forest was without the aid of moonlight. Perhaps Edgar was right to be concerned because, as they both knew, the other prisoner released into his custody was Hawk.

"That's where he went, lord," said Hawk, indicating a narrow track through the wall of trees. "Perhaps he was killed by outlaws."

"We'd have heard," said Thomas. "Come on, we'll go deeper into the forest."

"What, just the two of us?" said Hawk.

"I'll lead," said Thomas. "Just keep quiet and follow close."

Staying on the winding track in the dark was easier said than done for, in places, they had to push their way through bramble and thorn. After fifty yards of slow progress, their hands and faces were badly lacerated; though at least Thomas knew, from the occasional yelps and curses, that Hawk was following him. Just as Thomas was close to abandoning the search, however, the path opened out into a tiny clearing, in which a grey figure awaited him.

"Renold?" he enquired warily. "Is that you?"

"Aye," acknowledged Renold.

"What in God's name are you doing out here?"

"I'm waiting," murmured the man at arms. "Waiting for you…"

As Thomas's eyes adjusted to the gloom, he realised that Renold's sword was out. It was hardly a shock, since he had wondered all along whether he could trust a felon; yet, it was still a disappointment. William had warned him against taking the two prisoners from the castle gaol – as had Edgar. Yet, how could he reject them when, for all he knew, half the outlaws already defending Schaftesberia had committed even worse crimes? Nonetheless, it appeared that he had been wrong to trust these two for there was no doubting the menace in Renold's stance.

Ah well, he thought, the world was full of pissmaggots like these two and it wouldn't be the last time he misjudged a man. Though, with Master Hawk lurking behind him, perhaps it might be...

45

20th August, late afternoon at Schaftesberia Castle

Despite what she had achieved in partnership with the abbess, Adeline yearned only for her husband's safe return. Three or four days, he had promised, yet he'd now been gone a week and with each additional day, she could feel her belief ebbing away a little more. A nagging voice in her head insisted that he was already dead and that she was ever more likely to follow him. Even in the stoic Enric she sensed a similar concern; but, in truth, he did not seem the same man after his parting from Avice. Adeline did not need to hear their exchange to see two people whose vain hope of love had been dashed to oblivion.

That day more wagons had arrived carrying newly-milled grain and more precious barrels of water. It should have been a cause for much rejoicing, yet no-one in the castle seemed to celebrate it and their mood remained sombre. Like Adeline, many feared their enemies would arrive before their lord returned with reinforcements. And then there were some who believed they would never see Thomas FitzRobert alive again.

When one of Enric's daily scouts arrived to report the approach of soldiers, Adeline dared to hope that it might be her husband returning at the head of a small army. But that hope was dashed by her first glimpse of the advancing column, for she knew Sir Roger's banners well enough. Somehow, the appearance at last of a genuine threat seemed, for no reason she could understand, to rejuvenate Enric. In moments, he was flinging out orders in all directions: gates to be closed and ramparts to be manned. Adeline might have claimed nominal authority over the castle, but she knew when to leave matters to Enric. Hurrying up to the tower rampart, she joined him there to peer down the steep slope to the north-west.

"Do you think it's just Sir Roger," she asked him, "or could it be the king too?"

"No royal banners there," replied Enric, "nor even those of the Earl of Leicester. I see only the arms of Sir Roger; though, since he has few men left, most of these arsewipes must have been supplied by the earl."

"Does he have enough 'arsewipes' to take the castle?" she enquired, aware of the tremor in her voice.

"Perhaps not, but he can lay siege to it," replied Enric.

"Then we must be ready," murmured Adeline.

"We are ready, lady," Enric assured her. "At least we're as ready as we can be with Thomas and several of our best men lost."

"Enric!" she chided. "They're not 'lost'; they will be back."

But, despite her brave words she, like Enric, was not sure that they would.

Looking her in the eye, he said: "Now's the time to be honest with each other, lady; it's been too long. Brystole should be a day and half ride at most…"

"You believe he's dead then?" she asked.

"Perhaps not dead, but very likely taken. Either way, I think we're on our own now."

"Then I should address the company," she told him. "Be plain with them."

"Is that wise, my lady?"

She wasn't sure that it was, but she did know that if she didn't do it at once, she would lose what little nerve she still possessed.

he "I can do it well enough from up here," she told Enric and strode swiftly across to the rampart overlooking the yard. To her surprise, he didn't try to stop her; instead, he followed to stand by her side as she stared down at the busy courtyard.

"Deep breath, lady," he murmured.

Trembling all over. she was never more grateful for his support than at that moment. So she followed his advice and then shouted down to the folk below: "Hear me, friends!"

Some were at the ramparts, while others were at work in the courtyard or elsewhere; but all looked up in surprise when her voice rang out. Even she was surprised how loud and clear it sounded. The sight of all their expectant faces, however, utterly swept away her confidence and, whatever she intended to say simply vanished from her head.

As the silence lengthened, Enric stepped closer and, with a sinking feeling, she assumed he was going to take control, until he said: "Just speak from the heart, lady; that's all you have to do."

And, from somewhere deep inside, she found the strength to speak.

"Hear me, loyal friends of Thomas FitzRobert. Those who have come to lay siege to this castle would bend me – and you - to their will. Our lord, Thomas, has not yet returned; so, until he does, it falls to us to defend this place. But, don't defend it for him, nor for me. This is our last sanctuary, so we must defend it for us all."

Her rousing declaration was greeted not by the acclamation for which she had hoped, but by a low murmur of concern.

"Who are you to tell us what to do?" bellowed a raucous voice from the yard.

In the face of such stark dissent, Adeline hesitated; for who indeed was she?

"Go on, lass," hissed Enric. "God's nails! You can't piss it away now."

Sweat trickled down her face and her mouth felt dry as dust but, as Enric had so eloquently put it, she couldn't stop now. So, after another deep breath, she answered the challenge.

"You all know who I am: I am Thomas FitzRobert's lady," she cried. "I am no warrior, but I will fight for this sanctuary. I will stand with you all; aye, and if God demands it, I will bleed to defend this place. For where else can I go? Where else can any of us go now? Our lives have taken root here in this castle and I, for one, will die before I'll surrender it!"

"Well said," said Enric.

But to Adeline, the crushing silence that followed the dying echoes of her plea seemed to last forever until a single voice rang out, from a woman somewhere in the yard, who called out: 'Well said, lady!"

After a moment, further endorsements sounded which so filled her heart with pride, that she raised an arm aloft and screamed: "Prepare to fight!"

A great cheer rose up and when, after a while, it died down, Enric bellowed: "Men, to your posts; women and children to the hall!"

"So, now what do we do?" murmured Adeline.

"We do what we've been doing since Thomas left," replied Enric. "We wait."

"But shouldn't we do something?"

"Waiting *is* doing something, lady," said Enric. "All our preparations are made; so, I shall wait where the men can see me - calm and assured. Perhaps you could wait down in the hall and take charge of our provisions. Over the days, perhaps weeks, rationing our supplies will decide our fate as much as blades and blood…"

"I shall do my best, Master Enric," she said.

When she descended to the hall with Edith following in her wake, Adeline was shocked by the confusion she discovered there. Poor Wilflaed was attempting to bring some order but the healer darted her a look of despair, for it seemed that every woman there had her own idea of what they should do and how they should do it.

Pausing at the foot of the stairs, Adeline was tempted to cry out for peace; but something stopped her, some intuition she didn't fully comprehend. After a few moments, several women noticed her standing there and, as more saw her, the raucous rattle of argument began to subside. Adeline was not foolish enough to imagine that she had somehow won them all over with her fine words, but she could see that they were at least curious to know what she was going to do next.

Knowing that the respectful silence was likely to be short-lived, she seized the opportunity with both hands.

"Friends," she began, keeping her voice soft and low. "We always knew this siege was coming, didn't we? But we're well provisioned now and together we shall endure. Still, there is work to be done. Some of you can help Wilflaed make ready tables to bear the wounded; others can be making and rolling bandages. Mothers, watch each other's children so that some can help."

Before anyone moved, she took a deep breath and continued: "We shall also need to make our provisions and water last as long as we can."

That provoked a groan from some and one woman demanded: "And who decides how much we can eat and drink?"

"I do," replied Adeline at once, recognising the woman as one who always had much to say but who also worked harder than most.

"You'll be alright then, won't you?" retorted the woman.

Adeline left the stair and passed through the crowd until she stood only a yard from the woman.

"It's Margaret, isn't it?" she said, feeling all eyes upon her. "Well Margaret, Edith and our cook, Selima, will help me take charge of the provisions and they shall give me no more than anyone else here. Now, shall we go about our work?"

Though Margaret nodded, no-one moved until, mercifully, Wilflaed called out: "Who will help me with the table boards?"

To Adeline's immense relief, several women shuffled forward to do so and others followed their lead. Margaret, she noted, was among the first to help. So far so good, thought Adeline but now for the difficult part. She was dreading dealing with Selima for, somehow, it was always a struggle to talk to the girl. Where Edith was gentle and compliant, Selima seemed forever cool and distrustful. Thomas had instructed her to serve Adeline by taking responsibility for the food but, every conversation the two women had, seemed to end in a dispute.

She had no need to search for Selima, however, because the latter was even now wading through the throng towards her wearing a thunderous frown.

"I look after the food," she declared, daring Adeline to challenge her. "Our lord told me so; and I need no help from others. They'll only try to steal everything - unless it's me you don't trust, lady?"

"Of course, I trust you," Adeline assured her, "and I shall need you to advise me on our food supplies but the responsibility is mine – and only mine."

"But-"

Cutting across the next protest, Adeline said: "You are our trusted servant, but now you will need others I trust to help you. So, together you, Edith and I shall decide upon daily food and water rations. Above all, it must be seen to be fairly done."

A grudging nod from Selima was probably the best outcome Adeline was going to get and she was almost relieved when Enric entered the hall and guided her out through the great door into the yard.

"What is it?" she asked.

"Sir Roger is approaching the gate, lady," Enric told her. "It seems he wants to parley."

"Well, I don't want to talk to him," declared Adeline.

"*Well*, you wanted to be the lady," Enric pointed out. "And I doubt he'll speak to me."

"Since I rejected his proposal, I'm no more than a whore to him," said Adeline. "He despises me…"

"All the better," said Enric, with a dark gleam in his eye. "Let's raise you up then; we'll prepare a dais for you to receive him."

"Receive him?" mumbled Adeline.

"Aye, he clearly wants to talk – which suits me - and since, in the absence of Thomas, you're the lady of this castle, it has to be you," explained Enric. "Believe me, lady, the knight won't enjoy this at all."

"But I can't… see him like this," she protested, "dressed in rags."

"You're right about that," he agreed, before darting back into the hall to reappear moments later with Wilflaed and Edith.

"Don't just stand there," he ordered, "make her look more… like a lady…"

Quickly, Edith ensured that Adeline's long, lush braids of hair were displayed to best advantage and arranged the pale linen covering over most of her head. Wilflaed borrowed a long woollen shawl which she draped over Adeline's shoulders to cover her threadbare tunic.

After a few moments, they both stepped back to admire their work but Adeline was not encouraged by their glum faces.

"Well, lady," said Wilflaed, "I think that's all we can do."

"I must still look terrible," muttered Adeline.

"You could never look anything but wonderful, my lady," cried Edith, with tears in her eyes.

"Act like a lady and you'll appear to be one," advised Wilflaed.

"He's almost at the gate," announced Enric. "Are you ready, lady?"

Though Adeline knew she would never truly be ready for such an ordeal, she dutifully took her place on the high seat which had been fetched from the hall and gave Enric a nod. She settled herself but her calm demeanour lasted only until she heard Sir Roger bellowing at the gate.

Stomach churning with anxiety, she felt like a small child and was grateful for the solid oak chair beneath her. As the gates were opened, she felt ever more apprehensive and, perhaps Enric noticed, for he motioned two spear men to stand either side of her. It was a small gesture, but it helped. A glance across the courtyard and up to the ramparts told her that everyone was now watching.

She feared that, at the very sight of Sir Roger, her willpower would evaporate but, when Enric led him in, it was the limping knight who looked more ill at ease. Be brave, she told herself; above all, be brave…

"Adeline-" began Sir Roger.

"Lady Adeline," interrupted Enric at once. "You'll address the mistress of this castle as 'my lady'."

Sir Roger, visibly wincing at the prospect, made no response.

Undaunted, Enric continued: "You'll be respectful, or you'll be tossed out of the gates on your arse."

Clearly struggling to rein in his anger, Sir Roger addressed Adeline again.

"My *lady*, this is my castle by right, granted to me by the authority of King Stephen himself and I require you to return it to me at once and disperse your rabble of outlaws."

With heart pounding in her breast, Adeline said nothing, partly because she was heeding Enric's advice that she, not Sir Roger, was in charge; but mainly because she couldn't think of an appropriate response. However, when she observed how much her silence irritated Sir Roger, she delayed her answer even further and merely fixed him with what she hoped was a steely glare.

His impatience soon got the better of him. "Come then, lady," he barked. "What is your answer, for I act with the full support of Earl Robert of Leicester – and the king himself?"

"Sir Roger," she began, "my lord, Thomas FitzRobert, does not accept the authority of Stephen of Blois, who presently calls himself king; and thus, I cannot accept your right to this castle."

"He's a traitor then like his father," growled Sir Roger. "And where is he? Where is your traitorous lover?"

"Call him traitor again," warned Enric, "and you'll lose a hand..."

"My lord... and husband... will return very soon," replied Adeline, "But, in his absence, I bid you leave Schaftesberia in peace."

"Peace?" Sir Roger spat out the word. "There can be no peace with rebels. I'll rip this castle from your... lord - aye, and have his whore whipped through the market place of Schaftesberia."

Adeline was shaking as she stood up. "Get out," she ordered, "for I've no more to say to you. If you come through those gates again, Sir Roger, it will be to die."

A cheer sounded around the yard but Sir Roger shouted above the din: "You have two days, lady; because on the third day, I shall take back this castle. You have until then either to surrender or to send out all your women and children. After that, every soul who remains here will be hanged."

Without waiting for a response, the knight turned upon his heel and stalked out of the castle gates. Adeline, drained from the encounter, watched him go while the castle folk, with the show over, returned to their work.

"What have I done? gasped Adeline. "I've condemned us all, haven't I?"

But to her surprise, Enric was grinning broadly. "No, lady, you said what a brave lady should: you've told him we won't bend to his will – and, believe me, nothing you could say would stop what's coming."

46

22nd August, in the early hours near Gyllengeham, north of Schaftesberia

"Only an oath breaker draws his sword against his sworn lord," growled Thomas, as he faced Renold armed only with his seax.

"I'm no oath breaker," retorted Renold. "I swore an oath to your father and never once broke it."

"Then sheathe your weapon and I'll forgive the fault," said Thomas.

"But I also swore to defend my comrades – even after their deaths. Hawk and me… we were good comrades of the de Burgh brothers… and we fought beside them many a time."

"I'd no quarrel with them either," replied Thomas, "till they tried to kill me."

"But in the end, you killed 'em both," declared Renold, whose steely demeanour suggested there was no possibility of a reconciliation.

"Only Roland had a right to seek vengeance," declared Thomas, "and he did so, to his cost. I killed him in fair combat - as I'll certainly kill you, if you don't put up that blade."

So far Hawk had remained silent but Thomas was acutely aware of his presence at his back.

"I hold you both to your oaths to me," insisted Thomas. "Hawk, what say you?"

"Aye, time you spoke up, Hawk," grumbled Renold.

Sensing perhaps some reluctance in Hawk, Thomas told him: "You've done little wrong yet, Master Hawk."

The ensuing long silence must have weighed heavily upon Renold especially when Hawk murmured: "Is it worth it, Renold?"

"Forgotten your old loyalties, have you, Hawk?" scorned Renold, moving a pace closer to Thomas.

"There's no honour in this," protested Hawk. "He's not even got his sword."

"More fool him," snarled Renold, "But, if you're not up to bloody work, then just keep out of my way."

"Hawk," said Thomas. "If your oath means anything to you, then go back to the camp and tell Edgar to assemble the company."

"Don't listen to the coward's begging, Hawk," warned Renold.

"Very well, lord," agreed Hawk, "but… you should take my sword."

"No, just go," ordered Thomas wearily, wishing he had heeded his half-brother's warning about loyal friends of the de Burghs.

The instant Hawk slipped away in the darkness, Renold pressed home his advantage, but Thomas was ready to meet his initial onslaught with his seax. The skirmish, months before, at the dead of night in Escewich, had taught Thomas the importance of keeping on the move. If he couldn't see his opponent, then he must rely upon sound and touch. Hence, he danced around the small patch of clear ground and, unencumbered by a heavy sword, he was light on his feet. With his own breathing slow and shallow, he listened for the rasping breaths and heavy tread of his frustrated opponent.

Out of the darkness, a sword point arrowed at his chest but, just in time, the seax flicked it aside. Next moment the lunging shaft of steel carved across him, coming close – damned close – to slicing through his neck. Barely deflected by the tip of the seax, it must have given Renold much encouragement; but though another sweeping blow followed it, the outcome was the same. And, while

Renold muttered and snarled throughout, Thomas made no sound at all.

When the vengeful blade speared out of the darkness yet again, Thomas stepped aside and let it graze past his mail shirt. Then swiftly grasping the extended sword arm, he hauled his adversary to him and, in a heartbeat, the bout was over. Renold jerked in shock as the seax punched under the mail protecting his belly and ripped upwards from his groin. Releasing Renold's arm, Thomas stepped back, allowing the gutted traitor to drop to his haunches. The sword fell onto the bloodied earth and all Renold could do was clutch at his torn midriff in vain.

Staring down sadly at the dying man, Thomas said: "You may have satisfied your oath to the de Burghs, but it's a damned pity you had to sacrifice yourself to do so."

There could be no elation in such a kill, only regret at the loss of a brave man who might, in other circumstances, have served him well. How many more revenge-seekers would he have to butcher, wondered Thomas? He was just about to leave the clearing, when a snarling and thrashing in the undergrowth announced the arrival of another warrior with sword drawn.

After a cursory glance at Renold's still groaning body, Edgar sheathed his sword and enquired: "You alright, lord?"

"Aye," said Thomas, who noted that the light in the forest was changing subtly with the approach of dawn. "Get Hawk and someone else to bear the body back to the camp; we'll bury him before we leave."

"He's not dead yet, lord," Edgar pointed out.

"No," agreed Thomas, "but he will be by the time he reaches the camp."

And he was.

After the burial, Thomas challenged the whole company: "Renold sought revenge for the de Burghs," he told them. "If any other man here regrets his oath to me, then I will free him now from that allegiance and bid him leave here in peace."

It was a gamble, as Edgar's astonished face testified; but, mercifully, no-one took up his offer and he was mightily relieved for he could hardly afford to lose any more of his few precious men at arms.

"Then get ready to leave," he told them but, while the men gathered up their heavy loads, both Edgar and Tancred cornered him.

"Are you sure you can trust the rest of these new men?" Edgar challenged him.

"Aye," hissed Tancred, "if one can break his oath, so can others."

A glare from Thomas silenced them both. "I'm more confident than I was before," he told them. "Though Renold tried to strike me down, Hawk could have stabbed me in the back if he wished; but he chose not to. I believe all the rest will remain loyal – so, that's an end to it."

Before the subdued column set off, he announced: "By midday, we'll be at Schaftesberia Castle. But lest you've forgotten, this is no game we play. Your sworn lord is at war and hence, you are all at war. So, by God's truth, stay alert – for all our lives depend upon it."

Only now as, yard by yard, he drew closer to Schaftesberia, did Thomas allow his mind to concentrate upon what must happen in the coming days and weeks. There would be much to prepare at the castle; though he hoped that Adeline and Enric would have made a start. His brother, William, had told him of the desperate privations at Schrosberie where the garrison had eventually sent out all the women and children. Now he must contemplate doing the same for, once a royal army arrived, the struggle would be bitter indeed.

With that terrible thought in the forefront of his mind, Thomas appraised the rough mix of men travelling with him. All had trained, as he had, in Brystole Castle yard; but only a handful had experienced fierce combat – and one of those was now dead. He could hardly have expected any better, for William was understandably reluctant to spare his most effective men in what he probably supposed was a losing cause. However much William wanted to believe in Thomas, he had warned him that Schaftesberia was, like the other small forts, almost certain to fall. Only Brystole, he argued, could withstand the power of the king until their father returned.

Though Thomas feared that his half-brother might well be right, he had promised to lead the defence of Schaftesberia and that was what he was going to do. He was still pondering how to ensure the safety of his stubborn wife, when the company came to an abrupt halt. When Thomas joined Edgar, at the head of the column, he saw the swathe of tortured ground that cut across their route. There was no mistaking its cause and so many recent tracks heading south told Thomas that an army must already have arrived at Schaftesberia. His greatest fear, that his enemies would descend upon the castle in his absence, had come to pass.

Thomas roared: "We make for the castle with all speed!"

But he took only one pace forward and then stopped dead.

"Lord?" murmured Edgar. "What is it?"

Thomas gave a shake of the head. "You know, six months ago, Edgar, I would have run till my heart bled to get to that castle as fast as I could," he replied. "I'd have hurled myself against my enemies, reckless of my life and those of any men unfortunate enough to be with me."

"So, what's changed?" prompted Edgar.

"I'm not sure," confessed Thomas, "but perhaps, in these past months I've had to live with all the mistakes I've made."

Whilst that was undoubtedly true, Thomas knew in his heart that Adeline was the difference; she alone had wrought the change in him. And, though he was desperate to return to her, he was learning that a leader must see beyond such selfish desires – and he was trying hard to be that leader.

"We'll approach with caution," he told them. "Where we can, we'll keep among the trees; but stay watchful - and silent."

In single file he led them through the woodland to the west of the town until, where the tree cover grew thin, he called a halt. While he despatched the fleet-footed Eadwulf ahead to discover what was happening at the castle, the remainder laid down their heavy burdens to take a well-earned rest.

When Eadwulf returned to report what he had observed, Thomas drew him apart from the others.

"They're already under siege, lord," whispered Eadwulf. "And it's Sir Roger back again; for I've seen his banners."

"Then, by Christ, we've come too late," gasped Thomas.

"No, not yet," replied Eadwulf. "The castle's still in our hands and there's no sign of any assault yet."

"So, you think perhaps they've just arrived?" asked Thomas.

"Either that or they're trying to starve the castle out," said Eadwulf.

Tancred, who had been listening in to their conversation, blurted out. "Lord, we need to get inside to help our comrades."

"Aye, we do have to get in there somehow, but not yet," replied Thomas.

"But surely the sooner the better," insisted Tancred.

"And what if most of us perish trying to get inside?" enquired Thomas. "Out here, we have an advantage; so, let's not be so eager to surrender it, eh?"

"But-" Tancred continued to protest.

Thomas put a hand upon the young soldier's shoulder. "Don't be so hot, Tancred. First, we need to know if the women and children are still inside and how well the castle is supplied with food and water. We must also take account of our enemy's strength. Such things can be done from outside the castle."

"Aye, lord," acknowledged Tancred glumly.

Thomas clapped the youth on the back, knowing he was only concerned for Edith. Then he gave a wry smile, for here was he, the incarnation of rash behaviour, counselling the lovesick youth to be patient.

Gathering the men around him once more, he told them: "You may look at me and think: what does this half-Saxon, bastard youth know about fighting? Well, as it happens, I know more than any of you; so, your lives will hang upon doing exactly what I tell you. Remember that."

"But there's scarcely a dozen of us, lord," observed one of the youngest recruits.

"Remind me of your name?" said Thomas, annoyed that he had forgotten it.

"Bernard, lord," replied the young man, lowering his eyes.

"Well, Bernard, we dozen aren't going to take on the whole enemy host on our own… at least, not yet."

Bernard looked suitably confused as Thomas continued: "Edgar and Eadwulf will get close enough to the enemy to assess how they are arrayed, while the rest of us make our way to the abbey."

"But when shall we strike?" asked Tancred.

"When we give up our one advantage of surprise," replied Thomas, "we must make damned sure that we strike the besiegers a mortal blow."

Getting a dozen men into the abbey unseen was not going to be easy since Sir Roger was certain to have men posted in the old burh. So, only at dusk did Thomas risk leading his nervous men at arms north of the town to approach the abbey through the market place. Once they were within fifty yards, they moved as fast as their heavy loads allowed, ghosting towards the main abbey gate with Tancred watching out for any of Sir Roger's men.

Though he wanted to pound thunderously upon the gate timbers, Thomas contented himself with what he hoped was a firm, but respectful knock. After a few moments, a small door opened at head height to reveal a worried-looking gatekeeper peering out at him.

"You know who I am?" asked Thomas.

"Aye, lord," mumbled the keeper.

"Then open the gate fast."

"But the abbess said-" protested the keeper.

"As soon as you let me in, I'll be speaking to her," promised Thomas, forcing a smile. "So, make haste, man."

"It'll soon be Compline," advised the keeper.

"I need to see the abbess urgently," replied Thomas.

Finally, the keeper was persuaded to open the gate but warned: "Only you though, lord."

Thomas, however, pushed the gate wider open and replied: "I think not." Thus, ignoring the half-hearted protests of the gatekeeper and one of the ushers, he shepherded his men at arms inside. Posting Tancred just inside the gate, he led the others along torchlit passages into the yard before the malthouse.

"How dare you bring all these armed men into the abbey?" complained the usher.

"I'm bringing them into this yard, that's all," declared Thomas.

"I shall report this to the abbess at once," warned the usher.

"Aye, please make haste to do so," growled a stern-faced Thomas. "And tell her Thomas FitzRobert is on his way to see her - but mind you don't report our arrival to anyone else."

After the usher scuttled away into the depths of the abbey, Thomas reassured his men: "You can take your ease here; but keep quiet and stay together. And don't steal anything - food will be brought soon enough…"

Knowing his way to the abbess' chamber, he did not wait to be escorted there, for he could ill afford any delay. He doubted that his sudden arrival, armed and in full mail, would please Abbess Bella and, sure enough, she greeted him with dismay.

"I'm shocked, Thomas, that you have entered the abbey by force," she cried.

"In haste and in secret, Reverend Mother, but not, I think, by force," he explained. "I can't risk being seen by Sir Roger's spies. But you should not fear the presence of my men at arms; they'll soon be gone."

"This abbey is not an occasional camp for your soldiers," declared the abbess, bristling with indignation. "And, after all I have done for those at the castle."

"So, what have you done for them?" enquired Thomas.

"I agreed to provide provisions and water – and I've kept my word."

"So, the castle is well-provisioned," he said, much relieved to hear it.

"The last wagon went there just before Sir Roger's army arrived," she told him.

"How long ago was that?"

"Two days," she replied.

"Then you have my grateful thanks, Reverend Mother," said Thomas, "for I confess that I doubted you'd be able to reach any agreement with Master Enric."

"I've not seen Master Enric since he returned the hostages," replied the abbess. "It was Lady Adeline who came to see me."

Thomas grinned. "The lady is persuasive, is she not?" he remarked.

"Aside from the food and water," said the abbess, "there was another arrangement agreed between us. In the event of a siege, I agreed that the women and children would be admitted here. Since this has now… come to pass, I expected to receive them, but none have yet been sent out."

"Sir Roger has the castle surrounded," said Thomas. "Perhaps he won't allow them out."

"No, on the contrary, Sir Roger assured me that the women and children had been given leave to come here."

"Yet they haven't," mused Thomas. "So, I shall have to look into that."

"I fear it may be too late," replied the abbess, "for I believe that he gave Lady Adeline until today. He may attack, Thomas, at any moment."

"Perhaps he should have known that my lady is not so easily cowed," said Thomas, his heart warming at the thought of his wife's determination.

"So, what do you intend?" enquired the abbess. "Your men can't stay here… I want you out by Compline."

Thomas heard in her voice the desperation of an abbess who found herself embroiled in a struggle which threatened to overwhelm her abbey.

"If you can feed my men, I give you my word that we shall be gone by Compline. Rest assured: we shall not bring the fight to this holy place."

The abbess gave a sigh. "I fear, Thomas, that you already have."

Shortly after his meeting with the abbess, Edgar and Eadwulf slipped into the abbey while their fellow men at arms were enjoying the abbey's refreshments.

"What news?" demanded Thomas at once.

"Good news, lord," replied Edgar. "Sir Roger's only got thirty or so men at arms and no siege engines at all."

"He must be expecting an easy victory then," murmured Thomas. "The abbess told me he's been inside the castle so he'll have an idea how many he's up against."

"Except, he doesn't know we're here, does he?" said Eadwulf, with a sly grin.

"I assume from your late return that he's not going to make an assault today," remarked Thomas.

"Not likely, lord, for his men are well bedded down."

"In the same place we attacked them before?"

"Aye, lord, same place and, by God, there's still dried blood on some of the branches."

"So, on the morrow then, you think?" Thomas asked Edgar.

"Dawn, or just before, I'd say," replied Edgar.

"Aye, my thought too," agreed Thomas. "Encourage our men to get an hour's sleep, while I take a look in the old burh."

"You're not going out there alone, lord?" said Edgar.

"Aye, I am, I need to see for myself. Keep the men in this yard. I'll be back before the bell sounds for Compline."

Slipping out of the privy gate, Thomas pulled his cloak more tightly around him and hauled the hood up over his head. Though it was too late in the evening for law-abiding folk to be at large, Thomas dared not be recognised in the old burh. Thus, he kept to the shadows as he walked up the short lane to what had once been Schaftesberia's main thoroughfare. But those prosperous days were long gone and now it was a poorly-lit, rundown neighbourhood. During the hours of darkness, he knew that it would be frequented mainly by thieves and whores – just the sort of folk who would cheerfully earn some coin by informing Sir Roger that Thomas FitzRobert had been spotted in the old town.

With care, therefore, he made his way to the west end of the burh, though he decided to keep clear of the old gateway, for that was the most likely place for Sir Roger to post watchers. In any case, Thomas found a position on a section of the rotting town rampart twenty yards or so along from the gate where he could observe the castle well enough. Here and there a wavering glow showed where sentries stood upon the battlements; and Enric, he suspected, would be pacing across the top of the tower anticipating the likely attack to come.

Somewhere, perhaps in her privy chamber, would be Adeline - how he longed to see her… and not just see her either. He was so proud of her for winning over the abbess – probably more easily than he could have done. But he was worried now that she lay outside his protection and, once the expected assault began, only God could keep someone from harm. A stray arrow or crossbow quarrel might tear into her soft flesh and there was nothing he could do to stop it.

Studying how the castle and the burh were arranged with a very wide but shallow ditch between them, he struggled to put together any sort of plan. Since Sir Roger had no siege engines to soften up the defenders, he would have to rely upon battering down the gates. All the knight would need was a small breach, though he would know better than anyone how sturdy the gates were. All the same, there were certainly enough trees about for his men to have fashioned a suitable ram in two days.

No doubt, he would place archers or crossbowmen on the hill beside St John's to cover the attack upon the gates. Then, once the breach was made, the rest of his men, massed in the nearby burh, would pour across the ditch and force their way into the castle.

Thomas was surprised by the lack of siege engines which he knew from William had been employed elsewhere by King Stephen. Perhaps Sir Roger, impatient to return, reckoned that, facing only ill-trained outlaws, he would not need trebuchets to ensure a swift victory.

It was a chill night for mid-August, which perhaps added to Thomas's apprehension. He knew that, even if the defenders repulsed Sir Roger's first attack, another would follow soon enough. After a time, growing ever more worried, he trudged back to the abbey.

47

23rd August 1138, in the old burh at Schaftesberia

Watching the cool, drizzle-laden dawn cast a grey glimmer over the old burh, Thomas fiddled idly with the uneven patch of his mail shirt. Somehow, just touching the unyielding iron rings which Adeline's determined fingers had repaired, brought her a little closer. All night, he had lain there in the damp and derelict building with the rest of his comrades. But now Edgar was silently rousing the others, one by one, which brought forth a few groans of misery.

"Peace," warned Thomas softly.

The men's sombre mood was not improved by the enticing smell of freshly-baked loaves, wafting down the street on the gentle east wind. Hiding a dozen men in mail shirts and armed with spears, shields and crossbows had not been easy. However, when Thomas scouted the burh the previous evening, he identified the half-ruined cottage which would suit their purpose well enough.

Though the abbey offered far greater comfort, they could not have remained there all night. Not only would it have infuriated the abbess, but also, they needed to be much closer to the castle when Sir Roger's attack came. During the night, Eadwulf, Edgar and Tancred had taken turns to watch the western rampart of the old town with orders to report any sign of movement there. Shortly after dawn, Eadwulf returned.

"Well?" enquired Thomas.

"As you thought, lord, he's moving some of his archers onto the burh's west rampart," reported Eadwulf.

Thomas nodded thoughtfully. "How many?" he asked.

"About half a dozen."

Six men did not sound many but, overlooking the castle gate, they would be able to rain down a hail of arrows upon the defenders – unless, of course, someone removed them before they could do so... However, Thomas dared not show his hand too soon; patience would be needed if he was to extract the most advantage. Timing was all. The rampart would need to be cleared of its archers with the utmost stealth.

"Anyone else near the rampart we need to worry about?" he asked Eadwulf.

"There were two sentries, lord, but they'll not trouble us now."

"You know your part?" said Thomas.

"Aye, lord."

"Very well, let's move," he announced. "And, by Christ, not a sound."

While most of the men followed Eadwulf to outflank Sir Roger's archers, Thomas passed, with several others, behind a row of adjacent houses towards the dilapidated west gate where Edgar and Tancred awaited him. So well were they hidden, that Thomas almost fell over them. Edgar grinned and nodded a silent greeting, as they settled down to observe Eadwulf's men who were creeping up on Sir Roger's archers from behind. By God, thought Thomas, how carelessly he now condemned men to death. But, as he had told his recruits, they were at war now…

The archers would be the first casualties of the day but, if even one managed to cry out in alarm, the precious element of surprise would be lost. Thomas watched with grim satisfaction as, one by one, the unfortunate archers died without uttering a sound. Soon Eadwulf joined Thomas and confirmed that six of his comrades, all armed with crossbows, were now deployed in their stead.

"No man moves – or even shows himself - till I command it," Thomas reminded them all.

"What if there are too many of them, lord?" whispered a pale youth, whose name Thomas struggled to remember.

"Then we'll very likely die," Thomas told the lad. "But a man who goes into a fight expecting to lose, almost certainly will. We came here to defeat Sir Roger of Schaftesberia; and that's exactly what we shall do."

A glance at Edgar brought a wry smile from the older man.

"What?" hissed Thomas.

"They'll be fine, lord," said Edgar. "I reckon they're mostly good lads – but it's as well their first blooding won't be in some great field, else fear might get the better of a few of the younger men."

Observing the broad ditch and the slope below it, Thomas nervously eased his sword in and out of its scabbard, as was his habit. The tension among the men around him was palpable and he felt it keenly too: that heady brew of excited anticipation and abject terror. It was almost a relief when, finally, he noticed the host of men gathering at the base of the slope to launch their assault.

Fortified by several deep inhalations of moisture-laden air, Thomas, as was his habit, eased his sword an inch or two out of its scabbard. Next moment, he spied a second company of men at arms advancing up the steep road past St John's to gather just outside the burh rampart. This was the shock force he expected; but, as they moved into position, he realised that they would pass worryingly close to where he and his men squatted with only the frail timber rampart to hide them from view.

As the men of Sir Roger's main assault force neared the top of the slope, their battle cries gradually grew from a ripple into a loud, staccato outpouring of venom. With them, they lugged a crudely-fashioned battering ram and Thomas did not envy them the task, for the light drizzle had made the ground underfoot greasy and the tree trunk was, of necessity, very heavy.

REBEL SWORD

On either side of the burh rampart, not a soul uttered a word. Sir Roger's men waited for their comrades to ascend the slope, while Thomas's company crouched like carved figures, weapons gripped tightly in their sweating hands.

As the ram was hauled ever closer to the castle gate, with no reaction yet from within, young Bernard whispered: "Why do the defenders not plague them with arrows, lord?"

"Because they've few arrows," hissed Thomas crossly. "Now hold your tongue."

At that moment the ram struck the gate with a resounding crash and Thomas winced to see that it had damaged the timbers. Yet, he dared not risk intervening until Sir Roger had committed all his men to the assault. Acting too soon would rob his attack of the impact required to overwhelm the besiegers; but, if he acted too late, the castle would be all but overrun. He must seize the right moment but there was no certainty to it, just a feeling in his gut as the battle ebbed and flowed.

Peering through a gap in the rampart, he stared across to the top of the castle tower where several figures stood. It was easy enough to pick out his uncle for Enric was pacing up and down, pausing only to hurl down the occasional gobbet of abuse at his enemies. With a gasp, Thomas realised who else was standing there beside Enric and, at first, he cursed to see her in such a perilous position. Yet, he reflected, perhaps she was exactly where Thomas FitzRobert's lady ought to be: where every man defending the castle could see her. And by God, she looked so wondrously determined and brave.

Only the sudden, and disturbing, groan of timbers being torn asunder forced him to drag his eyes away from her. The second impact of the mighty tree trunk had hewn a great gash in one of the gates. At once, a roar went up and the ram was abandoned to allow the front-rank men at arms to race forward and hack at the damaged timbers with their axes. Every blow resounded inside Thomas's helm as he watched the attacking force advance to form up at the shattered gates.

Risking a final glance up to the tower, Thomas saw that, though Adeline still remained there, Enric had gone. No doubt, his uncle would be down in the yard preparing to meet the besiegers head on.

Sir Roger's second company, concealed only a few yards from his own men, now began to shuffle forward.

"Lord?" whispered Tancred. "Surely we must attack."

"Not yet," murmured Thomas, whose eyes were fixed upon Sir Roger for only when the knight committed his hidden reserve, could Thomas risk launching a counterattack.

Hampered by the deepened ditches on either side of the gateway, Sir Roger's men at arms formed a wedge of heavily armed men attempting to squeeze through a gap scarcely wide enough for a brace of them at a time. Hence, most of his soldiers remained uncommitted to the fight and Thomas, his heart heavy with regret, knew he could not strike until the gate was entirely destroyed. At that dread moment, the superior weight of numbers outside would begin to drive back those within.

"Lord," pleaded Tancred.

But Thomas, raising his hand, hissed: "Hold, damn you!"

Unblinking, he stared at the brutal, close-fought struggle unfolding in the gateway until, almost before he knew it, the whole gate caved inwards. At once, Sir Roger waved forward his reserve of men at arms. Needing no encouragement, they raced across the broad shallow ditch, whooping and yelling as they joined their comrades pressing forward into the fort.

Praying that Eadwulf was paying attention, Thomas dropped his hand.

An instant later, six crossbows delivered their lethal missiles and four of those bent upon joining the fray were halted in their tracks. Another two staggered back towards the burh, but they never reached it for Thomas and his comrades swept out of the burh's west gate to cut them down. Tancred would have charged on down into the mêlée had Thomas not gripped his arm and snarled: "Hold! Unless you want a quarrel in your back!"

The second volley from his crossbowmen cut down half a dozen more combatants and, more important, spread panic in Sir Roger's ranks.

"Now," cried Thomas, "forward!"

With the gateway itself already hopelessly crammed with fighting men, Thomas made for the rearmost ranks of Sir Roger's men at arms. Some were still standing with idle spears or axes whilst their comrades ahead hacked at the defenders in the gateway. As Thomas hoped, his arrival caused even more confusion so that, by the time the truth dawned on their opponents, they were trapped.

"Traitors!" roared one man, who might have continued his outraged protest had Bernard not driven a spear through his throat.

Knowing that Sir Roger would have sworn to hang the garrison, Thomas yelled. "No quarter! Give no quarter!"

"No quarter!" Edgar picked up the cry and others followed his example.

"For the Empress!" shouted Thomas, who had never met the Empress Matilda. But then, of course, she was not the woman for whom he was risking all. A few of his fellows echoed the call as they tore into the rear of the besieging force. Moments later, they were reinforced by Eadwulf and several of his men; but the task was far from over for Sir Roger's vanguard was still attempting to break through into the castle yard.

Breathing hard, Thomas carved a merciless path into the milling men at arms, some of whom scarcely had time to turn before they were cut down from behind. Shattering one opponent's shield with his sword, he crashed his own into the face of another. Flecks of blood splashed across his face, but he drove on with Roland's sword wreaking carnage upon the poor bastards herded into the broad ditch.

Eadwulf must have left a couple of the crossbowmen to continue sniping for, every now and then, Thomas noticed quarrels thudding into several of Sir Roger's men fighting in the gateway. Aware now of the riotous clamour behind them, those attacking at the gates began, for the first time, to falter; and Enric – God bless the old warrior – led the defenders in a charge to recapture the gateway.

When Enric's thrust drove their adversaries back a few yards, Sir Roger became trapped in the middle with several of his leading knights. As Thomas battered his way closer, he could tell by the way the knight moved that, under that blood-smeared helm, was a man seething with raw anger. He must fear that victory was being snatched from his grasp and that his small army was likely to be annihilated. So, he did exactly what Thomas expected: he chose to make his escape.

"Fall back! Fall back, damn you!" the knight bawled wildly, as he hammered at the encircling men at arms.

With only a handful of companions, he bludgeoned a path out of the broad ditch towards the slope. For one brief moment, scarcely two yards from Thomas, he hesitated, peering at the outlaw in disbelief. But whatever the furious knight intended; his two companions drew him away down the hill towards his camp, leaving Thomas cursing that yet again his enemy was escaping.

Many of Sir Roger's men at arms, however, were not so fortunate; caught between the exultant defenders and the stern-faced, mail-clad warriors with Thomas, many were butchered before they could even offer to yield. For a short time, the blood-letting continued unchecked and, though Thomas was sickened by the relentless killing, he knew that, for his grim message to strike home, it had to be written in blood. Schaftesberia must not be seen as another Castle Cary or Richmont; it was a stronghold to be reckoned with.

Yet, to carry that message to those who mattered, there also had to be survivors…

"Hold!" he roared.

At first no man seemed to notice his order and more of the defeated were cut down, until he bellowed the command again and, to his relief, heard it taken up by his uncle. Slowly, the fighting ceased leaving the battered rump of Sir Roger's army, barely a dozen men, completely surrounded in the blood and gore of the corpse-filled ditch.

Sheathing his sword, Thomas removed his bloodied helm and tossed it to the nearby Bernard. Then, stepping forward to address the trapped men, he announced: "I am Thomas FitzRobert, Lord of Schaftesberia and son of Earl Robert of Gloucester. I serve the rightful ruler of England, the Empress Matilda. And this castle, over which you have shed so much blood, is hers. If you yield to me now and swear not to take up arms against the Empress again, you may leave this field with your lives."

His words drew a murmur of concern from some of the castle defenders who, knowing that a victorious Sir Roger would not have been so generous, were puzzled by this act of mercy. But Thomas had not finished.

"If even one of you does not throw down his weapon and yield," he added, "I shall hang you all. So, choose now: submit on your knees, or die."

It was with some relief that he watched all of them sink to their knees at once, indeed some could hardly stand from fatigue or injury.

"You will remain here, under guard until I order your release but… you may sit."

By then many of those from the castle had spilled out into the ditches and the slope below. First among them was Enric who embraced Thomas warmly. "That was well done, nephew," he said, voice gruff with emotion. "Though I wish to God, I'd known you were there."

Thomas smiled, but his troubled mind was already moving on to the next challenge. "The gate needs to be repaired, uncle," he observed, "and it clearly needs to be much, much stronger."

After a pause, Enric said: "Aye, I'll get on with that then, shall I?"

"If you would," replied Thomas, who then cast around for Edgar and, spotting him amid a swathe of broken bodies, called out: "How goes the count of our new recruits, Edgar?"

Trudging across to him, Edgar said: "Two men lost, lord; and another with a bad wound."

"I'm glad that young Bernard survived his first fight," confided Thomas, "though I've no idea how."

"I think he just followed you about, lord," replied Edgar, with a grin.

"God help him; that sounds like a very dangerous idea. Get the new men settled in, will you."

Without waiting for any acknowledgement from Edgar, Thomas moved towards the gateway, knowing that many eyes would be upon him. When he entered the castle, a great cheer went up followed by chants of "Fitz, Fitz, Fitz!"

More important to Thomas, he saw Adeline descending the steps from the hall to greet him. Ribald shouts assailed the pair as they drew closer and the urge to race to her and lift her off her feet was almost irresistible. Yet, he observed that she was walking towards him with measured step and vowed to show similar restraint. In that moment somehow his love for her deepened. She was no longer a young girl; she was his lady and she was in the struggle with him till the end - however long and bitter it might become.

By the time he clasped her hands in his, the bawdy cries had stopped and, when the pair did finally embrace, it was with such tenderness that all those witnessing the moment fell strangely silent.

With Adeline at his side, he declared solemnly: "Friends, we've won a battle, but it will not be the last. More men will come against us - perhaps the usurper king himself. But we shall endure here; this is our place for as long as we choose to defend it."

More cheers broke out again as he led Adeline into the hall and then, just for a moment, they were alone.

"You've changed," she murmured.

"Aye, and so have you… lady," he replied.

"But, despite all," she grinned, "I find that I still love you…"

"And, merciful God, I too am still thus afflicted."

"Then I have one thing I must ask of you," she told him.

"Name it," he cried.

"Before we put our lives at risk again, I would like our wedding vows to be sanctified," she said.

"Of course," he assured her. "Of course…"

"Your words say one thing, Thomas," she murmured, "but your eyes say another."

"Well, it may not be easy to find a priest willing to do it, but we can ask the advice of the abbess."

"Aye," she agreed, "though I pray I haven't pressed the abbess too far already."

Part Six: Lord of Schaftesberia

48

26th October 1138, in the late afternoon, at Schaftesberia Castle

Leaning against the tower rampart beside his uncle, Thomas looked down with some satisfaction upon what they had achieved since the siege was lifted. Although more than two months had passed without any further attempt to take the castle, he understood that the fight was by no means over; in truth, it had scarcely begun.

They had used the time to improve the castle's defences as much as they could, which meant completely rebuilding the gates. To strengthen the entrance further, they added a sturdy rampart above the gateway which could make all the difference when they faced the next attempt to batter it down. The perimeter ditch outside the palisade had been scoured out even deeper and its sides made much steeper. At the same time, the manufacture of more arrows and crossbow quarrels was proceeding at an encouraging pace.

Enric insisted that finding useful work for the whole castle community was essential if they were to sustain their high morale after the victory over Sir Roger.

"They all know worse is to come," he argued, "but the less time they have to think on it, the better."

Thomas needed no persuading for he saw his company for what it was: a disparate collection of souls condemned by their king, abandoned by the law and united only in a fight for their very survival. They cared nothing for Robert, Earl of Gloucester and even less for the Empress Matilda, but they did care about their own lives and those of their families. For all of them, the world outside Schaftesberia Castle offered only poverty, misery and almost certain death. Yet, within the castle's fragile timber palisade, they could still harbour a frail hope.

It would be a different matter, of course, when the fight started again in earnest; because then, their burgeoning fellowship would be put to the most severe test. His resistance so far had thrown down a public challenge to King Stephen's authority and no king could allow such open defiance to go unpunished. Thus, sooner or later, a far better equipped army would be despatched to crush Schaftesberia.

All through a fine September and the crisp October that followed, they awaited their fate; but no royal army appeared and Thomas dared to hope that the scale of Sir Roger's defeat might have persuaded the king to wait until the spring. That morning, however, his vain optimism evaporated when reports came in from his scouts further north that an army was being mustered at Salesberie. Perhaps, after all, time might be running out for the Schaftesberia rebels.

"What's she doing here?" asked Enric abruptly.

Glancing down to the gate, Thomas saw the Abbess Bella entering with Avice, Berner and several others in attendance. Swiftly, he descended to the yard to greet her, for it was the first time he could recall her visiting the castle herself.

"Reverend Mother, you honour us with this visit," he said, attempting to convey a delight he did not particularly feel, because he suspected that, for the abbess to come in person, she must be the bearer of grim tidings.

"Edith, fetch Lady Adeline," he ordered, as he led the abbess into the hall, struggling to contain his impatience. He seated her on a chair on the raised dais, partly as a mark of respect, but chiefly because it was the only sturdy chair the castle possessed.

"This is a matter for you and your lady only," the abbess told him.

Waving away his uncle and the others, Thomas waited for Adeline, who had been slow to rise of late, to descend from her chamber to the hall. The abbess, Thomas observed, shifted restlessly in her seat and, the moment Adeline reached the foot of the steps, she blurted out the reason for her visit.

"I had to tell you myself," she announced, "that the Bishop of Salesberie will not allow your marriage to be blessed by a priest."

"What do you mean, he won't allow it?" snarled Thomas, with a sudden savagery that caused the abbess to shrink away from him. "It's got nothing to do with him – Lady Adeline isn't his ward."

Moving swiftly to his side, Adeline clasped his hand in hers and gave it a sharp squeeze of warning.

"My love," she murmured, "the Reverend Mother is merely the messenger…"

"Any religious ceremony held in the abbey is a matter for the bishop," explained the abbess. "Services, prayers and, even a simple blessing such as this, must be conducted by an ordained priest."

Calmed, as ever, by Adeline's presence, Thomas strove to bury his anger when he grumbled: "So, what is the bishop's objection?"

"It is twofold, though either cause would be enough," replied the abbess. "Since you, Thomas, are declared an outlaw and a traitor, to bless your marriage would be to flout both the law and the church."

While Thomas might contest the charge, he understood that it was futile to do so until the Empress reigned; and only God knew when, or even if, that would happen.

"And his other complaint?" he muttered.

"Lady Adeline's father made her a ward of the abbey in his will, but, after her… abduction, Sir Roger petitioned the king - through the Earl of Leicester - to grant him wardship over Lady Adeline."

"Aye, and you did not oppose that," remarked Adeline coldly.

"No, but I knew nothing of you then, my dear," said the abbess, with genuine sadness in her eyes. "I believed Sir Roger's account of what you had done… in the forest… with…"

"Even so, with, or without Sir Roger's permission, we are already wed," asserted Thomas.

"But not as far as the bishop is concerned," replied the abbess.

Yet something in her demeanour suggested to Thomas that the bishop's refusal might not quite be the end of the matter. Meeting the nervous stare of the abbess, he enquired: "What if the blessing was done… without his approval?"

The abbess was clearly prepared for the question, for she replied swiftly: "You would still need to find an ordained priest willing to bless your marriage."

"And, would you happen to know of such a priest?" asked Thomas, feeling Adeline's fingers tighten around his.

"Me? I could not possibly countenance such a deliberate flouting of the bishop's authority," declared the abbess. "I condemn the very suggestion of it. However…"

"However?" breathed Adeline.

"Perhaps others you know may be aware of such a renegade priest…"

The abbess was already rising from her chair when Adeline whispered: "But would such a ceremony be recognised by the law and the church, Reverend Mother?"

As the abbess passed Adeline, she rested a hand upon the girl's shoulder and replied: "As God's poor servant, my lady, I cannot judge the right or wrong of such matters but, if an ordained priest blesses your union, then surely only God can part you..."

After the abbess left, the pair fell silent for a time, deep in contemplation. But moments after the abbess left, the hall door opened again to admit Avice and Wilflaed. Sensing that Adeline was in no mood for conversation, Thomas told them: "We are retiring to our chamber."

"Wait, lord," said Wilflaed. "Avice has reminded me of a priest who might just be willing to carry out the blessing."

Thomas could not resist a smile, for he saw the hand of the abbess in the timely intervention of Avice and Wilflaed. "A local man?" he asked.

"Aye," said Wilflaed, "he lives as a hermit at the summit of Duncliffe Forest, not so far from my cottage."

"A hermit?" groaned Adeline. "But we need a properly ordained priest."

"Father Edric was ordained, lady," Wilflaed assured her. "Though I doubt he's practised his faith for years. Yet, surely what matters is what the eye of God sees."

"Aye, that's what troubles me," lamented Adeline.

"But would he do it in the face of the bishop's opposition?" enquired Thomas.

Wilflaed gave a wry smile. "I think he might, since his falling out with the Bishop of Salesberie was the very reason that Edric turned from the church. I recall that his most recent judgement upon his old enemy was quite memorable; the bishop, he said, was: 'an arsewipe not fit to lick shit from the Lord's stable…'"

With a grin, Thomas replied: "This fellow sounds like my sort of priest; but what do you say, my lady?"

With a worried frown, Adeline drew him apart from the others and, looking deep into his eyes, whispered: "This Father Edric sounds appalling, but I think we have little choice now for, if a priest doesn't bless our marriage very soon, I fear that some might claim that our first child - like his father and grandfather - is born a bastard…."

"Oh!" he said, with a gulp of shock. Then he smiled. "Does anyone else know?"

"Only Wilflaed and Edith, for I could never hide much from those two."

"Very well then, we shall fetch this lapsed priest at once to bless our union," he said, and after a moment's hesitation, added: "And you should know that there's another reason for haste; just this morning, our watchers reported a large force assembling to the north."

"Is it coming for us?" she murmured.

"Aye, most likely; and, if it is, then we've only a few days before it arrives. So, if there's going to be a blessing, it must be tomorrow before you and the other women have to leave for the abbey."

Though he was slow to observe the change in Adeline's expression, when Thomas realised that her face no longer radiated accord, he gasped: "What is it?"

"If you believe that I'm fleeing to the abbey when the castle comes under siege," she growled, "then you don't know me very well, Thomas."

"But a lady should obey-"

"I'd rather be your whore and decide my own fate," she growled, "than be your lady, sent away like a child."

"But I just thought – and now, even more so…"

Squeezing his hand with all her strength, she hissed: "Hear me well, Thomas: I will not cower in some safe corner, when they storm our castle. I shall be right here. I shall be here if they breach the gates and, by God, however much of a shambles this place becomes, I will stand with you and only surrender my place at your side when I'm dead. Do you understand me?"

Though he had always known that she was strong-willed, and loved her all the more for it, her vehemence still astonished him. And how could he stand by while she put their child at risk?

"We'll talk further on that later," he told her. "Now, are we agreed about the priest?"

"No, we're not," she retorted, fierce eyes flashing. "Because, if I don't have your trust, then we've no need of a priest."

"Of course, you have my trust, but this-"

"Trust has no 'buts', Thomas," she insisted. "I made no conditions when I stepped into your world of blood and treason; so, pray let me stay with you to the very end."

"But, how can I fight," he whispered, "when all I'll be thinking about is that you're in danger?"

"Because, my love, if I'm in the castle, you'll have even more reason to fight with all you have…"

Only when he saw flecks of gold sparkling in her eyes, did Thomas admit defeat. This was, after all, the brave girl he had fallen for at Scireburne and, however much he loved her, he could never rob her of that indomitable spirit.

"Very well," he agreed. "Your fate will rest in your own hands; but you are quite impossible, you know that, don't you? So, can we fetch this fellow, Father Edric now?"

Adeline made no reply but kissed him on the cheek and then swept away, calling to Edith: "Come, we've a blessing to prepare for."

Thomas feared that the reclusive priest, having for so long withdrawn to a forest hermitage, would have no interest in the affairs of men. Such an aloof figure would very likely refuse outright to conduct the blessing. Hence, the following morning he had given his uncle strict instructions to bring the priest to the castle, no matter how much he might protest.

However, when Wilflaed and Enric dragged the wayward cleric through the gateway, Thomas encountered a man who seemed neither aloof nor especially spiritual. By his appearance, Father Edric had not fallen from the church he had plummeted from it. Indeed, Thomas was far from certain that the fellow was even capable of conducting a marriage blessing since he struggled even to stand without assistance. Nor was he at all sure that Adeline would want her marriage blessed by a man who appeared to have abandoned not only his faith, but also his sobriety and cleanliness.

"Are you sure he's a priest?" he cried. "By Christ, he stinks. For all our sakes, find a pond and toss the beggar in. Let's see if the Lord thinks he's worth saving from drowning."

When Enric hesitated, Thomas snarled: "Well?"

"Oh, you were serious," muttered his uncle, before snatching the priest away.

When he returned, hauling the sodden, bedraggled Edric with him, Thomas was not much more impressed. It seemed though that, if his marriage was to be blessed at all – and Adeline insisted that it must be – this excuse of a priest was their only hope.

"You," he said, addressing the priest. "Can you remember how to carry out a blessing for a marriage?"

Father Edric, splttering as he spat out some water, snarled back at him: "Who are you to have me taken against my will from my home-"

"Your 'home' is a hole in the ground full of pismires," observed Enric.

"I'm Thomas FitzRobert, Lord of Schaftesberia," said Thomas.

"Who says?" protested Father Edric. "I've never heard of you…"

"Yet, here I am," replied Thomas, his patience ebbing away a little more with every word the priest uttered.

"So, what you mean is, you're calling yourself lord of Schaftesberia," argued the priest.

"As long as I hold this castle, I am lord here," insisted Thomas.

Edric gave a nod of acknowledgement. "True enough, I suppose, but you've no authority over me."

"Nor do I claim any," replied Thomas, treading a little more carefully since he could hardly have the priest conduct the ceremony at the point of a sword. "I just want you to bless my marriage."

The priest studied him thoughtfully for a moment before chortling with laughter. "By Christ, you must be a desperate man."

"Will you do it, or not?" demanded Thomas.

"Do I have a choice?"

Only for an instant did Thomas pause before replying: "Aye, you do; you can walk away now but know that, if you do, I shall never forgive you – and, more of a concern to you, neither will my lady."

Thomas never discovered whether Father Edric would have walked away because Adeline arrived and, ignoring his damp clothes, took him by the arm as if he were a favourite uncle.

As she swept him away into the hall, Thomas exchanged a puzzled look with his uncle, but conceded: "I think we'll leave persuading the priest to the ladies."

"Wise," agreed Enric. "Very wise…"

Elsewhere in the castle, two sets of preparations proceeded alongside each other. The majority of folk were still working hard to further enhance the castle's defences and hone their weapons, while another, smaller team was bringing in additional supplies from the abbey. Ostensibly, these goods were for consumption at the marriage celebration, but all of it was, in fact, added to the stores the castle would require when it came under siege. More livestock was also brought into the castle, making it more overcrowded and rank-smelling than ever. Additional tuns of water arrived, accompanied by two hogsheads, which Thomas suspected were filled with rather stronger liquids earmarked for the imminent festivities.

Enric, who was focussed only upon their defence, objected to the distraction caused by the nuptials, but both Thomas and Adeline hoped that it would provide a welcome salve for the wounds already taken and those still to be borne.

"A celebration's all well and good," declared Enric, "as long as our enemies don't catch us like a load of fartwits with our braies round our ankles."

"My marriage is no light matter, uncle," replied Thomas, "so, I shall rely upon you to ensure that your braies are well secured."

Despite his glib response to Enric, Thomas was becoming rather nervous about the ceremony which seemed to have grown in significance. No longer was it simply a commitment to a girl with whom, in the blink of an eye, he had fallen in love; it marked the creation of a new family. Then there was the matter of his father who would, in the usual way of such things, have arranged a suitable marriage for his son. Adeline, though an heiress, might well never inherit the de Sarne estates at all. Would his father condemn his choice of bride?

The ceremony was to take place later that afternoon, partly because Enric insisted that as much work was done as possible before the occupants of the castle surrendered to celebration, but also because Adeline insisted that she could not possibly be ready any earlier. For his part,

Thomas wondered what she was doing to prepare that took so many hours but, the moment she descended the stair to the hall, accompanied by her sister Isabel, he understood.

He hardly recognised his bride for, gone was the ragged, threadbare overtunic that she had mostly been wearing since they first met and, in its stead, she wore a richly-sewn kirtle of deep blue. Her long raven hair, which he had mostly seen hanging loose or tied back carelessly with a tattered green ribbon, was now braided with new red ribbons and crowned by a band of crimson cloth beneath a circlet of flowers. Her beauty quite took his breath away as it had done the very first time he saw her in the flickering torchlight at Scireburne Abbey.

"You… look…"

"Well enough, I hope," said Adeline, grinning broadly.

"But where did you find such clothes?" he gasped.

"You must ask Avice and Isabel that," she replied, "for they won't tell me and I fear that some poor young lady of Schaftesberia lacks some of her attire."

"I shall be the envy of every man in the kingdom," he breathed.

"Aye, because they'd all like to be such a notorious outlaw and traitor," she teased.

A cough from Father Edric suggested he was growing impatient. Perhaps it was the shock of wearing freshly laundered clothing or, more likely, his enforced sobriety, reckoned Thomas.

"Come then," said Adeline, "let us say our vows again before the priest."

So, they did and, surrounded by a host of witnesses including Isabel, Ralph, Avice and Enric, Thomas and Adeline's marriage received its blessing from Father Edric.

Though the ceremony was short, the revelry after it continued long into the night fuelled by the refreshments supplied by the abbey. Long before the festivities ended,

Lady Isabel said a tearful farewell to her sister and Berner escorted her back to the abbey precinct. Thomas hoped that neither would give the abbess too detailed a report of the event; for, if she learned how far the copious quantities of ale and wine had loosened propriety, she might well regret her generosity. Yet, as Thomas and his lady presided in the hall, he was glad of the occasion to lift the spirits of his loyal supporters.

Peter, the gleeman, entertained the assembly with bawdy songs though, as the evening drew to a close, he told tales of lost love and regret; so that the mood became more melancholy. Perhaps, like everyone else, Peter was beginning to contemplate what would come next. It was natural enough then for many to seek solace in a jug of ale, or in the arms of another frightened soul. Later, before Thomas fell asleep with his bride in his arms, he thanked the Lord for giving them that one uplifting day together.

With the knowledge that the approaching royal army's arrival was imminent, arrangements had already been put in place for the morrow. In the morning, yet more barrels of precious water would be delivered after which, the women and children would say their tearful goodbyes and ride the wagons back to the abbey. And, for those who remained, the final, agonising wait would begin.

49

Dusk on 28ᵗʰ October 1138, at Schaftesberia Castle

With the inhabitants desperate for any scrap of news, every hour a new and darker rumour engulfed the castle. For all Thomas knew, some had a kernel of truth at their heart, but there was simply no way of knowing for certain. First, it was suggested that Robert, Earl of Leicester was in Normandy with his twin brother, Waleran in which case he could not be leading an assault on Schaftesberia. Other reports told of Schrosberie Castle's capitulation and the slaughter of its garrison to the last man. Though such stories could not make their perilous situation any worse, they did much to undermine morale. But, that afternoon, all speculation ended because, at last, their enemies arrived.

Thomas had expected an overwhelming force to descend upon Schaftesberia but, in the end, there were far fewer than he feared. Nonetheless, there were still scores of men at arms and, before nightfall, feverish work began to assemble two great siege machines at the foot of the hill. The only banners anyone could pick out were those of Sir Roger so, perhaps rumours of Robert of Leicester's absence were true after all.

Flanked by Enric and Edgar, Thomas surveyed the growing army camp below, daring to hope that the absence of royal banners meant that the king viewed the trouble at Schaftesberia as a merely local matter. He prayed that was so for, the moment the king became directly involved, it would be a matter of royal reputation to crush Thomas and his rebels.

"Do you think we can keep them out, lord?" enquired Edgar.

"Likely not," replied Enric bluntly, before Thomas had a chance to respond.

"If we could cripple their throwing machines," suggested Thomas, "we might…"

"Aye, nephew," replied Enric, "but we could lose half our men trying to do that."

"I suppose," agreed Thomas. "How far do you think those engines can hurl a rock?"

"Not far enough," concluded Enric. "So, unless they move 'em closer, which they can't 'cos of the slope, they'll have to use small rocks."

"So, that's good then," said Edgar.

"Not if you get hit by one," Thomas pointed out.

"Oh, aye," agreed Enric. "We'd best warn folk to keep their heads down."

"What about our bows, can they shoot that far?" enquired Thomas.

"Aye," replied Enric, "if you want to use up all the arrows that we've spent so many hours making."

"So, we'll just have to put up with the rocks," grumbled Thomas.

"We can't waste men wrecking a couple of trebuchets that don't even threaten our walls," advised Enric.

"Will he attack at once, do you think?" asked Edgar.

"He won't waste much time," said Enric. "Don't forget, he's got to feed his army too. Some will likely be mercenaries; so, the longer they stay there, the more he'll have to pay them – or his master, the earl, will. So, no, Sir Roger won't want a long siege."

By dawn, it became clear that Sir Roger's men must have laboured through the night to make the siege engines ready. As soon as it was light enough to see, the engineers began to test their machines. Thomas and Enric looked on with some trepidation as, with a great groan, the first of the trebuchets let fly its load. Moments later, when a rock the size of a man's head dropped at least twenty yards short of the castle and rolled back down the hill, its impact was greeted with an ironic cheer from the castle ramparts.

It did not take long, however, for the besiegers to identify ammunition of a more suitable size. Within an hour, teams of men clustered again around both trebuchets and soon the two great beams were hauled down and a brace of slightly smaller stones was hurled towards the castle.

"Look out below!" yelled Enric, as the two projectiles flew over the timber palisade and landed in the yard.

"Keep in the lee of the walls, or stay inside," ordered Thomas, though his instruction was hardly necessary since those in the yard had moved faster than stoats down a burrow.

For a time, the two men observed the bombardment from the tower for none of the missiles struck higher than half way up the structure. Even when a rock did hit the ramparts, Thomas noted that it inflicted only superficial damage.

"You were right, uncle: they won't break our walls down with those," he declared, smiling.

"Aye, but they'll keep our heads down," replied Enric grimly.

"So, what do we do?"

"We keep our damned heads down, of course," scoffed Enric, before stalking off to descend the stair to the yard.

Remaining there alone, Thomas considered the possible approaches to the castle, which he knew very well from his own attempts to gain entry. To the north and west, the steep slope made any assault difficult since men would have to trudge uphill, carrying their weapons and shields even before they reached the deep ditch and stout rampart. The best they could hope to achieve there was loose arrows at the defenders on the ramparts. From the south, though the slope was gentler, it was still a challenge; especially for men lugging up a battering ram, though Sir Roger had used one successfully before.

The real worry for Thomas, however, was an attack launched from the old burh on his east flank – exactly the same approach he had used to thwart Sir Roger. But, beyond posting sentries along the west wall of the burh, there was little more he could do; for he simply did not have enough men to defend the entire burh.

During the afternoon, the trebuchets ceased lobbing stones over the ramparts and a relieved silence fell upon the castle. In the evening, a sparse meal was consumed in the hall, not far from the trestle table where several bloodied casualties from airborne rocks had been treated earlier. It was a miracle that no-one had been killed but, now that the long-awaited siege was real, the atmosphere in the hall was much subdued. Thomas observed that many more folk than usual found a reason to speak to Father Edric that night. It had been a great surprise when the priest had decided to remain at the castle, yet Thomas could not deny that the defenders needed him.

When Edith accompanied Adeline up to their chamber, he went out into the yard, seeking his uncle. The latter, however, was walking arm in arm with Avice – and her continued presence there had been yet another shock. When he urged his uncle to persuade Avice to leave with the other women, Enric replied with a dark grin: "Aye, lad, 'cos that worked so well with your lady, didn't it?"

Perhaps, Thomas reflected, some madness had afflicted them all that they were so driven to risk death. Leaving Enric and Avice to savour whatever time remained to them, he walked across to the gate where the guards scrambled to appear alert. Ascending to the newly built rampart above the gate, he stared across to the fragile west wall of the old burh. They had placed torches there to illuminate the broad shallow ditch between the two fortifications which lay no more than about thirty yards apart. Praying it was enough to give them warning of any incursion towards the gateway during the night, Thomas returned to the yard and wandered back to the hall.

Outside the hall door, he found Selima, one of the women who had also chosen to remain behind after most left for the abbey. While he understood that some women, like Adeline, had stayed to support their menfolk, Selima had no such attachment; yet she refused to leave despite his offer to release her from her oath.

As he passed, he caught the scent of her and stopped.

"Lord?" she murmured.

"Tell me, Selima, why did you stay?" he asked.

"You think I would go to that abbey?" she scorned. "And I am still your servant – till death, lord."

"You've already saved my life once; I'd say you owe me nothing."

"I fear you will need saving again," she replied.

It was a simple statement yet delivered somehow with the intimacy of a lover and the awkward silence that followed troubled Thomas. There had been more than a few girls before Adeline, but none like Selima, whose beauty - so sultry and mysterious - he could not deny.

"You should be abed by now," he said, his voice sounding husky in the cool night air.

She made no reply, but merely smiled before mounting the steps to the hall where she would lay her head with Wilflaed and some of the other remaining women.

"Christ's bones," he breathed, entranced by the sway of her hips as she moved.

Overwhelmed by a sudden desire to see Adeline, he followed Selima inside, half-expecting she might be waiting for him. But she wasn't and reason told him that she would already be in the screened-off area at the far end of the hall. Ascending the stair to the chamber he shared with Adeline, which had once been Sir Roger's, he removed his boots and undressed before sliding into the bed beside her. When he gently cradled her in his arms, the mother of his unborn child stirred only enough to murmur: "You're cold…" and then slumbered on.

Thomas, as ever, did not fall asleep so easily, haunted not only by his fears for what the dawn might bring, but also by a pang of guilt for even glancing at another girl – and, in truth, he had done more than glance.

Long before dawn, cries of alarm from the gateway caused him to stagger out of bed, haul on his boots and clothing and snatch up his sword.

Adeline, too was wide awake. "Has it begun?" she whispered.

"Aye, better get dressed," he told her. "But promise me you'll stay up here."

Before he could leave, she flung her arms around him and gasped: "Take care, my love."

By the time Thomas hurtled through the hall, he knew something was badly wrong for the warning shouts from the yard were growing ever more panic-stricken. Stumbling down the steps outside, the first thing he saw was a wall of fire at the gateway. Though Enric was already overseeing efforts to quell the flames, Thomas was astonished how swiftly they were spreading.

Seizing his uncle by the arm, he cried: "How was it fired so fast?"

"Sir Roger's got men in the old burh," snarled Enric. "The sowsarding arsewipes tossed our own torches from the burh rampart down at the gate. They must have crept into the ditch with a few buckets of oil for that's the only way the wood could burn so fierce."

"So, our sentries in the old burh?" asked Thomas.

"Long dead," replied his uncle.

"I should have put more men over there," groaned Thomas.

"Then you'd just have lost more men," barked Enric.

They had, of course, prepared for an attack by fire and piles of earth stood ready to be shovelled onto any burning timbers. But though the gatekeepers and many others were hard at work, the oil on the outside of the gates was clearly hampering their efforts greatly. The rising flames were already scorching the rampart above the gate, forcing the guards there to leap down into the yard.

Enric, patently livid at being caught out by their opponent, railed at the defenders to redouble their efforts, but Thomas could see that, even if they quelled the fire now, the gates would be badly weakened.

"God's nails!" cried Enric in fury. "At dawn, they'll hurl more rocks at our ramparts and bring up a battering ram to smash what's left of those gates to pieces."

"Aye, and once they get into the yard…" muttered Thomas.

"We're dead," confirmed Enric. "And without giving them so much as a bloodied nose, God rot their shitmongering souls."

"What if we go out to face them," suggested Thomas.

"We could - if we were a pack of fartwits," retorted Enric. "They'll have crossbows on the burh rampart now – just as you did. We'd be cut down before we even crossed the ditch."

"But what else can we do?" hissed Thomas.

Enric paused for what seemed to Thomas an age, then he said softly: "We could invite the sheepswiving bastards in…"

"Aye, and break our fast with them, no doubt," growled Thomas.

"I mean it," insisted Enric. "We need to cut their numbers first, Thomas or we're done. So, we let them break apart the gates and mass all our archers and crossbowmen on the ramparts."

"But why not just rain arrows down upon them as they try to get in?" argued Thomas.

"Aye, we'd kill a few that way, but most of our arrows and quarrels would be wasted. This way, when they charge in fast, eager to draw blood – we trap 'em in the yard and then let fly with all we have."

"But they'll only fall back and attack again later for our gates will still have been breached."

"Ah, but the men coming up behind will be desperate to get in here too, Thomas. That'll make it harder for the front ranks to fall back – as it did last time."

"Aye, but last time some of us were behind them outside."

When Enric outlined the rest of his plan, Thomas was more doubtful than ever. "Even with our archers, many will still make it across the yard and, if our men at arms can't hold them back…"

"Well I didn't say it would work," lamented Enric, "but better a fight we've planned for than a wild panic when they break in."

Thomas gave a sigh. "We'll risk the lives of every man and woman here."

"God's bones, we're already doing that!"

"Aye, but by Christ, I thought we were so well-prepared…"

"We did what we could; but the old burh was always the weak spot."

"So, we gamble the lives of all on this one ruse," breathed Thomas.

"That's war, nephew; one long series of damned foolish gambles," said Enric. "Now, are we doing it, or not?"

"Aye, we're doing it," agreed Thomas. "I'll get the men at arms ready in the yard while you tell the archers and crossbowmen… They'll all think we've lost our wits."

"We lost those months ago, lad," murmured Enric.

50

30th October 1138, at Schaftesberia Castle

By mid-morning the flaming castle gates were smashed open in an explosion of glowing timber shards. A horde of snarling men rushed inside and tore across the yard. But, after a dozen or so paces, the attackers slowed up, for stretched across the yard in front of the hall was a makeshift barricade which extended from one palisade to the other. It was constructed out of any object the defenders could find, but mostly boards and trestles from the hall. Behind it, waited two ranks of men at arms.

After only a moment's hesitation, the onrushing soldiers charged at the barrier, roaring their battle cries. Only when the first volley from the adjacent ramparts thudded into them, cutting down half their number, did they see the trap. As more men, however, piled in behind them, the survivors of the first wave, knowing that crossbows would be slow to reload, launched themselves at the obstacle barring their way. There they were met by the castle's men at arms who stabbed their spearpoints fiercely between the timbers to slice through the bellies or thighs of their opponents.

Unable to close tight to their enemies, Sir Roger's men at arms, urged on from behind by their comrades, tried to dismantle the barricade. For a few moments they had some success, until the reloaded crossbows were discharged once again. Quarrels flew into the close press of men where it was almost impossible to miss. They took such a heavy toll that some in Sir Roger's vanguard began to cry out for a retreat.

Enric, in command on the rampart, ordered Edwin and the other archers to turn their longbows upon those still outside the gates waiting now to get inside. The crush of men there also provided a wealth of easy targets even for poorly-trained archers. As a result, the whole assault soon came to a bloody standstill in the charred gateway.

"Now!" bellowed Thomas, drawing out his sword.

At once, parts of the barricade were hauled aside to allow Thomas and the men at arms to pour through into the killing ground. Thomas leapt over a row of bodies to launch himself into the fray, chopping a desperately-raised shield in half with Roland's heavy sword. Beside him were men he had come to respect: young Bernard, who fought like a crazed lion… the two giants, Garth and Jonas, wielding their axes to hew a bloody path into the mêlée. There were many others too that he did not know so well, who hurled themselves valiantly against Sir Roger's seasoned warriors.

Enric had warned that there would only be one chance to win, by destroying the siege in a single, decisive blow.

"You can't let them fall back and regroup, Thomas," he had insisted, "or you'll just have to face them again and they won't be trapped a second time. Let them come onto your swords and spears until Sir Roger is compelled to join the attack himself."

Though Enric's advice might have made sense in theory, in the cramped press of the yard, it was impossible for Thomas to control the ebb and flow of the fighting. Disaster struck when the besiegers surged forward on their right flank, forcing the defenders back against the barricade. Half a dozen of them, unable to find their way back through the barrier, were butchered to a man. Their comrades, attempting in vain to extricate them, unwittingly made matters worse by creating more gaps in the barricade which were quickly exploited by their enemies. Only when a volley of arrows sent several men reeling back, were the castle men at arms able to rally and close the breach. But the cost was high.

Despite all the blood they had spilled so far, Thomas feared they had no answer to the greater numbers Sir Roger could bring to bear. However many they killed, more seemed to come in through the still-smouldering gates - perhaps not in a flood, but certainly in a constant trickle. He and his comrades strained every sinew to fight on until, to his surprise, Sir Roger recalled his men to the open gateway and asked for a halt to retrieve his wounded. Thomas readily agreed, grateful for the opportunity to recover several of the bodies strewn in the yard. But he could see that his surviving men were already exhausted and the barricade was broken apart in too many places to defend.

Enric, breathing hard, came down from the rampart to join his nephew. "Sir Roger couldn't give a toss for his wounded," he gasped. "He's getting ready to launch another attack."

"I know," snapped Thomas.

"We can't hold them," admitted Enric.

"I know," said Thomas. "So, go to the tower and take Avice with you."

"What?" cried Enric. "I'm not leaving your side."

"You are - by Christ, you are," ordered Thomas.

"But I swore to your father," pleaded Enric. "Your father-"

"-is safe in Normandy," rasped Thomas. "Now, do as I bid you."

"I will not," declared Enric.

Thomas seized his uncle by the shoulders and hissed: "You will do me this one last service and make sure that my lady - and her yet to be born child - get out of this graveyard alive."

"She's... with child?" groaned Enric.

"Aye; so, do whatever you must to keep her safe. You hear me?"

"Aye, but-"

"And go now, before it's too late," urged Thomas.

Torn between two unconditional loyalties, Enric looked utterly bereft. But, perhaps aware of Sir Roger's forces massing for their final assault, he clasped his nephew's hand and whispered: "God be with you then… lord."

"And with you, uncle…"

Looking about him, Thomas studied the ragged remnant of his army. On his right hand stood Eadwulf, while Tancred protected his left flank with Edgar just behind. Those men would, he knew, fight beside him till they spat out their very last breath. But, among many of the others still manning the defences, he observed a change; their drawn faces, many streaked with blood, eyed each other nervously. And, though they still held their spears ready to meet fresh opponents, where once there had been conviction, Thomas found in their half-shuttered eyes only the stoic resignation of beaten men. He knew then that they would not survive the next assault.

"Lend me your shields a moment, my friends," he said to those nearest him and smiled at the confusion evident upon the faces of both Eadwulf and Tancred.

"You just need to raise your shields a little," he reassured them, as he used them as stepping stones to clamber up onto part of the barricade.

"Cousin," protested Eadwulf, in alarm, "What are you doing? You put yourself at grave risk."

But soon enough his cousin followed Tancred and Edgar in raising his shield to cover the lower half of Thomas's body.

Up on the barricade, Thomas looked down upon his company of assorted warriors and noticed that there were even one or two women among them, gripping spear hafts as if born to such bloody work.

"Before us lie the torn bodies of our enemies," roared Thomas, "men that God has condemned with His mighty sword. Stand with me now and I swear we'll cast these dogs back whence they came!"

A few cries of "Fitz, Fitz, Fitz!" rose up as Thomas leapt down to join his comrades. But Sir Roger, perhaps prompted by Thomas's speech, decided to delay no longer. Scarcely had Enric disappeared into the hall, when raucous cries of 'Traitors!' went up and the besiegers raced across the yard once more to tear into the barricade with renewed vigour. Though several were struck down by quarrels or arrows, most reached the barrier and, this time, those in the front rank wielded axes to hack aside any stubborn remnants of the defensive wall.

But even as the renewed assault began, another voice screamed out across the castle yard from atop the tower rampart – a railing, haunting voice which caused the attack on the barricade to falter.

"Hear me, folk of Schaftesberia!" cried Adeline de Sarne. "And know that I, who bear your lord's heir in my belly, will never surrender."

Though a collective gasp greeted her revelation, Adeline was far from finished.

"Know that I will stand here and fight to the end with you – and, even if I and my unborn child are torn apart in a river of blood, my spirit will live on. So, pray do not lose heart, for I shall never lose mine!"

The impassioned fire of her words filled Thomas in equal measure with pride and terror. So much for sending Enric to protect the girl, he lamented; but then what else should he expect from his courageous and passionate lady?

The deathly silence that followed her outburst was broken only when Sir Roger, waving forward his last archers and crossbowmen, bellowed: "Kill that whore!"

So, though grim-faced men at arms still faced each other across the barricade, all eyes flicked upward to the tower as a flurry of arrows and quarrels struck home.

When Edwin fell, Thomas was horrified but, when an arrow struck Adeline down, he was thrust into a deep sea of despair. He could neither speak nor move; for, if she was gone, what did his life matter? And all he could do was stare up at the space on the rampart where, a moment earlier, she had so gloriously radiated her defiance. Lost in his grief, only an exultant shout from Sir Roger reverberating around the yard hauled him from his bottomless pit of sorrow.

"Finish them!" bellowed Sir Roger. "And bring me the head of that damned Saxon!"

In moments, the first of the knight's men were almost through the failing barricade and Sir Roger urged them on: "Get up there and make sure that bitch is dead."

"Lord!" pleaded Eadwulf, seizing his distracted cousin by the arm. "If she still lives, will you let those dogs go and kill her?"

"Aye, she may yet live, lord," cried Edgar.

Thomas, having witnessed her sudden fall, knew different; but Eadwulf was right: he would not let the bastards have her even in death.

Sir Roger's whole battle line was pressing forward now and a few men at arms succeeded in breaking through. Ignoring their immediate opponents, they made straight for the hall steps to carry out their lord's dread command.

"Ralph, look to your sister," barked Thomas. "Tancred, go with him."

While the young pair set off for the hall, Thomas, his tortured heart suffused with anger, sucked in a long, deep breath as he eyed the mass of warriors before him.

"So be it then, my love," he murmured and, snatching up the blood-caked spear he had employed from behind the barrier, he hurled it at the nearest man at arms with all the venom he could muster.

"But, 'tis no time for spears," he grumbled and unsheathed his sword once more.

"Take my shield, cousin," offered Eadwulf, holding it out to him.

But with a brisk shake of the head, Thomas instead took the familiar hilt of his seax in his left hand. Even as he started to clamber through the tangle of timber debris and blood-smeared corpses, he vowed that Sir Roger and his henchmen would pay the very highest price for taking the life of his love.

"On me!" he bellowed. "On me!" and drove straight into the midst of the enemy host.

His startled comrades behind the barricade had little choice but to charge out after him to meet their enemies head on in a murderous clash of steel and blood. With savage power and frightening ferocity, Thomas hacked down his first opponent and, with nothing left to lose, unleashed his demons.

51

30th October 1138, at Schaftesberia Castle

With Sir Roger's men at arms already crashing through the hall ahead of him, Ralph, stricken by his sister's fall, gave chase with Tancred close behind. The soldiers barrelled through Father Edric, Wilflaed and others tending to the wounded, before mounting the stair to the upper floors.

Ralph, inspired by Adeline's fierce, unyielding outburst, found the courage that had so often eluded him and leapt up the steps two at a time. One of the three men ahead, glancing back, came to a halt on the first landing whilst his two comrades continued to climb up.

"God's blood!" cried Ralph. "We daren't delay."

"Leave this fellow to me," replied Tancred, charging past Ralph to drive their lone opponent back.

Seizing the opportunity, Ralph raced past the grappling pair, but he was already gasping for breath and only the dread thud of boots pounding up ahead forced him on. At the next landing he half-expected another man to be waiting; but the two must have forged on together. Even before he reached the top of the stair, Ralph heard an alarming clash of swords; and, when he finally stumbled through the door out onto the rampart, he almost wept at the bloody scene before him.

While Enric was trying to parry swingeing sword strokes from one man, Edith, standing over the lifeless body of Adeline, faced down the other with just a small knife in her hand.

Edith screamed at her assailant: "Leave us be, or God will surely curse your wicked soul for killing a woman with child."

But the pitiless soldier, growling: "I've done worse.", thrust his sword at her.

Ralph, dragging his gaze from Adeline's death-white, bloodstained face, shouted: "No!" and charged across the rampart.

But he was too late to stop the blade slicing through Edith's slim torso. Crumpling down onto boards already spattered with blood, the girl threw her body over Adeline.

Driven out of his wits by the terrible sight of his sister, Ralph aimed a wild slash at the man at arms, only to see it parried with ease.

"Think you can take me on," taunted the soldier, who proceeded to batter Ralph back against the timber parapet. "I don't think so, boy…"

Clubbing Ralph down with the hilt of his sword, he then plunged his dagger under the youth's ribs. With a groan, Ralph let fall his sword and sank onto the rampart, his breathing short and rasping, while his adversary grinned down at him, admiring his handiwork. But, before he could deliver the killing blow, the soldier was obliged to turn his attention to Enric, who had just hacked down his comrade.

Ralph could only watch, helpless, as the older man, already looking utterly drained, confronted his new opponent. Out of the corner of his eye, Ralph fancied he saw his half-sister move and croaked: "Ade…"

But then he remembered she was dead and it was just his eyes failing. He could only pray that, after death, his soul might be judged worthy enough to join hers. His wandering mind was slow to register that Enric was lying on the floor, clutching a wound in his side. In despair, Ralph tried to retrieve his sword, but neither of his numbed arms would move more than a few inches. The victorious warrior smiled and took a pace back towards him until halted by a sudden howl of anguish.

Adeline gasped awake and, finding Edith in her arms, with her breast cut and bleeding, gave a despairing cry. She was sitting up, still cradling Edith, when her horror-filled eyes met Ralph's and she wept at the sight of her dying half-brother. In two strides the soldier crossed the rampart to loom over Adeline; but Ralph, astonished that she still lived, was powerless to help her.

However, as the swordsman raised his blade to plunge down into Adeline, footsteps thudded on the rampart behind him. Clearly hampered by an ugly wound in his thigh, Tancred stopped dead when he saw his beloved Edith so cruelly butchered. Then, his face darkened by rage, he took several lurching steps towards the lone man at arms. The latter was already swivelling to meet the attack and the two swords clashed angrily.

Ralph blinked, having lost consciousness for a moment, but was heartened to see that Tancred had not succumbed easily to his powerful adversary. Ever more distracted by the ribbon of blood dribbling steadily from his own belly, Ralph was finding it hard to discern what was happening, especially as his vision became ever more blurred. The pair still fighting looked spent but, in a sluggish exchange of blows, Tancred was struck hard on the helm and slumped down, dazed, onto his knees. Another crack upon his head felled him and he lay still.

Adeline had clambered to her feet and was now clutching Edith's small blade. When had that happened, Ralph wondered? Tears rolled down his pale cheeks as he watched her, blood dripping from her hair, back away towards the parapet. The surviving soldier, though his mail was torn and bloodied at the shoulder, pursued her one languid step at a time. At first, he attempted to drag his sword with him, its point scraping across the timber; but weariness compelled him to relinquish his grip upon it.

"Time… to end this sport," he muttered, raising his dagger.

In silent disbelief, Ralph rejoiced as his sister thrust her blade up towards her adversary's chin – until he saw that the brute had a hand clamped about her wrist. Though clearly hampered by the pain in his shoulder, he still possessed more than enough strength to prevent her knifepoint from piercing the skin above his mail shirt.

With a shake of the head, he told her: "Women are just too weak to play such mortal games…"

Barely clinging to life, Ralph heard a new voice: the infidel servant, Selima was snarling: "Not these women!"

The last thing Ralph saw before a dark shadow engulfed him, was a glint of steel captured by the rays of the midday sun. His eyes, now sightless and bereft of tears, closed as he grieved for his doomed sister.

But then, somehow, a cool, soft hand caressed his cheek and she whispered: "When I said I would never surrender, I meant it. And I'll carry you with me always, brother…"

52

30th October 1138, at Schaftesberia Castle

Wading into his baying enemies, Thomas had only one prize in mind: to raise aloft the head of Sir Roger as he had that of Sir Thorold. He cared not how many others he must slaughter to reach the knight and, within minutes, both his blades were dripping blood. Though his head pounded from a glancing blow to his helm, the only sound in his head was the roar of blind rage. Heedless of cuts and jabs at his mail, he shunned the pain and fought on until his blood-soaked fury propelled him into the visceral heart of Sir Roger's force.

Yet, his strained sinews and aching muscles could only hold for so long. A brace of men at arms, perhaps marking his weariness, came at him together; but though his body was weary, Thomas was far from finished. With disdain, he raked his sword down across one opponent's neck, before ripping the seax up through the groin of the other.

"God give you thanks, Roland, for your mighty sword," he muttered to himself, "But by God, it grows heavy..."

He knew that his relentless surge forward must soon begin to eat away at the enemy's resolve – if only he could keep his legs pumping one after the other. Time and again he heard Sir Roger exhorting his men to: "Kill the Saxon." But the desperation in the knight's cry only gave Thomas fresh hope. And every man who turned to strike at him, exposed his flank to the spears and axes of those who had followed Thomas into the deadly mêlée.

With every yard Thomas advanced, his comrades staggered forward in his bloody wake and he heard their lifted spirits in the chant: "Fitz! Fitz! Fitz!"

Carving aside another opponent with Roland's sword, Thomas wondered vaguely how they still had the energy to shout. Then, with a sudden, belligerent shout of joy, he saw Sir Roger a mere two yards away from him.

"Crossbows! Cut him down," screamed Sir Roger. "Two marks for the man who puts that youth down."

"So wails the craven dog!" snarled Thomas, driving into the thick press of Sir Roger's household knights. Even as he bludgeoned men aside, he felt several blades force gaps in his mail shirt, and prayed only that none would kill him before he reached his adversary. But, when he lunged out again, a blade chopped down upon his right arm, and he let fall Roland's weighty blade. Heedless of the blood dripping from his arm, he swooped forward to slash the seax across his opponent's wrist. It was enough to discourage the fellow who fell back a pace, yielding to the relentless and demonic menace of Thomas FitzRobert.

Behind the Lord of Schaftesberia swarmed his comrades, finishing off the wounded souls he abandoned and driving home the advantage gained by his remorseless onslaught. God had smiled upon him, he decided, until a sudden, sharp pain in his thigh brought him to a wretched halt. When the spear point pulled back to lunge again, Thomas lurched sideways to evade the second thrust and then sliced his seax across the spearman's gullet. With a gurgle of protest, his assailant fell but, for the first time, Thomas feared he had sustained a mortal wound.

Enric told him once that a man wounded in the thigh should count to two score and, if he was still alive, he was not going to bleed to death. But who, in Christ's name, had time to count to four in the heat of battle - let alone forty. Nonetheless, he survived the spear thrust, though it hindered his movement and he was limping badly when he finally caught up with Sir Roger at the charred castle gateway.

Both men knew that if the knight dared to flee the contest now, he would forever be branded a coward. As if by common assent, all other men, bloody and utterly fatigued, gradually ceased their combat and fell back in the knowledge that their leaders must settle the day. But Sir Roger came fresh to the fight, while Thomas was beyond exhaustion.

Indeed, as soon as he stopped, his battered body burned with the sting of every cut, every torn patch of skin, and bleeding, punctured flesh. His sword arm hung by his side, next to useless and, now that he faced his rival in single combat, the savage demons that had driven him to slaughter a score of men, chose to desert him. Yet, despite all, Thomas felt strangely calm.

"So, Saxon," declared Sir Roger, "at last it falls to me to slay you – as my men slew your whore."

Outraged cries greeted that taunt, but Thomas, feeling more at peace than he had for months, raised a hand to silence his men. Several offered their shields, but he knew he had not the strength to carry one. Nor could he wield Roland's sword for, wonderful blade though it was, it was simply beyond him.

So, removing the helm from his aching head, he tossed it carelessly aside.

"Lord!" cried several of his comrades in dismay.

But, with a shake of the head, Thomas took a step towards his adversary, armed only with his seax. Breathe deep, he told himself, lest these few breaths should be your last. Without the weight of shield, helm or sword, Thomas, despite his tired limbs, was able to move more lightly on his feet and, when Sir Roger aimed a sudden thrust at his breast, he evaded it easily. Yet, though he parried the next blow with his seax, his torn leg reminded him that his fragile agility could not last long.

At first, the two adversaries sparred in silence but, the longer Thomas survived, the more confident his men became and the cry of: "Fitz, Fitz, Fitz!" began once more to echo around the wooden palisade. And, however much Sir Roger tried to ignore it, Thomas could see that the low, insistent refrain was beginning to unsettle him. Several times, the knight's sword carved only through thin air and Thomas observed that some of the men at Sir Roger's back, looked a little disquieted that their experienced captain had not yet been able to put down his wounded and barely-armed, opponent.

When the knight stopped moving to stare beyond him, Thomas suspected some ruse or other but then the chanting of his name stopped and he heard a rustle of movement behind him. Glancing back, he watched the ranks part to reveal Adeline, hair and clothing matted with blood and, close behind her, daubed in similar fashion, walked Selima with a curved, blood-stained, Saracen knife clutched in her hand.

Thomas could only stare, open-mouthed, at Adeline - at once appalled by her appearance yet elated that she still lived. An almost imperceptible nod from Selina confirmed that his servant had carried out the task he had entrusted to her.

Perhaps Sir Roger's face registered almost equal shock, but it was he who recovered his composure first, snarling: "So, the whore who began all this bloodletting isn't dead after all – well, I swear, she very soon will be."

Perhaps the knight might have taunted Adeline again when he took a step forward, had Thomas not swept his arm around in a lightning swift arc. Sir Roger's hand flew to his throat but, when his fingers came away with only a trace of blood upon them, his grinning face betrayed his relief. Absently, he brushed a hand across his neck and raised his sword. But the seax must have lacerated some vital conduit of blood; for Sir Roger's heavy touch, instead of stopping the dribble, made it gush forth in a flood. Thomas watched the knight collapse onto his haunches, as his blood pooled in the castle yard.

Cries of: "Fitz, Fitz, Fitz!" rang out again while the knight's remaining men looked on, transfixed by their lord's sudden demise. Only one or two found the presence of mind to flee at once, before their fellows were pressed back and trapped by the defenders.

Thomas wrapped his blood-stained wife in a hungry embrace, fearful each moment that she might dissolve in his arms. Only when he felt the warmth of her, did he truly believe that she was alive. And only then, did he raise a tired arm aloft and call for silence.

To the vanquished, he declared: "Yield now and surrender your weapons; swear never again to take up arms against me - or the Empress Matilda - and you may leave here in peace. Refuse to do either and we'll hang you all. And, I pray you, tell all my enemies what they should expect if they seek to destroy Thomas FitzRobert."

Epilogue

53

21st November 1138 at Schaftesberia Castle

For many weeks there had been no reaction from outside Schaftesberia to the shocking events at the castle. Every one of Sir Roger's surviving men at arms had yielded, sworn oaths for their future conduct and departed, leaving behind all they possessed save their undertunics and braies. Their oaths, of course, would most likely not be adhered to since the men at arms could – and surely would – argue they had been exacted under duress. But all that mattered at the time was that they left Schaftesberia in peace.

Though the besieged had won a significant, and wholly unlikely, victory, the cost in lives was so great that the euphoric moment of triumph faded all too swiftly. More than a third of their fighting men were dead, including young Ralph de Sarne, and many of the wounded would never take up arms again. Indeed, Thomas suspected that neither Enric nor Tancred would ever fully recover from their wounds. Among the score of women who had remained to stand by their menfolk, almost half succumbed to their wounds and others, such as Edith and Adeline, would forever bear the scars of war.

Burying so many comrades in arms brought an outpouring of grief the like of which Thomas had never before witnessed. With so many dead, Avice fetched folk from the abbey to help prepare the bodies. This, reflected Thomas, was the grim cost of war… the high toll exacted in the quest for power. And he must accept his share of the responsibility for it was only his refusal to abandon Adeline that began the carnage. If this was what a hard-fought victory looked like, Thomas reckoned he would be content never to see another.

Yet, the besieged had done what few other rebel strongholds had done: repulsed a determined attempt to capture the castle. News of their success spread very far and brought a few more recruits to their newly-repaired gates. Indeed, his half-brother, William, sent another half-dozen men at arms from Brystole. It was a mark of respect which moved Thomas more than any words could.

Yet the very notoriety of Thomas and his garrison also increased the likelihood of overwhelming royal retaliation and thus, not for the first time, he was faced with an impossible dilemma. With the fate of the whole garrison in his hands, Thomas knew that, whatever he decided, folk would die – if not by war, then by the winter's cold or, God help them, starvation.

Leaning upon the rail of the tower rampart, his leg still heavily bandaged, he considered what he must do next. He had no need to consult his uncle who would, no doubt, recommend leaving at once for Normandy despite the fact that he couldn't even ride yet. But Thomas had long ago abandoned that path and, whatever happened now, he had an obligation to others.

Only when a cold hand pressed upon his did he realise that he had not heard Adeline's approach. Grasping her hand in his, he asked: "What say you, my dear – do you still stand by what you shouted in the midst of the fight?"

"Aye, husband, I do; we'll live or die here," she said. "Will the king come now do you think?"

"Before winter? I doubt it – unless he intends to starve us out."

"Then we must make sure we've supplies and stock enough to see us through the winter," she declared. "For your father will come in the spring, will he not?"

"Aye," agreed Thomas, yet he wondered how much he could rely upon his father's promise – and, in any case, could they truly hold out all winter?

Perhaps Adeline sensed his doubts for she asked: "Do you truly believe he will come?"

"Nothing is certain," he conceded.

"But what if he doesn't come?" she pressed him.

"Then we'll worry about that in the spring," he told her. "But first we must survive the winter."

Indeed, only one thing was certain: for all those who remained at Schaftesberia Castle, it would be a long and bitter winter.

∞ ∞ ∞ - ∞ ∞ ∞

Historical Notes

The Anarchy

The name the Anarchy is used these days to describe the civil war between King Stephen who succeeded his uncle, Henry I, in 1135 and the adherents of Empress Matilda, Henry I's daughter. Though he had an enormous number of illegitimate children, Henry's only legitimate son died in the White Ship disaster and he prepared for his daughter to succeed him. But Matilda was not able to do so when Henry died and it was his nephew, Stephen of Blois, who seized the opportunity.

Most barons, including Matilda's half-brother, Robert FitzRoy, Earl of Gloucester, accepted the fait accompli partly because Matilda's husband, Geoffrey of Anjou, was viewed as an enemy who had gone to war with King Henry over Normandy. But after a year or two, Robert became disenchanted with Stephen because, whereas under his father, King Henry, the illegitimate Robert had been a key advisor, his influence during Stephen's rule was waning. He saw other men – notably the Beaumont twins – rise in power as his position was weakened.

By announcing in May 1138 that he would support Matilda against Stephen, he effectively began a civil war. However, he was ill-placed to do much at first and – as this story reveals – his supporters in England were mainly defeated in his absence. The exception was Bristol Castle held by his son, William, as described in the book; and, of course the fictional heroics of his little-known bastard son, Thomas FitzRobert at Shaftesbury.

I hope you have enjoyed reading about this period which I think is far too often ignored in medieval history. After all, without the civil war, the Plantagenets would almost certainly not have ruled England at all, because at the end of the anarchy, it was Empress Matilda's son, Henry II, who emerged as king.

Places

Schaftesberia [Shaftesbury]

The Old Burh

Shaftesbury was one of the Saxon burhs founded to defend Wessex and initially included only the settlement on the hill plateau which was protected by a wooden rampart. By the twelfth century, the original settlement there, and its fortifications, were in decline and the town had grown eastwards towards the abbey and market place.

The Castle

The archaeological evidence reveals that during the twelfth century there was indeed a small castle built on the spur northwest of the town, as described in this book. The supposition is that it was an adulterine castle – one raised without royal permission. Since very little is known about this castle, I've re-constructed it from the evidence of other similar forts built during this period. It was almost certainly made of wood with a palisade around a large tower as its keep. It would have been cramped at the best of times and I may have exaggerated a little how many souls it could house. My descriptions, however, are largely consistent with what the meagre archaeological remains suggest.

The Abbey

Shaftesbury Abbey was a very prestigious nunnery, partly because it was founded by Saxon royalty, but also because it housed the remains of St Edward which was a big draw with pilgrims. Little remains now above ground and, though the abbey has been excavated more than once, there is much — even about the basic layout — which is still not clear. As I have indicated in the book, the abbey was undergoing extensive building work in this period.

Scireburne [Sherborne]

Sherborne had a Benedictine Abbey which became independent of Salisbury in 1122. Shortly afterwards, the ambitious re-building programme referred to in this story began. Much of the abbey, including the cloisters mentioned, was replaced as part of another rebuild in the fourteenth century, so it is difficult now to establish the exact layout and nature of the buildings or cloisters in 1138.

Sturministra [Sturminster Marshall]

By the standards of the day, Sturminster was a fair-sized settlement, named for its 'church on the River Stour'. It was in the hands of the Beaumont family who — in my story at least — gave it to the newly-knighted Sir Thorold Le Breton.

Brystole [Bristol]

Bristol Castle, which was the stronghold of Robert Earl of Gloucester, was heavily fortified and virtually impregnable. Though King Stephen did try to besiege it, he quickly realised that he would not succeed. Its port allowed the castle to be supplied by means of the River Avon — which is also the means by which Thomas leaves the castle on two occasions in the story.

Warham [Wareham]

Wareham was a relatively small settlement which had been a useful port for centuries using the River Frome out to sea via Poole Harbour. It was still being used in early Norman times when it was in Beaumont hands and was thus, to Thomas, a potentially hostile place.

REBEL SWORD

Archet [West Orchard] Blaneford [Blandford Forum] Gyllengeham [Gillingham] and Escewich [Ashwick]

These are all real places though it is almost impossible now to have any genuine sense of what each looked like though Escewich was certainly an ancient settlement.

Duncliffe Forest

This was a forest on a hill just west of Shaftesbury which was very extensive in early Norman times and it still is quite large today.

Castle Cary and Richmont

These were castles, south of Brystole, taken by King Stephen in 1138 much as referred to in the book.

People

The only historical figures who actually appear in this story are: Robert, Earl of Gloucester, his son, William and his bastard son, Thomas. All other characters are fictional. Though King Stephen, Empress Matilda and the Beaumont twins are mentioned, they do not actually appear in this story.

Thomas FitzRobert

Our hero Thomas was a bastard son of Robert, Earl of Gloucester; however, hardly a trace of Thomas remains in the historical record, so almost everything about him in this story is, inevitably, fictional.

Robert FitzRoy, Earl of Gloucester

Robert was an illegitimate son of King Henry I and was prominent at his father's court. After his father's death, he accepted like most barons the succession of his cousin, Stephen of Blois. But, after several years during which his influence at court was dwindling, he became a champion of his half-sister Matilda who was Henry I's only legitimate child. His declaration for Matilda in 1138 prompted the civil war known as the Anarchy.

William FitzRobert, son and heir of Robert of Gloucester

William was Robert's eldest legitimate son and the half-brother of Thomas. Though still quite young – there seems to be much argument about when he was born - William held his father's fortress city of Bristol and also acted for his father in other areas.

The Beaumont Twins

The twins Waleran and Robert de Beaumont became very powerful and influential at the start of Stephen's reign, largely at the expense of Robert of Gloucester – as he saw it. Waleran, the elder brother, was Count of Meulan and later Earl of Worcester. Like many Anglo-Norman barons in this period, Waleran divided his time between England and Normandy. In 1138, it was he who trapped the traitor, Robert of Gloucester at Caen in Normandy. The younger twin, Robert de Beaumont, was Earl of Leicester and also held extensive estates in south-west England. Both brothers were resented by Robert of Gloucester.

Abbess Bella

The abbess is a fictional character – largely because it is not at all clear from the historical record who was abbess at the time. There is - conveniently for me, I suppose - a gap in the list. However, in creating the character, I have tried to present her situation authentically - as the controller of a very important royal abbey caught very much in the middle of the dispute between Robert of Gloucester and the Beaumonts.

Other Books by Derek Birks

The *Wars of the Roses* series [in order]:
Feud
A Traitor's Fate
Kingdom of Rebels
The Last Shroud
Scars from the Past
The Blood of Princes
Echoes of Treason
Shadow of Doubt - novella
Crown of Fear

The Last of the Romans series [in order]:
Aquileia – short story published in the *Imperium* collection.
The Emperor's Sister – short story in *Triumphs & Tragedies*
The Last of the Romans
Britannia: World's End
New Dawn – a novella
Death At the Feet of Venus – short story
Land of Fire

With historian, Sharon Bennett Connolly, I also co-host the Slice of Medieval Podcast

To find out more about the books and my other work, you can go to my website: **http://www.derekbirks.com**

Printed in Great Britain
by Amazon